NORTH
SEA

FRIESLAND

Bremen

SAXONY

Danzig

Utrecht

Münster

Rhine

Elbe

POLAND

Cologne

Dresden

Reims

Frankfurt

Paris

Verdun

Prague

Worms

Châlons

Metz

Strassburg

Danube

Dijon

Ulm

Vienna

Geneva

Bern

Salzburg

Lyon

HUNGARY

LOMBARDY

Rhône

Milan

Arles

Venice

Belgrade

Marseille

Arno

Tiber

ADRIATIC
SEA

Loire

CORSICA

Spoleto

Rome

SARDINIA

SEA

SICILY

A Journey to the End
of the Millennium

A Journey to the End
of the Millennium

A. B. Yehoshua

TRANSLATED FROM THE HEBREW
BY NICHOLAS DE LANGE

Doubleday
New York London Toronto Sydney Auckland

PUBLISHED BY DOUBLEDAY
a division of Random House, Inc.
1540 Broadway, New York, New York 10036

BOOK DESIGN BY JENNIFER ANN DADDIO

Library of Congress Cataloging-in-Publication Data
Yehoshua, Abraham B.
[Masaʻ el tom ha-elef. English]
A journey to the end of the millennium / A. B.
Yehoshua; translated from the Hebrew
by Nicholas de Lange. — 1st ed.
p.   cm.
I. De Lange, N. R. M. (Nicholas Robert
Michael), 1944– . II. Title.
PJ5054.Y42M3713   1999
892.4′36—dc21   98-28619
                                              CIP

ISBN 0-385-48882-3

Printed in the United States of America

February 1999

3   5   7   9   10   8   6   4

For Ika

But will there be anyone to remember us in another thousand years? Will that ancient soul, in whose moist, private womb flickers the transient shadow of our deeds and dreams, still exist then? Whatever it is called, lacking internal organs, crammed full of computerized liquids, miniaturized in wisdom and happiness, will it still feel the urge or the longing to travel back a thousand years and look for us, as you are looking for your heroes now? But will it be possible to find anything at all? Surely a thousand years then will be like thousands of years now. Who knows whether in a thousand years' time clear, concrete understanding will not have removed its responsibility for our abstruse and muddled history, just as we have got rid of the "history" of the cavemen? Still, surely we won't just be forgotten like that. Surely it's not possible that not a single molecule of memory will be found for us, like a yellowing manuscript at the bottom of a forgotten drawer, whose very cataloguing guarantees its eternity even if not a single reader ever discovers it. But will the catalogue itself survive? Or will some totally different cipher fuse and scramble everything that has gone, so that our image can never again be intertwined as we imagine it to ourselves?

PART ONE

The Journey to Paris, or the New Wife

1.

In the second watch of the night, finding himself woken by a caress, Ben Attar thought to himself that even in her sleep his first wife had not forgotten to thank him for the pleasure he had afforded her. He brought the caressing hand to his lips in the deliciously swaying darkness, intending to plant another kiss upon it, but the touch of its dry heat on his lips soon corrected his error, and disgustedly he thrust away the hand of the black slave, who, sensing his master's revulsion, vanished. Lying where he was, naked and very drowsy, Ben Attar was once more tormented by anxiety about the journey. He reached out to check whether the youth, who had dared to intrude so far into his bed to wake him, had not also touched the belt full of precious stones, which he now hastily buckled on before donning his robe. Silently, without a word of parting, he slipped out of the tiny cabin and climbed the rope ladder onto the deck. Even though he knew perfectly well that his departure, however silent it was, would wake his wife, he was confident that she would have the self-control not to detain him. Not only was she aware of where his duty now lay, but it was even possible she shared his hope that he would be in time to discharge it before the dawn of day.

But to judge by the twinkling summer stars that filled the firmament, the dawn was still far off. The breeze that was gently clearing the sleep from his eyes as he climbed on deck was not the kind of breeze that blew up suddenly toward the third watch, but just a gentle billow that soon vanished into the void they had identified the previous day, by the intersection of the winds and the smell of the water, as the mouth of the River Seine, for which their hearts had been yearning ever since they first set sail from the Maghreb more than forty days before. So as not to miss the precise opening of the river that would take them into the heart of the Frankish lands, the captain had given orders before sunset to stop the ship, drop anchor, tie up the two steering oars, and wrap the great sail around the long yard that hovered about the gently slanting mast. In the space on deck, freed of the suffocating motion of the great triangle of canvas, the rope ladders became improvised hammocks for the crew, who, unable to abandon their curiosity even at this deep and intimate hour of the night, squinted drowsily to watch the Jew, the ship's owner, recharging his desire, anxious not to let himself down or to fail his second wife, who was expecting him in the stern of the ship.

Meanwhile, a faint tinkle of bells accompanied the shadowy figure of the slave who had woken his master with a long, impudent caress, as he slipped out now from among the baskets of merchandise, proffering without expression a basin of pure water. Surely, Ben Attar brooded resentfully as he freshened his face in the icy water, the slave could have made do with the little bells attached to his tunic instead of intruding into Attar's cabin to steal a look at his nakedness and that of his wife. And without a word of warning or reproof, he suddenly slapped the slave's black face with all his strength. The boy reeled from the blow but showed no surprise; nor did he ask for any explanation. Since the beginning of the voyage he had become used to the fact that no man spared the rod upon him, if only to restrain this son of the desert, who ever since he had been taken onto the high seas had lost his stability and, like a small, lithe wild animal, terrified the moment it is caged, had taken to roaming the labyrinthine crannies of the ship day and night to nestle up to any living creature, whether man or beast. In despair Ben Attar and his partner had resolved to put him ashore in some harbor and pick him up again on the return journey, but the fair wind that had filled the sail during the first two weeks had carried them far from the Iberian Peninsula, and when they stopped at a fishing village near Santiago de Compostela to take on fresh water no Muslim could be found to take the bewildered boy even temporarily under his wing. The Arabs refused to leave him in the hands of Christians, for they knew well that with the approach of the millennium they would not receive back what they had left, but a cowed little new Christian.

It was on account of the rumors that had been flooding Andalus and the Maghreb this last year, about a new fanaticism spreading through the Christian principalities and kingdoms, that the Jewish merchant and his Arab partner Abu Lutfi had decided to minimize their travels by land, so as not to endanger themselves and their merchandise by journeying among hamlets, villages, estates, and monasteries swarming with Christians who were feverishly yearning for their wounded Messiah to descend from heaven to celebrate the thousandth anniversary of his birth but who still feared that that moment would be a day of reckoning for accumulated sins, particularly for the stiff-necked Jews and Muslims who walked freely and calmly in their midst, not believing in the crucified godhead nor expecting any salvation from it. And so, in these twilight days, as faiths were sharpened in the join between one millennium and the next, it was preferable to restrict encounters with adherents of another faith and to be content, at least for the greater part of the way, to travel by sea, for the sea, which can reveal itself at times to be capricious and cruel, owes no obligation to what is beyond its reach. Instead of heading east through the Straits of Gibraltar and sailing northward along the Mediterranean coast to the mouth of the Rhone, and then going up that great river swarming with local craft, and thence seeking the distant harbor town along ruined roads thronged with zealots in search of sacrificial victims, they had decided to hearken to the counsel of an ancient, much-traveled mariner. This man, Abd el-Shafi by name, whose great-grandfather had been taken captive during one of the last Viking raids on Andalus and had been compelled to accompany his captors for many long years upon the seas and rivers of Europe, had brought them two old maps painted on parchment, with green seas and yellow continents abounding in red bays and blue rivers on which one could travel almost anywhere. On close scrutiny the two maps were slightly different—for instance, the land of the Scots appeared on one but was missing from the other, its place being occupied by sea—but both maps agreed as to the existence of a winding northern river, although they called it by slightly different names, which would enable the North African traders to sail, without their feet touching dry land, from the harbor of Tangier all the way to the distant town of Paris, to which a year previously their third partner, Raphael Abulafia, had withdrawn himself.

And so, on the advice of that ancient mariner of captive pirate stock, who showed mounting interest in their journey, they had purchased in the port of Salé a big ship, old but built of sound timber, which had served in bygone days as a guardship in the fleet of the caliph Hashem the First. Without removing the old bridge in its bow or the row of rusting shields that adorned its sides, they prepared it for its civilian mission. They installed separate cabins amidships, cleared out the hold, reinforced the timbers with large wooden rivets, increased the height of the mast, and fitted a larger, triangular lateen sail. They waited for the summer to manifest itself, and then Abu Lutfi selected six experienced sailors to take the ship on a trial run back and forth near the Straits of Gibraltar. It passed the test, and so they loaded it with the great mass of merchandise that had accumulated in the warehouses over the past two years, and with further goods as well. Jars full of pickled fish-cheeks and olive oil, camel skins and leopard skins, embroidered cloth and skillfully made brassware. Also sacks of condiments, and sugar canes, and fastened baskets full of figs and dates and honeycombs, and leather containers brimming with desert salt, in the depths of which they had concealed daggers inlaid with precious stones and flasks of rare perfumes. It was late June when they set sail, turning their backs for the first time in their lives on the rising sun and setting their faces to the west, to the great expanse of the ocean. Clinging cautiously to the coast of southern Andalus, they began to sail northward along the califate of Cordoba and the kingdom of Leon, turning eastward somewhat along the northern coast of Castile and Navarre to the port of Bayonne. From here, after a short rest, they sailed along the coast of Aquitaine and the duchies of Gascony and Guyenne, touched the coast of Belle Île, and turned northwest, into the heart of the ocean, so as to give a wide berth to the dangerous craggy headlands of Brittany. So weary were they from the long voyage that they momentarily disregarded the old pirates' map and hunted for the mouth of the river they were seeking in the big gulf that they had come upon. But they had been overhasty, and pressed on northward for ten long days more, skirting the great duchy of Normandy until at last they were able to turn east, into the crocodile jaws of a new bay that appeared at dawn in all its splendor, and into which flowed the longed-for river named the Seine, which would conduct them circuitously but safely to the place where their third partner had vanished, after submitting to his wife's repudiation.

Even though there was no reason why the Christian millennium should trouble Jews or Muslims sailing alone upon the universal ocean, the Moroccan ship, advancing at the pace of a fast horse, seemed to have absorbed something of the new religious fervor radiating from the nearby Christian coasts. How else are we to explain the fanaticism with which the sailors harried the black boy, who attempted occasionally to commune with his ancient gods, which the dread of the wide ocean was forcing out of the memory of his pagan childhood? Ben Attar sometimes thought that this panic-stricken youth might be able to find peace in his outlandish prayers, and even bestow it upon others. But this is not what the Arab sailors thought, for whenever they caught the boy prostrating himself in supplication to the sun or the moon or the stars or bowing down at the base of the old bridge, facing the animal head carved at the top of the mast, they would drag him to his feet and flog him for idolatrously polluting the worship of the one invisible God, who here, on the high seas, seemed to his worshippers not merely a necessity but the only rational divinity. Fearing that the young African might secretly betray them, they attached little brass bells to his coat, so as to keep track of his movements. And even now, as he brought Ben Attar the light meal he had cooked for him, the soft chimes dissolved the silence of the night.

On a round brass tray lay an earthenware bowl full to overflowing with a yellowish stew with some pieces of white cheese floating on it. Beside it was a fine silver basket replete with figs that had been picked and dried in Seville, on which lay a grilled fish that had been netted earlier in the night, its eye still gleaming in the dark as though it were not yet reconciled to its death. At such a deep hour of the night Ben Attar did not feel like tackling a full-scale meal, but he forced himself to swallow some of the scalding stew and picked at the white flesh of the fish, so as not to drink on an empty stomach the wine that the young slave was pouring for him, despite the rabbinic prohibition on drinking wine poured by idolaters. Even though he sought to temper his spirit, and even to befuddle it enough to encourage the carefree humor that gives rise to a proper desire, well balanced between shyness and assertiveness—like that which had guided him in his coupling earlier in the night—he still had to be cautious with an unfamiliar wine, whose effects had not yet been fully tested.

At first, out of consideration for the faith of his fellow travelers, he had thought of declining the large wine jar he had been offered in exchange for a jar of olive oil twenty days since in the port of Bordeaux, and to content himself with sipping the sweet spiced wine he had brought from home for ritual purposes. It was the ship's captain who had urged him not to turn down the Frankish wine, whose smell and taste were very seductive. For seafaring men, even if they are Mohammedans, the drinking of wine is not a sin, explained Abd el-Shafi, whose many years at sea had made him not only a tough old sea salt but also an expert in maritime law. If in truth all mankind may be divided into three classes, the living, the dead, and seafarers, who are neither living nor dead but merely hopeful, surely there is nothing like wine for inspiring hope. Therefore even now, observing the Jew tippling in the silence of the night, the captain leaned down from his hammock with an agile movement to inspire himself with a little hope, not for a waiting wife but for the mouth of the river, which he hoped the summer had left deep and wide enough to let the potbellied ship pass through without disgrace or mishap.

He did not venture to serve himself without asking the owner's permission. But once invited, he started to gulp the wine down so lustily that the young slave had to be repeatedly dispatched to refill the pitcher, until even Abu Lutfi, who was sleeping the sleep of the just among the sacks of condiments and the camel skins so as to keep an eye on the hidden swords and daggers, awoke at the sound of the swilled wine and emerged from the bowels of the ship—not, heaven forfend, to transgress against the Prophet's prohibition, but to content himself with contemplating the ruby liquid and perhaps sniffing its unfamiliar odor. Unable, however, to contain himself at the sight of Abd el-Shafi calmly drinking, he raised his eyes to the dark vault of the sky to discover whether at such a distance from his native country, on the threshold of a backward Christian land, unstable of government and possessed by vain beliefs, there was anyone who might rebuke him for tasting this beverage that was so beloved of the inhabitants of the place. Not for the sake of pleasure, he reasoned, but to judge for himself the nature of this juice that colored the thoughts and feelings of those whom he would soon be called upon to pit himself against. He closed his eyes as he raised the goblet to his lips and took a small sip of the cool liquid, and then his face paled as he understood how sublime the taste of the forbidden drink was, and how easily one might become enslaved to it. There and then he resolved to abjure it totally. But it was such a pity to throw the wonderful wine into the sea that he passed the goblet to the captain, who drained it delightedly and by way of thanks pointed to a pair of new stars that had appeared over the northern horizon to confirm how far they had sailed under the vault of heaven.

Meanwhile, the young slave was clearing away the remains of the Jew's meal. Before he threw the fishbones overboard, he could not help kneeling and praying secretly to them to have pity on him now that they had met their appointed end. The soft tinkling of the bells on his lithe body betrayed him to the men on deck, but they were all too weary to rise and cut short his forbidden prayer. Perhaps now that they were about to enter the Frankish kingdom, it would be best not to disdain any possible source of salvation, even if it was disguised in the form of a fish's skeleton. Straight ahead of them, not far from the place where the mouth of the river must be, a fire had been burning since nightfall, as though someone on the shore had already spotted the strange ship and was hastening to wreathe himself in fire in preparation for the meeting.

What form would this meeting take? The eyes of the men on the deck gazed fixedly at the bright red sign. Up to now the voyage had been pleasant and safe, as though the God of the Jews and the God of the Muslims had combined their forces upon the sea to supply each other's lack. Nature had smiled upon the travelers, and if occasionally the skies had darkened and the ship had been lashed by showers of rain, these had been short-lived and refreshing, and had not deterred the captain from spreading the great sail to the favorable winds and garnering their full blessing. Nor had they been troubled by the curiosity of passing craft, for despite the ship's unusual appearance, it was immediately apparent that she was a stray, threatening no harm. Even though the signs of her previous military career could still be discerned, her rounded belly betokened peace, and even those who had been so consumed by suspicion that they had come aboard to inspect what was truly hidden in the ship's bowels could find no menace in the camel skins or brassware, or in the dried figs and carobs that they were promptly offered. Taking the packet of salt that Abu Lutfi offered them wrapped in thin paper, the visitors would depart with thanks, not imagining the concealed daggers, curved and lovingly honed. True, the sight of a woman or two in colorful robes and fine veils, strolling on deck or sitting on the old bridge, might have aroused some unease in the minds of the curious, but even this was a personal, not a religious or military, worry.

But now, as they left the open sea behind them and sailed upriver into the heart of the continent, they were bound to attract hard looks from the local inhabitants on either bank. How should they comport themselves? Should they display all the passengers on deck so as to reveal, besides their commercial aims, the domestic harmony that prevailed, or should they dissemble the luxurious character of the human and material cargo that they were bringing from the prosperous south of the Maghreb, leaving visible only a handful of tough-looking sailors hanging from the ropes like long-armed monkeys, to deter anyone who might attempt to meddle with them? Ben Attar, Abu Lutfi, and the captain debated the matter anxiously, for despite their great combined experience, not one of them had ever sailed farther north than the Bay of Barcelona.

They had been to the Bay of Barcelona once a year for the past ten years, at the beginning of August, in sailing ships laden with merchandise, to meet Abulafia, partner and nephew to Ben Attar, who came to meet them from Toulouse. He crossed the Pyrenees on his own, disguised sometimes as a monk, sometimes as a leper, the better to conceal in the folds of his robe, whether from the extortionate customs men of the little duchies on his way or from genuine robbers, the silver coins and precious stones that he had received in return for the merchandise he had distributed the previous year throughout Provence and Aquitaine.

These meetings were very pleasant for Ben Attar, because the joy of seeing his dear nephew was combined with the flash of gold and silver coins from the Christian states in the north. Abu Lutfi too was excited each time to discover afresh how the brassware, jars of oil, camel skins, perfumes, and condiments that he had gathered so busily in the villages and hamlets of the Middle Atlas had been transformed in the space of a year into shining silver and gold coins. No wonder, therefore, that year by year the two partners became more and more impatient. So fearful were they of leaving Abulafia alone for a single minute in the meeting place with his hidden treasures that they brought forward their departure, leaving Tangier before the end of July, and covered the intervening miles in six or seven days' travel, with short night stops in deserted coves along the Iberian coast. As soon as they reached the Bay of Barcelona, they left the new merchandise in a stable adjoining a tavern belonging to a local Jewish trader by the name of Raphael Benveniste, and paid the sailors' wages with a cargo of timber that they loaded onto the ships for the return journey. Not only did the partners not entrust their return to the same sailors who had brought them, but for fear of treachery they refused to return by sea at all. Lightened of their merchandise, they would hire a pair of fine horses and ride up a nearby hill. There, in a charming, secluded wood, stood the ancient, partly ruined inn where they would meet Abulafia. Some said that the last Roman emperors, six centuries earlier, had passed the autumn there. In the darkness of its large dank rooms the two partners first tried to sleep, exhausted as they were from the fierceness of the sun, which had scorched their eyes and seared their flesh during the long hours they had spent suspended between the blue of the sky and the blue of the sea. But this sleep did not last long, for all too soon their anxiety for Abulafia woke them, dispelled their tiredness, and sent them running to the paths all around, trying to determine by which route he would come. After five or six years, this good-hearted man had taken to being not only a day or two but three or four days late, generally with the pretext of real or imagined fears that had forced him into hiding or made him change his disguise repeatedly so as to evade whoever it was who was secretly planning to harm him, or so he thought.

So strong had Abulafia's love of disguise become that he began to deceive not only menacing strangers but even his two anxiously waiting partners. He tricked them not only with his disguises but also with his angle of approach to the meeting place. Even though Ben Attar and Abu Lutfi would comb every possible path to intercept their partner, he would outwit them and slip past without their spotting him, so that it was only in the evening, when they returned, disappointed, to the inn, their souls consumed with fear for his safety and that of the gold and silver he was carrying, that they discovered to their amazement that he had already arrived and had even finished his supper and was now resting from his stratagems, sunk in a deep slumber. But later in the night, unable to restrain himself, Ben Attar would creep into the sleeper's room, smiling at the discarded disguises scattered around the bed, and without a word would gently lay a hand on the curls that reminded him so much of his late father's, so that Abulafia, forced to abandon his pretense, would open his smiling eyes and begin to talk.

Then the stories would start to flow like a gushing spring. Abulafia would begin with a highly colored account of the eventful journey from Toulouse to Barcelona, boasting particularly about how he had succeeded in outwitting the border guards of the little counties and duchies, who imposed a heavy tax on all those who entered or left so as to sustain those who remained. Despite the lateness of the hour, Abu Lutfi would hasten to join his two Jewish partners, asking Abulafia to show him at once the silver and gold he had brought and to tell the story of each coin, its value, where it had come from, and for what it had been traded. Because the Arab had an excellent and precise memory of the merchandise he had entrusted to Abulafia the previous year, he was on his guard when he demanded it back item by item, and it was necessary to concentrate hard to track the fate of each, since most of the goods had not been sold outright but exchanged repeatedly in a succession of strange and complicated deals. To satisfy Abu Lutfi's inexhaustible curiosity, Abulafia recalled each and every one of the purchasers, identifying them by name, relating where they dwelled, what their business was, how they had haggled, on what they had compromised, and he was even persuaded in the course of his account to describe their facial appearance and their dress. Occasionally he also expatiated upon their beliefs and opinions, and by the time dawn broke, the destiny of the merchandise had become inextricably entangled with the destiny of the world. So it was that the men from Tangier learned of this count or of that duke, born in Gascony, Toulouse, or the Valley of the Loire; who was stubbornly fighting on, and who had wearied of war and sued for peace; which river had flooded the previous winter, or what plague had broken out in the spring; what the monks were thinking, how the nobles were comporting themselves, and whither the Jews were migrating. And the most important thing of all, what had and had not changed in people's taste and in women's whims, so that they would know what to seek out and bring with them the following year.

The next day, when the year that had passed had been fully gone over and the hope for the year to come had been cautiously adumbrated, the delicate moment arrived when Ben Attar had to decide how to apportion the year's profit among the three partners. To free his mind from all distractions he would dispatch his two partners back to the coast, to the stable adjoining Benveniste's tavern, so that Abu Lutfi might explain to Abulafia the nature of the new merchandise they had brought with them, justify its choice, and discuss the price it should fetch. Meanwhile Ben Attar himself would bolt the door, cover the window, light two large candles, spread out on the table the booty of coins, gold bars, and precious stones from the Frankish lands, and begin to let his mind roam over the year that had elapsed, so as to scrutinize honestly the share of each of the partners in the labor that had been expended and the profit that had been made. So he sat in that ancient Roman inn, in the depths of a thick wood, tracing first in his imagination the travels of the Arab, wandering among the tribes on the fringes of the Sahara, collecting spices and condiments, animal skins and daggers. The more harshly the sun beat down in the Jew's imagination and the fiercer the desert nomads appeared, the more his heart went out to the Ishmaelite, and he added more and more coins and jewels to his little pile, which grew accordingly—until Abulafia's spirit became resentful, and he compelled his senior partner's thoughts to turn northward, to the wind and the rain and the muddy roads. After allocating him several large gold coins for his travels among the estates and castles of the lovers of the cross in the Touraine, Ben Attar added a few small silver ones on account of Abulafia's talent for evasion and disguise, his knowledge of languages, and his dexterity. Still not satisfied, in his compassion for his nephew's wandering alone among gentiles filled with hatred and contempt, he reached out and transferred to Abulafia's pile two sparkling jewels from that of the Muslim.

But as the candles on the table burned down, he would realize that he had been so carried away by sympathy for his trusty friends that he had neglected his own share. Surely he should not forget that the source of all this wealth was not only his own money but his initiative, his connections, and his ample warehouses. Even if he himself did not take to the roads, his far-ranging concern protected the other partners from danger. He thought also of his wives and children, of his many servants and his large houses, which demanded not merely subsistence but luxury and beauty, and as he weighed these

13

considerations against the simplicity of Abu Lutfi's life and Abulafia's tragic loneliness, by the light of the guttering flames he carefully diminished the piles he had made for his partners and increased his own. By the time the light had flickered and died, there lay before him on the table three leopard-skin pouches, two of which he concealed in the luggage of his partners, whom in his heart of hearts he still considered to be agents rather than true partners. Only then was his mind at peace, and he unbarred the heavy door, unshuttered the window, and feasted his eyes on the pleasant afternoon light filtering through the trees, composing himself after the struggle that had divided his soul against itself in pursuit of justice.

Already he could hear the hoofbeats of the horses coming up from the bay. The two men seemed worn out by their discussions, and Abu Lutfi's face was somewhat sullen because of a slight contempt displayed by Abulafia toward the new merchandise, and his low estimate of the expected prices. But out of a sense of nobility and pride, the Ishmaelite did not examine the contents of the leopard-skin pouch concealed in his baggage, nor did he weigh it against that of Abulafia or Ben Attar. He did not wish to betray any hint of a suspicion of unfairness, which would involve him in calculations that the two Jews would handle so adroitly that he would be unable to keep up. Instead he chose to take his leave forthwith and be on his way, for in any case he and Ben Attar never returned together, so as not to tempt the devil. He fastened his possessions onto his horse, concealed the leopard-skin pouch close to the fleshly pouch that held the tokens of his manhood, and after partaking of the Jewish food that Benveniste's wife had sent for their supper, he withdrew, took his bearings, prostrated himself in the direction of the holy city of Mecca far away in the desert, cupped his hands to his ears, and delivered himself loudly and clearly of a prayer in praise of God and the Prophet, concluding with an extravagant curse upon anyone who had done or would do him any hurt. He slapped the two Jews heartily on the shoulder, and then, since he disdained to disguise himself even for safety's sake, he contented himself with wrapping his head in the scarf that his distant forebears had brought from the desert, so that anyone lying in wait would not recognize him and anyone pursuing him would not know whom he was pursuing. As twilight fell, he mounted his horse and galloped off in the direction of Granada, whither he would travel only under cover of night.

Even though Ben Attar trusted his Ishmaelite partner—indeed, felt affection and friendship toward him—he was pleased as the sound of Abu Lutfi's horse's hooves faded into the red of the dying day, for only then did he feel free to leave aside concern with commerce, coin, and news of the world and hear what had happened in the previous year to his beloved kinsman, who had been sundered by a cruel fate from his native land and his family. Although it was not prudent for two strangers, and Jews to boot, to stray too far from the inn in the darkness, the eager pair, after first taking care to conceal their respective leopard-skin pouches, pressed on into the thick of the wood, making for a spot that had become dear to them ever since their first meeting. There, among jutting rocks in the mouth of a cave hollowed out by some ancient earthquake, they lit a fire, not only to ward off any local wolf or inquisitive fox, but also to sprinkle the embers with fragrant herbs, whose smoke curling around them might perfume the joys and sorrows of the year that had passed. Notwithstanding his great curiosity to hear all about the private life of the exile, who had years before abandoned the sun and sea of North Africa in favor of the loneliness and backwardness of Christendom, Ben Attar knew well that his seniority conferred the obligation to speak first. He was duty-bound to give an account of kinsfolk—wives and mothers, sons and daughters, brothers and sisters, and other relatives and friends—whom Abulafia was keen to learn all about precisely because they had betrayed him, and then to slake his nephew's thirst for his native town, with its white houses and narrow alleys, its olive trees and palms, its vegetable gardens, its golden beach and its pink harbor. And finally to help Abulafia weep again, across the years, for his beautiful young wife, who had drowned herself because of the bewitched, feeble-witted child she had brought into the world, doubling and redoubling by her scandalous death the shame she had brought upon her husband, so that he had been compelled to banish himself.

And so, in the sweet sadness of remembrance of the past, they spent a wonderful summer's evening together on the border of the Spanish March, which neatly divided the two great faiths from each other. And although they both felt an occasional flickering anxiety for

15

the fate of the third partner, who was at this moment galloping into the depth of the night with his leopard-skin pouch dangling near his privy parts, they were also pleased that the Muslim was no longer with them, for now they were free to season their conversation with words from the holy tongue, and on the morrow, the eve of the fast of the month of Ab, when Benveniste came up together with a quorum of Jews hired especially for the purpose of praying and wailing for the ruin of the Temple, they would forget the purses full of gold and the wiles of commerce, and taking ash from the fire and smearing it on their foreheads, they would join in the eternal fear and mourning of their people.

2.

On the eastern horizon the firmament was sinking somewhat, and the moon had declined to the height of a man. Even though the captain's sole responsibility was to sail the ship, he had caught Ben Attar's anxiety about the secret, noncommercial purpose of the journey, and he rose and woke Abu Lutfi, who had been put to sleep by the mere smell of the wine, so that he should stir the ship's owner, sprawled in a drunken stupor on the deck, to visit the wife who was waiting for him in the stern. Soon dawn would break and put an end to their last night on the open sea, and from now on they would lose their anonymity; on either side of the Seine they would be tracked by suspicious natives, full of the panic of the approaching millennium, who would certainly try to board the alien ship to inspect her and find out what she was about. As Ben Attar slowly rose from the depths of his slumber, he not only felt on his face the cool, urgent breeze of the last hours of the night but also found himself looking into his partner's anxious eyes as Abu Lutfi shook him roughly. He thought painfully how wrinkled the Ishmaelite's face had become these last years, perhaps on account of the repudiation emanating from the northern partner.

Though Ben Attar wondered how he would manage to spread the wings of his desire a second time, he nevertheless hurriedly stood up, swaying at first and leaning on the side for support, staring at the dark water lapping at the stationary ship. The fire was still burning at the mouth of the invisible river, and on the shimmering water could be seen the enchanted silhouette of a gigantic bird. All the Jew's senses were opening up toward the night, which was filling with new signs, and he was almost driven to kneel, as though he had been infected by the pagan faith of the young slave, who was now standing nearby, awake as ever, with his bells tinkling in the breeze, ready to raise aloft the oil lamp and light the way before the dawn should break.

Here in the stern of the ship he had great need of the guiding light, for the breadth of the ship's hindquarters added to the confusion and deepened the darkness. He had to beware not only of the piles of cloth, the bulging sacks of condiments, and the large oil jars roped together like captives, but also of animals, which stood up as he approached, their sad eyes flickering in the darkness. The space that had opened up in the hold of this old guardship after the soldiers' bunks had been removed had inspired Abu Lutfi to add to the sheep and chickens intended for consumption a pair of very young camels, a male and a female, tethered to each other with flaxen ropes, as a present for Abulafia's new wife, to soothe her mind and help her feel and smell the essence of the Africa from which her young husband had come. At first Ben Attar had rejected this notion, but eventually he had agreed, not because he believed that the woman really wanted a pair of camels, but from a vague hope that the strange, rare animals might arouse sympathy among those of high class, who liked to buttress their nobility by means of wonderful things. But are these little camels really capable of surviving the journey? wondered Ben Attar, watching the black slave, who could not refrain from either worshipping or affectionately embracing their delicate little heads. True, Abu Lutfi did not forget to feed them a small bundle of hay every week, to which he occasionally added slices of greenish rancid butter churned before they set sail, but their bloodshot eyes and the incessant trembling of their little humps did not seem to bode well. And when will the end of the journey be? A sigh escaped from Ben Attar's heart as he descended lower and lower. Would he ever manage to return to his beloved Tangier and embrace his children again?

Upon entering his second wife's chamber, Ben Attar tried to waken and expel the rabbi's young son, who instead of sleeping next to his father in the bow had recently become fond of falling asleep in this very spot, by the dark curtain. But the boy, who spent most of the daylight hours helping the sailors, either climbing up to the crow's nest to scan the wide expanse of sea or pumping bilgewater, was sleeping so deeply that Ben Attar decided to let him be. He took the lamp from the black slave and ordered him back up on deck. Only when he was certain that the slave's footsteps were fading into the space overhead did he draw the curtain aside. Behind it was another curtain, so that he had to bend double and almost crawl on all fours to enter his second wife's bedchamber.

In this place that she had sought out for herself, so close to the bottom of the ship that you could hear the gurgle of the water, Ben Attar was assailed by the special odor not only of her body but of the rooms of her home so many miles distant. It was as if even in this cramped cabin she managed to cook her stews, air her bedding, and cultivate her flowerbeds. By the shadowy lamplight cast on the ancient, soot-blackened timbers of the guardship, which had almost gone up in flames in one of the great caliph's battles, amid rumpled bedclothes, discarded garments, and candle ends, it occurred to him that this woman had been waiting for him to come to her ever since the beginning of the night. His heart sank at the thought that all this prolonged, eager waiting might have sharpened needles of resentment that would frighten away his desire. He had hoped to enter unobserved and grope his way quietly into her bed, so as to become part of her sleep before he became one with her body, so that she would dream him before she sensed him. Only then would she be able to forgive him for bringing with him tonight the smell of the first wife's body, which he was always careful not to do.

But she was awake. Her long, fin-shaped, amber-colored eyes were bloodshot from lack of sleep, like those of a newly trapped wild beast. In the city a veritable maze of alleys separated his two houses, so that each wife could feel that her universe was separate and self-contained—although he, who plied between the two, knew that the distance was less than it appeared to them, and in fact he was sometimes amazed at how little it was. Some nights, smitten with the anxiety of delicious longing, he climbed up onto the roof and floated across to the roof of the other house over the domes of the white city,

which lay still in the moonlight like the breasts of pale maidens floating on a lake, as though he were a sailor leaping from prow to stern.
That may have been the reason why at the beginning of the spring,
when, at first desperately and later enthusiastically, he had first
thought of gathering together the merchandise that had been sadly
idle for nearly two years, sailing with it to that faraway town called
Paris, and having a face-to-face meeting with the partner who had
been severed from them, it had not seemed strange to take both his
wives with him. He was convinced that the calm, harmonious presence of the two wives side by side would prove to Abulafia's new,
knowledgeable wife better than any rhetorical argument how far she
was from understanding the quality of love that prevailed on the
southern shore of the Mediterranean Sea.

Of one thing Ben Attar was always certain: his deep and precise
knowledge of the nature of the care and love that inspired happiness
and security in his wives. Every act of love with one of them involved
an anxious concern for the other. Otherwise, how could he have asked
them to leave their children and do without servants, to give up the
scented warmth of spacious homes with beautiful tableware and luxurious beds, and squeeze like fugitives from a war into tiny, rocking
cabins on board a ship sailing north instead of east, on an unknown
route? If he himself, who had passed his fortieth year and was entitled
to contemplate seriously the approach of death, was prepared to endure the hardships of such a lengthy journey, were they, being so much
younger than he, entitled to refuse? Surely they knew well that it was
also for their sakes that he was undertaking this daring voyage. Even if
they felt apprehension about their ability to withstand the hardships,
surely they should feel no less apprehension about the wandering of a
solitary man, who for many long days would be not only without a
bedmate but without a kind word to caress his careworn brow. If he
were to take with him only the first wife, whose two sons were now old
enough to fend for themselves, and spare the second, whose only child
was five years old and still tied to the hem of her robe, surely he would
be undermining the living and compelling proof of the stability and
equilibrium of his double marriage, by means of which he wished to
surprise his nephew's sanctimonious wife, who could not imagine even
now, in this dawn when he was at the mouth of the river, that in a few

more days he would glide on his strange guardship to the very threshold of her house, to bring her this living proof.

Ben Attar's uncle, however, the famous scholar Ben Ghiyyat, was not entirely happy about the idea of subjecting two wives who had scarcely met to prolonged and indelicate proximity in the narrow confines of a small ship. Surely it would be an assured source of storms and troubles over and above those caused by the winds and the waves. So that his nephew would not be left alone in the company of sailors, who were in the habit of seeking sin in every port, the good uncle had a mind to send a letter to his friends in Andalus asking them to prepare for the honored voyager, from his first port of call, Cadiz, a third, temporary wife, for the purpose of this journey only. A woman who would be at home on the ship and happy dwelling on the sea, with the waves as her companions. A woman whose bill of divorce would be signed together with her marriage deed and would be waiting for her on her return, in the port in which her married life had begun. Politely, with due respect to his distinguished uncle, whose white hair and beard he greatly admired, Ben Attar swiftly declined this well-intentioned initiative, which would only add fuel to the fire that was already burning against him far away. He was absolutely confident of the power of his understanding love to quell any storm caused by loneliness or jealousy, like that which was now pent up in the confines of this cabin.

At home he was always careful not to lie down beside his second wife, let alone touch her, until he was certain of her utter reconciliation, for even a grain of resentment can reduce desire to mere ardor incapable of bringing relief. Consequently, whenever back in Tangier he entered her delightful bedchamber, with its high, blue-washed ceiling and its window looking out on the sea, he would first scrutinize her long, lovely face, whose angularity sometimes recalled that of a sad man, and if he observed the slightest shadow around her eyes or her mouth he preferred not to approach her, even if the sweet pain of desire was already burgeoning in his loins. First he would go over to the window to look at the boats in the bay, then he would return and walk slowly around her bed, which was covered in striking colorful blankets that Abu Lutfi found especially for her among the nomadic tribes of the northern Sahara. Softly and casually he would start talking to her about the troubles and pains of kith and kin, so that the miseries of the world would enter into her and soothe away any resentment or grudge that she felt toward him. Only then, when he could see the dim amber hue of her eyes sparkling with moisture brought out by the duty of compassion, would he permit himself to sit down on the end of her bed, which was also his own bed, and quivering with excitement, as though traveling back in time to his wedding night, he would delicately draw her perfumed legs, their down smoothed and softened by warm honey, one at a time out of the rumpled covers, and press them to his face as though trying to identify with his lips the legs of the young woman who had stamped on the dust of the small yard of her home when he had come and indicated to her father his wish to marry her. Only then did he permit himself to begin to caress her from the top of her long thighs down to her toes, talking all the while softly and unhurriedly about the prospect of his death, which in the case of a man like him, who had passed his fortieth year, was not only possible but indeed natural. And only thus, with the permission he gave her to contemplate without any sense of guilt a new young husband who would wed her after his approaching death, did her shuddering acceptance begin, and he would feel her foot clench in his hands. Unlike the first wife, who was shaken to the core of her being by any talk of death concerning himself or others, this one, who was younger and sadder, was attracted by talk about his death, which not only stirred her curiosity and hope for herself but also aroused her tender desire for him, which he promptly took up and sprinkled upon himself like fragrant powdered garlic.

But now he was afraid to mention the reassuring prospect of his death even in a lighthearted or jocular way. The subject might appear brightly lit and charged with sweet sadness by the window looking out over the Bay of Tangier, but here, in this cramped little cabin in the very bottom of the creaking ship, it filled even him with dread. Therefore, without a further unnecessary word of apology, he entered, hung the lamp on an iron hook above her bed, unbuckled the belt full of jewels and laid it by her head, then boldly removed all his clothes. But before lying down naked next to his wife he tied his ankles with some coils of yellow rope left over from those with which the caliph's admiral had reinforced the ship's timbers, and then he took off the heavy silver chain that hung around his neck and bound his wrists together with it, so that she would understand that nothing prevented her from taking whatever she wanted from his body and his soul. Maybe like this she would be able, if not to forgive him, at least to reconcile herself to the fact that he had married her as his second, not his first, wife.

Although she was surprised that he surrendered himself to her so unconditionally, stripped and bound, which he had never done before, she still recoiled from him and was in no hurry to remove her shift, but took down the lamp to shed light on the body stretched out at her feet, to check whether since their last lovemaking any more curls on his chest had turned that silver color that always excited her so, because it was given to so few men to have their hair turn white before death cut them off. Now she confirmed what she had imagined. The same days of sun and clear skies that had ruthlessly tanned her own skin had whitened the hair on her husband's head and chest, so that it was hard to know whether to lament the new signs of his approaching demise or to rejoice over the mysterious beauty with which they endowed him. A sweet sadness flooded her soul, and she could not refrain from laying her curly head upon the chest of the man who had come to her so late in the night.

In the silence that encompassed her, she was unable to feel, as she had hoped, the beating of her husband's heart. All she could feel was the painful and unfamiliar outline of his ribs. With a strange selfish thrill she reflected that not only had her own body become gaunt from seasickness and meager rations, but her husband's sturdy frame too was becoming lean from constant worry about the future of his business, which was threatened, more than anything else, by his marriage to her. And now a venomous gleam flickered in her beautiful, slightly myopic eyes, which had so far been narrowed to slits and now opened in offense. She looked contentedly at what in her bedroom at home merely appeared and disappeared between her body and the sheets, whereas here it was entirely revealed, shrunk into itself, as though it had changed into a mouse. So sorry did she feel for that part of her husband's body and for herself that she lifted her head a little, and still without looking at the face of the man who had bound himself before her, she began to speak about the first wife, which she had never dared to do before.

22

A shiver of fear shook Ben Attar, and his eyes closed. He had become accustomed on this long voyage, in the evening twilight, when the waves swallowed the last traces of the sun, to sometimes finding the two women sitting on the bridge where in bygone days captains had commanded battles. With their gaudy veils fluttering in the sea breeze, they exchanged words without looking at each other, with blank faces, like a pair of spies. He had the feeling that throughout this long sea voyage they were passing to each other the most hidden secrets touching him, and his heart swelled with dread, and also with excitement, at the thought of the horizons of desire that extended before the three of them. And sometimes he went so far as to imagine that he could bring to Abulafia's new wife in Paris, who was pitting herself against him, not only a living proof that would overcome her opposition but a new, sharp temptation that she would have no defense against—a temptation that he could now feel upon his flesh, in his loins, here in the swaying cabin, between the slurping of the water, the smells of the spices, and the quiet groaning of the young camels, as the young wife questioned him about his lovemaking earlier in the night and answered her own questions.

Her answers caught the picture and the feeling as accurately as if she had somehow participated in that lovemaking, and as if even now that she was alone she did not want to let go, at least in speech, of what he had done to the first wife. Panic-stricken, he tried to free his hands, which were coiled in his silver chain, and take hold of her face and stop her mouth. But the coils that had been meant to be symbolic had become all too real, and as soon as she discerned his purpose she started to struggle, as fiercely and desperately as if he were to be made to pay not just for what he had done earlier to the first wife but for all the unrequited excitement that had quickened within her as she watched the sailors wandering around half naked on deck.

Angrily she reached out to catch the minuscule mouse, as though she wanted to strangle it or even to tear it apart, but the mouse disappeared, and in its place there reared up a gentle young snake, which soon hardened into a fierce lizard that tried to escape from between her fingers and lay its thin vertical lips upon her eyeballs. Then, from the lust that moved painfully before her, she knew that her husband was regretting having tied himself up, and her spirit began to be appeased, for now that he was bound helplessly, not spontaneously, she was able to remove her shift and take from him slowly and right to the end everything that he owed her, not only since they had set sail on this voyage but ever since her father had given her to him as wife, even if she ended up dragging out of herself a wild moan that would rouse the boy sleeping on the other side of the curtain.

But the loud groan that almost turned into a shriek of pleasure did not even scrape the outer shell of Rabbi Elbaz's son's consciousness, so deeply was he immersed in youthful slumber. Instead, it startled the young slave, who had crept back to warm himself against the lordly bodies of the young camels and to remind himself of the smell of the desert from which he had been snatched. Virgin though he was, he understood only too well the meaning of the groans, which flooded his heart, as though through two curtains his master's rod had pierced him too. He stroked the hindparts of the two camels, who also, to judge by their closed eyes, understood what it was that was echoing around them. Who knew, he thought, if they too would not be slaughtered and cooked before the ship reached the city? He wanted to bow his head and pray to the spirit of the fragrant bones that death would draw out of them, but eventually he gave up and shinned up the rope ladder to disappear before the Jew came out and flogged him, even though this time he had sinned by hearing alone and not by seeing. He was suddenly seized with a longing to enter the little cabin in the bow and see the smile of the first wife, whose white body he had seen gleaming earlier in the night. At this time he could go wherever his spirit wished, for the ship was still, every last sailor was asleep, himself excepted. He was kept awake and alert from the start of the night to its end by the divinity that emanated from everything, so that in these last moments of the night he became the true master of the ship, and if he wished he could even weigh anchor and hoist the triangular sail, and instead of sailing east along the river and into the heart of Europe he could head due west and sail beyond the horizon into a new world.

But a little bird striking a rope with its wings proclaimed that dawn was nigh. Before he had time to bow down and worship before its tiny holiness, it gave a chirp and sped off toward a new speck of light moving into the horizon of the new continent. Even though it was but a speck, it was sufficient to wake Rabbi Elbaz, of whom the rhyming words of the poem that had been swaying all night between his thoughts and his dreams demanded order and logic. But since the fine rays of light drawn slowly from the land were still too faint to illuminate the lines rustling on the paper concealed among the sheepskins that were his bed, he took on deck only his quill pen, which soon, as the light grew stronger, he would be able to sharpen and dip into his inkhorn, and then he would be able to insert the correct word in place of the empty space that had been waiting for it for several days. He bowed his head in shamed gratitude to the black slave, who now handed him the morning dish, fat olives drowned in an oily sauce in which to dip pieces of the warm bread that lay beside it. For forty days now he had sailed in this boat, and still he felt embarrassed whenever this slave waited on him, as though he were unworthy of it. After the birth of his only son, his wife had been so weak that he had assumed all the household chores himself. And he had enjoyed the housework that he was forced to do in her place, openly or secretly, so much that since her death he had found it hard to remarry, for where would he find a healthy wife who would consent to be waited on by him?

And so now, as bundles of gray cloud floated in the air, he ate with bowed head, holding the platter between his hands, careful not to make a movement or say a word that might encourage the young slave to continue to wait upon him, lest the slave would get carried away and prostrate himself and kiss the hem of the rabbi's threadbare robe. He had done this one evening, seized by a powerful religious feeling, and the rabbi had been compelled to complain about him to Abu Lutfi, who had flogged his protégé prodigiously. But no, this time the young man did not seem to be returning to his old ways. As the morning mist thickened, with his master's two acts of lovemaking and the smell of wine, which still wafted around the deck, a mighty tiredness had befallen him, and now, for all his youth, he would have gladly lain down and died upon the sail folded at his feet. But he still had to carry out Ben Attar's orders and make certain that the rabbi did not toss all his olive stones overboard but hide one in the pouch suspended near his heart, to ensure the correct counting of the days, for it had already happened that the Jews had lost count of their sacred seventh day. This morning the rabbi did not neglect his task as timekeeper, and after sucking the juicy flesh of the last olive he placed the stone with the five others and smiled cordially at the young slave, who was so exhausted that he could scarcely stagger to the first wife, who had just climbed up, her heavy body draped in a red embroidered robe, onto the old bridge, where she stood as splendidly as though she were the caliph himself. He did not know if she wanted some of the honey drink that he concocted for her each morning, or if she wished first to discover whether all had passed well there in the stern of the ship. He stood motionless for a moment, his weary young body torn asunder by conflicting forces. But Abu Lutfi's stern voice, as he came to rouse the sleeping crew, spurred the slave's legs on toward the regal woman, around whom the mist that was thickening as the daylight grew brighter wafted like incense. Already he could discern an unfamiliar hint of anxiety clouding her round, bright face, which was lit as always by a pleasant smile, and his soul longed to soothe her care, but he did not know what to say or how to say it, and so he closed his eyes and began to sigh deeply, once and then once more, as though he were trying to transmit to her all the second wife's sighs of satisfaction and cries of pleasure.

3.

But where would this poem meander to next, Rabbi Elbaz asked himself as the sailors toiled in the morning mist to hoist the sail, which had been reduced in size during the night in readiness for the delicate task of sailing up the river. For the rabbi, the mere fact of writing a poem was something wonderful; he had never imagined that he himself would be able or eager to do such a thing. But during the previous week six lines had put themselves together, all in Hebrew, following the meter and rhyme scheme that had been brought to Andalus from the east by Dunash Ben Labrat. Right from the start, from the moment he embarked with his son on Ben Attar's ship, which had come to the port of Cadiz especially to fetch him, he had had a feeling that his life was about to undergo some great change. At first he had been alarmed and depressed at the sight of the cramped little cabins, the swaying deck fenced around with ropes, and the sacks of condiments and jars tied together in the dark hold, which gave off unfamiliar, pungent African odors at night. Accustomed as he was to the bright beauty of his home town, Seville, and to the elegant courtesy of its inhabitants, he was terror-stricken at the sight of the half-naked Arab sailors with yellow flaxen ropes wrapped around their bodies, shouting orders gruffly to each other and cuffing the black slave who ran in and out among them. The two veiled women too, sitting on the bridge barefoot in colorful robes, did not reassure the new traveler as he tried in vain to control his son, who shinned blithely up and down the ropes like a little monkey. In the twilight, as the ship set sail slowly into the vast ocean that he had never so much as set eyes on before, and as it began to heave beneath him relentlessly in a previously unknown rhythm, he was overcome with dizziness and nausea. Shamefully, privately, through a small porthole, he cast forth upon the waters illumined by the reddish glow of the sunset the morning meal that the congregation in the house of study in Cadiz had offered him in gratitude for the homily he had delivered to them, and at midnight he spewed out from the depths of his bowels the remains of the farewell dinner that his late wife's family had held for him in Seville. By dawn, exhausted by a sleepless night, he felt that he might make his peace with the sea, but when he set eyes on the empty eye sockets of the baked fish the black slave set before him, his stomach erupted all over again. He immediately vowed to fast. He was accustomed to vows and fasts from the time of his wife's illness. But still the nausea did not abate. Pale, gaunt, with sunken eyes, he no longer tried to conceal his suffering but openly leaned over the ropes with his mouth wide open and his eyes fluttering, staring wildly, like a fish taken from the sea, dreaming of the day they would reach the port of Lisbon, where he could withdraw from this maritime adventure. He was not made for this. He was just like the prophet Jonah, he said apologetically to the owner of the ship, who had hired him and pinned his hopes on him: the sea was not happy with him. Only God did not summon a great fish to swallow him whole.

Ben Attar was accustoming himself to the idea that he might have to do without the help of religion in the confrontation that lay ahead with the new wife and the sages she mustered on her side, for if he sent the rabbi overland from Lisbon to Paris he would arrive only in the autumn, by which time they would be on their way home, when to his surprise Abd el-Shafi intervened. Knowing nothing of the part of the rabbi in the expedition, he felt responsible as captain for the suffering that his ship was causing the new passenger. First he took it upon himself to slow the ship, but seeing that the rabbi continued to suffer, he obtained permission from Ben Attar to halt for a whole day. He turned into a quiet cove, furled the sail so that not even the slightest breeze would rock the ship, cast anchor, and fixed the two steering oars opposite each other so the ship would be perfectly stationary. On the old bridge, from which the caliph's officers had once kept watch on the Christian ships to make sure they did not cross the invisible line that divided the Mediterranean between the two opposing faiths, he set a comfortable couch stuffed with wool and straw and draped with soft, gently colored rugs for the thirty-three-year-old rabbi, whom he saw as ringed around with a fine aura of sanctity. There they settled the suffering passenger, whose very beard had turned green. Then the captain began to boil up a special brew that the Vikings had used to allay the panic of those captives whom they did not kill: a decoction of fish fins flavored with finely ground scales, quenched with lemon juice, to which was added green seaweed that a diver brought up from the sea bed. When it was ready, the patient's hands were bound, and Abd el-Shafi insisted on personally pouring the acrid, steaming liquid down the convulsed rabbi's throat with his own wooden spoon. Indeed, by evening the vomiting had begun to cease, and the rabbi's son, Samuel, who had taken the opportunity afforded by his father's illness to climb to the top of the mast, was able to see from his aerie the pink gradually returning to his father's broad brow. As for the rabbi, he had a clear sense of the purgative and even spiritual quality of the Viking broth that had been poured inside him.

And so, on board a stilled ship not far from the port of Lisbon, a deep sleep fell upon Rabbi Elbaz, and so peaceful was his slumber that the captain did not wait for dawn but gave orders for the sail to be hoisted and the anchor weighed, so that the ship would forge ahead and when the rabbi awoke after a day's sleep he would feel the rocking of the waves beneath him to be a natural and even necessary part of the world's being.

Indeed, the vomiting did not return to plague the rabbi from Seville, even on stormy days, and from that time on he learned to take pleasure in sailing on the sea. He preferred, even at night, to remain on deck so as not to miss the movement of the glittering sky as it led the ship on. At midnight, when Abd el-Shafi turned in in his own hammock, leaving a sailor or two to navigate by the stars, the rabbi would take a leopard skin and a sheepskin and lay them one on top of the other on the old bridge, which was warmed by the bodies of the two barefoot women who had sat there during the day, and there he would sink into an open-air sleep in search of a dream—either a real dream, if one came, or if not, then at least a waking dream combining snatches of memory with bundles of wishes. All unawares, his mind began to shed layer after layer, losing some of its scholarly clarity and curiosity in favor of a new philosophical introspection blended with a certain sentimentality.

The sharp-eyed owner had begun to notice signs of lethargy and indolence every time he told the slave to take the rabbi the ivory casket crammed with strips of parchment inscribed with the teachings of the sages and sayings of local saints, which had been selected especially for him by the famous uncle, Ben Ghiyyat, to season Andalusian scholarship and wisdom with North African wit and mystery. It did not seem as though the rabbi was interested in reading or studying anything new on the issue of dual marriage, which he had been hired to defend. The arguments he had prepared back in Seville seemed perfectly sound, and if there were any need to reinforce them, it was preferable not to use the Scriptures but the unwritten law, which billowed up first in the mind, then turned sometimes into chance, long-drawn-out conversations with Ben Attar, who may perhaps only have been waiting for an encounter with a bored sea traveler to speak openly about himself and his life. Whatever Ben Attar did not or could not tell, his two wives sometimes related, especially the first, but sometimes the second too, who for some reason was still somewhat afraid of the rabbi, who was only seven years her senior. And whatever the wives were unable to see or understand, the partner, Abu Lutfi, could add from his own Ishmaelite perspective. If even he omitted or concealed some detail, perhaps from an excess of loyalty, the captain or some clever sailor could often supply it, for anyone, if he is compelled, is able to deduce one thing from another. Even the black slave would have been regarded by the rabbi as a qualified witness, if he would only cease kneeling before him in the heart of the night.

But some ten days before, as the ship began to sail past the jagged coves of Brittany, Ben Attar had noticed that the rabbi was holding between his fingers a goose quill that he constantly sharpened with a penknife, licking the sharpened tip with an expression of wistful shrewdness on his face, as though his soul had been stung by a genuine idea. Not a day had passed before Ben Attar observed that the rabbi was using it to inscribe words upon an unfamiliar strip of parchment. The slowness of the writing, on the one hand, and the speed with which the parchment was concealed whenever Ben Attar approached, on the other, attested to the fact that it was not some new homily that was being indited, or a commentary on a difficult text, or an elaborate ethical argument, but something else. Ben Attar kept watch from a distance and noticed how a line was added or deleted and replaced by another, which was crossed out in its turn. Eventually his curiosity got the better of him, and he instructed the son of the desert to approach the rabbi's bed while he slept and extract the parchment. What he saw confirmed his fears. He discovered the disjointed lines of a poem or hymn, which began in Arabic and continued in the holy tongue.

Secretly, by the light of a candle, Ben Attar attempted to decipher the writing, at first word by word and eventually line by line. What he read filled him with sadness. The hints of the rabbi's desire for Ben Attar's wives in the last two lines impugned his honor, but as he was about to tear up the parchment and throw it overboard, he remarked to himself that a poem composed so laboriously was indubitably etched on the mind of the author, who would write it out again and take all the more pains to conceal it. So he had the parchment restored to its place, so that he could continue to watch over it. While the black slave unfastened the robe of the sleeping poet so as to reinsert the poem furtively in the inside pocket and in doing so perhaps absorb some of the heat that the unseen god vouchsafes to those who believe in him, the ship's owner continued to reflect on the rabbi whom his uncle had attached to him. Would he really be of any help? Surely he was supposed to pay him not for writing verses of unrequited longing, but for compiling subtle and persuasive textual arguments against his partner

Abulafia's new wife, who had come between them and had left him in a spot, with no buyers for his merchandise. Overcome once more with pity for his rejected wares, he found himself making his way under the triangular canvas of the sail to peer into the hold. Here, in the fragrant darkness pierced by rays of moonlight filtering through the timbers of the deck, the ropes binding the great jars and sacks seemed to have dissolved, and the containers stood before him like a company of men possessed by a sense of fellowship in the face of common misfortune, for which their master would soon be called to account. One of the great sacks suddenly stood erect and strode toward the trembling Jew, who strangled a scream. But it was only Abu Lutfi, who liked to sleep close to his hidden store of daggers encrusted with precious stones. He too was unable to sleep, as in the Roman inn in the hills above Barcelona on those summer nights of the years 4756 and 4757 of the creation of the world, according to the Jewish way of reckoning, when Abulafia was arriving later and later for their appointed meetings.

It was only two years later that Ben Attar had realized that if he had only taken the trouble to understand the cause of the delays, he might have reached an earlier appraisal of the repudiation that was taking concrete shape in the north. For it was during those years that the first threads were being spun that were to tie Abulafia to a new woman, a widow who had come to Francia from a small town on the banks of the River Rhine. At that stage Abulafia was mentioning her only as a loyal customer, not as a possible bride, but by reading between the lines it should have been evident that a new hand was involved, wittingly or unwittingly, in Abulafia's ever-lengthening delays. Abu Lutfi, to his credit, did not delude himself, and was skeptical from the outset about Abulafia's pretexts and explanations. Right from the start of the partnership he was convinced that sooner or later a day would come when Abulafia would vanish with the goods. So strong was this belief that the delays only seemed to him like a foretaste of the eventual disappearance that the northern partner was preparing for his associates. Consequently, when Abulafia recounted the hardships of his journey owing to new conflicts between warring duchies, which kept altering the frontiers and so delaying his progress, Abu Lutfi would turn his eyes away from the speaker and fix them on the flame of the campfire to purge them from the polluting falsehood. If Abulafia embroiled himself in further complexities, the Ishmaelite would wind his headscarf around his head and ears and move even closer to the flames, which almost scorched his clothes, as if to say, *And this is a partner! Go to someone who is willing to believe whatever you say!* Indeed, Ben Attar was so excited and happy at the appearance of his beloved nephew, whom his anxiety and fear had already depicted in his imagination as— heaven forbid—dead or injured or taken captive, that he strained his hardest to believe every word of Abulafia's explanations. To strengthen his faith he would inquire repeatedly about the signs of the famous millennium, which was already suspended, Abulafia claimed, in the heavens like a huge cloud containing a great glimmering red cross. Even though it was still a few years off, men's minds were already confused from thinking about it. Even Abulafia should have known that one who had failed to rise from the dead a thousand years ago would not suddenly come on a visit a thousand years later. In any case, Jews had nothing to fear from thunders and lightnings in the sky, since they had been promised from time immemorial that heaven would always stand at their right hand. But still, there was no certainty that on the face of the earth they would be able to abate the zealots' fury at not being permitted to eat the messianic banquet for which they had been toiling for so many years.

While Abulafia told his partners about the mounting fear of the Christians over the approaching millennium, Ben Attar laid his hand lightly on Abu Lutfi's shoulder as he lay almost in the campfire and reflected on how easy relations between Ishmaelites and Israelites were. Before the thousandth anniversary of the birth of their prophet, the Messiah son of Joseph and the Messiah son of David would have arrived to put every spurious prophet in his proper place. For Abulafia's safety, Ben Attar advised him to come back across the border between the two great faiths in preparation for the millennium and take a house close to Benveniste's tavern, where he could also lodge his wretched daughter and her nurse, so as to spend the millennial year in the company of those who counted the years differently. Who knew whether the unusual nature of the child, whom Ben Attar himself had not set eyes upon these seven years, might not arouse evil thoughts in the heart of someone who wished in this holy year to rid the world of all his own demons? Ben Attar couched his thoughts in cautious words so as not to offend his beloved nephew. Although he might have been the first to notice that the face of the baby born to his nephew thirteen years before the impending millennium was not right, he would never have presumed of his own accord to associate her, by so much as a hint, with the demonic world.

It was her beautiful mother, Abulafia's late wife, who in her despair had soon called her baby "my she-devil" or "the little witch," so as to negate the evil thoughts of others by anticipating them. The poor woman thought she would show her family and friends that she was not afraid of her child, and was even prepared to see her strangeness as a kind of comical gift sent by heaven to try her. Not only did she make no attempt to hide the baby with the bulging eyes and the narrow forehead, but she made a point of taking her around, dressed in a shiny silk gown and adorned with colored ribbons, in an effort to include her kinsfolk and companions in the trial that God had sent her way. But it seemed that even if they tried, none could extract affection from a baby who cried in a deep, dull voice that made their hearts shudder. In particular, her grandmother, Abulafia's mother and Ben Attar's older sister, did not take to her. The old woman sank into depression at the sight of her demonic granddaughter, whom her daughter-in-law brought to see her every day, to show her how she was growing and developing. Abulafia was soon obliged to intervene so as to prevent his wife from making the poor child into the sole test of the world's humanity. As he had difficulty in exercising his authority over her and getting her to cease her wanderings, particularly her daily visits to his mother, one morning he locked the iron-clad door of the house when he went out to Ben Ghiyyat's little house of study, where he would intone the morning prayers in his beautiful voice before going off to serve in Ben Attar's shop. At first he felt pangs of remorse for what he had done, then he believed that his wife would manage to escape, and eventually he was so busy that he forgot all about her. But when he returned that evening he found his house locked as he had left it, with the baby asleep in her cradle and his wife's beautiful face pale and sunken in silent sadness. That night she knelt before him and promised not to disobey him again and not to take the baby to his mother, so long as he swore never again to lock her in alone with the baby, and he acceded to her request.

Consequently, not a soul suspected her motives when on the next day, before the time of the afternoon prayer, she appeared with her baby at Ben Attar's shop and asked her husband to watch over the fruit of his loins for a short while, so that she might stroll in the market square and seek fresh amulets from the nomads coming in from the desert, in the hope that they might counteract the spells that were bewitching her daughter. In the meantime, Abulafia went as usual to chant the afternoon and evening prayers in his melodious voice in Ben Ghiyyat's prayer house, and so Uncle Ben Attar was called upon to watch over the bundle that had been deposited among the bolts of cloth until her mother returned. But she was in no hurry to come back. At first she did indeed walk to the city gate and wander among the stalls of the nomads from the distant Sahara, but she recoiled from the twisted, hairy amulets of the idolaters, not even daring to pick them up and feel them. Instead she was attracted for some reason by an old fishhook made from an elephant's tail, which she purchased, and she hastened outside the walls of the city to the seashore to try to catch a real fish. At that twilight hour there was not a soul to be seen on the shore except a Muslim fisherman, who was startled by her, for it was not usual on the seashore at Tangier to see a young woman wandering on her own, not to mention a Jewess, especially one holding a fishhook. And so when she addressed him and asked him to show her how to prepare the hook and cast it into the water, he hesitated at first to become involved with her, but because she was very beautiful he could not refuse her, and after learning from him what she learned, she removed her sandals, rolled up her robe, and clambered onto a rock, where she sat down and dropped her hook into the waves of the sea, which occasionally broke violently and splashed her. Her luck was with her, and in the first few minutes she managed to catch a large fish. Flushed with her unexpected success, she refused to leave the shore, which was wrapped in the glow of the setting sun, and the fisherman, who had begun to fear that this would not end well, wondered whether to remain where he was and see that the waves did not wash her away or hurry to carry news of her to whoever by now must surely be looking for her. But when darkness fell and the shadowy figure on the rock became blurred, he was afraid that if anything happened to her he would be held to blame, and so he ran inside the walls to tell one of the Jews about her. Right inside the gate he stumbled on Abulafia and Ben Attar and the Jews from the yeshiva, who were looking for her, but when they hurried to the rock where she was said to be sitting, all they found was the fishhook thrust into a crevice. At first Abulafia turned on the fisherman, and then he demanded that he be bound and forced to confess the truth, but when at high tide the sea gave up his wife's body, with her hands and feet tied with the colored ribbons she had used to adorn her daughter's clothing, all knew at once that she had taken her own life and that no man's hand had touched her for evil.

It was not only shame at his wife's grievous sin and guilt at his own indifference and strictness which had caused it but also a terrible anger at his mother that made Abulafia ask to be banished from his native city. He thought at first to punish his mother by secretly leaving the accursed child in her house and going off himself to the Land of Israel, whose sanctity would atone for all their transgressions. But Ben Attar, suspecting his intentions, caught the poor wretch hiding in the hold of an Egyptian ship, and with the assistance of Ben Ghiyyat he compelled him at the last moment to return to dry land. To make up for the unsuccessful flight and to prevent a future recurrence, he proposed a small commercial expedition—to take some camel hides and skins of wild beasts from the desert to some merchants in Granada. As for the bewitched babe, if Abulafia's mother indeed refused to take her into her home, Ben Attar himself would take care of her for the time being. Thus, instead of sailing eastward to the Holy Land, which almost certainly would have atoned for nothing and might even in its holiness have embroiled the sinner in additional sins, the grieving widower went to Andalus with a large and heavy cargo of hides, freed of bearing the reproaches of his kith and kin. Since Ben Attar's first wife, who at that time was his only wife, was afraid to keep the deformed child in her home in case the new fetus that was or would be in her belly should peep out, behold his destined playmate, and refuse to emerge into the light of day, Abu Lutfi went to a nearby village and brought back for Ben Attar a distant kinswoman, an elderly, experienced nurse, who would look after the child in Abulafia's empty house until the widowed father returned from his journey.

Abulafia, however, was in no hurry to return from his journey, but extended it considerably on his own initiative. When he learned that people in the Christian country of Catalonia were eager for such hides as he had brought from the desert, he contained himself and did not sell the merchandise in Granada but traveled north and crossed the frontier of the faiths near Barcelona so as to meet Christian merchants, who indeed leapt upon his wares and doubled his profit. Instead of returning at once to Tangier, the young trader decided to exploit the breach he had made. He sent the proceeds back to his uncle with a pair of trustworthy Jews from Tarragona and requested fresh merchandise, while he himself pressed on into the villages and estates of southern Provence to identify new customers and gain a sense of their wants, taking advantage of the protection afforded by the signing in those years of a new treaty among the Christians known as the "Peace of God," which was made with the aim of protecting traders and wayfarers. He did not inquire about the baby he had left behind. It was as if she did not exist.

This may have been the secret reason for the rapid success of Ben Attar's trading network, whose head was in the Bay of Tangier while its two arms embraced the Atlas Mountains in the south and Provence and Gascony in the north. Afraid and ashamed to return to his native town and grateful to his uncle for looking after the infant, Abulafia had resolved to repay Ben Attar, his benefactor and employer, with feverish energy and imaginative resourcefulness, which year by year widened both the circle of his customers and the range of his merchandise. Abu Lutfi could no longer make do with his traditional spring journey to the northern Atlas but had to penetrate deeper into the valleys and the villages, and even inside the nomads' tents, in search of polished brassware, curved daggers, and pungent condiments, for the smell of the desert sufficed to attract and excite the new Christian customers, who began to remember as their millennium approached that their crucified Lord too had come to them from the desert. Meanwhile, the Ishmaelite nurse stayed with the bewitched child, who had been forgotten by everyone except Ben Attar, who looked in occasionally to check that she still existed and that he was not paying money to maintain a ghost.

But the baby, despite her many defects, did not seem to want to turn into a ghost. She insisted on remaining as real as always. Even though she was very backward in her development and limited in her movements, and her eyes remained bulging and blank, as though she belonged to a different race, nevertheless she increased the range of her movement so that the stern-faced Ishmaelite nurse was obliged to take great care to see that there was no loophole in the house through which her charge might accidentally escape into a world that was not expecting her. At this point the uncle's uncle, the sage Ben Ghiyyat, intervened, when he went in the spring to prepare Abulafia's house for Passover. Whatever might have been the Creator's purpose in forming such a creature, the covenant made at Mount Sinai still embraced her too, and her father who begot her could not be replaced by an Ishmaelite nurse, who owed nothing to the God of Israel except her inferiority. And even though Ben Attar was by now accustomed to the responsibility he had taken upon himself, and feared that if Abulafia were forced to take his child back his sense of guilt would be diminished and with it his energy and resourcefulness, which in the past two years had made Ben Attar into one of the grandees of the city, he did not wish to disobey his great uncle, who at fifty-five years of age seemed to frighten death itself. Although Abulafia could not be compelled to return to Tangier and take back his offspring, Ben Attar decided to take her to her father himself, in person and without prior warning.

And so, ten years before the millennium, Ben Attar and Abu Lutfi set out on their first journey from Tangier to the port of Barcelona. Although they repeated the journey summer after summer, increasing the number of ships each year, the memory of the first trip was engraved deeply in Ben Attar's heart, and not only because of the novelty of the voyage, which showed him close up how the natural forces—the sun, the moon, the galaxies, the wind, the waves—contended silently opposite the lazily moving shoreline, but because of the intimacy that grew up in the narrow confines of the ship between him and his fellow travelers, especially the strange, dumb child, for even though she was attached by a cord to the nurse who accompanied her, it was not short enough to prevent her from toddling to him from time to time and attempting to thrust her little fingers into his eyes. Sailing slowly among the bolts of cloth, hides, and oil jars, against the background of the monotonous prattle of a Jew from Barcelona who was traveling with them, he forged a bond with Abulafia's child, so that occasionally he even let her snuggle mutely against his chest and watch the forms of the two Ishmaelite sailors, who in the midday heat removed their

clothes and stood on the prow as naked as on the day of their birth.
Occasionally, when they camped in some desolate bay on the way and
he saw the child walking slowly along the shore in the evening twilight,
he remembered her mother, who despite everything had bequeathed
something of her great beauty to her defective child—a soft line on the
cheek, a certain hue, the molding of a thigh. Indeed, on this voyage
Ben Attar thought a great deal about Abulafia's suicidal wife, as though
he too bore some guilt, until one night on the sea, in pain and desire,
she burst into his dreams.

As it turned out, he was very careful not to let the least hint of this
dream escape from his mouth, precisely because the meeting with
Abulafia was so emotional, so brimming with love and friendship, that
the three of them wept real tears. Yes, all three of them. Abu Lutfi was
the first to give in and burst into tears as he embraced his long-haired
comrade, who was waiting for them in a new black Christian habit at
the entrance to the Roman inn, to which the Jew from Barcelona had
taken them. The sobbing of the manly Ishmaelite was so surprising
that Abulafia was carried away. Then Ben Attar too felt a lump in his
throat, but not enough to make him forget the final return of the child
to her father's care. He gave a signal, and the large nurse, who was
standing a few paces away, drew forth the child who was hiding in her
skirts and gestured to her to approach Abulafia, who first of all uttered
a cry of panic at the unfamiliar bird that was fluttering toward him but
then closed his eyes in pain and clasped his child to his chest warmly,
strongly, as though he had just realized that he too had been longing
for her in her loneliness. But on the next day, in between talking about
merchandise and rates of exchange, about merchants' hopes and purchasers' fickleness, it struck Ben Attar that Abulafia imagined that they
had brought the child there only to see him, and that she would eventually return whence she had come. Delicately but decisively, he had
to remind his nephew of his duties as a father, supporting his words
with texts supplied by the sage Ben Ghiyyat. Abulafia listened in silence and read the texts, nodding his head, and after reflection consented to take the child back. Was it only from a simple sense of
paternal duty, or was it also because Ben Attar shrewdly offered him
promotion from agent to full partner, so he would share in the profits
of his work? Either way, there is no doubt that the old Ishmaelite

nurse's agreement to go with Abulafia and continue looking after the child in his home in Toulouse until a replacement could be found also helped the widowed father reach his decision.

This furnished an excuse for a further meeting, since Ben Attar and Abu Lutfi promised the Ishmaelite woman that they themselves would come the following year to take her back to North Africa. Behind that promise no doubt lay the satisfaction and enthusiasm arising from the present meeting. After two years of new and exciting commercial business conducted thus far by means of occasional envoys, through letters, some of which had gone astray, and on the basis of unreliable rumors, Ben Attar now realized that there was no substitute for Abulafia's living, gushing words, describing the adventures of each bolt of brightly colored cloth, each sack of rare condiments, each inlaid dagger, which was the source of a veritable saga of exchanges unwinding like a snake until the final transaction resulted in a coin of silver or gold, or a heavy precious stone. No orderly narrative delivered by a trustworthy and clever emissary could replace that leisurely, relaxed conversation with the agent, whose stories hatched a whole clutch of subtle insights, suppositions, and hopes, which persuaded the merchant from Tangier that there really was a change in the air and that the poor benighted souls of the Christians beyond the mountains wanted at this time to be joined to the south and the east by means of their hides, cloths, and copperware. To these practical factors must be added, of course, the joy of reunion of kinsmen and comrades in that pleasant spot steeped in the azure of the Bay of Barcelona and reached by a smooth, calm sea voyage. Now that uncle and nephew had become in a sense partners, although not yet equal ones, it seemed that a summer meeting of these members of a small but ancient faith on the frontier between two great faiths that sought to swallow each other would become a fixed custom.

On the return voyage from Barcelona to Tangier, however, on board the ship that was now lightened of its cargo, Ben Attar was suddenly stricken with fear. He felt himself to be naked and exposed. He missed the company of those bolts of cloth and sacks of condiments, which always warmed his heart and gave him a sense of security, and he needed that assurance all the more now that his belt and pockets were full of the coins and precious stones that Abulafia had brought him.

True, Abu Lutfi was beside him, although from the moment they had embarked his old assistant had seemed for some reason to be alienated and displeased, whispering a great deal with the two Ishmaelite sailors, who seemed to have been smitten with a kind of religious fervor on the return journey, for instead of dancing naked on the prow of their boat they now knelt in prayer five times a day. It was not surprising that Ben Attar had forgotten how tedious the prattle of the Jew who had accompanied them to Barcelona was, and now he missed his company. In his newfound loneliness he even felt a pang of longing for the backward child, remembering with an ache in his heart how she had toddled toward him, tied by a cord, to peer into his eyes. He thought now that if the child were once again lying in his bosom, the Ishmaelite sailors would refrain from attacking him in his sleep, stealing his money, and throwing him overboard. But the little girl was now beyond the Pyrenees, and all Ben Attar could do was to order the sailors to hug the coast, in the hope that there would be someone nearby who could testify against them if they tried to harm him. But they adamantly refused, supposedly for fear of hitting a sandbar, and Abu Lutfi not only refused to intervene but even defended their decision. Had the Ishmaelite managed to follow Ben Attar's conversation in Hebrew with Abulafia when he had promoted him to partner, while Abu Lutfi had to content himself with the leftovers? Ben Attar's fear grew stronger, and by nightfall he had come to regret the whole expedition. He sat hunched in the stern of the boat with a dagger hidden in the folds of his robe, straining to keep his eyes open, waiting for the attack.

Abu Lutfi sensed his Jewish master's new fear, but did nothing to allay it. He had not managed to understand the Hebrew words spoken by the campfire at the old Roman inn, but he was sensitive enough to infer that if his employer was afraid not only of the sailors but of himself as well, it was a sign that he felt some new guilt toward him, so that when Ben Attar summoned him after a sleepless night and offered him a large gold coin he refused it, on the assumption that it was worth less than his forgiveness for an unspecified guilt. Ben Attar, startled by his refusal, was convinced that when the attack came Abu Lutfi would abandon him to his fate. So it was that after a second night without sleep, realizing that his strength was waning, he made up his mind to appoint the Ishmaelite as a partner as well, so that from now on the silver and gold would be as precious to Abu Lutfi as the apple of his eye.

Although in the course of this voyage Ben Attar had acquired two partners to share his profit, he felt that he was not returning to Tangier diminished but, on the contrary, increased and strengthened. And when the fast sailing ship passed through the Straits of Gibraltar and to the calm, steady blue of the Mediterranean was added the wicked, dreamy green of the great ocean that lapped at the walls of his fast-approaching native town, he understood how long the arm he had stretched out toward the distant northern horizon was, and he knew too, as he remembered the new confidence and earnestness that had radiated from Abulafia, that from now on the new partner in the north would stimulate the new partner in the south, and that the new partner in the south would charm the new partner in the north, while he himself, remaining where he was, would cast his protection over the two of them, keeping an intelligent pressure on the reins and receiving his share. The outline of the great cliff was still shimmering behind them like a tawny idol, and already the yellowish African midday light was flooding them, soaking the white walls of the city with a pleasant warmth. And they were ringed with the fishing boats of Tangier, and the fishermen, identifying the newcomers, greeted them happily on their return from their long journey. As Ben Attar disembarked onto dry land, he kissed the sand and gave thanks to his God for bringing him home safely, but instead of proceeding directly to his house, he handed his bundles to a young man and told him to inform his wife and servants that they should prepare a celebration for his arrival, while he for some reason headed for Abulafia's house, which was now emptied of the last vestige of its owner. As he opened the iron-clad door with the key that was concealed on his person, he reflected that at this very moment, in the far north, Abulafia, dressed in black, might be taking his bewitched daughter with her tall nurse into a dark, gloomy house in Toulouse, no doubt surrounded with frightening crosses, and he felt sorry for them, because the house he was standing in was flooded with light and warmth, its floor was clean, and in a corner, neatly folded and tied into a bundle, was the bedding and clothing of the old nurse, who was still unaware that she would never return here. But nothing at all remained of the child's things: it was as though she had never existed.

He strode from room to room and looked at the arches of the small inner courtyard. Most of the flowers had withered, because there was no one to water them. Again he recalled Abulafia's dead wife, and her child who had made strange growling sounds here. He was holding an authorization signed by Abulafia to sell this accursed house on his behalf, and he suddenly felt sorry for the empty house, which at this pleasant summer hour revealed nothing but charm and pleasantness everywhere. He fondled the pouches of gold and silver bound to his loins, concealed under his robe, and calculated what he would do with all that money. Suddenly he had the idea of not selling the house to a stranger but buying it himself. But what would he do with another house, which was much too lovely to use as a storehouse for the new goods that Abu Lutfi would send him from the south during the year ahead? Perhaps he would lend it to his famous uncle as a meeting place for his pupils, and thus gain the credit for a meritorious act. But Ben Attar knew only too well that Ben Ghiyyat sometimes had difficulty in bringing together even the minimum number of ten worshippers, so where would he suddenly find enough disciples for a second house of study?

Then, standing alone and at peace in this courtyard drenched in the sweet light of late summer, watching the little fountain quietly playing, Ben Attar felt that the fears of the journey that had just come to an end had been transformed within him into a gentle desire. Why should he not take another wife and install her in this house? The thought of marrying a second wife had occasionally flitted through his head, and he had sometimes conjured up an image of this or that woman whom he knew from a snatched glance or by hearsay. But now he felt that the decision had been taken in his mind. His wealth would probably continue to increase, he still had strength in his loins, and his wife had begun to weaken a little. Several of his kinsmen and his Jewish friends, not to mention Muslim acquaintances, kept two and sometimes even three wives, in some cases under a single roof. He was now thirty-five years old, and if he managed to exceed the lifespan of his father, who had died at the age of forty, he still had ten years ahead of him, or even more. This was the right moment to widen his horizons. When his time came and his children stood around his deathbed, the leavetaking would be easier, because the wealth he would have amassed by then would enable them to part on easy and generous terms.

The sudden new thought so captured his heart that after locking the door behind him he did not hasten to his home but entered Ben Ghiyyat's synagogue. His uncle interrupted his meal to greet him, and Ben Attar, stooping to kiss his hand and receive his blessing, was on the point of taking a few coins out of his pocket as a gift to the poor students who sat around the table when he suddenly thought better of it and decided to tell Ben Ghiyyat first about the new desire that had seized his heart, and then to fix the size of the gift in proportion to his uncle's reaction. The sage listened with a smiling countenance, nodded his agreement, and only inquired whether he had spoken to his first wife yet about the second one. As he responded in the negative, he immediately offered to go and tell her and receive her approval, so that the announcement might seem to be an invitation to a meritorious act rather than an order. Who knew, she might even agree to help him select a suitable woman, so that there would be twice as much joy for all of them.

4.

Slowly the dawn began to break and the European continent opened up before them, sucking in the remains of the fog and enchanting the passengers on the old guardship with the lush greenery of the banks of the River Seine emptying lazily into the ocean. Small, unfamiliar birds with multicolored wings filled the air with their chirping, as though they had only been waiting for this ship. Everything that had appeared inscrutable and menacing in the night became clear and friendly with the gathering daylight. The flame that had burned so threateningly in the night had turned into a pleasant curl of grayish smoke, and the outline of a giant bird hovering in the darkness over the sea was now revealed as a wreck, which, to judge by the seaweed that had invaded it, had evidently been lying at the mouth of the river for many a year.

43

Although Abd el-Shafi took pains to give it a wide berth, for fear of unseen projections, his heart drew him closer to it, because his sharp eyes had recognized excitedly the beautiful carvings of the savage Vikings. Even without the wreck he would have had no doubt that he was steering the ship into the right estuary, but the greenish presence of this living ancient testimony confirmed with the sweetness of certainty his confidence about the whole journey. He nearly shouted something about this to the ship's owner, but he held himself back at the last minute so as not to arouse the memory of his forebear the captive pirate, which was liable to undermine the trust he had acquired in the course of the voyage from the two women too, who were now sitting on the old bridge, quiet and thoughtful after the double night, staring with fresh-eyed curiosity not only at each other but at the first bend of the river, which was now approaching.

It was at this time, as the ship began to penetrate the River Seine, solemnly raising the spirits of passengers and crew alike, that the chimes of the black slave's little bells died down, for after a night replete with activity he now sank into slumber in the hold, sprawled like a black octopus among the jars of oil and sacks of condiments and heaps of sheep's wool close to the two little camels, who eyed their young lover anxiously. With the rising and falling rhythm of his breathing he now became the hidden heart of this Muslim guardship that had come from so far away and was now sailing slowly through the Christian lands. Abd el-Shafi, who for several days had feared the opposing force of the expected current, was surprised not only by the gentleness of the summer stream but also by the unexpected generosity of the northwesterly wind that blew from behind them, whose good intentions he had discovered from its caress on his naked back. If these infidels are so successful, he mused with the strange jealousy of a veteran sea salt, at balancing current and wind to facilitate the passage of travelers on this river, why then, despite their primitive faith in a divinity who vanished from his tomb, they have a slight advantage over the Muslims, who are drawn to the decrees of fate. But despite the hope aroused in him by the northwesterly wind, his anxiety did not leave him, for he had never before sailed such a wide ship up such a narrow waterway, and his reckless wine-bibbing of the night before now bound his head with bands of iron, and each one of the unnumbered cups of Bordeaux wine that he had downed in the night had become a needle to stab his brain. He decided to talk or shout as little as possible, to avoid disturbing his brain, and preferred to give his orders in silence. With help from his sailors he lashed himself to the great mast, so that he would feel the sail on his body and know the precise direction of the wind and so that he could estimate from a height the safe distance between the two banks of the river. In order not to lose contact with his sailors he attached cord harnesses to them, and by lightly tugging on the cords he could transmit his orders to them, as though he were in charge of a great chariot rather than a ship, with its horses contained within it. And so, softly and silently, the ship traversed the first five bends of the river.

Ben Attar and Abu Lutfi, however, were untroubled by the river and its bends. After forty days of successfully sailing the ocean, they had absolute confidence in their captain's skill; indeed, they would have trusted him, had it been needed, to steer his ship up the very steps of Abulafia's house. However, they nervously awaited the first encounter with Franks, if only to discover whether merchandise coming from abroad was taxed in these remote and savage lands, or whether it was merely a matter of generous hospitality. But until the afternoon deep silence reigned all around, and there was not a living soul to be seen apart from the cheerful birds, as though the progress of a Moroccan ship down the arteries of Francia did not stir enough curiosity in any inhabitant that he should ask himself about its intentions. Where were all the new customers that Abulafia talked about so hopefully? True, little Samuel Elbaz, who since dawn had occupied his favorite spot at the masthead, high above Abd el-Shafi, and could see beyond the wall of trees and undergrowth, was constantly observing things that the other travelers could not, such as the sails of a water mill, or a goose girl leading her charges down a hill, a peasant plowing in a field, or children playing next to a thatched cottage. But for the time being he was silent, because it seemed as if none of the inhabitants had noticed the outlandish ship sailing secretly so close to their homes. Surely even if someone had happened to raise his eyes and catch sight of the tip of a white triangle swaying above the tops of the trees, topped by a naked youth half merged with the pinkish sky, he would not have hastened to verify the import of this apparition but would have simply fallen to his knees, crossed himself, and bowed his head in excited gratitude for this portent announcing the advent of the approaching millennium.

This is what the young local couple did at first; even though their little boat was almost crushed by the prow of an alien ship, they did not seem surprised by the sudden encounter in the river, as though it was entirely unremarkable that a strange potbellied ship should suddenly appear, with a huge triangle of canvas for a sail and half-naked Ishmaelites scurrying up and down its ropes. Thus they did not flee but merely stood gaping and smiling, as though this were not a real ship but a picture floating against the background of a dream that projected its wild fantasies for its own entertainment. But when Ben Attar hailed the young lovers from the deck they were panic-stricken, as though his voice had shattered the dream and a terrifying reality had come bursting out of it. First they tried to escape, but their way was blocked by the large ship. Then they hurriedly doffed their hats and fell to their knees, pleading for their lives in a strange, lilting tongue. But since no one on board knew how to reply so as to calm their spirits, the two women were told to stand on deck and wave peaceably in greeting, so the local couple would realize that the fear and panic were inside them and had nothing to do with the peaceful reality of those on board. However, the spectacle of two barefoot women in brightly colored robes waving to them did nothing to allay the young couple's fears but if anything aggravated them, and Rabbi Elbaz had to be summoned to scatter over them a few verses in Latin that he recalled from the prayers of Christian friends in the little church in Seville, to let the terrified couple know that even if this was no Christian ship, it was not an anti-Christian ship either. The fears of the young lovers were gradually calmed. The smiles returned to their faces, and they rose to their feet, crossed themselves gracefully, and chanted a Latin prayer to a captivating tune, so endearing themselves to Ben Attar that he could not resist inviting them on board. They were very hesitant at first, afraid that the strangers might seize them and, who could tell, perhaps cook them alive and eat them, but their curiosity got the better of their reluctance, and they clambered on deck, careful not to be separated from each other. Seeing them close up, the people on board were astonished at their youth, and Rabbi Elbaz attempted to ask them in sign language if in these lands love was habitually so precocious, but the pair did not appear to comprehend the meaning of the question, or perhaps they did not see any connection between a person's age and his capacity to love. Eventually they were seated on the old bridge and given a greenish herbal brew to drink, which they sipped politely despite its unfamiliar taste. Then they were offered dried Andalusian figs and lemons preserved in sugar, which they ate with evident delight, while the crew and passengers surrounded them, enjoying their enjoyment. Rabbi Elbaz was particularly attracted to them, partly because he still hoped that they might react to a word or sentence in Latin, and partly because their evident love for each other captivated his heart and reminded him of the lost days of his own love. In an effort to extend their stay he suggested they should be taken down into the hold, to enjoy the spectacle of the pair of young camels. But Ben Attar refused. He was afraid that they might spread the news of the rich cargo to customs officers who would lie in wait for them farther up the river. So as not to let the charming young pair depart empty-handed, he spread before them some embroidered cloths, to judge their reaction as potential purchasers. And so the voyagers amused themselves with the couple for a while, and then they gave them a little salt wrapped in a twist of paper and asked them how far Rouen was and what the city was like. To judge by their reply and their gestures, the distance was not great. Abu Lutfi, who had stood apart scowling all the while, approached and told Elbaz to ask them how far it was to Paris. Although the rabbi hesitated at first to ask such young people about such a faraway place, he did put the question. The young couple's faces at once lit up. Paris: they repeated the name over and over again in a smiling cadence and a charming accent, pointing reverentially toward the east, as to a Jerusalem or Mecca of their own. Not only did they know how far it was, even though they had never been there, but their joy was evident at this opportunity to pronounce the name of a place whose enchantment extended even to those who would never behold it. But while Ben Attar and the rabbi smiled at the couple, delighted with their answer, Abu Lutfi continued to glower at them skeptically, as though notwithstanding the many wearisome days and nights that he had invested in the voyage to that distant city, he still nursed a hope that it would finally emerge that it had never existed.

In truth, even Ben Attar at first had not understood what his nephew had been getting at when he pronounced the name of Paris so enthusiastically, even before he had been there. This Paris had been first named at the second summer meeting in the Spanish March, the year after the bewitched child was returned to the care of her blood father. The Moroccans had reached the Bay of Barcelona on the first day of the month of Ab, and after leaving their merchandise at Benveniste's tavern, loading their two boats with timber, and sending them back to North Africa, they took three horses and rode up to the old Roman inn, faithful to the promise they had given the previous year to take the nurse back to her home. But to their surprise, Abulafia came alone. The nurse had consented to remain a further year in Toulouse, since every effort to replace her by a local woman, whether Jewish or gentile, had met with frantic opposition from the wretched child herself, who in the darkness of her soul had probably assimilated the tattooed face of her nurse to the spirit of the mother who had abandoned her.

At first Abulafia had had difficulty persuading the elderly nurse to exchange the sighing of the waves and the scent of citrus orchards steeped in the limpid copper-hued light of the North African coast for a pent-up existence in an alien Christian town with a creature whose inscrutable wishes could be compensated for only by sorrow and pity. Indeed, whenever the Ishmaelite woman took the child out into the narrow streets around the castle of Toulouse, dressed in the white robe that Abu Lutfi had brought her and a fine veil of bluish silk that half concealed the large ring in her nose, the local inhabitants would screw up their eyes and mumble suitable phrases of advice and reproof from the Gospels to reinforce their human toleration in the face of the strange sight. To persuade the nurse not to abandon her charge, Abulafia was obliged to raise her wages and make her into a sort of super-numerary junior partner, paying her a large coin every time the moon was full and a small coin each Sabbath and agreeing to move from the foot of the castle to the street of the Jews in the heart of the city, not only because Toulouse had no street of Ishmaelites, but because the nurse herself opined that the Jews, who from their early childhood consorted with Asmodeus and delved into his lore, would be bound to find within themselves some sympathy for one who was caught in his thrall.

In the end, the special effort that Abulafia made to keep her paid off, not only in terms of his own peace of mind but in terms of the partnership as well. It was only this that made possible his long absences from home, which he needed because it was hard for him to put up with his daughter's hopeless presence and also because his rich imagination and his restless nature pushed him on to find new and ever more sophisticated customers, demanding refined goods, light in weight but of great value, such as little daggers studded with precious stones, snakes' skins, or shiny necklaces made from elephants' teeth. His soul was weary of the carts sinking into the mud under the weight of the great sacks and jars that Abu Lutfi brought from the desert. Therefore, after winning over the nurse and attaching her to the community of the Jews, he started to travel to the north, at first heading east, toward the Burgundian kingdom, on the road leading from Rodez to Lyons, turning off to Viviers and joining the trade route of the Rhone Valley. But he realized that he would not make his fortune here, for there was too much traffic, and quick-witted merchants from Byzantium who came up from Italy via Toulon offered treasures for sale that originated in the real, Asiatic East, brilliant merchandise compared to which his African wares seemed shoddy and dull. And so he changed direction and headed northwest, toward out-of-the-way places in the heart of Aquitaine, to the duchy of Guienne and the townships of Agen, Angoulême, and Périgueux, via Poitiers and Bourges, and from there to Lusignan and as far as Limoges, and there he was shown a way through to the Loire Valley and the border of the Capetian kingdom, where new towns such as Tours, Orléans, Chartres, and Paris were springing up and beginning to attract him.

When Abu Lutfi returned and asked Abulafia during their summer meetings to draw a new map of his peregrinations and locate the places that would suck in so lustily the other, lighter, more valuable merchandise, Abulafia became confused, and each map he drew for Abu Lutfi was different. He had particular difficulty fixing the precise place of Paris, the port town in the midst of the river that so attracted and excited him even though he had not yet been there. It is hardly surprising that this confusion kindled antagonism and suspicion toward the city and its surroundings in the breast of the Muslim partner, for with his keen mind he understood that the further the Jew pressed northward, the further he, the Muslim, would have to push desertward, so as to supply him with the light but valuable merchandise that would capture the hearts of the new customers. Ben Attar too, who always tried to achieve a compromise between his two partners, sometimes wondered where Abulafia's adventurous spirit would lead them. Unlike Abu Lutfi, however, he did not oppose his partner's northward thrust, not particularly out of commercial considerations, whose benefits were still in the realm of speculation, but in the hope that the further Abulafia traveled from North Africa, the easier he would find it finally to give up a strange, childish delusion that had pervaded his soul since he had abandoned his native town: that he would amass enough money, return to his town, and avenge himself on all those who had mocked his wife, particularly his mother. This was why, even after crossing the Pyrenees and entering a new world, he had chosen to avoid the company of Jews, who might enmesh him in the coils of a new marriage and undermine his vision of a vengeful homecoming. In the first year Ben Attar had feared that someday the young widower might return, not from nostalgia or because he missed the little girl who had stayed on her own, but to sully the escutcheons of those who had forced him to bury his beloved wife outside the fence of the graveyard. Consequently Ben Attar rejoiced retrospectively that he had responded so swiftly to the advice of his wise uncle to travel to Barcelona and return the child to her father, because apart from the discovery of the pleasant summer voyage and the importance of the face-to-face meeting with the man who was disseminating his goods, he hoped that the contact between the child and her begetter would teach Abulafia to face up to the facts, so that the purposeless delusion of returning like an avenging spirit to his native town might be moderated and weakened.

Weakened, Ben Attar said to himself, but no more than that. When Abulafia's mother, his own elder sister, suddenly took to her bed, Ben Attar was in no hurry to tell her son, and even in their summer meeting in the Roman inn he concealed the seriousness of her illness, lest the morose son hasten to her sickbed to poison her last days with words of reproach. Only after her interment did Ben Attar dispatch a special messenger, who pursued the orphan along the highways of Provence for many days to take him news of her death, which was received as expected, without tears and even with a slight smile. Then indeed Ben Attar asked Abulafia to return, even for a short visit, to execute his mother's will and perhaps, who knew, to make his peace with his kinsmen, to whom he shortsightedly ascribed the blame that was his own. But Abulafia, who had lost the sweet kernel of the vision of his great revenge, was still far removed from any willingness to make his peace with anyone else, so he sent word to his uncle to sell his share of his mother's estate on his behalf and bring the proceeds with him to the next summer meeting.

By this time Ben Attar's heart was deeply moved by the loneliness of his kinsman, the balance of whose mind was disturbed by the combination of guilt and love for his wife. He had even begun to wonder whether he had behaved correctly in extracting his nephew from the hold of the ship bound for the Holy Land, for the sanctity of the ancestral land might possibly have sucked some of the poison out of his innards and imposed order on confusion. Even more he regretted the alacrity with which he had executed his famous uncle's orders to restore the child to her father, for her deformed presence repelled marriage brokers and continued to keep her mother's memory alive. Bound hand and foot, Abulafia's wife remained engraved on the memories of others too, including Ben Attar himself, who that terrible night on the seashore had been unable, despite himself, to avert his eyes from the naked woman who lay so wonderfully beautiful upon the sand. Since then, such were the thoughts that Ben Attar pondered in his heart: If I, who saw her so degraded, cannot forget her beauty to this day, what must her husband feel?

However, Ben Attar also recognized the benefit of the younger partner's loneliness, which delivered a special impulse to business, for a salesman who has no wife to draw him homeward but is tempted by every new place, however remote, in the hope of discovering there the reflection of the beloved image, goes where no other trader will go, and even if the goods he has for sale are strange and unneeded, the mere fact of their appearance there compels their purchase. The demand for Moroccan merchandise did indeed increase in Provence, so that every summer they were obliged to add another ship to the convoy setting sail from Tangier, and if ten years before the millennium, at the first meeting, when they brought the child and her nurse, one ship sufficed, now, five years later, five ships were scarcely enough. True, it was not only Abulafia's energy and resourcefulness that had achieved this, but also the rise in the Christian population, for as the millennium approached the dying strove to defer the day of their death and babies hastened their birth, so as to ensure their presence in the year that was said to bring an abundant quickening of the dead.

Yet despite the rapid enrichment of the three partners, or perhaps because of it, Ben Attar grieved for his nephew's loneliness. Refusing to give up hope, he persisted in seeking among his nephew's innumerable tales and plans the rustle of a woman's skirt. And so, when the evening of the ninth of Ab arrived, after Abu Lutfi mounted his steed and vanished into the afterglow of sunset on the long mountain path that wound its way to Granada, Ben Attar began to describe to his beloved nephew and business partner, carefully and delicately, using two interwoven languages, the terrible wilderness of loneliness that his stubbornly maintained widowhood would condemn him to. But in that summer of the year 4755, which was year 385 of the Hegira according to the Mohammedans, five years before the millennium of the Christians, when the lamentations for the loss of the twice-destroyed Temple had softened and sweetened the souls of the two Jews and at their feet in the ashes of the dry grass of late summer the flames of the campfire had become a fragrant Cyclops' eye, Abulafia wrapped his head in his scarf and laid it on a stone, thrust his legs out in front of him, and, still fingering the hidden purse of coins that had been given to him a few hours earlier and fixing his eyes on the glimmering sea of stars overhead, began to speak again of Paris. But this time he spoke not only about the town but also about a woman who lived there.

It transpired that it was not in vain that the nurse had insisted that Abulafia move to the street of the Jews, to whom he belonged by race and by faith, for only there could he have obtained the means to establish contacts with other Jews' streets, in Tours and Limoges, Angoulême and Orléans, in Chartres and perhaps also in Paris. These were not always real streets, but sometimes merely narrow little alleys, or no more than the entrance to an alley, or a single house, or perhaps only a single room in which dwelled a solitary Jew. And so Abulafia's eyes were schooled to discern in his surroundings not only the kings and dukes and counts who held sway but also the places where the Jews were scattered.

Slowly Abulafia was drawn back to his kith and kin, from whom in the early years he had distanced himself in the fear that they would try to marry him off and frustrate his dream of returning to his native town. He had already admitted to himself that this was not a concrete plan but a dream, and therefore he had nothing to fear from its being frustrated, because it is in the nature of a dream that it always remains in the power of the one dreaming it. Therefore, after moving to the street of the Jews in Toulouse and seeing that not only were there those who could exchange a word or two of Arabic with the nurse but some who would offer a smile or a caress to the bewitched child, his heart softened, and on his return from his journeys he would join the congregation in prayer, not only to recite—still with a raging heart—the memorial prayer for his wife, but also to question the Jewish worshippers about the roads to the north.

For the Jews, even those who had never traveled far from their town, always knew something about Jews from other towns, just as they always knew something that the gentiles did not yet know about themselves—for instance, that the devotees of the approaching millennium would be attracted particularly to goods coming from the desert, the sort of objects that Jesus and his companions in the Holy Land must have handled, for the faithful wished to make a welcoming home for the Son of God, who would soon descend from heaven with his apostles. Thus Abulafia, who could interpret the signs, no longer traveled from Toulouse to Agen or from Limoges to Bourges, but from one Jew to another, each of whom advised him not only about the new types of merchandise but about how to raise his prices. It was while he was traveling in this way, following the advice of the Jews, that he made the acquaintance in an inn in Orléans of a woman, Mistress Esther-Minna, the childless widow of a scholar who had passed away a few years previously in Worms, a small town called Vermaiza by the Jews, by the River Rhine in Ashkenaz. She had been invited after her husband's death by her brother, Master Yehiel Levitas, a dealer in jewels and precious stones, to reside with him and his family in Paris, both to lighten the gloom of her loneliness and so that she could occasionally assist him with her good sense on secret missions to the towns and villages in the surrounding country.

It appeared that it was not only because she was a widow and childless, nor only because she was exposed to him in the somewhat licentious air of a wayside inn, but particularly because she was some ten years his senior that Abulafia had given himself easily to a lengthy conversation, which led him to a deep association that he had not imagined himself capable of. From exchanging casual remarks in the twilight hour before the evening meal, commencing with the attempts of this elegant yet respectable woman, the widow of a distinguished scholar, to embellish her speech with a word or phrase in the holy tongue that she had learned from her late husband, and with some acute commercial observations that she let fall, there developed an intense conversation that continued until midnight. It was a licit exchange, in view of the widowed state of both the interlocutors, who were still nameless to each other, yet it contained a certain hint of boldness and even sexual license. When the cross on the belfry pierced the flesh of the moon, which was as round and pale as the famous local cheeses, and slowly let it drop behind the church, and total darkness fell in the chamber in which the pair were sitting, Abulafia felt a pleasant warmth spreading through his body. It was the first time he had met anyone who took the old story of his pain and affront seriously and listened with open sympathy to his continuing dream of revenge, while firmly and absolutely rejecting any suggestion that his daughter was the victim of a curse or enchantment.

If it was not a curse or enchantment, Ben Attar wondered, what was it? But even Abulafia could not answer that question. He could only talk of the astonishment and gratitude that had coursed through him at the end of that conversation. Here at last is somebody who gives rest to my soul, he had thought to himself as he inhaled the woman's unfamiliar scent, which he had not only become accustomed to but even begun to enjoy. And as, like a child reading his mother's lips, he sought the precise meaning of this slim, small woman's words, which had been spoken in the Frankish tongue but slowly and clearly enunciated, with quotations from Bible stories and rabbinic writings, she

54

seemed to become stripped in his mind of her enfolding femininity, not, heaven forfend, so as to take on male attributes, but to reveal her primal and fundamental humanity, which is the true source of sensual excitement.

But precisely because he was so contented and elated, was he able to imagine that this steady, rational woman, Mistress Esther-Minna daughter of Kalonymos, who had subtly lanced the boil of his hatred for his mother, had begun to be strongly attracted to the man sitting opposite her, so that perhaps this warmth that had begun to spread through him sprang not only from her wise words but also from the heat that glowed in her, and that she was beginning to catch fire from the spark of her desire? Three or four times in the ten years of her widowhood she had been assailed by such a sudden attraction, but always she had succeeded in stamping it out, perhaps because the men she had been attracted to had been not only worthy but married. This time she was surprised by the youth of the man who had aroused her interest, as if on this occasion it was a desire not for a strange man that had sprung up inside her, but for all the children she had not been able to bear, who seemed to have burst into the world of their own accord and merged in this young man, a southern Jew, with his dark curls and his swarthy skin, whose very being was transformed that night by the shadows moving between the flickering candles and the moonlight into something rich and attractive.

True, Abulafia had become accustomed in recent years to various kinds of snatched infatuations, generally involving gentile women, that had arisen in taverns or marketplaces, and sometimes even on the road. Even though he came from the south, women discovered something oriental in his melancholy, since it was in the east that the beloved Son of God had suffered, and even though in the course of the years he had spent in Christian Europe Abulafia had endeavored, for his safety's sake, to adapt his appearance to the places where he was trading, some traces of his alien origin could still be discerned in his way of dressing his curls or trimming his beard, or of selecting and matching the colors of his clothes, or even his manner of tying up his coat. Since his prosperity was apparent from the quality of his garb and the nature of his baggage, these liaisons flared up with particular intensity. However, they were short-lived, since Abulafia was careful to sever them in good time, so as not to surround himself with excessive fire. But not before he had managed to sell some goods that even his lovers had not intended to buy from him. Not a few homes of Provence and Aquitaine received sacks of condiments that would suffice not only to season their owners' last supper but even the dishes of their heirs' heirs.

But on that winter's night in Orléans, he was so moved by the older woman's curiosity that he refrained from qualifying as love her sensitive interest in his thoughts and deeds, which did not even omit an inquisition into the character of his partners and friends. *Me too?* Ben Attar asked in a whisper, with his head cocked and with a surprised laugh, his eyes likening the galaxies twinkling above his head to the glittering embers of the log in the campfire. It emerged that the woman had shown an interest not only in Ben Attar but in Abu Lutfi as well, and even in Benveniste and their summer rendezvous. She had been excited to hear, for example, of the total confidence that Abulafia and Abu Lutfi invested in Ben Attar to be the sole arbiter of the distribution of the proceeds of the previous year's business.

And so, on the eve of the fast of the ninth of Ab, Ben Attar learned for the first time about the meeting with the new, clever woman, but he could not yet imagine how decisive and fateful she would turn out to be for him, or how one day he would be compelled to purchase a big old guardship, load it with the merchandise that had piled up over two years, separate his wives from their children and their homes, and take them on a tiring and dangerous journey from North Africa into the heart of Europe, in the company not only of his partner but of a rabbi from Seville, hired to pit his wisdom against hers. In that summer five years before the millennium, when he first heard from Abulafia about his meeting with Mistress Esther-Minna, Ben Attar was interested in her words and her questions rather than in her form and the nature of her womanhood. But as he came to recognize the particular excitement that informed the speech of his partner, who did not even conceal his intention of accepting the new woman's invitation to visit her family home in Paris, Ben Attar also began to interest himself in the appearance of the woman from the Rhineland, and was surprised to learn that she was a small, elegant woman with her hair gathered at the back, perhaps so as to reveal her intelligent face and her pale eyes better.

Pale? Pale in what way? Ben Attar wondered. When Abulafia described the precise tinge of blue of the widow's eyes and the flaxen color of her hair, likening it poetically to the color of the ocean licking the golden sands of the North African coast, Ben Attar's soul trembled, for not only did he now sense Abulafia's responsive love for the new woman, but for the first time he understood that there might be Jews in the world whose most remote ancestors had never been in the Land of Israel.

Who could say that curiosity about these Jews, who may have had some Viking or Saxon blood in their veins, was not one of the unwitting causes of Ben Attar's journey, which, with the entry to the river, from the time when sea and land met, was taking on a special sweetness? The River Seine welcomed this ship that had traveled so far and carried it along like a father carrying his child. True, it was midsummer, and there was no knowing the depth of the river and whether there was some danger to the hull of the ship, but the warm brightness surrounding them spoke only of affection and hope, and without noticing, they had eaten up since dawn, despite the many bends, a very considerable distance. And the evening was still gradually drawing in the slowly fading redness. Back home the evening fell swiftly, whereas here the sunset was extended, and the twilight struggled for its life. Abd el-Shafi had noticed that two weeks had passed since the lengthening of the twilight hour began, but at sea the drawing-out of the twilight is not as spectacular as inland, where the trees cast reflections of reddish light upon the water. Since morning the captain had been lashed to the mainmast, and despite his worries he was enjoying this unusual form of navigation. And even though Ben Attar and Abu Lutfi were both of the opinion that it was high time to stop and encamp, the pleasure of sailing got the better of the captain's fears, and he steered the ship upstream into the darkness, relying on the young eyes of the rabbi's son, who remained at the masthead so as to be the first to cry "Rouen!"

As the darkness deepened all around, limiting the child's vision, new, unfamiliar sounds came from the river. The dull ringing of the bell of Rouen church echoed from afar, and they understood that the pair of young lovers who had been lowered from the ship a few hours earlier had already announced their coming, for all unawares the river had filled with small boats, which surrounded the ship as though attempting to imprison her.

<h1 style="text-align:center">5.</h1>

During the night there was no contact between the boats from Rouen and the strange ship, as though hosts and guests alike were reluctant to diffuse in darkness the excitement of the encounter. In silence the boats remained where they were, surrounding the Arab sailing ship in a semicircle, and it was unclear whether they were blocking her way or protecting her. Every now and again a boat changed its position for no apparent reason, the plash of oars sounding clear and pure in the warm night air. Around midnight Ben Attar tried to halt the flow of his thoughts by entering his first wife's cabin, laying his head between her legs, and waiting for slumber to sever his soul from his worries, but they refused to depart, and compelled him again to seek the deck and Abd el-Shafi and Abu Lutfi, who were sleeping peacefully upon the lowered mainsail, watched over by the black idol-worshipper, who crouched at their feet. Ben Attar looked at them enviously. Their worries were not his worries, he mused as he listened to the boats that surrounded his ship, trying to discern their purpose from their melodious sound.

Eventually he roused the two Arabs and quietly told them of his decision. Until the true intentions of the people of Rouen were revealed, and also so as not to impose too heavy a burden on their minds, it would be better if all the passengers aboard the ship should be deemed to share the same faith. A faint laugh lit up the captain's white teeth. Could the Mohammedans then be changed to Jews by morning? *Neither by morning nor by Judgment Day,* Ben Attar muttered to himself, but he patiently explained to his partners that so long as the Umayyad caliph Hashim II, who was supposed to protect them, clung stubbornly to his Islamic faith, it was for all his subjects in times of adversity to cloak their own faith in his. What, even Rabbi Elbaz? Yes indeed, came back the resolute reply, both the rabbi and the rabbi's son.

In the case of young Elbaz, the rabbi's son, it would seem the change had already taken place some time before. From the moment he had come aboard in the harbor of Cadiz and felt the motion of the deck, his soul had understood that this was where he would rediscover the rocking and cradling that his late mother had deprived him of, and so he had clung to the ship as though it were the swing he had swung on in his lost childhood. When his father had subsided into seasickness, and in his terrible confusion had lost contact with his son, the frightened boy had looked for protection to the sailors, who unhesitatingly sent him to climb the mast, both to keep him occupied and to test his strength. And there it was, atop the mast, that the young traveler began to grow. For he sometimes imagined, at that great height, that the erect shaft of the ship was stirring between his skinny, naked legs, so that he was unable to resist the idea that he was its true master and the men scampering about far below on the deck were under his command. It was on account of this vision that the crew treated him with affection and respect, adopting him as a young sailor.

He rapidly adopted them in return. The boy immersed himself in the sailors' ways, learned the secrets of their tongue, and imitated their manner, so that he looked, in his short breeches and red turban, as though he had been born into the light of day not from his mother's womb in Seville but from the ancient belly of the guardship. Nevertheless, the rabbi was pleased with his son. He had not forgotten the reproaches of his kinsfolk, who had pleaded with him to leave the motherless child behind and not subject him to the tedium and perils of the lengthy voyage. But the rabbi had insisted. After enduring the death of his wife, he was not willing to face a further parting. And when he beheld the boy's limbs filling out in the light of the sunshine and the azure sea, his skin growing dark and smooth, and his happy, eager sharing in the work of the ship, he knew that he had been right to obey his own instincts rather than hearken to his family and friends. But once each day, at the time of the evening prayer, he firmly removed the little sailor from the ropes and steering oars, seated him on the old bridge between Ben Attar's two wives, facing the prow which cleaved the ocean's reddening waters, and read a psalm or two with him, lest he forget that there was dry land beyond the vast deep.

At first the rabbi had thought to study some simple texts of Mishnah and Talmud with the boy, but once the sea journey had aroused such powerful poetic feelings in him, he had postponed rational studies until they were on shore again, and in consequence it was no wonder that when Ben Attar roused him from his sleep and asked him to dissemble his true nature in the morning, so as not to muddle the minds of the local folk by confronting them with the spectacle of two alien and possibly incompatible faiths sharing a single ship, the rabbi manifested no alarm at the surprising request. The verses he had composed during the past days had rendered his personality gentler and more pliant, and so long as he was not required to consume forbidden foods he was ready to shroud his head like Abu Lutfi and disguise himself as a Muslim, until it became plain what kind of welcome the inhabitants of Rouen were reserving for them.

With the light of dawn, however, the only token of welcome in Rouen was the insistent, solemn clangor of bells that filled the air of the small port. Was the ringing intended to gather the faithful for Sunday mass, or to encourage the oarsmen on the boats to board the strange ship and ascertain its true nature? Either way, Abd el-Shafi gave orders for the mainmast to be adorned with some colored pennants that had been hoisted in the ship's engagements with Christian fleets in the past, but as a token of peace he also lowered a large rope ladder, so as to encourage the ship's night jailers to become her morning guests. Eventually some armed men came on board, headed by one of the lords of the town, who was amazed not only by the distance the ship had traveled from the Maghreb but also by its original form. It was immediately apparent that here in the port of Rouen there were great experts on ships—how else to explain the chief man's protracted and minute inquisition into the nature and use of the great sail, the Arab lateen sail, which performed on its own more than a number of small sails did on a Christian ship? Eventually the man went down with his men to inspect the hold and to gape at the two young camels, whose trembling increased so much at the touch of the Christians that the slave was compelled to quieten them with gurgling sounds. Since these Christians had never set eyes on a real camel, they were treated to an account of its qualities, and especially its ability to do without water and food. Then they were offered the usual visitors' tour. They were invited to sniff the spices, to feel the skins and cloths, to test the blades of the daggers with their thumbs, which they also dipped in the olive oil, and then they were asked to taste the dried figs and dates and carobs and raisins, and to conclude with a pinch of white salt, which was also wrapped for them in a fine paper as a gift.

It was only when they climbed back up on deck and looked around to see if there was anything left to examine on this wonderful ship that they peered cautiously at the two women, who hurriedly veiled their faces to hide their blushing smiles. The lord bowed deeply, while the Jewish merchant, unable to contain himself, asked the rabbi, who served as translator from Arabic to the mixture of Latin and Frankish of the men of Rouen, to invite the visitors to examine the rest of his fabrics, from which the women's dresses were made. But the lord happened to be more impressed by the women themselves than by what they were clothed in, and so the invitation to do business was politely declined on the grounds that they had shortly to attend mass, and instead Rabbi Elbaz was asked to write on a parchment the names of all the travelers and the animals and their personal relationship to one another.

Only after the lord had left the ship, not before insisting cordially but firmly that the travelers should honor them by visiting the city and its churches, did Elbaz whisper to Ben Attar that he had taken it upon himself to inscribe the second wife as the sister of the first, to prevent unnecessary gossip among the Christians, whom the approaching millennium was infecting with excessive piety. At first Ben Attar was shocked. Was this not a retreat or even a betrayal of the principle in whose name the whole expedition had been conceived? But once he had grasped the rabbi's considered caution, he said to himself that there was no reason to despair of him. Even if the sea had changed him into a poet, the dry land would restore his senses.

And so, their personal and religious status having been especially adapted to the purpose of visiting the infidel town and particularly of participating in the mass of an alien faith, twelve travelers disembarked, leaving only a single sailor with Abu Lutfi to guard the ship. To protect the Jews, Abd el-Shafi insisted on accompanying them ashore, and indeed on reinforcing their disguise by adding four of his crew. They also decided to take the young slave with them, lest he escape during their absence to the shore that he so longed for. They stripped him of his tatters and clothed him in a white robe, which emphasized the blackness of his face and his hands and feet.

After so many wave-tossed days, the voyagers' minds were dizzied somewhat by the solidity of the cobbles they walked on, and so they tended to huddle together at first, if only to allay the terror caused by the sound of the bells, which from a distance, on board ship, had seemed soothing and kindly, but here, among the narrow streets of Rouen, shook the gray air with an insistent menace. Indeed, the streets of Rouen were narrow and winding, and the houses seemed miserable and small to the North Africans, who wondered not only at the unpainted and unplastered gray stone but also at the absence of flowerbeds and ornamental trees. Only occasionally did they halt to feast their eyes on a thick blackened beam that reinforced and adorned the small doorway of a mean house.

Since most of the folk of Rouen were at the mass, the travelers soon lost their way in the empty streets, but a local lad, who at first stood rooted to the spot at the sight of the visitors, bestirred himself and ran to announce their arrival. At once a pair of monks came to meet them and addressed them cordially in clear Latin phrases. It was for the glory and joy of Christ that the honored unbelievers should take part in their worship, they announced to the newcomers, opening for them the heavy great door of the cathedral.

By comparison with the spacious mosques that the visitors were familiar with in North Africa and Andalus, their soft couches and the blue arabesques that adorned their walls, the cathedral of Rouen seemed cramped and sad in its dark severity, and it had a sweet-sour smell blended of incense and sweat, for even on this summer day the congregation was dressed in heavy, dark clothes. The two women had a moment of revulsion as they entered, but it was already too late, all eyes were upon them, and the service was interrupted to allow a ripple of astonishment to spread down the rows of worshippers, as the women's softly billowing robes and the men's baggy trousers passed through their ranks. The sight of the black pagan in his hooded coat and the brightly colored oriental silks made it seem as though the mythological figures painted on the walls of the church had descended and come to life in their midst.

It may have been then, in the gloomy cathedral of Rouen, that the rabbi first noticed the special thing that women brought to the land of the Franks, particularly such flowering, exotic women as Ben Attar's wives, whose fine scented veils might have been intended to shield their modesty or, alternatively, to heighten their seductiveness. When the newcomers had taken their places in the seats that the monks had reserved for them and an invisible choir had burst into virile yet gentle song, accompanied by a totally unfamiliar musical instrument, the North Africans raised their heads in search of the origin of the un-known sound, in the realization that despite the simplicity of the church it could be a place of complex artistry, blending the clear monotones of the chant with the severity of the thin-limbed images that stared with profound and eternal melancholy at the splendidly robed figure of the priest with turned back, who prostrated himself, rang a little bell, prostrated himself again, rang his bell again, and so on.

He has a bell too, thought the black slave, his eyes fixed devotedly on the priest, who, after completing his repeated prostrations, removed his gold-embroidered stole and ascended a small dais to address the congregation. He spoke to them in Latin, but whenever he noticed that his listeners had difficulty in understanding him, he introduced a word or phrase in the local language, at which the people sighed with plea-sure at the suddenly revealed meaning. At first the rabbi tried to follow what he was saying, so as to know if it contained any menace to the voyagers, who sat motionless—except for the young pagan, who, over-come by idolatrous fervor, was kneeling before the image of a gilded man spreading his arms out like a bat's wings behind the altar.

The priest was moved by the sight of the black youth suddenly kneeling in such a spontaneous fashion, but he had too much consid-eration for the other guests to interpret it as a sign from heaven or an omen concerning them. He merely smiled contentedly, rubbed his palms together, and pronounced a special greeting to the visitors, call-ing them in each sentence by a different epithet—Africans, Arabs, Muslims, Mohammedans, Ishmaelites, colorful, dusky southerners, sailors, merchants, voyagers, pilgrims, and unbelievers. He did this so much that the congregation must have had the impression that instead of a dozen weary travelers they were welcoming representatives of the whole wide world.

Afterward, at a special reception in their honor in a large hall behind the altar, the monks insisted on making them taste some little pieces of strange, very fine bread, which had a wonderful flavor. But when they also invited them to sip from a large goblet of wine, Ben Attar and the rabbi hurriedly interrupted them. The Prophet's command prevented the drinking of wine, they explained, signaling cautiously to Abd el-Shafi and the sailors to refrain from drinking the little beakers they were offered. Then a tall, black-clad palmer, a monk who had spent many years roaming the lands of Islam and had learned a little Arabic, was summoned. Even though his Arabic was meager and very strange, so that even the rabbi could hardly understand it, he insisted on improving his acquaintance not only with the rabbi-interpreter but also with the two women, whom he addressed directly, and even with Abd el-Shafi and his men, who here in this hall, as they stood quiet and very apprehensive, but also on a level with the other travelers, revealed their true character, which for eight long weeks at sea had been concealed, as it were, among the ship's tackle. The palmer wanted to know whether the infidels had enjoyed the divine worship. The rabbi attempted to give a single answer on behalf of the whole party, but the crusader insisted on extracting an individual reply from each of them. It emerged that the ringing of bells had impressed and moved the North African sailors particularly. *In a mosque there are no bells,* Abd el-Shafi said, summing up the opinion of the true Muslims, *and so when we return to the Umayyad caliphate we shall suggest adding some bells to the call of the muezzin.* The palmer smiled slyly at this reply. He too believed that the sound of bells could bring people closer to prayer, but prayer to whom? To that Muhammad? Admittedly an important man, and a great prophet, who beheld the angel of God from a short distance, yet he died a long time ago, whereas the bells here called people to pray to one who will never die and now sits in the bosom of God. Like a son with his father. The visitors from far-off lands had been vouchsafed a rare opportunity, because their good fortune had brought them here close to the thousandth anniversary of his birth, when he would save all mankind from its wretched state. *And we thought the Jews killed him long ago,* Abd el-Shafi exclaimed, shocking Ben Attar and the rabbi. The crusader smiled calmly. Is it possible to kill the Son of God? Even the most evil imagination cannot conceive his death. That is why the Christians had resolved to leave the accursed Jews in their debased condition, so they would witness their own wickedness and folly.

Now, as the sea captain began to nod to the crusader in deep agreement, Ben Attar realized that it was better to cut short the theological discussion, for there was no knowing where it would lead. So he stood up and asked the Andalusian rabbi to thank their hosts in Latin for their hospitality. When they returned to their distant city, they would not forget the cathedral of Rouen and its fine worship. When the millennium dawned and the hosts' Christ descended from heaven, would they kindly ask him, if it was not too hard for him, to come south and visit the people in Tangier? There too he would be welcomed with great honor. For sometimes those whose prophet is dead and buried long for somebody living who can comfort them for the troubles of the world, which did not allow them, for example, to sit here any longer and enjoy the interesting conversation, but compelled them to hasten to the river and press on to Paris, which was waiting impatiently for their merchandise.

Yes, Paris, Paris, muttered the crusader, as though he were wrestling again with something that always got the better of him, and reluctantly he was forced to interrupt his tortuous conversation and let the stubborn Muslims return to their ship. Outside a summer shower was falling, which soaked the women's silken robes, and their hems were soiled with mud from the puddles, in some of which pink pigs that had emerged from a nearby graveyard were already wallowing, getting under the visitors' feet and alarming the women. The sight of their distress moved Abd el-Shafi to request Ben Attar's permission to allow his strong sailors to make a kind of living hammock with their hands and raise the women a little way off the ground. And so the two of them floated down the narrow streets of houses and the country lanes, where the travelers lost their way, until the black slave shook himself free from the idolatrous dream inspired by the mass, and with the instinct of a desert tracker led them back to the ship, which Abu Lutfi had already loaded with fresh water, apples and grapes, and those long thin loaves of bread whose crisp taste he adored.

In the afternoon Ben Attar decided to weigh anchor and slip quietly out of Rouen, under the cover of the local people's sacred Sunday rest, but a small boat approached, bearing two of the lord's men together with a Jew clad in a tricorn hat trimmed with blue lace, who had been sent on this, his working day, to purchase something for his master. And although Ben Attar would have preferred to wait for Abulafia to price the goods, he realized that if he refused he would add anger to the suspicions of the Jew, who seemed in the grip of a spasm of suspicion as he boarded the ship.

This Jew of Rouen, having never set eyes on a real Muslim, was unable to distinguish a true from a false one, but the hidden identity of his disguised kinsmen penetrated his innermost being, and his feet faltered as he climbed down the ladder into the hold, and he slipped and fell down among the sacks and the young camels, who sniffed at the newcomer's face with friendly curiosity. But Ben Attar chose not to reveal to the Jewish agent in the afternoon what had been hidden in the morning from his Christian master. So as not to increase the confusion, he left the hold in darkness, without lamp or candle, to prevent the Jew from testing the truth of his suspicions and peering behind the oil jars and the sacks of condiments, because then he might discover goods that were definitely not for sale. Gradually those on board managed to calm him down, and after he had groped in the dark and asked for prices, the true purpose of his mission emerged. His lord had set his heart on one of the camels, whose economy and modesty had captivated him. But why not both of them? thought Ben Attar. It turned out that the lord was content with the female alone, on the supposition that the young creature might already have conceived during the long sea voyage, and so she might deliver him another young camel with no further expense on his part.

Ben Attar eyed the two animals. From the way they were lying, the look in their eyes, and the angle of their little heads, it seemed to him again that their death was not far off. Was it right to separate them? he wondered. And surely if he made a present to the lord of the male as well, he might give him a document that would enable the ship to proceed up the river unimpeded. But he also recalled all Abu Lutfi's care for the camels on the long voyage, so that Abulafia's new wife might feel and smell at first hand something of the desert lands from which her husband had come, and so he called to the black boy to help separate the female from her companion and take her up on deck.

But the evening twilight was upon them before the sailors managed, thanks to the experience and patience of the young slave, to separate the enfeebled little she-camel from her stubborn and panic-stricken mate, who groaned and sneezed in her direction. Placing her in a special rope cradle, they slowly raised her out of the hold, then hoisted her up over the deck and into the waiting boat of the Jew, who, to judge by his roving glances, had not yet abandoned his secret hope of discovering the true identity of the ship's owner. But Ben Attar clung stubbornly to his Mohammedan disguise, which by evening he seemed to be enjoying, and after going down on his knees before the Jew and directing his face southeastward toward an imaginary point midway between Mecca and Jerusalem, and whispering the afternoon prayers silently to himself before darkness fell, he rose to his feet and firmly declined the greenish silver coins stamped with the effigy of an unfamiliar ruler. Instead he demanded payment in kind for the rare beast, namely, besides letters guaranteeing safe passage, two sheep, ten hens, and some large, strong-smelling cheeses. Only when all these were safely on board and the business was concluded did the lord and his companions appear on the shore, shouting drunkenly and carrying torches, to haul in the boat carrying the bound she-camel, which looked magical in the silvery moonlight.

And in the same magical, silvery moonlight Abd el-Shafi weighed anchor and gently sailed away from the city of Rouen, whose attractions the visitors had exhausted. On the bushy southern bank, amid the croaking of frogs and the barking of clever Frankish foxes, Ben Attar and the rabbi lost no time in returning to the faith of their forefathers, and despite the late hour they did not dispense with the evening prayer, so as to bless God, who had distinguished light from darkness and the people of Israel from the other nations. And the first wife, her large face calm from peaceful sleep, emerged from her cabin in the bow, wrapped in a white sheet and carrying in her arms, like a swaddled girl, her splendid embroidered robe, washed of the mire that had clung to it from the morning. She hung it up near the sail to dry in the warm night breeze. Meanwhile the second wife too approached from the bowels of the ship, still clad in her soiled and crumpled silk gown, her sleepy face disturbed by a strange dream in which Abulafia's new wife was among the stern-faced images adorning the walls of the church, and from an abstraction became an angry, living visage. In her distraught state she sought the company of Rabbi Elbaz, who was leaning on the rope and staring down into the water. Would this gentle man, who occasionally shot her a shy glance, really be able to annul or soften the repudiation that awaited them?

Repudiation. That word was heard for the first time in the summer meeting at the Spanish March in the year 4756 of the creation of the world, which was year 386 of the Hegira of the Prophet, four years before the longed-for Christian millennium. And in the small, sinewy womb of this simple word that escaped hesitantly from the mouth of Abulafia in the name of Mistress Esther-Minna, there already lay curled the embryo of the struggle that was to engage the partners so fiercely in the years to come. But in the year 996 of the Christian reckoning it was still a tiny embryo, blind and weak, which did not imagine the seriousness and toughness of its widowed mother, the repudiatrix herself, whose new presence allied itself easily with the exalted mood that had taken hold of all the partners. For Abulafia's expansion toward northern Francia and his new contacts with Jewish traders in Orléans and Paris had forced Abu Lutfi to enlarge the circuit of his wanderings in the Atlas Mountains and to increase his merchandise. Consequently, it was not four or five but six ships that hoisted their sails that summer in the port of Tangier, filling the hearts of the partners with apprehensive joy as they watched the commercial power spreading from south to north.

That year Abulafia was a whole week late at the old Roman inn. Still it occurred to no one to interpret the delay as a sign of disfavor, only as an understandable hitch in the calculation of time and distance on the part of the cordial, loyal partner, who was now compelled not only to come from farther away but also to take his leave of someone he loved. The delay forced Ben Attar to recite the dirges of the Book of Lamentations on his own, but Abu Lutfi, deeply moved by the double measure of sadness that had fallen upon the Jew and by the melancholy tone of his chant, showed true comradeship by sharing his Jewish partner's fast, to relieve some of his sorrow. And indeed the sadness lifted as though it had never been when Abulafia arrived two days later with a very respectable quantity of coins and precious stones, the proceeds of the past year's successful trading. This time he had dispensed with camouflage and appeared to his partners in his true guise, as a handsome young Jewish merchant who had honestly and generously acquitted all the dues levied at each border crossing in return for protection from highway robbers until the next station. Having made himself legal in the eyes of the world, he seemed more at peace with himself. After resting from his long journey and examining with emotion and embarrassment the fine gifts that his partners lavished upon him and his bride, and after recounting, as usual, albeit briefly, the events of the previous year, which had been exceptional not only in terms of business, he went down to Benveniste's tavern to look over the new merchandise that had arrived from the south. Unlike his usual custom, he did not discuss either the prices of the goods or their qualities with the Ishmaelite, but after casting a remote and distracted glance over them, he listened in grim silence to Abu Lutfi's explanations and then returned to the old inn.

Only in the evening, after the distribution of the profits, when the Ishmaelite had disappeared on his horse on the road to Granada, was Abulafia smitten with a new unease, and even though the ninth of Ab was over and gone, he asked Ben Attar to stay with him at the Roman inn and light their fire as usual. When he started to speak, he told his kinsman and former patron first of all about his marriage ceremony, whose modesty had only increased its sanctity. Since he was alone, without kith or kin, the members of the bride's family had doubled their affection toward him and had presented him with costly gifts: a prayer shawl of silk embroidered with silver thread, phylacteries of fine leather that caressed the arm as gently as a woman's hand, a silver goblet engraved with the words of the benediction, a velvet sash, and a black velvet cap. Abulafia also spoke of his new wife's jewelry, of her headscarf; he repeated the admonitory words of the bride's brother, Master Levitas, who was both a merchant and a scholar, and between one description and the next, beside a fire that was too fierce for a summer evening, the uncle began to direct his mind to a new word that kept recurring on Abulafia's lips, hesitantly at first, but with a kind of strange persistence, as though he too were now of one mind with the new wife's repudiation of the partnership between north and south.

At first it was hard to understand whether the repudiation was directed against the partnership or against the partners—whether it was due to a wife's personal resentment over the hardships of her husband-to-be's travels and the implied protracted absences from his new bridal chamber or to a more commercial reaction, derived from a calculation of the profits and their distribution. There flickered for a moment a suspicion that Abu Lutfi might be the source of the revulsion felt by this widow from the Rhineland, who might be accustomed to Huns but frightened of Ishmaelites. But gradually, from Abulafia's careful words, which like the wood of their campfire smoldered slowly until every now and then they suddenly flared up and crackled, it became clear that its true source was the uncle himself, Ben Attar— Abulafia's patron and benefactor, the guiding force behind the partnership and the architect of its success—who was now painfully and sadly lifting a glowing ember from the fire and turning it over and over.

If Ben Attar had taken the trouble the previous year to consider Abulafia's story about that unforgettable nocturnal encounter in the Jewish tavern in Orléans and carefully turned it over, as he was now turning the ember between his scorched fingers, he would have discovered the bewilderment that had begotten the repudiation. For then, beside the campfire near the entrance to the Roman inn, between one dirge and the next, Abulafia had recounted to his partner how attentively Mistress Esther-Minna had absorbed everything that was offered her on the subject of the black-curled man, who, not yet imagining the strength of the love and affection that he was stirring up, had prattled on not only about his thoughts and deeds but also about his faraway kinsmen and business partners, what they were like, what they wanted, what they looked like, and how they lived. And when, innocently carried away by the spate of his words, he had mentioned the second wife whom Ben Attar had married a few years previously, whom he himself had never met, he had felt his delicate questioner momentarily hold her breath.

A *second wife?* Mistress Esther-Minna had whispered in Hebrew, as though fearful of uttering the words in the local tongue, lest she arouse the Frankish servant who slept by the doorway. *Why not?* Abulafia had whispered in reply, with a faint, provocative smile. But from the crimson tinge that suffused her cheeks and her haste to reach up to adjust her headscarf, he had understood how much his answer had frightened her. So he had immediately attempted to broaden the woman's mind, for despite her experience of business trips with her brother, she had never traveled farther south than Orléans, let alone visited the wonderful, luxuriant south and informed herself about the customs of the awesome Arab grandees, not only in North Africa but also in the verdant cities of Andalus, replete with wisdom and song, where some, not content with possessing two wives, wed three or sometimes even four. Mistress Esther-Minna had looked up, her thin lips twisted slightly in a smile of curiosity tinged with disgust. And were there, she inquired, in the land where Abulafia had been born and from which he came, Jews who had three or four wives? Abulafia had been unable to give her a clear answer, for so many years had passed since he had left North Africa and Andalus. But the woman, her bewilderment and curiosity by now wrapped up in her love, had refused to let him be and had insisted on knowing whether the uncle, Ben Attar, the director of their partnership, might someday up and take, say, a third wife in addition to the two he already possessed. *God alone knows,* Abulafia had said, trying to evade the strange question. But seeing that God did not dispel the widow's curiosity, he was impelled to answer: *Perhaps, who knows?* If the partnership continued to prosper and to bring great wealth to the partners, Ben Attar might take another wife, for Ben Attar's expansive, love-filled heart was different from his own. He himself had not yet recovered from the blows that he had suffered in his life, and so he had hardly managed to have one wife.

Then Abulafia had felt the light touch of a small hand in the semi-darkness, and had realized that only a natural, self-confident humanity could find the courage to touch him. It was this humanity that had given him no rest during the year that had elapsed, so at the beginning of the spring he had turned his horses northward and at last headed with his wares to Paris, to seek out his acquaintance from the tavern in Orléans and to find out whether that tiny white hand that had reached out and touched him so generously in the darkness would deign to touch him also in the light of day. Even though her younger brother, who saw himself as her guardian, was hostile to the young North African's offer of marriage, his sister succeeded in allaying his doubts, and when they had satisfied themselves that despite Abulafia's years of wandering he had not forgotten his prayers and was still able to chant (although in an unfamiliar melody) the blessings to welcome the Sabbath and those that bade it farewell, as well as the long grace after food, the younger brother had given his consent to the match, on the condition that the couple set up house in a wing of his own home, not only so that his sister would continue to be close to him and his family but also so that she would not feel lonely when her husband resumed his traveling life.

Because the new household was to include Abulafia's daughter, whom henceforth he was forbidden to call, even jokingly, "bewitched" or "she-demon" but only, at most, "poor creature," it would be necessary to extend somewhat the house situated on the south bank of the river of Paris, close to the castle, with its law court and its execution chamber. In the meantime Abulafia was in a hurry to leave for the south, for his summer meeting in the Spanish March, but it became plain to him that Esther-Minna's bewilderment of the previous year had not vanished but had now changed into a feeling of panic. The very thought that the man who was soon to be her husband was partner to a savage Jew who, out of ignorance or unbridled lust, possessed two wives, to whom he might one day add a third, terrified this woman who was no longer young, and she demanded before Abulafia left that after the distribution of the previous year's profits he should not take the new merchandise but should share out his part between the other two partners and bid farewell to his uncle, who now, hearing these words, was so startled that he almost put the crumbling ember into his mouth.

But why? Ben Attar's voice was choked. His northern partner tried to mumble a reply that would set his mind at rest—that he had deliberately waited until Abu Lutfi had left them, so as not to embarrass his kinsman on a matter that the Ishmaelite too took pride in. Since he himself was still far not only from becoming accustomed to Mistress Esther-Minna's capricious demand, whose firmness was already visible in a slight softening of his black pupils, but even from understanding her reasons, he tried first to explain her repudiation by her peculiar quality of human sensitivity, for her heart grieved for all that the first wife was denied when a second wife arrived. *But how so?* Ben Attar retorted at once. Two wives might help each other to support their husband in every way and might on occasion transform their conjugal desires into a longing that only enriched and purified their love. And who knew better than Abulafia himself how miserable a single wife might also be? Abulafia listened very attentively and nodded his head in agreement. How sad, he said, that Ben Attar could not explain these delicate matters to his fiancée himself, for he himself had forgotten them in his long years as a widower. But since he had not yet made up his mind to accede to her demand and dissolve their partnership, he would endeavor to remember Ben Attar's words and use them to assuage his bride, and when he came to the next summer's meeting, if God willed it, he would bring with him her acceptance.

And so, in the year 4756 according to the Jewish era of the creation, corresponding to the year 386 of the Prophet's Hegira, four years before the millennium that so thrilled the Christians, instead of dissolving the partnership that was so dear to him, Abulafia loaded the merchandise upon six carts, one for each of the boats that had brought it, and on reaching Perpignan he sent one cart, laden with condiments, westward, to the duchy of Gascony, and a second cart, bearing copper bowls and pans, eastward into southern Provence, while he himself went with the three remaining carts to Toulouse, trading the olive oil, honeycombs, and strings of dried carobs and figs of Andalus in the villages along the way and bartering in turn with the goods he received in exchange for them. By the time he reached Toulouse he already had two empty carts on which to load his mute daughter and her Ishmaelite nurse, who demanded five gold bracelets in exchange for her agreement to abandon her southern dream in favor of a winter journey through Edomite kingdoms to a faraway town like Paris, to which they were taking a luxurious consignment of vials of fragrant perfumes from the desert, lion and leopard skins, and embroidered cloth in which lay concealed curved daggers encrusted with precious stones.

Early in the spring of 997, Abulafia returned to that same Paris, not alone this time but bringing with him his dumb ten-year-old daughter, who, if she was no longer bewitched, was assuredly a poor creature.

Again he discovered that his future wife was not only older than he was in years, but was also experienced and worldly-wise. Although she immediately folded the poor creature in her arms and hugged her to her bosom, and inclined her head in respect and wonder before the elderly Ishmaelite nurse, agleam with golden bangles, and even though all winter long her soul had yearned for the young man with his black ringlets, she did not hasten to undertake the promised marriage but returned to the theme of her repudiation of the twice-wed partner. So saying, she introduced a black-robed personage who had come to Paris from the province of Lotharingia in Ashkenaz, wearing a hat from which arose a horn of black velvet. This man, Rabbi Kalonymos son of Kalonymos, a kinsman of her late husband's, a resident of her native town of Worms, had been invited to Paris especially by her younger brother, Master Levitas, to conduct the marriage according to the rites and ceremonies of their forefathers. He sought first to test the nature and firmness of the southern bridegroom's faith, in case it required strengthening or completion, correction or purging, before it was joined to the unshakeable faith of the respected woman from his home town.

To this end he engaged Abulafia in a lengthy conversation, and because the mute child trembled and moaned at the sight of the horn nodding on his head, Abulafia took him outside and walked with him amid the mud and mire of Paris, among swine, horses, and asses. Leading him across a small wooden bridge, he strolled with him along a wide dirt track known as the Road of Saint James, along which the pilgrims departed on their way to the shrine of Saint James of Compostela at the tip of Iberia. The cold-mannered German pointed out to Abulafia the pilgrims clad in thick capes, with their broad-brimmed felt hats adorned with a scallop shell, holding long poles with leather water bottles attached to the tips, preparing themselves for their long and arduous journey. Then he showed him the women bidding them farewell while braiding their hair and wrapping their ankles in scarlet leggings above their feet, which were shod in stout sandals. All this was meant to indicate to the Moroccan Jew that true faith requires meticulous preparation. Then he explained to the bridegroom the steps of the marriage ceremony in due order, lest any exotic desert whim or Mediterranean habit disrupt the sacrosanct ritual. He introduced some anecdotes from Worms, which, while it might lack the attraction of

74

Paris, and though its houses still rested on gnarled piles, was not lacking in one thing: Jewish scholars. Dead scholars, who watched over living scholars, who in their turn were preparing the world for future generations of scholars still unborn. Clearly, it was vitally important that the future generations should be born in the purity of wedlock, and what purity could there be without security and peace, which were protected by interdict and ban against a man who might seek to take to himself a second wife, or to divorce his wife against her will?

Abulafia understood that the visitor whom his bride and her brother had summoned from the Rhineland was drawing a clear connection between the annulment of the partnership with Ben Attar and the marriage with Mistress Esther-Minna. Consequently, he was not surprised when, upon their return to the inn—after the pilgrims, who had at first taken the German for a man of consequence, had eventually recognized the Jew in him and pelted him with rotten apples as a first virtuous deed on their arduous journey—Master Kalonymos drew forth from his luggage two strips of dark parchment inscribed in red ink, one for the bridegroom, to remind him of what he had just learned, and the second for the rejected partner, to be sent to him that summer by hand of messenger, together with what was due to him by proper reckoning in exchange for the merchandise that had been sold the previous year.

And so, on Thursday the eighteenth of Iyar, the thirty-third day of the Omer in the year 4757, after he had promised to his new kinsfolk to dissolve the partnership, final consent was given and the marriage took place. But when the summer month of Tammuz came and the messenger was due to leave for the Spanish March, Abulafia, overcome by a powerful longing for the Bay of Barcelona, repented of the promise he had given. Notwithstanding the grim expression that overtook the pallid face of his new wife, to whom he had been drawn with a mixture of fear and strong desire ever since their wedding night, he was not prepared to part from his old partners by means of a letter, nor did he dare to take it upon himself to divide up the proceeds of the year's trade and send it by the hand of a stranger. Consequently, after swearing again to his wife and his new brother-in-law that this time he really would take his leave and dissolve the successful partnership so that the repudiation might take effect, he took to the road himself. So divided was his heart between the awesome oath he had sworn and the pain and sorrow that awaited him that he lost his way, and in the Sierra de Andorra he was saved from falling into the hands of highway robbers only by a black leper's coat that he had bought at the last moment and now donned. And so his delay was extended by ten more days, and for a second year Abu Lutfi joined in marking the fast of the ninth of Ab.

Clad in his leper's habit, sounding a clapper so as to keep healthy folk at a distance, Abulafia found his two business partners lying prostrate in the heat of the day between two ruined marble columns that had once adorned the Roman inn. Despite the words of joyful greeting, the embraces and the bows, the southerners could already discern in their northern partner's lovely eyes the grim signs of separation. When the Ishmaelite heard that Abulafia wished to cut the partnership off in its prime, and was not intending this time to accept the six boatloads of merchandise, he lost his self-control and, getting to his feet, began to wheel around in a rage, until he suddenly stopped in front of a huge olive tree and hit his head against it, the tears coursing down his cheeks, quite different from the tears of joy of the first meeting that had taken place at this very spot eight years before.

It was not easy for Abulafia to comfort him, both because he was not reconciled in his own mind to parting and dissolving the partnership and because he knew how hard it would be for a Muslim man, who could marry wives according to the state of his wealth and divorce them at will, to understand, let alone respect, the spirit that had animated the new rules, which he now presented to Ben Attar upon a sheet of parchment darkened by the shade of the Black Forest. So they waited as the Ishmaelite's sobs gradually subsided. Before he could emerge from his grief and reach a false notion that all this was merely a trick that the two Jews were playing on him so as to exclude him from the partnership, Ben Attar decided to subvert the new orders from the north by freely making over his share of the new merchandise to Abu Lutfi, so that Abulafia could accept it without any difficulty from the hands of a non-Jew, who was not subject to the edicts emanating from the Rhineland, or indeed to those coming from Babylon or from the Land of Israel.

At first Abulafia hesitated to consent to a solution whose southern simplicity would be laughingly dismissed by his fastidious kinsfolk. However, since the boats had already been sent back to Tangier and the goods that had been piled up in Benveniste's stables for more than three weeks were already enraging the horses and asses whose living quarters they were crowding, he could not be indifferent to the distress of his old partners, and so he consented to accept the merchandise from the hand of the Ishmaelite, who had suddenly, uncomprehendingly, become the owner of everything. But all this, Abulafia warned them once more, was only on condition that all the goods be transported as they were straight to Paris, there to receive the stamp of approval from his kin before being sold to gentiles. His trader's instincts whispered to him that the higher prices he would receive for them in the Île de France would amply compensate him for the additional hardships and expenses of the long journey.

While Abu Lutfi was hurriedly mounting his horse to gallop south to Granada, confident that the solution the Jews had found to their problem would also hold good for the wares he would gather during the following year, and despite the lateness of the season, with the first cool signs of autumn already discernible in the air, uncle and nephew found it hard to take leave of each other, for who knew whether this might be their last parting? Since they had been deprived of their joint prayers for the ninth of Ab, with its lamentations and its grief, they wanted to be together to recollect the joy of the daughters of Israel who in bygone times had gone out in search of love and a marriage partner on the fifteenth of the month. But the melody of Abulafia's prayer turned gloomy at the sight of Ben Attar's sad face, and so, without being bidden, unable to contain himself, in the darkness gathering around them at the end of their prayers, without campfire or stars in the sky, he began to speak out in praise of the new Mistress Abulafia, so that Ben Attar would not start to hate her. He spoke at length of her wisdom, her refinement, and her charitable deeds, and he dwelled especially on her tender care for his poor child, who had found shelter in her home. Little by little there emerged between the lines his wonder at his desire for the blue-eyed, fair-haired woman, until, carried away in ever more confessional speech, he let fly little secrets of his bedchamber like sparks from a bonfire.

They parted from each other with mixed emotions. On chilly autumnal roads, journeying with purposeful determination, Abulafia took his six heavily laden carts to his new home in Paris, to hear from his beloved wife and her brother a clear and decisive verdict, which, as expected, dismissed any Ishmaelite subterfuge to dissimulate the continuation of the partnership with the twice-wed southern Jew. To thwart any further attempt at Mediterranean sophistry, they insisted on confiscating the whole of his stock in trade and selling it themselves, so as to be satisfied that the partnership had been broken once and for all, at their own hands. They agreed to send the proceeds of the sale, after deduction of expenses, southward in its entirety, to the two partners who were now deemed *past* partners, along with the Ishmaelite nurse whose time had elapsed.

When the two southern partners arrived once more at Benveniste's tavern in Barcelona, this time with seven boatloads, in the hope of renewing their trade, they were informed by Benveniste that Mistress Esther-Minna had anticipated them. He led them, excited at the thought of finally meeting the new wife face to face, to a small cubicle in his stable, and there, in the darkness full of smells of straw and hay, knelt the old Ishmaelite woman calmly surrounded by her bundles, gleaming with the golden bangles she had amassed in the course of her years of service, a broad grin exposing the single tooth that remained in her mouth. And before they could recover their senses, she drew from her bosom a familiar leopard-skin pouch containing gold coins, the proceeds of the highly successful sale of the merchandise, to be divided now between two instead of three. And so, in the year 4758 of the creation according to the reckoning of the Jews, 388 of the Prophet's removal from Mecca to Medina, two years before the portentous millennium of the Christians, Abulafia's delays turned into utter absence.

6.

After so many days of soaring and heaving between the mast and the ropes of a swaying ship, it was small wonder the dry land exercised such a powerful pull even on light, nimble legs that they refused to go on standing silently atop the wide hill that rose gently on the north bank of the river, and without asking permission they sank slowly and carefully into a full oriental kneeling position on the ground, toward the thrill of grass, stones, and clods of earth, whose smell had been all but forgotten during the long voyage. Even the joyful dampness that now bedewed those young eyes did not dim one whit the attentive look the rabbi's son directed at his master, who from all his men that afternoon had selected the boy from Seville as his sole companion on an early, somewhat furtive reconnaissance, intended to prepare for the first stage of the contest with the business partner who had withdrawn into the nearby city.

By the ruins of a stone arch, perhaps left over from an ancient Roman temple, the Jewish merchant from North Africa now stood gazing with contained excitement at the fields and woods exposed in this saffron-colored light of lazy summer, already tinged with the fresh gray droplets of autumn. From his minute inspection, it appeared for an instant that Paris, the city toward which he had been sailing for so many weeks, was not only situated there to his east, entrenched on a little island in the River Seine, but could also be to the north of the hill he was standing on, and even to the west, and certainly to the south, where the beautiful bend of the river glowed like soft steel, as if every one of the dirt tracks that kissed the little stone arch like rays of light meeting at their star could in its own way lead the two foreign Jews to that radiant city.

But for the small boy, who was following the ship's owner attentively and with interest the whole time, there was no doubt that as the first twilight came on, Ben Attar would choose the track that led eastward, not only because it led straight to the gray island with its huddled houses, but because this was not a mere track but a real road, so resolutely straight that it had carved a broad passage for itself between fields and trees that seemed to make way for it, and it seemed to invite not only a man and a boy to stride along it safely in the gathering twilight, but whole marching armies. Before the moment came when they set forth to seek out the people his father was supposed to admonish with his learned arguments, the child knew that they still had to study well, before dark, the appearance of the stray buildings scattered on both sides of the river. A church tower rose stiffly on the right bank in the clear light not far from the water's edge. Now, as they looked at it, her bells sounded toward the distant Jews.

For several days Ben Attar had known that his first meeting with his nephew and business partner had to take place in total privacy, without the presence of the new wife or any of her stern kinsfolk. Nevertheless, it must not be a chance or secret encounter, in an alley or a field, but upon the very threshold of Abulafia's house, so that the sacred duty of hospitality, which was supposed to be ingrained in a southern man like second nature, would overcome, by the force of tradition and habit, any attempt on the part of the new wife or her severe young brother to extend the repudiation that had been pronounced against him into a veritable interdict, which would instantly dash all the hopes of the bold expedition. Consequently, it was not only an element of agility and surprise that was needed, but also detailed prior knowledge of the house to which the merchant from Tangier was intending to introduce not only himself but also his two wives, who, once their way had been smoothed by the rabbi from Seville with appropriate scriptural verses, would express merely through their placid existence the image of happiness and love that the arbitrary edict emanating from a small town in Ashkenaz sought to destroy.

And so, on learning that afternoon from a pair of fishermen that the town of Paris was waiting to appear around the next bend in the river, Ben Attar had instructed Abd el-Shafi to halt the ship, and prepared himself to go ashore. He had briefly entertained a mischievous thought of surprising Abulafia in his own disguise of a monk or a leper, but he had immediately dismissed it, fearing some theological question he would be unable to answer. Thus he had made do with the garb of an Andalusian Christian who, weary of the Ishmaelites, was seeking out holy places—although, according to Abulafia, it did not seem that this town was particularly notable for sacred sites that might attract a pilgrim from far-off lands. He got his wives to stitch him together a multicolored robe compounded of various styles, so that it would be hard to pin him down to a single identity.

Yet he knew he must not venture alone into a strange city, for a man on his own may vanish without a trace, while two men can always testify for each other, if not in this world then in the next. At first he thought of taking the rabbi from Seville with him, in order to interpret the unfamiliar Capetian environment by means of the Latin he commanded, and also to exercise some legal authority over the Jews whose repudiation he had come to contest. But on further reflection Ben Attar decided that it would be better not to reveal all his weaponry at the outset, and he did not know whether Rabbi Elbaz had recovered from the poetic intoxication that had laid hold of him on the ocean. He thought of taking Abu Lutfi, in the hope that his wronged Ishmaelite presence might make Abulafia feel some remorse for the merchandise that had been so laboriously amassed and so casually brushed aside. But eventually he abandoned this thought too. It was not right that he should leave two tender women and a rabbi utterly transported by poesy to the mercy of sailors who, notwithstanding their honest comportment in the course of the voyage, were nevertheless total strangers; and it was also fitting to ensure that there would be somebody on the ship who would be able to sail her back to North Africa if, heaven forbid, he should disappear in this unknown city.

Whom did he have left? In his heart of hearts Ben Attar would have liked to take his sea captain, not only because he would probably have somewhere in his mind some useful ancient lore from the Viking attacks on Paris at the end of the previous century, but because of his pleasing disposition and his honest, open look. But how could one leave a sailing ship laden with merchandise in a coursing river without a captain? As a last resort he thought of taking one of Abd el-Shafi's burly seamen with him. But again doubts began to nag. This might be just what the stern new wife was waiting for, that he should turn up on her doorstep with a simple, rough, threadbare Arab seaman, so that she could say, *So this is the living wild source of your partner's desire.* Or should he take the young black along with him? The slave's sharp desert senses would certainly guide him straight to the house on the strength of a whiff of Abulafia's scarf, but his rampant thirst for idolatry would have him prostrating himself before the silver ritual chalice in the home of the Parisian Jews, kneeling before the Sabbath candlesticks, and rendering Ben Attar's own religion profoundly suspect. Consequently, it might be best for him to go on his own. But as he raised his eyes heavenward to seek encouragement from his God, who had been so kind to him and his ship during the long voyage, he noticed young Elbaz swaying at the masthead, and said to himself in the words of Scripture, *It seems that this was the lad I was praying for,* not only because a man who has a child with him preserves his humanity even in a strange city, but also because if Abulafia insisted on rejecting him, the child might remind him of his own childhood, when his uncle had taken him to the seaside and held him in the waves, yet always took him home safe and sound.

And so they walked, the ship owner and the little rabbi's son, on this mild evening toward the city. The road they were following was so wide and straight that it might be properly termed an avenue, and after a long time there opened out before them a huge square, and Ben Attar asked the boy to help him erect a small column of stones in its center, as a landmark for their return, in case they were obliged to return alone. From there, still in the same eastward direction, they walked between little squares of green and neatly trimmed bushes, and past a pool of water behind which another stone arch could be seen, only this was a tiny one, only chest height, perhaps a miniature copy of the big one on the hill. If the two travelers had turned around, they would have seen, even at this twilight hour, the straight line that extended between the two arches, but their faces were looking straight ahead, toward the lights of little lanterns swaying all along the river toward the city, and the first faces of the somewhat noisy Parisians themselves, with their sharp features, their watchful eyes, a bald patch at the top of their skulls and shaven faces after the manner of players.

Meantime the island was filled with little lights, as though the inhabitants were vying with one another to display their personal light. In the throng of men and women strolling vociferously along the river, little Elbaz suddenly lost his self-confidence, and the hand that upon the ocean had held firmly to the tip of the mast gave way to panic and now laid hold of Ben Attar's robe, which despite its striking colors attracted no attention from anyone, as though these strangers were walking not into a remote provincial town in darkest Europe but into a real metropolis, like Cordoba or Granada in Andalus, cities that receive many foreign visitors every single day without favoring them with so much as a second glance. Is it the boy who is inspiring such trust all around us, Ben Attar wondered, or do the local folk possess such self-confidence that they can receive any stranger without hostility, so long as he is ready to converse with them?

Indeed, Ben Attar, and even his young companion, began to feel that not only the traders standing at their stalls but even the people

walking along the riverbank were constantly exchanging rapid remarks, and occasionally even uttering a word or two in the direction
of the two strangers, as though the mere fact of speaking in such a
musical language was a source of pleasure and blessing and whoever
said nothing was the poorer for it. But since the two southerners had
no words with which to reply and an ungarnished smile was no longer
sufficient, they kept their heads bowed and began to look down at the
rounded cobbles, upon which the feet of men and women, bound in
curious leather leggings, pranced lithely, so as not to tread in the
horse, swine, and dog droppings scattered everywhere. So intent were
their eyes on the legs all around them that the rabbi's son fancied he
found among them those of his father, who had remained on board
the ship—that is to say, his manner of walking—and stirred by this
discovery, the boy tugged on Ben Attar's robe, and in his soft Andalusian Arabic he whispered excitedly, *Sir, the man walking in front of us
could well be a Jew.*

Surprisingly, Ben Attar was attracted by the boy's idea, not because
of the man's gait but because of the hat that was pulled down on his
head. Without further reflection he turned to follow the man, who, if
he really was a Jew, might be expected not to turn into one of the
taverns whose dim lights flickered around them, but would head for his
home, which would certainly be found in a street in which other Jews
lived, and so, unsuspected, they might arrive at the Levitas house,
where Abulafia resided, for it was not possible that Jews who maintained their faith did not live close to other Jews. Even if it emerged
that the man walking in front of them was not a Jew, to judge by the
gentleness of his step there was no doubt that he was a kindly person,
who would not object to serving unwittingly as a guide.

But a guide to what place? At first their Jew followed the river,
which now revealed to them the walls of the large island, resembling
for an instant a gigantic illuminated ship sailing along beside them.
Even though the majority of the people went down the steps that led to
a ferry that would convey them to the island, their Jew chose instead to
continue on his way along the riverbank, until they reached a dark spot
where the water almost licked at the earth, and there was a modest
bridge of planks, half of it floating in the air and the rest immersed in
the water. Their anonymous guide led them straight into the heart of

the island crowded with houses and winding lanes and full of dark-uniformed guards, who were playing dice at the corners of the lanes and jabbering ceaselessly in their beloved language. From basement windows rose smells of dinner cooking, as though it were not so much the heart of the city that they had reached as its belly. The child, who had eaten nothing since midday, hesitantly turned his steps aside until, half afraid and half hopeful, he halted in front of a portly Parisian who was engaged in dissecting a whole roast piglet into fine pink slices.

When Ben Attar saw that the fragrant morsels of suckling pig failed to distract their chosen guide and that on the contrary he hastened his steps and lowered his eyes, muttering something as he did so, he was confirmed in his view that the boy had guessed right and this really was a Jew. So he continued to dog the man's footsteps when he turned into a long dark alley, which led them through a small opening in the wall of the island to another bridge, no less dilapidated than the first, which took them to the southern bank. Even though it seemed more desolate than the northern bank, it had something gay and liberated about it, at least to judge by the merry, casually dressed young people who sat in the square by a fountain that ran into a stone basin adorned with torches, listening to a musician who was playing a small harp and bestowing friendly glances on Ben Attar and the boy, who were tailing their Jew. No longer able to ignore the pair following him, this man halted in a dark alleyway beside a large stone that projected from one of the houses and considered whether to say something, but he merely looked straight at them out of the darkness.

Abulafia? Ben Attar pleadingly whispered the name of the man who for more than a year had steeped his soul in sadness. A relieved smile flitted across the Jew's face as he realized that there had been a purpose in his being pressed into service as a guide. Raising his arm, he gestured firmly toward the largest dwelling in this small alley, and without saying a word he opened a wicket hidden behind the stone and vanished inside.

Ben Attar was immediately alert. The presence nearby of Abulafia and his new wife had pricked all his senses. But then he admonished himself, for a hasty, unconsidered entrance at this evening hour was liable to confound his hopes of paying a formal visit with his two wives to the home of this woman who found him so repugnant. Accordingly, instead of making for the front door, he lingered and even retreated somewhat, inspecting the new home that his nephew and business partner was inhabiting and considering the best way to draw him out of it. But the windows of this house were small and out of reach, as though they belonged to a fortress rather than a dwelling. Little Elbaz, his impudence aggravated by the hunger that had been haunting him since the afternoon, offered the fruit of his great experience, and boldly laying hold of the heavy, dark wall with his skinny hands, he located hidden projections that enabled him to raise himself to one of the windowsills. For a long while he stayed there, hanging in silence, unable to break free of the attraction of the view afforded to anyone who happens to peep into someone else's house. Meanwhile, Ben Attar, careful to make no sound, was stealthily pacing around the rear courtyard, attracted by familiar smells, and eventually recognized among the logs and broken cartwheels some of the sacks and brassware and skins that had been sold to Benveniste at half-price on the last ill-fated trip to Barcelona.

By now jealousy had rekindled his pain and longing. Unable to restrain himself, he called in a firm whisper to the boy to come down and tell him what he had seen. It transpired that the boy's eyes had been transfixed by those of a girl about his own age, who had stared at him without uttering a word. In that case I have reached my goal, Ben Attar thought excitedly, and concealing his face with his scarf and placing the boy in front of him, he knocked on the door, which was very soon opened by an old servant woman with a kindly expression. While she was wondering whether she ought to be alarmed at the shrouded figure standing before her, the boy, who had learned his part well, bowed deeply and gracefully, and with a gentleness that would dispel any unseemly fear pronounced the name that had floated soundlessly before the advancing prow of the ship for the past eight weeks.

Although only two years had passed since the partners' last meeting, Ben Attar had prepared himself to find Abulafia changed. Even so, he was surprised at the appearance of the man who came toward them. This was not because of his long hair or the pallor and gauntness of his face, but because of a new expression, a kind of inner, spiritual, somewhat artificial smile, as if he were forever attempting to understand the secret of the world yet did not believe that it was possible to do so. Had the new wife really managed to exchange the memory of pain over the drowned wife for a spiritual smile? The nephew's eyes had not yet noticed his uncle, who had withdrawn into the shadow of the doorway, but they were drawn toward the boy, who had begun to prattle to the master of the house in Arabic, so stirring Abulafia with emotion that he could not refrain from touching the child to make sure it was not a dream standing on the threshold of his house. Then Ben Attar lowered his scarf, enjoying not so much the astonishment but the pain that suffused his nephew's beautiful face as he closed his eyes as though he were about to faint.

But Abulafia immediately reined himself in. He knew only too well that fainting on his own doorstep would be considered an escape not only by his guest but also by his wife and her brother, who would come running at once, and so he changed his plan and hastened to embrace Ben Attar, not with that strong, natural embrace of the summer meetings in the woods near Barcelona, but with a soft, desperate hug tinged with guilt and pain, and also with a new repudiation, a hug that repelled even as it clasped the North African traveler. Ben Attar had covered such a vast, impossible distance to come here that he had earned a high status in the eyes of the master of the house, a status that instantly relieved Abulafia of any scruples concerning the nature of the reply that he must give his twice-wed uncle when the latter made his request for hospitality. *My house is your house,* he said clearly, repeating the words in Hebrew so as to avoid any possible misunderstanding, whether on the part of the business partner who had returned or on that of his new wife, whose gown now rustled at his side.

The generous host did not yet know that behind the solitary uncle stood an old guardship lying at anchor not far away. But it was clear from the flash that lit his eyes and the blush that suffused his cheeks that he would not have modified his generous invitation if he had known that hospitality was being requested not just for a young, ill-defined child but for an entire household. For it became more evident by the minute that he was animated by joy at the sight of this guest who had descended upon him with almost magical suddenness, and his excitement caused him to bend down affectionately once again toward the unknown, suntanned child and hoist him tenderly in the air, this child who for many days had swayed at the masthead of a doughty ship. And the new wife, Mistress Esther-Minna, realizing that she had been bested in the first, lightning-quick engagement of the present campaign, smiled too at the uplifted child, who lay gripped in the arms of the master of the house, perhaps in hopes of receiving, once he was back on the ground, something to eat.

Not once but many times in the course of the voyage Ben Attar had asked himself, when the ship was becalmed at night, creaking to herself upon the darkling sea beneath a heaven pregnant with stars, which of Satan's brood had tempted him into abandoning his home and his children and endangering both his two beloved wives and his merchandise on such a ghastly escapade. Why should he insist on winning back the heart of his partner Abulafia, when he might have found a replacement for him, or even two replacements, who, even if they might not have traded with the same talent or reliability as his dear nephew, could have dealt with the old markets of Provence and Toulouse and made him a decent profit, which would preserve his good and honored name and the prosperity of both his houses? And each time he had reminded himself once again that in truth it was not Abulafia's heart that he was trying to win back by means of this crazy journey, but that his new wife, who, though he had never beheld her face nor heard her voice, was extremely important to him, particularly from the moment she had reached out so surely from a distance to impugn his honor.

It was because of the importance of this unknown, distant woman, which had only increased as the journey dragged on and its tribulations became more severe, that he had not only held firm to his purpose but even managed to instill confidence and faith in the other travelers and the crew. So when he finally stood in the entrance of the house, clad in the multicolored robe that his two wives had made for him and inspecting his new kinswoman, who had come up from the Rhine Valley and united herself with his nephew, he knew clearly that this daring adventure had not been in vain. It was indeed right for him to have come from so far away to pit himself against such a woman, who, even though she was ten years older than her young husband, even though fine wrinkles showed on her face, still retained in her high cheekbones and her bright pearl-like eyes traces of a peculiar, exotic beauty, like that of a fine white hound or a fox. Who could say, he reflected with an inward chuckle, whether some savage Viking or Saxon blood might not be coursing in her pious veins, or glimmering in the deep blue stare with which her eyes were now fixing his own?

7.

Supper was laid for them in a large, overfurnished room with woolen rugs on the floor. So astonished was the North African traveler, however, at the rapidity and ease with which he had been accepted into this dreamed-of house that he was incapable of tasting the food that was set before him in heavy dull copper dishes. Instead, he watched the boy from Seville attack the chunks of cock served in a large pot and slake his thirst eagerly from a large crystal goblet that Mistress Esther-Minna casually refilled for him as though she were pouring water rather than wine. Was it the savor of roast pork in the street that had given the lad such a lusty appetite? Ben Attar asked himself as he smiled with embarrassment at his hosts, as though he himself were somehow guilty of this imported hunger. As he watched and wondered, the good wine gradually overcame the young diner, the fork slipped from his hand, his eyelids drooped, and the little pigtail that he had grown on the voyage began to nod, until full-blown slumber unceremoniously overtook him as he was, at table, converting the promised hospitality from a pious gesture to a necessity.

Mistress Esther-Minna, not having been vouchsafed any fruit of her own womb, was moved by any child who fell into her hands, especially such a dusky lad as this, whose locks were as curly as those of her husband, and who was also a half-orphan, according to his companion. Consequently, it was not surprising that she forgot, or at any rate deferred, the repudiation she had imposed upon her guest and called the two old Christian maids to pick up the boy and carefully remove his trousers, not realizing that children's sleep is made of cast iron and not spun from cobwebs like her own—particularly because in this house they were accustomed to dealing with a girl whose slumber deserted her at the slightest sudden movement, to be replaced by raucous, tormented grunts. Even though it was forbidden in this house to call Abulafia's daughter bewitched or accursed, her fundamental nature had still not changed.

Even Ben Attar minded his language when he caught sight of the child standing in the doorway, conjuring up a flickering image of a baby crawling in the bottom of the boat on the first trip to Barcelona, trying to dig her little fingers into his eyes. His heart warmed toward her, and he surreptitiously signaled to the girl, in whose face her late mother's beauty struggled with the blankness of her deformed soul, to come closer to him. Perhaps something really did sparkle in the foggy rage of her memory, since she did not flee in haste as usual from the strange visitor but stood fixed in the doorway, retreating before the master of the house. The moment he learned of the alarming appearance of the rejected business partner, Master Yehiel Levitas, Mistress Esther-Minna's younger brother, shrewdly grasped not only that the first round was lost but that the second too was in jeopardy, and so he hastened to introduce himself politely, if somewhat coolly, to this distant, strange kinsman, who now gave a shallow bow of greeting. The brother did not delay but at once addressed the North African in clear, simple, and very slow Hebrew, as though the worry was not only about some difference in accent, dialect, or vocabulary but about a mental gap dividing north from south. Since, unlike his brother-in-law, he felt no guilt toward the visitor, he was not afraid to ask, after some brief courtesies, a direct question aimed at elucidating the purpose of his visit. Abulafia's face reddened in embarrassment at the coarse question posed by his brother-in-law, who was short and fair-haired like his sister but lacked the jewel-like quality of her eyes, and before Ben Attar managed to reply, Abulafia was attempting to soften the question in trilingual speech. First, in Frankish, he indicated to his precipitate brother-in-law the boundaries of correct comportment. Then, in Arabic, he addressed the dear man who had come from so far away and restored his faith in the expanse of friendship that had been spread out before him here. Finally, in the holy tongue that they could all understand, he urged the weary uncle to sit down at last and taste the food that was growing cold on the table.

Ben Attar was satisfied, however, with the directness shown by Master Levitas, supported by his sister's beautiful, limpid eyes. He was worried now not for himself, his hunger and his tiredness, but for his ship, concealed in the vegetation of the riverbank, whose anxiety for her master, vanished in a strange city, floated above her like an additional sail. Little unexpected tears welled up at the sight of these Jews, whose repudiation had forced him not only to make this long, dangerous journey but also to conceal from them the existence of his companions, and to insinuate himself into their home by night, alone with a strange child. He stared straight into the other's yellow, foxlike eyes and tried to answer him also in clear, simple, and very slow Hebrew, as though his worry too was not only about a difference in accent, dialect, and vocabulary but about a deep religious gap dividing north from south. *We have come to demand divine justice against you and your repudiation,* he said, *and to that end we have brought with us a learned rabbi from Seville.* He was careful not to add any more, so that the plural speech he had adopted, surprising even himself for a moment, might remain vague. Although he was not yet ready to reveal the two wives he had brought with him, to introduce them as daring guests in the house that had opened its doors to him, he was reluctant to impugn their honor by ignoring them.

It turned out that his vagueness was successful. Despite the plural speech, neither the clever Mistress Esther-Minna nor her wary brother could imagine two real wives, but they were excited at the news of the arrival of a learned, virtuous rabbi, who would want to worship with them until he was sent packing. They had grown up in a home of brilliant scholars, who were sometimes so carried away by a discussion of a biblical text that they forgot to lay the table for supper. Hence they were already exchanging delighted glances. And the southern Jew in his multicolored robe struck them as a possible interlocutor, for he had come to plead not for mercy but for justice, like a true Jew. So relieved did they feel that they added their voices to Abulafia's request for the swarthy uncle to eat his fill, recover his strength, and then go to bed, and in the morning to go and fetch the rabbi, whom they wished to receive with great respect, because they could already sense the sweet taste of victory.

Ben Attar too, however, believed that he would prevail—not because of the high hopes he pinned on the rabbi, but chiefly because he could already see in his mind's eye the living, colorful presence of his two wives in this gloomy, dark house, gradually wearing down the

opposition, not by means of an unexpected proof-text or sophistic casu-
istry but simply through the naturalness of the triangular love relationship, which would flow in its full humanity before anyone who tried to
cast a slur on it. This vision of the impending encounter so revived him
that he wished to return to his ship at once. But since his hosts pressed
him to sit at table, he washed his hands over a silver basin that the
Christian maid brought to him, blessed bread in a quiet old chant, and
began to eat the two halves of a hard-boiled egg spread with a thick,
creamy sauce. Then he turned to the chunks of cock stewed in a
brown sauce, surrounded by beans, and continued with a bowl of green
leaves sprinkled with crumbled almonds, and rounded the meal off
with pears baked in honey. He ate slowly and politely, as though to
atone for the child's frantic haste, and for that very reason he was so
taken by the pleasure of eating that he felt a powerful and urgent
desire to share it with the women he had left behind on board ship.

But his hosts, who had welcomed him into their home, were also
responsible for his safety, and they forbade him to go outside at this
late hour. Instead they offered him a bed not far from that of the child,
whose drinking had caused him to snore like a drunken sailor. However, after so many days and nights during which the whole world had
been swaying all around him, the North African was unable to find rest
in a stationary, boxlike room. Small wonder, then, that when the first
glimmer of light caught the window he was ready to set off, leaving the
rabbi's son with Mistress Abulafia, either as a scout ahead of those who
might appear later in the day or as a pledge for the safe return of her
husband, who gladly accompanied his uncle and former partner. Since
the house stood on the southern bank of the river, there was no need
to wait for the gates in the walls to be opened and cross to the north
bank—or right bank, as Abulafia called it, looking at the river from the
point of view of the direction of its flow—for they could simply walk
along the south bank—which Abulafia termed the left bank—until
they reached the bend where the ship lurked. It was now time to reveal
the ship to Ben Attar's astonished nephew, and not merely the fact of
its existence but the richness of its material and human cargo.

Throughout the two years of separation, Abulafia had never given
up hope that his partner and uncle might try to fight against the repudiation that his new wife and her kinsfolk had decreed. In the first

months after the non-meeting that summer at Benveniste's, he had been haunted by false visions of his uncle's splendid robe in the alleys of the Cité in Paris, or among the stalls of the great market in Saint Denis, or occasionally along the walls of the convent of Sainte Geneviève. But knowing his uncle's character well, Abulafia was convinced that someone who was accustomed to the comfort and luxury of two fine houses in a calm and temperate seaside town would recoil from the hardships and dangers that lay in wait for travelers on the long and ill-repaired roads of the Christian kingdoms in the twilight years of the millennium.

Only now, as he stood with his dear uncle in a field beside the fountain of Saint Michel, did he realize how feeble and limited his imagination had been, looking always toward the land and not thinking of the sea, even though it was a genuine ocean. The boldness and daring of his partner, who had persisted in sailing secretly to his very home not only with merchandise but even with his wives, with no prior guarantee or clear chance of winning over the stubborn zealots, moved him with such joy and compassion that he wanted to fall on his knees and beg for pardon for everything he had done to his benefactor. But he stopped himself at the last minute, knowing that begging for pardon would indirectly incriminate his wife and would negate everything she had tried to teach him since their marriage. So he held back and merely threw a friendly arm around his uncle's sturdy shoulders, as though to support him gently as they walked down the slippery winding path toward the river.

And so, in the morning chill of early September, in the year 999 of the birth of the Nazarene, corresponding to the last days of Elul of the year 4759 of the Jewish era of the creation, the two hurried to join the ship, which had passed its first night on this long voyage without the presence of its master. So deeply immersed were they in excited speech, interrupting each other constantly in their desire to finish the two conversations they had missed in the past two summers in that ruined inn looking out over the Bay of Barcelona, that they did not feel the ground hurrying past under their feet, nor did they notice the sound of the bells of the great abbey of Saint Germain des Prés, whose high walls touched the water of the river. They were deep in a business discussion in which Ben Attar was attempting to discover the open and secret desires of the Parisian market, so as to know how much he could expect to make from the goods hidden in the hold of his ship. Even though the ship itself was not far off, the merchant could not refrain from enumerating in advance not only all that his estranged partner would soon see with his own eyes, but also those things that had been and were no longer, such as a little she-camel that had been separated from its mate by the lord of Rouen.

Abulafia was aflame with excitement, not at the thought of seeing the young male camel or the sacks of condiments but at meeting his two aunts, the elder one from whom he had parted years before, and the new one whom he had never seen, even though she had been living since her marriage in his old home, the house of his great lost love. But as he drew near to the big-bellied, tawny ship, well hidden by her captain in the vegetation overhanging the river, he forgot the women for a moment, and a great cry of wonder burst from him at the resourcefulness of blending the military with the civilian in order to undertake an adventure of which even now only God knew what the outcome might be.

Once again he embraced the brave uncle who had not given him up, and he fell into the arms of Abu Lutfi, who had recognized him from afar and hurried down from the deck to greet him with a loud exclamation, shaking his long-lost partner so angrily and affectionately that he almost strangled him. Then he was taken up the rope ladder to the deck, where the captain bowed ceremoniously before him, ordering a sailor to wave a small blue flag in honor of the guest who would soon become their host. They told the black slave to summon the rabbi, who emerged from his cabin all threadbare and confused, and Abulafia's eyes widened at the sight of the Andalusian sage, and he kissed his hand and asked his blessing and gave him greetings from his little boy, who was resting under the reliable care of Abulafia's wife. Then he was led down into the hold, where he was assailed by the powerful Moroccan smells of his childhood, and he felt as though this scarred Arab guardship were a real and precious part of himself, and his eyes filled with tears of sorrow at the parting he had had to undergo and the other parting that was to come.

Then the women came up on deck. First the first wife, in whom, although she had put on weight and her face had grown rounder in the years since he had last seen her, he recognized an affection that radiated toward the whole world. Even though as a child he had sometimes been hugged to her bosom, he was careful not to approach her now, but bowed before her time and again, his hand describing a threefold movement of respect from his forehead to his mouth to his heart, and he greeted her repeatedly, asking after her children in a confused mumble, because his other aunt was now approaching, shyly, fearfully, smiling with her brilliant, perfect teeth. Reddening, he hastily lowered his eyes, for her youth clutched at his heart, not only because he thought about himself but also because of the anticipated pain and anger of his wife, who would not agree to submit to Ben Attar. Yes, he knew this for certain now. His wife would on no account agree to abrogate her repudiation, even if the Andalusian rabbi floored them all with his texts.

But he knew he could not retract his offer of hospitality, even if it had been exacted somewhat deviously. Even if the thought of his uncle staying in his home with his two wives made him shudder, he knew that he would never forgive himself if he allowed his own flesh and blood, whom the good Lord himself had wafted hither from his native land, to lodge in some strange hostelry. That was ruled out from the start for the five Jews by reason of its questionable food, and even for Abu Lutfi, who dogged his heels, eager as ever to show his northern partner the wonderful goods he had collected in the folds of the Atlas Mountains.

For a while things went back to being as they had been in the past, except that the half-darkness of the ship's hold had been exchanged for that of Benveniste's stable, and the low groans of a lonely camel replaced the neighing and braying of the horses and donkeys. Once again the pungent smells of the spices burst from the opened sacks, and the golden honeycombs displayed their delicate tracery, while graceful little daggers inlaid with tiny jewels were extracted from their hiding places, and Abulafia was carried away by the sight of the new merchandise exposed to his gaze and hastened to appraise its quality and calculate how much it would fetch. All the time he spoke to the Arab, the floorboards undulated beneath his feet and the wooden walls swayed gently around him, for the order had covertly been given to Abd el-

Shafi to weigh anchor and carry the travelers forward to the house where the new wife awaited them.

Even though the wife in question was incapable of imagining the two women sailing toward the hospitality of her roof, already an arrow of anxiety had lodged in her heart on account of the North African who had crossed her threshold, and finding no rest for her soul she went into the yard to detain her brother, who was saddling his horse so as to ride south, a distance of three hours' journey, to the place named Villa Le Juif, where a couple of days previously a merchant from the Land of Israel had arrived with a precious pearl. This young man, who always knew how to keep precise track of what occurred in his sister's soul, was amazed to find her pleading with him not to leave before Abulafia returned with Ben Attar and the rabbi. Who was she afraid of, asked the brother, Ben Attar or the rabbi? But she made no reply and said nothing, for even though she was not able to visualize on this bright morning the menace that was sailing lazily into the heart of the Île de France, she could sense it, which is why she mumbled confusedly, *The rabbi . . .* , and wondered at her own reply. The brother's explosion of laughter startled even the horse. What could an Andalusian rabbi say that could frighten her, the daughter and widow of famous scholars? Surely no exegetical sophistry, no well-known biblical tale, no ancient parchment could deflect a clear, new, right decree that was demanded by the circumstances and endorsed by great luminaries. In any case—and here the brother lightly touched his sister's slight shoulder—no debate should be entertained with anyone before he had set up a special court, which might convert their vague repudiation into a definite ban.

With these clear words he mounted his horse and set off, but the sister he left behind was not calmed, for she was too clever to believe that the twice-wed partner who had traveled all the way from North Africa would release them from the affront he had suffered merely with a court hearing. She had already understood last night, from his slow, determined movements and his gentle gaze, which had not left her, that this man, whose resemblance to her husband could not be denied, and who had demanded divine justice, was only too well acquainted with human justice, which is why he had penetrated her home—to reveal to her some secret about human nature, although she refused to guess at what it was, unless the child awoke and revealed it to her. But the wine that had been poured like water into the boy's cup had turned to lead in his veins during the night, and when she attempted to rouse and question him, he only sank deeper into slumber. Even the mute girl, who all morning had followed her like a shadow, now broke into the persistent loud howl of lamentation that she had first uttered two years before, when her Ishmaelite nurse was sent away.

Into this howl, which had continued since morning and now pierced the noonday silence, entered the two wives, carrying their bundles and following close behind Abulafia, who had decided to accompany them into his home himself, with a presentiment of imminent disaster but also with the confident belief that the right thing was being done here, even if it was temporary. Ben Attar had remained on board to help Abu Lutfi and Abd el-Shafi allay the suspicions of the royal guardsmen who had boarded the ship, which was anchored by the little bridge. Now, left alone, Abulafia's manner to his wife became all the more bold, and she was not only angry with him but also excited and fascinated by his new commanding tone, as he ordered her to make ready three rooms, two for the two women and a third for the rabbi, who entered with a light, shy step and greeted in poetic and musical language the graceful housewife, whose blue eyes already made him miss the river he had just left.

And Abulafia repeated to his wife, *My aunts,* not only to stress the family bond by which he was bound but also to moderate somewhat the reduplicated sexuality, which between the gray walls and the dark furniture received such a powerful, colorful, and scented intensification that the mistress of the house felt the ground opening up under her feet and reached out to the nearest chair for support. But it was neither the new firm look in her young husband's eyes nor the timorous smile flitting over the rabbi's pale face but rather the mute presence, so submissive yet so serious, of two veiled women standing before her that suddenly softened her heart and caused her resistance to evaporate and curl slowly heavenward like the smoke from her kitchen chimney.

As though to demonstrate to her husband that she was not to be

outdone by him in fulfilling the sacred duty of hospitality, she unhesitatingly gave orders in the local language to the maids to take her
bedding out of her own bedchamber and prepare the room to receive
the first wife, and to remove the girl with her belongings and her rag
toys from her small room so the second wife might also have a private
apartment. She herself led the gaping rabbi, with his meager bundle of
clothes, to his son's bed, where by dint of his parental authority he
might shatter the boy's epic slumber. If it appeared to Abulafia now
that his dear wife had accepted defeat in the second round, so that he
could leave her calmly and return to the ship to continue rummaging
among the merchandise, this was only because of her resolute inner
confidence in divine justice, which would soon stand up against the
human spirit that had so rudely invaded her house.

Perhaps it was precisely because of her confidence in the temporary character of her defeat that Mistress Esther-Minna was willing to
be so cooperative, that it seemed as though she were seeking to retreat
further in order to double the sweetness of her victory when the time
came. Instead of standing on her honor in the presence of the two
wives, she joined her maidservants in changing the bedspread on her
own marriage bed. From the moment this duplication of wives, which
had aroused her repudiation from afar, had become a reality in her own
home, she sought not to flee from it but, on the contrary, to attack it.
And so she told the maids to fetch a large tub and fill it with warm
water, and she half seduced and half ordered her guests to undress
themselves and wash their bodies, so as to separate the fragrant duski-
ness produced by the African sun from the filth added to it by their
long journey.

Thus it was not through the eyes of their joint husband but in the
gentle but bright noonday sunlight, in such a distant and strange
house, that the first wife and the second wife were asked for the first
time in their lives to reveal to each other the hidden secrets of their
nakedness, and in the presence of a third woman, a stranger, blue of
eye and short of stature, who was not content with looking from afar,
from a corner of the room, but approached and took the jug from her
maidservant's hand to rinse the tangled braids and to scrape with niter
and soap the curved backs and soft bellies, the breasts, heavy hind
parts, shapely long thighs. She dried everything that had been exposed

with soft towels, so as to be satisfied that the accumulated dirt of the journey had not distinguished one wife from the other but had merely dulled the deep, true difference between them, which, now that they were gleaming with cleanliness, was revealed in full force, although still without elucidating the secret that joined them in the perfection of a single love.

But Mistress Esther-Minna could not wait for the master of this secret to return, for he was busy now, on the orders of the city guards, cleaning the caliph's ancient guardship of any old military insignia or accessory, real or imaginary, so that it would have the appearance of a civilian ship alone, qualified by its nonmilitary character to anchor in the port of Paris. Dinnertime came, but despite her sternness, Mistress Esther-Minna did not disturb the rabbi from Seville, who instead of waking his son had joined him in slumber. So only the two freshly bathed wives were summoned to table. And since Ben Attar had never seen fit to endow his wives with any words of the holy tongue, there was no question of any table talk, which grieved the hostess greatly, for both her dear departed father and her husband of blessed memory had always admonished her that a meal without words of Torah was likened by the sages to eating the sacrifices of the dead.

The three women ate in deep silence. While the two guests, as they tasted cautiously and with wonder the delicious "sacrifices of the dead," had the feeling that they were floating into a sweet dream, their hostess, who could not dispense with words of Torah, ascended to the upper story and asked permission from her brother's wife to seek among his parchments the faded copy of the last song of Moses, whose ancient reproofs she read slowly, verse after verse, to the two women, who had meanwhile finished eating. They listened in total silence, feeling the heavy drowsiness that had fallen on the adjoining chamber enfolding them too, for it was only now, in this closed, motionless room crowded with dark furniture made from the wood of the Black Forest, that they made the same discovery as the rabbi and his young son—that all the sleep they had known during their long voyage on the sea had not been real sleep, because the waves had never, ever let them forget, for a fraction of a moment, the existence of the world outside their dreams. And so it was best, before the abundant newly washed tresses sank into the empty dishes, to interrupt the reading of the ancient song, say a hasty grace, and hurry the two drowsy women into their separate rooms. Mistress Esther-Minna, who now remained alone at table, did not yet burst into tears of despair, but only because her long years of widowhood had taught her, among other things, the godly quality of patience.

Later that afternoon, when a soft knock was heard at the outer door and the gentile maidservant ushered in the uncle, Ben Attar, who had returned by himself and now stood before his nephew's wife completely naturally, like a welcome guest who had become used to his place, she rose hurriedly to her feet beside the cleared table, on which there lay only the yellowing parchment bearing the last song of Moses. She trembled at the sudden intimacy that the twice-wed partner had thus forced upon her, after insinuating himself cunningly into her home through an imperfectly sealed crack of guilt in her husband's soul. She could see that he was in a contented state, his eyes bright and calm, not only because he had found a suitable berth for his ship and her crew, but also because he had noticed how the new merchandise lying in the ship's hold had attracted Abulafia and rekindled the old spark in his eyes. Now, offering Mistress Esther-Minna a chance to turn the defeat of her repudiation into a new, shared victory of closeness and amity, he smiled and bowed before her politely, as if to say, *Even though you have forced me to make this long journey, I forgive you.* She, however, could stand the man's proximity no longer. A wave of fear and disgust rose up inside her, her composure deserted her, and impatiently she left the room.

But Ben Attar's spirits did not flag. Rather the contrary, as though neither the woman's sudden abject departure nor even the blue of her eyes convinced him now of its authenticity. But he stood perplexed in the empty room, not knowing where in this house full of narrow dark passages she had hidden his wives. Just as he was hungrily eyeing the strip of parchment, which looked like a sheet of baked pastry, he heard behind a curtain the voice of the first wife, who always woke at his approach, as though even in the depths of sleep she was always ready for him. Was she alone there, or was the second wife with her? Very carefully he drew aside the curtain, and found himself in Abulafia's marital bedchamber, a room with curved walls dotted with narrow little windows that seemed like eyes squinting in sunlight. The semidarkness and the strange smells seemed to mask the familiar scent of the first wife, who at her husband's entrance pushed the light bedspread off her large bare legs, which she crossed in a relaxed but explicit posture. From the sound of his footsteps as he entered, she knew that he was in a contented mood, which meant that not only had the door of this house opened easily and even respectfully before her and the second wife, accompanied by the rabbi who would justify her existence, but a fitting resting place had been found for the ship and her crew. In which case, she thought to herself with amazement, it might yet turn out that this crazy journey Ben Attar had forced them to make had not been in vain, and that the business partnership between north and south might yet come back to life. In which case, she continued to herself, I was mistaken to imagine that the gloom and melancholy that have laid him so low these past two years have robbed him of his wits. In the softness of the wide bed and the pleasure of the high ceiling above her, her feeling of regret was combined with a sense of pride in the success of the father of her children, the wise and strong and therefore desired husband, who was now penetrating deeper into the darkness of the curved bedchamber toward the first wife, who was removing her shift so as to offer him her large, washed breasts.

At first he recoiled from her, not only because he did not feel ready to make love so precipitately, and in a strange room, on the bedding of his hosts, his kin, with whose hearts and minds he still had to engage in battle, but also because he did not know where or how far away the other wife was. But when he tried to push her away with a strangled whisper of affection, she caressed him all the harder and her sighing turned into moaning, so that he was obliged to stop her mouth with one hand while the other tried to soothe with caresses the heavy, inflamed breasts that pressed against his face and flooded him with a fresh smell of soap. But now, in this curved chamber in this strange city, he discovered that the long voyage had made the first wife, like the second, stronger than he. While the anxieties of the journey had sapped the marrow of his bones day and night, the two women sitting on the old bridge had been freed of all responsibility, and with nothing to do, poised between sea and sky, they had accumulated strength flavored with a hint of wildness, so that this woman now grabbed handfuls of his hair and pulled them hard toward her, not only to force the obstructing hand to release the sounds of her desire but also to enable her more easily to remove the robe that covered his virility. Because of the existence of a second wife, he owed her more than if she had remained the only one.

Dazed and unready, at first he struggled silently with the desire of his first wife in the darkened room, until his heart longed for her and he took her, placing his mouth on hers in place of his hand to confine her moans. Afterward he hastened to cover her, wondering about the whereabouts of the second wife and thinking of what he had to do and wanted to do to preserve the perfect love that he had been forced to demonstrate here in double proof. But when he attempted to rise, he discovered that the creeping fatigue that had overcome the other travelers since last night had reached him too. So again for a while he laid his head between the first wife's strong thighs, inhaling once more with surprised curiosity the smell of Mistress Esther-Minna's soap. Within the curved walls of the chamber, whose tiny windows admitted the pink light of the Parisian sky blended with a gay, guttural babble from the nearby riverbank, he closed his eyes, taking care not to fall asleep, so as not to lose control just now, when the babble outside was joined from inside the house by the clear voice of its excited mistress.

Gently, Ben Attar released himself from the warm, warming trap. While the first wife, thus innocently released, curled up and went back to sleep, he rose and dressed, trying to smooth his crumpled robe, and crept in quietly for his next encounter with Mistress Esther-Minna, who was sitting red-faced where she had been before, with her old maidservant, the yellow parchment of the song of Moses spread between them as though the shared contemplation of the Jewess and the gentile might soften the angry menace of the words. Now the mistress of the house did not hasten to rise and retreat from her guest, perhaps in part because she realized that her generous hospitality had left her no private corner of her house to withdraw to. And so she remained, looking at him. Had she been able to, she would have made him too, wash his body, which smelled not only of the salty ocean but also of a heady reek of spices and animal skins. Moreover, from the soft, thick look that clouded his eyes, and perhaps also from the presence of a telltale stain on the edge of his robe, she was suddenly pierced, as by a painful knife thrust, by the knowledge that, having just made love on her own bridal couch, he was now roaming in search of his second wife, so as to prove to the mistress of the house that she was both misguided and ignorant.

A powerful shudder shook her, as though the vengeful desert god who had just cursed the world in the last song of Moses were trying to test her too, not in the faraway desert but here in her own home, in her innermost chambers, revealing to her what was forbidden and out-lawed in the new edict from the Rhineland as one might expose a child to a sexual act. She lowered her head and put her fist to her mouth in a childlike gesture. And the blue of her eyes shone in deep amazement, which made them sparkle like true sapphires among the fine wrinkles that adorned the corners of her eyes. As Ben Attar looked at her, he could feel her shudder with moral revulsion against him, but when he remembered what Abulafia had told him by the campfire in the Span-ish March about the pleasure that he extracted from her, he said noth-ing, except to ask her gently for the whereabouts of the second wife.

From here he strode along a narrow, very dark passage to a cubicle between whose bare gray walls the girl's bewitched spirit still wafted, even though she herself had been taken away that morning. The twi-light that was beginning to descend on the island played slowly on the profile of the young second wife, who had been caught up in the universal slumber. Although Ben Attar had neither the strength of spirit nor the desire to draw her up from the depths, he did not relent, because he knew that on the other side of the door a woman who was seeking to convert her failed repudiation into a full-blown ban was waiting for him, and until the rabbi from Seville should wake from his sleep and know what to say to her, it was up to him to show her with deeds, not with words, that she was mistaken, and that love was possi-ble at any time or at any place where the lover was present. And so, exhausted as he was, he roused himself to rouse the woman who was lying before him. But the second wife was young enough to cling fanatically to her sleep, and when he tried to wake her with his kisses, she pushed him frantically away, apparently still unconsciously, de-fending her slumber with as much determination as though it were her virginity.

He did not relent, despite being so tired and hungry, for his desire for food was greater now than his desire for a woman. Since through the haze of tiredness he imagined that he had been ravaged by the first wife, he allowed himself to ravage the second one, and slowly he struggled with her while dragging her up from her depths, kissing every part of her body that might be kissed, which meant every part of her body. At last she took pity on him, licking his eyeballs to make him close his eyes and enter into her slumber and be embraced in her breathing, so that when he took her he would not know whether it was reality or a dream.

Meanwhile, Mistress Esther-Minna remained seated in the next room beside her parchment, which seemed even more severe in the evening shadows, impatiently waiting for the return of her husband, who was wandering around on the right bank with Abu Lutfi, who had come ashore to discover what did or did not attract the notice of the Parisians in the market of Saint Denis. Ever since the partnership had been disbanded, Abulafia had nurtured a sense of guilt not only toward his good uncle but also toward the partner from the desert, whose weeping at their parting he could not forget, and so he now treated the Ishmaelite with great patience. He showed him every stall, every object, translated every remark, as though he did not have important guests at home who might forgive his absence only because they were all wrapped up at the moment in their sleep. His wife, however, did not forgive him, and she went down to the front gate to see who would arrive first, her young husband or her young brother. As time wore on and the darkness deepened, the space carved out inside her by worry increased, and for an instant she was seized by a terrible fear that neither of the men would ever return and that she would become the third wife of the North African merchant who had settled in her house. When the rabbi's son woke from his powerful sleep—for it was fitting that the first to wake should be he who had fallen asleep first, young though he was—and, approaching her in a daze, unthinkingly clung to her apron, she could not prevent herself from bursting into bitter tears, which were only assuaged by the whinnying of her brother's horse. She permitted herself to dispense with courtesies and announced to him at once what had taken place in the house from which he had been absent for a whole day. Her trusty brother listened expressionlessly, as usual, maintaining his inner peace and his clarity of mind so as to calm his distraught older sister with well-weighed words of moderation.

What was there to fear? The decrees were clear, and natural justice rendered them irreversible. And if those dusky Jews demanded a judgment according to the law of God, they would have it, and with great clarity too. For in between pearls—there had turned out to be two pearls, not one—he had managed to convene a special court at Villa Le Juif, which would convert the indecisive repudiation of the past into the definite ban of the future.

PART TWO

The Journey to the Rhine,
or the Second Wife

1.

In the second watch of the night, Rabbi Elbaz awoke, suddenly feeling so hungry that the heavy sleep fell away from him even before he realized where he was. At sea the stars in the heavens had caressed his opening eyes and helped him remember, whereas now his eyes were filled only with thick, coal-black darkness. But as he got up and groped at the world around him, he was startled by the warmth of the boy sleeping next to him. He had become accustomed to sleeping without him ever since the child had insisted on descending into the bowels of the ship at night and spreading his bedding near the second wife's curtain. But here he was beside him, just like in their little house in Seville, curled up lean and fetuslike and sighing occasionally like an old man.

Even though the chamber was warm, the rabbi piled his own coverlet on the young sleeper, then set off in search of something to quell his hunger before he went outside to feel the dome of heaven over his head and relieve the sense of suffocation. Where was Ben Attar? he asked himself, drifting like a sleepwalker along the long winding corridors of this large, complicated house in the hope of finding a stray crust of bread. Had his employer managed to arrive in the wake of his wives, or was he still being compelled to prove to the Parisian guards the innocence of his ship's intentions? For a moment he tried to locate the merchant by the odor of his clothes, but the new smells of the strange house had dulled the memory of the familiar scent of his fellow travelers. Then, inadvertently and in all innocence, he touched the soft plump back of the first wife, who responded by turning over on her bed with a luxuriant grumble.

When he finally found the kitchen, there was neither a crust of bread nor any other forgotten morsel on the table, but only a pile of bright iron cooking pots and a display of polished copper pans hanging on the wall, reddening with their gleam the pallid glow of the moonlight. But if the kitchen offered no hope of food, there was at least a spiral staircase leading down to the lower story. Only here the darkness was so dense that great resourcefulness was required not only to locate the outer door, which unlike the gracefully ornamented doors of the houses in Seville was clad in crude iron, but also to draw back silently the numerous bolts that restrained it, so as to escape from the hard darkness into the night with its caressing breeze and soft sounds. Despite the lateness of the hour, Paris was not entirely still between her twin banks, and even here, on the deserted southern bank, there could be heard a guttural gurgle of conversation between a man and a woman, who, to judge by the slow yet urgent pace of their talk, did not find the hour too advanced to lust after each other. For a moment the rabbi from Seville was tempted to approach them silently and perfume himself with their love, even if it was couched in a foreign tongue, but fearing that his sudden appearance might be misconstrued, he drew up a large log from the woodpile standing ready for winter and sat to enjoy the pleasant moonlight, first picking off a few pieces of soft bark to chew to still his hunger.

A light hand landed upon him. It was the child, who had woken and come out in search of him. He too pulled out a log, sat down on it, and began to ask questions, which came bursting out of him now, at the tail end of the second watch. Was this the house, were these the people for whom they had bobbed on the ocean waves for so many days and weeks? And would this really be their final stop, or would they sail on upstream to some other destination? Up to now the boy had seemed to ignore the purpose of the journey his father had imposed on him, surrendering his young being enthusiastically to the ship and her crew. But from the moment they had disembarked onto dry land his old nature had returned, and he felt homesick for his little house and everything else—his cousins and his friends, and the earthen flowerpots hanging on the bright blue-painted walls. Why had they gone onto that ship, he asked his father grumpily, and what was their business in this gloomy house? And if Ben Attar did decide to stay here with his wives, who would take them back to Andalus? Would another ship come to fetch them? Or would they go home overland? The father tried to revive his son's flagging spirits, and after promising him that the day was not far off when they would return to Seville, he tried to explain again the purpose of the expedition, telling him about the partnership that had been built up in the course of many years, and its disruption on account of Abulafia's remarriage and his new wife's alarm at the idea of two women being married to one man. When he saw that his son had difficulty comprehending Mistress Esther-Minna's animosity toward Ben Attar, Rabbi Elbaz drew the child's bowed head toward him, to look into his eyes and see whether, despite his youth and innocence, he was capable of both understanding the new wife's fears and guessing the meaning of the replies his father was preparing. Surely he had spent so many days close to the merchant and his two wives, both on deck and in the hold, that he would be better placed than anyone else to testify whether there was any suffering or sorrow there.

What sorrow? What suffering? the boy whispered to his father in astonishment. *That's just the point,* his father replied immediately with a smile. This was exactly how he must explain it to Abulafia's new wife, so that she would rescind her repudiation of the partnership. That was why Ben Attar had ventured upon the ocean waves and, not content with coming himself, had brought both his wives with him, so they too might testify in his favor. And that was why he himself had been hired for the journey, to bear witness that in the eyes of God too this double bond was pleasing. This new wife set great store by the will of God. And if—here the father winked at his son—the child too would testify to the easy and affectionate relations prevailing between the two wives . . . But the boy, alarmed at his father's intention of involving him, was seized by a vague terror, and with a new stubbornness he ducked out from under his father's caressing hand. No, he wouldn't say a word. He didn't know a thing. He would say nothing. The father's smile froze now on his face, not only because of his son's dogged refusal but at the sight of a line of black-clad, singing monks processing calmly down the narrow street, waving billowing censers, either to atone for the sins of the day that was past or to send abroad a fragrant enticement for the day that was to come. The sudden sight of two strangers sitting beside the door of the Jews' house in the middle of the night startled the monks so much that for a moment they stood rooted to the spot, before hurriedly crossing themselves and departing.

The child trembled at the sight of the monks vanishing toward the nearby monastery of Saint Germain, whose bell rang to greet them, and he entreated his father to go indoors. The father, however, was troubled by a new thought on account of the boy's firm refusal to support him in his testimony in favor of Ben Attar's double marriage. Is it

109

possible that the boy can see what I am not willing to see? he thought to himself, and he decided to take another look at the texts that Ben Attar had brought from Tangier in the name of the sage Ben Ghiyyat, in the hope of finding an apposite verse or a telling parable from the words of the sages and ancients to strengthen their case. Before the day dawned, he resolved to return to the ship and rummage in the ivory casket that had been left behind, and at the same time to relieve the hunger occasioned by his long sleep.

But the child refused to return alone to the strange dark house and insisted on going with his father, saying that he remembered the way back very well. Because he did not know that the ship he had left two days earlier had meanwhile been brought closer to the island, at first he denied it was the same one and insisted that it was a different one that simply resembled their own, which was moored farther away. Elbaz had difficulty in getting the boy to admit his mistake, perhaps because the old guardship really had changed and seemed to have shrunk in the intervening hours. The large triangular sail had completely disappeared, and the old shields and ornaments that had adorned the ship's sides had been removed. But when Abu Lutfi, hearing the sounds of argument breaking the still of the night, called to them from the deck, the boy was forced to admit that it really was the selfsame ship whose mast had slid between his skinny legs for so many days that it had become like a part of his body.

At once the black slave was sent ashore in a dinghy to fetch the returning passengers. Despite the short time that had elapsed since their last leavetaking, Abu Lutfi was glad to have the rabbi back on board, hoping that his holy presence might restore some order to the ship—for from the moment she had reached her final berth and been tied up on the northern shore of the Seine a certain licentiousness had begun to proliferate on board, not only because her owner was away but because of the absence of his two wives, whose quiet, courtly presence had held the winds in check. When the rabbi and his son climbed on board, they were confronted by a mess of dirty plates and a group of sleeping drunkards sprawled before Abd el-Shafi, who was seated aloft on the old bridge, wrapped in a leopard skin that he had helped himself to from the hold and humming an old tune that had probably been sung by the Vikings when they had attacked this town a hundred years before. Seeing the rabbi walking across the deck, the captain let fly a vulgar expression that he would never have used during the long journey. But the rabbi ignored it, hesitating as he was between looking for the ivory casket and quelling his hunger pangs. Fearing that immoderate eating might shed reproach on the hospitality of Abulafia and his wife, he decided to descend into the hold and slake his craving with dried figs and carobs. But Abu Lutfi, observing how hungry he was, gave orders for a meal of fish from the new river to be prepared for the two visitors.

While awaiting this meal of the third watch, which was already introducing a fine sliver of light into the sky over the darkened city, the rabbi went in search of the ivory casket. When the muse had taken hold of him off the rugged coast of Brittany, the casket had vanished, and he had completely forgotten about it. He could not locate it amid the jumble of clothes and objects in his cabin, nor was it in Ben Attar's. Climbing back up to the old bridge, he sought the little casket among the bundles and under the leopard skin that adorned Abd el-Shafi, who stared at him drunkenly, but there was no trace of it. Had Abu Lutfi included it among the merchandise to be offered for sale? Cautiously he questioned the Ishmaelite partner, who instantly swore that he would never dare to touch a casket containing holy words. Had one of the women taken it, then? the rabbi wondered. But they could not read. Out of respect, the rabbi considered sending his son to search their cabins, but eventually he mustered the determination to go himself, in case the search brought him some further helpful understanding. Entering first the first wife's cabin in the bow, he saw at once that it had been completely cleared, leaving behind nothing but a faint lingering hint of her fragrance in the air. Had she taken her clothes and possessions with her for fear of losing them, or was she preparing herself for a long stay ashore? Either way, most of her belongings had gone, and what little remained was neatly bundled and tied with a red cord and stowed beside her carefully folded bedclothes. The rabbi headed for the hold, where the young camel stood all alone, staring sadly between his front legs at a new Parisian mouse. Before the rabbi found the little cell draped with a curtain, he lost his bearings among the large sacks, but eventually with trembling hands he moved aside the rope mat, and with a lighted candle he stooped and entered and excitedly encountered the second wife's bed, which had been left covered in a mess of her clothes and other belongings, as though she had fled in a panic with the intention of returning at once. And here, among the smooth silk robes that perfumed his hands, he found the ivory casket, which might have been casually abandoned here or carefully concealed for the purpose of some secret ritual.

Elbaz had not been so close to a woman's clothes and objects since his wife's death, and for a moment he was shaken by desire. So he hastily departed, clutching the casket inside his robe and stroking the camel's delicate narrow head as he passed, out of compassion, and perhaps by way of atoning for the sinful thoughts that had flitted through his mind a moment earlier. On deck he found Abd el-Shafi, who had come down from his seat on the bridge to show the boy how to fillet a fish without damaging it. So well had the rabbi's son learned his lesson that without being asked he filleted the rabbi's fish too, and the rabbi, unable to contain himself any longer, threw himself upon the tender white flesh.

Only as dawn was breaking did the rabbi, sated and a little tipsy, manage to reexamine the parchments that Ben Ghiyyat had sent him and understand why he had so neglected them during the last days of the journey that he had almost lost them. The verses from the stories of the patriarchs, judges, and kings that the North African sage had selected and copied in his large, fair hand seemed childish and irksome, far removed from the nobility of the three-cornered love that had sailed beside the rabbi for so many days. Thus he asked Abu Lutfi, who had not taken his eyes off him, to replace the parchments in the ivory casket and keep it under his protection, hidden in a safe place beside his couch. While the Arab reverentially picked up the pieces of parchment, smoothed them, and arranged them in order of size, the rabbi screwed up his eyes in the brightening light and sensed the traces of the couplings that had taken place on the ship now riding quietly on the river. Suddenly he was assailed by a vague excitement, and he swore to himself by the beloved memory of his wife to devote all his power and wisdom to the defence of the integrity of his employer's family.

But the rabbi from Seville, as he sat deep in thought on the deck of the ship, did not imagine that this pledge of defense would have to be called upon this very day, which was dawning slowly and stirring deep fears not only in Mistress Esther-Minna, who had hardly closed her eyes all night, but also in her brother, Master Levitas, who despite his habitual equanimity and confidence was wondering whether the little tribunal that he had organized so hastily in Villa Le Juif would be able to get to the root of the matter and conclude its work before sunset, so that he would be able to rid his home speedily of this southern company that had taken up residence with excessive alacrity. Even though Ben Attar and his small retinue had made every effort to maintain a polite silence during the night, Mistress Esther-Minna was unable to avoid the feeling that her secure existence was being invaded. Since she had lain awake most of the night, she had been unable not to hear the groaning of the bolts of the front door in the middle of the night and the light footsteps disappearing outside. At first she had tried to restrain herself and had not stirred from her bed. But when a long time had passed and the footsteps did not return, she went downstairs and discovered that the door was wide open, the house was abandoned, and there was no one outside in the street. Then she experienced a strange feeling, joyful, yet painful too, that the second wife might have decided to disappear suddenly, either from fear at what the next day would bring or from a sense of guilt at her redundant status. The thought of that dark young woman wandering all alone outside upset her so much that she decided to waken Abulafia to go out and bring her back, for she now felt stirred by compassion.

Before waking her husband she went to confirm her suspicion, but she found Ben Attar's first wife sleeping peacefully in her place, and the second wife too in the place that had been allotted her, the wretched girl's cubicle, lying naked in her husband's embrace. When Mistress Esther-Minna realized her mistake, she found the courage to draw aside the curtain to the rabbi's bedchamber, and there she discovered an empty bed. Was it possible, she asked Abulafia as the morning dawned, that the legal genius who had been brought especially from Andalus had already fled the field of combat? But Abulafia refused to believe that. No, it was not, he said; why should he run away? It was evident that for some reason Abulafia was in a very good mood, as if he nursed another secret that his wife did not share.

Indeed, this new happy mood that had come upon Abulafia since his uncle's astonishing arrival exacerbated his new wife's constant anxiety for the well-being of her marriage, for despite its sweet and bitter moments, it was still impossible to tell whether its spiritual (as opposed to its emotional and physical) sanctity had yet penetrated her young husband's heart. Even though she was convinced that the hastily convened tribunal that her brother had arranged in Villa Le Juif would have the skill to repulse this bizarre and impertinent invasion that had originated in the south and attacked them from the west, whether it was personal or religious in nature, still she was nagged by a fear that lurking behind this was a new scheme to revive the proscribed partnership. That would revive Abulafia's traveling, and he would be once more exposed not merely to the menace of highway robbers but also to the temptation of dual matrimony, which the sturdy uncle was trying to demonstrate in the heart of her home could be undertaken without pain or effort.

In the intensifying light of day, when it was impossible to ignore the happiness not only of Ben Attar but of Abulafia too on seeing Rabbi Elbaz returning from his nocturnal visit to the ship, contented after roaming the narrow streets of the Parisian island and replete after his fish breakfast, Mistress Esther-Minna's beautiful eyes darkened, and biting her thin lips she went to the yard to gain encouragement from her brother, who was inspecting the wheels of the large wagon that was to transport the parties to their tribunal. Since Ben Attar insisted adamantly that the two wives must accompany them, firm in his faith that their presence at his side would strengthen, not weaken, his case, the driver must be asked to give additional power to the wagon by joining a partner to the stout, shaggy horse that was already standing harnessed and ready. How fortunate, Master Levitas chuckled to himself, that the Ishmaelite partner had remained on the ship and did not demand to be a party in the legal dispute, so that they were spared from having to order a third horse. Handing a coin to the Frankish wagoner, he sent him to hire one of the horses that were plowing a field close to the large monastery. And even though Villa Le Juif was not far away and the whole business should be over by evening, Mistress Esther-Minna's brother sensibly ordered the servants to make ready plenty of food and drink, as provisions for all the travelers, no matter which side of the barricades they stood on, so that the adjudication should be conducted in a mood of satiety and good cheer on all sides.

Indeed, both parties set forth together in good cheer and comradeship, three on one side of the wagon and four on the other, since the boy chose to sit next to the sturdy Frankish driver, who marveled without cease at the darkness of the little Jew's skin. As soon as they had laboriously climbed a steep hill, still scattered with the remains of Roman stones and columns from the fine houses of the city of Lutetia, which had been sacked by marauders from the north, the road ran level and smooth past a peasant hut, a field of barley, and a hedge of vines. Thanks to the pleasantness of the road they felt no weariness when at midday, after only three hours of traveling, Master Levitas called a halt so that they could eat in a charming wood, which had not only a stream winding among the trees but also a hillock from which one could see the estate of Villa Le Juif on the horizon. Perhaps because he was convinced that the clear verdict of the tribunal would make this their last meal together, he had decided to embellish it with fine embroidered tablecloths spread upon the ground and with elegant cutlery. And even though Mistress Esther-Minna was perfectly able to arrange everything herself, her brother helped her and sliced the long loaves of bread and the dark cheese and offered the large slices on his knife first to the three men and then, after a moment's hesitation, to the two women too, whom fear had brought closer to each other ever since they had disembarked from the ship. When Master Levitas felt that his usually firm hand was trembling slightly under the burning looks coming from behind the fine veils, he allowed himself to blush a little and to smile shyly into his little beard, before hastily drawing out of the folds of his robe a red leather-bound prayerbook in Amram Gaon's edition, which he wanted to compare with the one he had noticed in Ben Attar's bag, which turned out to be in the edition by Saadia Gaon. This was not merely because of a sudden upsurge of scholarly curiosity, but also so that religious conversation might ensure that this simple meal in the bosom of nature did not become a partaking of the sacrifices of the dead.

All at once Rabbi Elbaz, seized by a troubling thought, hastily thrust away the bread and cheese, which he placed on the plate of the ever-hungry child, and arose in agitation and went to the stream to refresh his face and hands. Then he addressed Master Levitas, who was still feeling the two prayerbooks with his thin fingers, with a question about the character and identity of the tribunal awaiting them on the horizon. Levitas seemed to hesitate slightly, as though he were afraid to enumerate the special merits of the judges, and contented himself with general praise of the good qualities of the Jews in Villa Le Juif, which was the large estate of an extensive family, containing various workmen, servants, and retainers and even a large winery, which made wine untouched by gentile hands for the benefit of those Jews who strictly observed the law concerning the wine of idolatry. A real law court was not needed in such a family estate, where any problems sorted themselves out. But for the sake of the visitors coming from so far, with their southern plaint, he had decided to assemble a special rustic law court.

Indeed, an impression of fertile fields and vineyards welcomed the party before they entered a gate in the moss-clad stone wall that surrounded Villa Le Juif, which consisted of no more than eight or nine single-story buildings arranged around a central courtyard. To judge by the long-haired children who came running up excitedly, the local Jews already seemed to know about the debate that was about to take place in their courtyard. There was no doubt that the knowledge that a rabbi had been specially brought from Andalus to assist in the contest particularly inflamed the locals' curiosity, which was already very excited, not only because of the pleasure of an argument but also because of the inherent attraction of the subject matter.

This attraction had even drawn in one or two Christians, like wasps to a honeycomb, from the neighboring estates; they pronounced their urgent desire to be present at a dispute between Jews and, who knew, maybe even to assist, thanks to their religious superiority, in the formulation of the verdict. Since word had got around that the two women who were at the center of the case would be present, it was clear to all and sundry that the little synagogue of Villa Le Juif would not suffice for such a gathering, and a more spacious and less sacred place that could contain such a large crowd would be required. Consequently, Meshullam the Priest, the proprietor of the winery and a close friend of Master Levitas, had given orders for the open main hall of the winery, which stood on a lower level, to be cleared, and already the large wooden vats and the jars had been removed, the small casks had been stacked one on top of another, and the piles of wood that had been prepared against the approaching cold weather had been dismantled in order to form a sort of small raised dais on which the judges would sit, so that they could survey not only the parties to the suit but also the feelings of the public standing behind them.

But who will be the judges? Rabbi Elbaz asked Ben Attar this time, but the merchant, who knew nothing, merely descended excitedly but in silence along the rough stone steps leading to the hall, whose dusty floor was stained pink by grape juice oozing from a large wooden press into a deep round basin, from which the foamy liquid exuded a perfumed sweetness. The audience was already waiting there, most of them presumably people who worked in the winery, bearded, bareheaded Jews dressed in faded, shabby clothes, and nearby a group of bare-faced women, their unkempt hair covered by small headscarves, their feet unshod and stained from stomping grapes. Unruly children were running to and fro between the men and women on little errands, their guttural babble mingled with occasional words of Hebrew, whose sounds were completely distorted. *But who will choose the judges?* the rabbi asked again, still delaying his descent to the lower level, refusing to believe that they were liable so hastily, without real preparation, to miss a fateful, longed-for moment for which they had bobbed on the ocean waves for nearly sixty days.

Have the judges already been appointed? Relentlessly he seized hold of the corner of Abulafia's black coat as the man shrugged his ignorance and gently guided his two aunts, who raised the hems of their colorful robes so that they should not sweep the dusty steps. He presented them to the proprietor of the winery, who in his turn proudly introduced them to a guest of his own, an oriental courier who had passed through the Land of Israel. A genuine Radhanite, this plump, alert man wearing a green turban was a dealer in precious stones who had arrived a few days previously from the east, bringing with him two large pearls, about whose value and price Master Levitas had not stopped speculating since the previous day. Both sides were now intermingled, and the Moroccan ladies were seated on wine barrels covered in soft tapestries next to the proprietor's wife, a tall woman with a delicate, sickly face. It was simply impossible to proceed in such haste, thought Rabbi Elbaz, his heart tormented by doubts and stirred by compassion for the second wife, who sat silently, erect, her veil fluttered by a slight breeze that might herald the advent of autumn.

But on what basis were the judges chosen? he repeated, demanding an immediate reply from Master Levitas, who now opened a side door and produced three gaunt men dressed in dusty black caftans, bearing a large parchment roll and a small sheet of green glass. They were scribes specializing in writing scrolls of the Law, phylacteries and amulets for doorposts, brought in from towns in the region to constitute the court. *Scribes?* the rabbi muttered disappointedly. *Men who try to discern what is written merely to copy it over and over again?* But Master Levitas thought highly of them. They would be able to judge on the basis of what was written in books. But what books? And what was the point of books? Rabbi Elbaz protested vehemently. If the answer was written explicitly in a book, would it have occurred to him to leave his city and entrust himself to the ocean to demand justice for his employer? Would he have allowed Ben Attar to put his wives at risk for something that was written in a book? But the words of the foreign rabbi made no impression on Master Levitas, and dismissing him with a polite smile, he continued to steer his three judges down to the lower level. The indignant Andalusian had no alternative but to hurry to anticipate them, and leaping onto the small dais, he demanded, in a wild shout that seemed unlikely to issue from such a pleasant, dreamy personality, that the judges should be changed forthwith.

A silence fell. Everyone had heard the shout, but because of his strange accent only a few understood what he was asking, and one of them was Master Levitas, who hastened to silence him. But Abulafia, shaken to the core by the rabbi's outcry, seized his brother-in-law's shoulder to restrain him. Even though in a short while he would be called upon to defend himself against the charges brought by the southerners, a strange hope was stirring in his heart that the case for the defense would not succeed, and that the honesty of his good, wronged uncle, combined with the rabbi's wisdom, would tip the scales against him, for then he would be able to renew his travels to the azure summer meeting in the Spanish March. Since he understood well the rabbi's shouted demand for the replacement of these judges, who had certainly prejudged the case, he turned to his wife, the blue of whose eyes had been so sharpened by fear since morning that now in the afternoon they looked like gray steel, and gently he pleaded with her to ask her brother to display magnanimity toward the plaintiffs, who had risked their lives to come from so far, and agree to exchange the judges for more suitable people.

Suitable for what? She turned in surprise to face her young, tousled husband, and, weary from her sleepless night, she scanned with a pained look the three gaunt scribes, who, confused by the repudiation that had suddenly attacked them, clung to one another, rolling their eyes in umbrage. *Suitable for what?* Mistress Esther-Minna asked again angrily, joined by her brother and the disappointed proprietor of the winery, who since yesterday had been doing the rounds of the neighboring villages and estates to assemble the three scribes. But while Abulafia was insisting on explaining to his wife how it might be possible to find true judges, scholars of outstanding wisdom, who would satisfy the visitors, who sought even in this out-of-the-way place the spirit of the wisdom of Andalus, Rabbi Elbaz hastened to pacify the ruffled participants by explaining that it would be proper to make do with the spirit of the ancient sages, which was the true spirit that could transform, say, the whole congregation of simple, goodhearted Jews into a public tribunal that might judge and save either the plaintiff or the defendant, as was stated in so many words in the book of Exodus: *to incline after the multitude.*

Even Master Levitas, who was a judicious and farsighted man, was confused by the rabbi's surprising suggestion, but first he tried to read in his sister's eyes her view about abandoning a dispute that he had seen as settled and sealed in favor of a motley assemblage of grape stampers, barrel rollers, and wine vendors. Before he had managed to catch her eye, he was startled by a softly yet clearly whispered question she put to the little rabbi. *All of them? Including the women?* And before he could contemplate toning down his sister's outrageous question, Rabbi Elbaz had astonishingly replied in an enthusiastic whisper, *The women? Why not?* After all, they too were created in God's image.

Is this rabbi's mind completely addled, or will he really lead us on the right path? The North African merchant sank deep in thought, watching closely as his nephew's beaming face approached his wives'

fine silk veils to whisper into their delicate, gold-ringed ears a translation of the surprising words spoken by a clever woman and a poetic
rabbi. The news seemed to arouse neither fear nor panic in Ben Attar's
wives, but only such a great curiosity that they could restrain themselves no longer, and the second wife, closely followed by the first,
stripped off her veil, the better to contemplate with kohl-darkened eyes
the men and women of Villa Le Juif, who gazed back at them with
smiling faces, little suspecting that the place where they were standing
was soon to become the judgment seat.

All of them? How is that possible? It will be total chaos, groaned
Master Levitas to his sister and the rabbi, suddenly united. The refined
Parisian was joined by the proprietor of the winery, who was alarmed at
the plan of converting his retainers into judges. And so, after a brief
exchange of words, it was agreed by both sides that in accordance with
the ancient spirit of the law, it would be sufficient to select seven
judges, corresponding to "trial by seven good men of the city." But
since this was not a city and the foreign travelers had no idea who were
the best folk among them, the judges would have to be selected by lot.
To this end young Elbaz, who had sat himself down in a corner on a
small barrel to inhale the fragrance of the wine maturing inside it, was
brought forward, blindfolded, and sent out into the sunlight dancing on
the treetops to choose seven people by means of a game of blind-man's
buff. A deep silence fell on one and all as the blindfolded child hesitated, then shuffled cautiously toward the tall woman with the sickly
face, the wife of the proprietor, and slowly laid his little hands on her
soft belly, as though he had decided even before his eyes were bound
to make her his first choice. At once, recoiling from this overbold
gesture, he collided as he stepped backward with one of the scribes,
who had positioned himself deliberately in his path to compel the boy
to choose him. Only then did the world beyond his blindfold seem
finally to become clear to the child, and discerning within the deep
silence the bated breath of the crowd, he turned resolutely toward it.
But for some reason the Jews recoiled from this blindfolded boy who
advanced fatefully toward them, all but a fair-faced young woman, one
of the wine stampers, who stood rooted to the spot as though inviting
the young stranger to touch her. He did indeed touch her face gently
with his little hand, until another woman, apparently jealous, took a

few paces toward him, and the boy turned toward her, and his fingers fluttered on her bosom. Unperturbed by this contact, he turned to his right, where a third woman was waiting for him, and he held her too for a moment, and while Master Levitas's sardonic laughter and his father the rabbi's rebuke rang out, yet a fourth woman, a toothless hag, hurried to his side, yearning also to be touched. But the child, startled by the feel of her wizened face, instantly buried his hands in the folds of his little robe and refused to stir. His father was obliged now to come forward and remove him from the women who were converging upon him. He turned him around and led him back toward the small dais, and it seemed for a moment as though he would once more approach the tall woman with the sickly face and touch her belly again, but his father steered him gently toward the Radhanite merchant from the Land of Israel, who was sitting immobile, his thick black beard lying calmly on his chest, seemingly taking great pleasure in the scene that was unfolding around him. Slowly the boy drew forth a single hand from the folds of his little robe and very cautiously held it out in front of him, until he encountered the large beard.

Now that the seventh judge had been chosen, the blindfold was removed and a new worry gripped Master Levitas's heart. Indicating the sunlight fading on the trees, he suggested that they should all, plaintiffs and defendants, witnesses and judges, join together in the afternoon prayer, which might also serve as a discreet hint to the Christian visitors that their presence was no longer appropriate.

2.

Then they all went to the well to draw water for the hand-washing. After that they stood for the afternoon prayer. It soon became evident that Abulafia's heart was so inflamed by the occasion that he yearned to lead the service with his pleasant voice. At first the proprietor of the winery and Master Levitas tried to undermine his precedence by chanting faster or slower, but eventually they desisted, not because Abulafia's singing was louder than theirs, but because concealed within it was a delightful, unique cadence that attracted the worshippers in

Villa Le Juif to follow his lead. His wife too, her mind confused by the ease with which the panel of judges had been filled with women, gave a silent signal to her younger brother to abandon the contest and let Abulafia surrender himself to his chant, which she found instantly appealing, although she could not imagine where it came from. But Ben Attar, who had never before stood in prayer so close to his two wives and could sense their overwhelmed souls, immediately identified the source of his nephew's tune as the muezzin's call in the mosque in Tangier. How amazing, he thought, that after all these years he still tries to preserve in his chant the Muslim cadence of that seashore, although he has also blended it with another melody, which to judge by its rhythm and tune must be taken from some local peasant song.

It may have been for this reason that the three Christians who had mingled with the Jews so as to enjoy the spectacle of two pretty, veiled women who belonged legally and naturally to a single man did not depart when the Jews began to pray, but lingered to wonder at the familiar melody, blending the Jews' Latin with an additional curling cadence. When Levitas saw that the three of them insisted on staying, he abbreviated the interval between the afternoon and evening prayers and gave a sign for the evening prayer to commence even before the first star appeared, in the hope that when they reached the *Hear O Israel* and the silent darkness filled with the profiles of motionless Jews standing in total separateness, with eyes closed and hands in front of their faces, looking like curious woodcocks, some vague dread might finally cause the uninvited guests to leave. Indeed, by the time torches were lit at the end of the service and the bunches of grapes suspended from hooks all around cast fantastic shadows on the walls, not a single stranger remained in the hall to seek entertainment from the Jews.

Perhaps it was the mood of earnest solemnity descending upon the Jews of Villa Le Juif after the two beautiful services had stamped upon the departing day a double seal of music and holiness that breathed fear into the four women selected by the game of blind-man's buff. When the president's wife, the tall mistress of the winery, was invited to mount the wooden dais, followed by the pleasant-faced oriental merchant, with the scribe close on his heels, looking gaunt and dusty in his black cloak but also earnestly determined to represent his two disqualified colleagues faithfully, the four women judges, who apparently failed now to understand the meaning of their desire for the touch of the dark boy, stood huddled in a corner, clinging to one another and too frightened to climb onto the dais. At this point Mistress Esther-Minna intervened. Desiring an additional female element, her faith in the justice of a verdict decided by three judges notwithstanding, she was filled with enough indignation and fury to echo in Abulafia's heart for the rest of his life, depriving him of any hint of regret that he might have doubled the number of his wives if he had not migrated from the south to the north. And so, with a gentle voice that concealed no little sternness, she induced the three young women and the elderly vintager to relax their hold on each other and join the three people who were already seated importantly on wine casks spread with old fox skins, with a torch blazing in front of them.

Everything was now ready. It was not the "seven good men of the city" demanded by writ who were seated upon the dais but merely seven ordinary men and women selected by a form of ballot, but this was simply because for close on a thousand years now there had been no wholly Jewish town but only small, dispersed communities, driven onward from one place to the next by troubles and dangers. There was nothing now to prevent Ben Attar from rising to his feet and setting forth his plea, for which he had come such a long way, although now, after the double service, it seemed to have shrunk. This may have been the reason that he seemed still to hesitate, sunk in thought, until Rabbi Elbaz was obliged to give him a sign of encouragement. Indeed, ever since the merchant and his entourage had entered the inner court of Villa Le Juif that afternoon and from there proceeded into the hall of the winery, his spirit had seemed to be failing. It was as if he had not imagined that he would really and truly come face to face with that repudiation, which from the vast distance separating Africa from Europe had seemed to him like the panic of Jews chiefly fearful of Christian opinion, or that only two days after disembarking from his ship he would be summoned before a strange, hastily convened court in the dark hall of a remote rustic winery. For the first time since he had conceived the idea of the journey, he experienced a vague fear of defeat.

Surprisingly, however, he felt pity not for himself, nor for his two wives, who had been forced to leave their children and their homes, but for his Ishmaelite partner, Abu Lutfi, whom Ben Attar now imagined sitting in the darkness of the ship's hold close to the solitary camel, praying to Allah for the success of his Jewish partner, although he would never, ever understand, however many times it was explained to him, why a Jewish merchant who lived with his wives and enjoyed the respect of Jews and Ishmaelites alike should care about the repudiation of faraway Jews living in dark forests on the shores of wild rivers, in the heart of a remote continent.

This feeling of guilt and compassion toward the Arab, who had given and would continue to give his own strength and money to a journey with whose purpose he could not identify, now charged Ben Attar with such powerful feelings of shame and sorrow that he sternly scrutinized the face of his nephew Abulafia, who was smiling at him with a kind of strange perplexity. Abulafia was standing before him not only as a defendant but also as an interpreter, who would be called upon to render his opponent's words faithfully. For a moment Ben Attar was filled with anger against his nephew, whom he had so lovingly reared, for his inability to stand up to his new wife, and for involving him not only in a long and wearisome voyage but also in this sad and unjust rift. So fiercely did his anger burn that he dispensed with the services of his nephew as interpreter, and in a deep voice that at once commanded silence in the hall he spoke a few hesitant words in the ancient tongue of the Jews, in the hope that those who understood would communicate his meaning to the others present. After a few sentences, however, he realized that it would be better for him to abandon his atrophied, jerky Hebrew in favor of fluent and colorful Arabic, which not surprisingly conveyed the full force of his distress.

Abulafia was surprised and troubled by the opening of his uncle's plea, which centered not on himself but on Abu Lutfi. But Ben Attar held firmly to his course. Yes, he wished to begin his plea with the pain and sorrow of a third party, a gentile, who every autumn for the past ten years had driven his camels to the northern slopes of the Atlas Mountains, wearying himself among tiny villages and remote tribes to seek out and discover the best and most beautiful wares to please his northern partner's customers.

Gradually Ben Attar's audience was able to apprehend the nature of that wonderful threefold partnership, which extended from the Atlas

Mountains beyond the Moroccan shores, wound through the towns and gardens of Andalus, then sailed slowly up to the Bay of Barcelona and to the enchanted meeting place in the Spanish March, climbing thence along the eastern slopes of the Pyrenees and spreading like a colored fan through Provence and Aquitaine, continuing along the routes of Burgundy and groping its way up to the Île de France. Ben Attar did not spare them the details. On the contrary, with rare precision he set forth the clever, rich framework devised by three partners who were joined together not only by understanding and trust but also by fellowship and friendship, trying to earn a living from the delights of the Mohammedans of the south, who sent their cumin, cassia, and cardamom to simmer in the steaming Christian stewpots of Narbonne and Perpignan.

This was the manner of Ben Attar's speaking: after a few sentences he would stop, fix his eyes on Abulafia's, and silently count the Frankish sentences as they came out of his mouth, fearing that the translation might omit some words. But his fears were unfounded, for not only did this interpreter not wish to leave anything out, but as one of the members of the legendary threesome, he contributed details on his own account to reinforce the story, so carried away by his words that he forgot that soon he would have to defend himself against the tale that he was so eagerly translating.

The face of the thick-bearded merchant from the Land of Israel, who drank the words straight from their Arabic source, was already beginning to darken as Ben Attar described the first signs of Abulafia's deceit—the curious disguises, the hints of his repudiation, the ever-increasing delays that opened gaping black chasms in the minds of those who awaited him, until the last summer, when that terrible, final, and definitive absence had occurred, leaving the two southern partners alone among the horses and donkeys in Benveniste's stable, alarmed at the huge quantity of merchandise that surrounded them. Amazingly, the plaintiff refrained from pointing an accusing finger at the new wife who had appeared from the Rhineland, or even from mentioning her name. It was as if Abulafia were alone in the world, and the blame were his alone—as though the accursed repudiation had been born only in the nephew's mind, and caused him to turn against his friends. So it was no wonder that it was now hard for the interpreter, who in

125

the course of translating was magnifying his own guilt, to continue interpreting faithfully while he was compelled to hear such harsh words from his uncle, who coldly, in rich but precise Arabic, attributed to his nephew the vile suspicion of simply trying to dissolve the old partnership in order to replace it with a new one that might turn out to be more lucrative. And since, Ben Attar's ruthless denunciation continued, it was hard for the traitor to abandon his loyal partners on some pretext of deception or unfairness, for their business relations had always been honest and just, he had invented a kind of strange repudiation of his uncle's double marriage, and, not daring to express this repudiation in his own name, he had put it into the mouth, so to speak, of his new, foreign wife.

For how could Abulafia complain now about his uncle's double marriage, when he had known for several years that his uncle had purchased his old house in his home town, to honor the grievous memory of the wife who had departed for the depths of the sea, and had installed there a second wife, a new aunt, whose existence he not only did not consider invalid but was openly pleased about, even if she was his own age? Since he could not suddenly protest against something that he had accepted and approved of for such a long time, he had been obliged to ask his new family to frighten him and to order him to feel revulsion toward his own flesh and blood.

At this point the interpreter's voice became so choked that nobody in the dark winery could understand a word of the last sentences, which had pierced him like sword thrusts. So the merchant from the Land of Israel, who had been listening attentively to the Arabic original, decided to venture a small shortcut. Turning to his neighbor, the scribe, who was gaping apprehensively, he very slowly, in a voice free from any guttural exaggeration, summarized what had been said so far in archaic Hebrew with the Jerusalem pronunciation, so that the scribe would spring to his feet, a gaunt figure dressed in black, and clothe the summary in the local language for the benefit of his fellow judges, who were sitting silently on the wooden dais, and for the benefit of the audience, which had been drawn by the heated dispute to emerge from among the wine casks and edge closer to the two disputants—and closer too to the new wife, who had immediately grasped Ben Attar's shrewd tactic in forcing her pained husband to leap to the defense of his loyalty to the partnership, and in so doing to expose to public gaze a crack (only a small one, she hoped) between him and her.

Into this crack Rabbi Elbaz now attempted to insert like a lance the sermon he had devised while rocked by the waves of the sea. But Mistress Esther-Minna hastily forestalled him. Her heart was seething at the sight of her husband standing stock-still, staring at his uncle with a strange, startled smile on his face, as though the terrible suspicion that had been laid at his door had spread through his body like a paralyzing poison. Without knowing whether she had the right to speak, she took the floor and passionately appealed to the court as a plaintiff, speaking volubly in the local Frankish dialect, first of all to dispel contemptuously any suspicion of another, secret partnership on her husband's part, and then to disclose at last the true, emotional source of the repudiation, which was even more important to her than the edicts that had arrived from the Rhineland.

Master Levitas, who had been well aware since the morning of his older sister's mental turmoil, and of her desire and indeed her ability to achieve a breakthrough, took a few cautious steps toward her, so that his calm presence and steady disposition, even if they were not expressed in words, might delineate a certain border, in case she were tempted to cross it. While Ben Attar had been speaking, this Parisian pearl-dealer had been looking neither at the accuser nor at the accused but at the faces of the four women who had volunteered to be selected by ballot as judges. By the look of sorrow that appeared briefly on their faces at the mention of all the unsold merchandise, and by the flicker of suspicion at the sight of Abulafia's pallor as he was held responsible, Master Levitas, a cautious, intelligent man, understood that from now on it would be a mistake to feel any certainty about the outcome of the case. Accordingly, it would be wise to restrain any sign of self-confidence or pride on the part of his small but ready-tongued and straight-backed sister, whose fair features, carved like those of a beautiful hound, were glowing in the torchlight.

But his fears were unfounded. His sister's opening words gave no hint of pride but merely a faint hint of shrewdness, borrowed this very moment from her southern adversary. And just as Ben Attar had begun his accusation not with his own pain but with that of his Arab partner, so she too sought to ground her defense not in herself or her abhorrence of double marriages but in the story of Abulafia's unfortunate daughter, who was still tormented by the puzzle of being abandoned by her young mother, a beautiful and beloved woman.

Here Master Levitas touched his sister lightly, not because he objected to her line of attack but to remind her that it was right and proper to give her opponents an opportunity to understand the words that would soon, with God's help, defeat them. Once more Abulafia, the accused, had to be asked to serve as interpreter, this time in the opposite direction, from Frankish to Arabic. Even though he now stood between his uncle and his wife, the two beings who were dearest to him in the world, he turned his gaze toward Rabbi Elbaz, who was standing facing him in his rabbinical robe, which was worn out by the nights and days on board ship, nodding his head slightly as though in prayer and swallowing every word that was uttered as if it were a sweetmeat. As earlier the younger partner's life had been conjured up in the deposition of his senior partner, now it continued to be recounted through the startling thoughts of his new, vivacious wife, who so embellished her argument with every small detail of her husband's life, even some he had forgotten himself, that at times he had to halt the spate of words in order to examine, before translating, whether what his wife was saying about him had really happened.

But what could such an examination avail, when it was only now, in the semidarkness of the winery, that he understood that his wife had devotedly collected every detail he had told her about his life and his travels, like someone compulsively gathering oysters on the seashore in the belief that each one must contain a small pearl? At their first meeting in Orléans, before that blazing hearth, when the proper widow had been startled by the willingness of this dark-skinned, curly-haired young merchant from North Africa to talk to her shyly but frankly about himself, she had asked herself how it was that this good-looking, easygoing man had been roaming the forests and villages of a strange land for seven years without attempting to marry and set up a home. On that first night, Mistress Esther-Minna explained, she had understood that only a man whose love for his wife continued to well up inside him like a gushing spring, even if that wife no longer existed, could behave in this way. But if that was truly so, she had continued to ask herself, how was it possible for that drowned wife, who had received such great love from her husband, to get up one day, dismiss so easily everything that had been lavished upon her, abandon her husband, pluck colored ribbons from the clothes of her baby daughter, who needed her so much, and bind her hands and feet and throw herself into the sea?

That night in the inn at Orléans, the new Mistress Abulafia did not hesitate to confess before the court, she had already experienced a great feeling of compassion for this child, abandoned with an Ishmaelite nurse in a small house in the street of the Jews, close to the castle in Toulouse. She felt a powerful urge not only to understand the mystery of what had happened but to share her understanding with the widower, who was continuing to wander the roads, confused by his own lack of understanding. A new love was needed to overcome the old, Mediterranean one—not, heaven forbid, to drive out the memory of the earlier love, but to enable Mistress Esther-Minna to reflect from close up on the secret of its vitality and also of its weakness and failure. But it was only at her second or third meeting with the young merchant, when the winter was past and the spring too was nearly over and gone and when Abulafia had innocently disclosed the existence of polygamous marriages in the lands of the Ishmaelites, not by way of metaphor but as a known fact, and even as a family matter, since the subject of conversation was his own uncle, the senior partner in the glorious partnership, that she had had a feeling that the nub of the secret that had caused the disaster had slipped out. But still she had said nothing, waiting until she was united body and soul to Abulafia, so as to satisfy herself that there was nothing weak in the man's powers of love, neither in respect to his new wife nor evidently in respect to his first wife, who, according to his testimony, had always known how to receive his love and believe in its faithfulness. It was only then that she had begun to draw a connection between the terrible, desperate deed of that dead wife and the threat that he might take a second wife, which would apparently neither require nor demand any break in or lessening of his love for his first wife. Yes, it was precisely when a second wife entered a household, through simple duplication, like the birth of another child, that she contained within herself a terrible destructive power, especially for a first wife who believes she has a curse on her womb. And so, did Esther-Minna have any need to justify

129

herself for the repudiation that had spread within her? It grew greater with time and sharpened like a spear which could not only defend her new husband against the disgrace of discovering among the sacks of spices and the copper vessels in Benveniste's stable an additional wife, brought for him in the ship by his uncle, but also, yes indeed, to avenge, however inadequately, the sorrow and fears of the drowned wife, who had been taken naked from the watery depths.

Here Mistress Esther-Minna's face suddenly reddened, and she lowered her head and fell silent. This not only gave the stunned interpreter time to digest the secret of his life before conveying it in Arabic to the other members of his household, but also evaded Ben Attar's openly offended look and the enigmatic veiled glances of his two wives, who were still sitting erect, calmly and submissively, where they had been placed. She had no way of telling whether the translation was able to penetrate their consciousness or whether it simply fluttered around them like a butterfly. Then Mistress Esther-Minna felt the feather-light touch of her brother's hand as he sought to give her a sign of encouragement, even though in his heart of hearts he would gladly have foregone the subtleties of her argument in favor of a short statement about the existence of a new rabbinical ordinance, stern but simple, which even though it had originated in the marshy swamps of the Rhineland was destined to enlighten and reform society everywhere.

It was this ordinance that the rabbi from Seville had been waiting for all along. He longed to speak about principles rather than details. His thoughts had turned so often to this ordinance in the course of the journey that he had begun to envisage it as a small, curved dagger of yellowish brass that needed to be kept firmly planted in the ground lest it take wing and fly away. But now, with the breeze of evening, he was assailed again by faint pangs of hunger, like a kind of echo of the powerful attack that had disturbed his senses in the middle of the night. Helpless to prevent himself, he held his hands in front of his face to see whether they held any lingering odor of the sweet fish that the black slave had cooked for him before dawn. Still, it was not a bad thing, he thought, to commence a discourse in a state of hunger, which sharpens the spirit and the wits. Moreover, Mistress Abulafia's forceful and unusual words had alerted all his senses.

Now the silence all around him seemed to become purified. Ben Attar's look was darkly suspicious, as though after Mistress Esther-Minna's virulent speech he had lost faith in what he would receive from the rabbi in exchange for the promised honorarium. And Master Levitas was touching his shoulder gently, to indicate that his moment had come. The rabbi had already noticed that this cold, reserved man always treated him with respect, as though any scholar, even if he hailed from the distant south and came with the obvious intention of aggressively disputing, were an important person. But were these strange, uncultivated Jews really capable of following the intricacies of his Andalusian thought? How was it possible that in all the dark expanse surrounding him there was no true sage to be found who might sit with him face to face and settle the matter? What could they really understand, these vintagers and winemakers, or these women whose bare feet as they sat facing him on the wooden dais were so stained from stomping the grapes that he had an urge to rinse them with clean water before he began to speak? Then his eyes happened upon his own son, who was sitting without sandals, slowly picking grapes off a large bunch and watching the fine stream of juice dribbling from the wine press into the inner tank. It was already two months since the child had been taken from his home, and it was unlikely that he would learn in the rest of his life as much as he had learned on this journey.

Then Ben Attar's second wife, unable to contain herself, rose to her feet, as though to see and hear the rabbi better. He said to himself excitedly that if she was so intent on his words that she was prepared to break the law and propel herself beyond what her own honor and that of the first wife demanded, it would be better if he began his speech not in the ancient holy tongue, as he had intended to do to attract the brother and sister, but rather in Arabic, so that the naked, untranslated words would reach straight into the heart of the young woman, who had hidden the ivory casket between the silken robes he had caressed last night with his hands. He did this not only to fortify and encourage the second wife but also for the sake of the first wife, who had raised her head, startled at her friend's sudden movement. By speaking in clear, intelligible Arabic, the rabbi may also have sought to erase something of the grimness that had taken hold of Ben Attar, who was behaving as if he genuinely believed the accusation he had launched against his nephew. Who could tell, the rabbi mused, perhaps his words could even persuade his skeptical son, if the boy was willing to listen to his father.

Once again the accused man had to be called on to interpret. It appeared that Abulafia would not manage this evening to utter a single word of his own or in his own favor, but would only transfer from one language to another what others said for or against him—if what his wife had said was indeed in his favor, rather than in favor of his previous wife. He had never imagined that his new wife might be concerning herself with the riddle of his first wife's death by drowning, as though this riddle threatened her too, even in a place where there was no sea but only a river. So even though Abulafia knew that the rabbi who had been brought from Seville was about to reprove him, to attack his wife's repudiation and condemn his sudden disappearance, he nevertheless felt a certain warmth toward him, not only because of the affection aroused by his slim, childlike figure, hardly taller than his own child, but also because of a hope that a rabbi's chastisement would always be wise and would therefore placate everyone. He therefore resolved not only to be as faithful as possible to the rabbi's actual words but also to be careful to preserve their spirit.

At first, however, there was no spirit in the rabbi's words, for thirst for that liquid whose fragrance scented the night air dried up the words in his mouth. While the owner of the winery was still trying to decide whether to serve the speaker a single glass or whether to open a cask for the whole company, Master Levitas, with the generosity of a guest who was also in some sense a host, decided for him: a cask. But a small one. It then transpired that the wine deemed most appropriate to the time and place was contained in the small barrel on which the child was seated, so that apparently it was no accident that he had been led to seat himself upon it. At once young Elbaz was made to stand up, and the barrel was rolled into the center of the hall and arranged so that it was possible to pour wine for all the sacred congregation without spilling a single drop wastefully on the ground. The first to be served was the rabbi, who pronounced aloud the blessing over the fruit of the vine, and he was followed by the judges and the disputants. While the first wife drank discreetly behind her veil, the second rolled hers back as though she had made up her mind to do without it, and with a new smile that lit up her finely sculpted features she drained her glass and waited for another.

Then it was, and only then, without any warning and still clutching his goblet that the rabbi began to speak in hope that the pink wine slipping down their throats would soften the thoughts of the Jews of Villa Le Juif and even stretch them to new and hitherto unknown horizons. For if the rabbi were to speak only in simple terms, using well-known and accepted notions, he need not multiply words but would merely state directly, *Frankish Jews, distant and strange, why are you so amazed? Why are you so alarmed? With all due respect, read in the rolled Scripture to whose holiness we are all in thrall and you will discover that the great patriarchs, Abraham, Isaac, and Jacob, each had two, three, or even four wives. Continue reading, and here is Elkanah with his two wives, and this is before we reach the kings with their numerous wives, and who was as great as Solomon? But if you object that these ancients were greater and mightier men than we, and able to discern between good and evil, then open the book of Deuteronomy, and there, not long before the end of the book, you will find the verse "If a man have two wives . . ." Any man. Everyman. Not a patriarch, a hero, a king, or an ancient.*

While Abulafia was endeavoring to translate this last sentence, the rabbi deftly drained his goblet, not so that he could put it down but so as to fill it again with the same blushing wine and continue without undue delay, in order not to give rise to any suspicion that he was evading the continuation of the quoted verse, "one beloved, and another hated," for all the confusion and terror that echoed in these words, to which he would come in due course. In the meantime he would merely express his anger that anyone should be so brazen, and in a faraway town like Paris at that, as to pass upon fellow Jews a verdict of repudiation and dissociation, which implied not only pride but ignorance, casting dishonor on men and women of old.

From the corner of his eye, Rabbi Elbaz now observed the anxiety in Ben Attar's face receding somewhat, and a short row of white teeth gleaming in the smile of a merchant who finally sees the hope of securing some return for his outlay. But was Ben Attar nothing more than a merchant? The rabbi suddenly put this fresh question to himself, and on the spur of the moment he repeated it out loud, enthralling his audience. No, he replied decisively to his own question,

Ben Attar had not come from so far away simply to demand satisfaction for loss of business. Nor would it have entered the rabbi's own head to undertake such a long and terrible journey for the sake of a mere merchant's dispute. If this man had just been motivated by love of money and the partnership, would it have occurred to him to undertake such a difficult and hazardous journey in pursuit of a defaulting partner, when he could easily have replaced him, for the same cost, with three new partners who would spread the news of the North African wares not only among the Franks and Burgundians but even among the Flemings and Saxons? No, Rabbi Elbaz saw Ben Attar not as a merchant but simply as a man disguised as a merchant. During the long days and nights at sea, he had not ceased to study this wonderful man, but only now, in Villa Le Juif, had he discovered the nub of his being: he was a loving man, a philosopher and sage of love, who had come from far away to declare publicly that it is possible to have two wives and to love them equally.

While Abulafia was translating the last sentence, he glanced toward his two aunts, and he was not the only one to do so. Everyone turned their gaze toward the shadowy figures of the two women, one of whom was still standing. Ben Attar, who had been very confused by the rabbi's last words, touched the standing woman on the arm to tell her to return to her place and sit down. But she remained standing, and although all looks were frozen for a moment on her disobedient refusal, she seemed unable to abandon the sight of the rabbi's small, lithe body as he paced up and down with short steps before the large torch, unable to content herself with his deep voice alone, which was now beginning to deal with Mistress Esther-Minna's last words.

For the second wife, the rabbi went on to declare confidently, *always exists. If she does not exist in reality, she exists in the imagination. Therefore no rabbinical edict is able to eradicate her. But because she exists only in the man's imagination, she is good, fair, submissive, wise, and pleasant, according to his fancy, and however hard his only real wife tries, she can never truly rival the imaginary one, and therefore she will always know anger and disappointment. However, when the second wife is not imaginary but exists in flesh and blood, the first wife can measure herself against her, and outdo her, and sometimes she can make her peace with her and, if she wishes, even love her.*

A faint, mocking smile now tightened Abulafia's wife's face. Her blue eyes never ceased earnestly scrutinizing the face of the interpreter, her young husband, to discover whether he was merely a passive translator or a secret accomplice to the crime. But the rabbi was not alarmed by this clever woman's smile. On the contrary, taking a small, confidential step toward her, he smiled straight into her blushing face, which suddenly looked childlike because of a stray golden lock that had escaped from her snood, and obdurately repeated his last words: Yes, even love her. For only the second wife is able to alleviate the man's infinite, tormenting desire and transform it from reproof into pleasure.

But now the faithful interpreter, suddenly alarmed, stretched his arms out desperately toward the speaker, whose ornate Arabic had begun to carry him away. Rabbi Elbaz stopped, gazing at Mistress Esther-Minna, whose tempestuous emotions reddened her face and made her more and more attractive. Out of the corner of his eye he could glimpse a strange look on the face of his son, who like everybody else was straining toward him so as not to miss a single word he was saying. Suddenly Elbaz was sorry that his son could hear and understand his words. If he were to remain faithful to the oath he had sworn that morning on the deck of the ship, to defend to the utmost the delicate double marriage that had sailed at his side for nearly sixty days at sea, he would have to change languages and ask the two disqualified scribes, who at present were unemployed, to come forward, take the place of the desperate interpreter, and translate straight from the holy tongue into the local language. For the rabbi felt that if he couched his speech in the beloved, forgotten ancient tongue from now on, he would not merely double his own authority in the mind of the impassioned little crowd, but he would also be able, like Mistress Esther-Minna, to make a confession that his son would not be able to understand.

Therefore, as the Jews assembled in the winery at Villa Le Juif gradually closed in around the parties to the suit, the rabbi from Seville began his confession about himself and his late wife, as though his life were not unique and accidental but universal and exemplary, able to shed light on other lives as well. By the magical light of the moon, which slowly embraced his confession, it became clear to his hearers that if the dead wife of the Andalusian rabbi were to rise from her grave in Seville to proclaim one thing alone to the world, she would complain because he had never taken a second wife—not only so that after her death her orphaned son would have another mother, but so that sufferings inflicted upon her by her husband would be alleviated, because he assumed the solemn responsibilities of a husband so religiously that he had begun to cleave to her as one flesh assiduously enough to be in danger of transforming himself, heaven forbid, into a female. When a wife does not have to face her husband alone and he has to pass continually from one to the other, he has no alternative but to renew his original manly nature repeatedly, since no two women are alike.

The rabbi now halted his Hebrew speech, which had poured wildly from his mouth as though the antiquity of the language absolved his words of any responsibility as to content. His two interpreters, the scribes, contended with each other about whether what had been heard was what had been said, and whether what had been said was what had been meant, and whether what had been meant could be translated. While they were deliberating on how best to proceed in dual responsibility along the treacherous path of translation, one with a word and the other with a sentence, one with a simile and the other with a parable, the rabbi from Seville could sense, if only from the flashing eyes of the merchant from the Land of Israel, that there was some hope the case might be decided this evening in Ben Attar's favor. The rabbi did not yet know why or how he would manage this, but he was suddenly filled with strength and confidence, and the beloved tongue pounded within him as though it were seeking to transform a speech into a new song. When the interpreters signaled to him that they were ready, he addressed these simple, direct words to the brother and sister, who understood every word:

We have not crossed the mighty ocean to enrage your spirit, nor have we any thought of urging you too to double or multiply your wives. If we have judged aright by appearances, the land in which you dwell is bleak, with such small houses and such meager produce, and the Christians who surround you inflict fear upon you beyond your control, so it is small wonder that you lack the power that flowers in a thousand roses in the southern lands basking in the light of the wise sun. But just as we refrain from judging you from our strength, so too you have no right to judge us from your weakness. Therefore, let each remain true to himself and faithful to his own nature: restore the old partnership and do not damage it further.

3.

In Worms, on the River Rhine, Rabbi Levitas and his wife had been in the habit of encouraging their children, Esther-Minna and Yehiel, first to seek in every setback that afflicted them their own guilt, and only then to scrutinize the actions of others. This training had become second nature to them, to the point that it sometimes seemed that the two children took a special pleasure in blaming themselves, even if secretly each of them examined the other and took care not to assume more blame than the other admitted. So too this night, when Mistress Abulafia began to torment herself for the foolishness and irresponsibility with which she had allowed matters to develop at Villa Le Juif, she still continued to inspect sternly, despite the darkness, every line on her brother's face, to see whether he appreciated the extent of the blame that he himself must accept. Even though in fact Master Levitas had said nothing of substance throughout the trial, but had only, like a choirmaster, given signs to others, indicating when they were to speak, when to refrain from speaking, and when to translate, there was no doubt that the original idea of setting up a tribunal at Villa Le Juif had been his. True, he could claim that if his sister had not interfered between him and the Andalusian rabbi and so inexplicably granted that strange permission to alter the constitution of the court, they might have been preserved from defeat. But Master Levitas, who now sat in darkness in a corner of the wagon returning to Paris, did not want to claim, even in his heart, anything in his own favor and to the discredit of his sister, but only to take more and more blame upon himself, as he had been brought up to do, like a child who piles food he does not like onto his plate just to please his mother.

It was not only a desire for blame that made him act thus, but also a suspicion that even if his original idea had been carried out and the panel of judges had consisted of the three scribes brought from Chartres, it was not certain that the Andalusian rabbi would have failed to confound them too. If there was one thing that Mistress Esther-Minna and her brother had agreed on that night, it was that the rabbi whom Ben Attar had brought from Seville, despite his childlike mien and threadbare gown, had been more cunning and shrewder than they had supposed, both in what he had said and in what he had left unsaid. How else to explain the treachery of the women, who had preferred Ben Attar to Abulafia and who had for some reason seemed smilingly content when judgment was given against the latter?

But could what had been pronounced there really be called a judgment? Or was another term more appropriate? Was it merely an emotional and forceful appeal by goodhearted folk to the nephew and his wife to renew the old family partnership with the uncle, or was there lurking behind the words something deep and daring, according to which double matrimony was not just a colorful private fact of faraway Jews but a practice that might deserve renewed interest? In that cool hour of the evening, heavily perfumed with the smell of the wine that had emerged from a second cask, there was scope to interpret the judgment, if indeed it could be called a judgment, in a lenient or a restrictive fashion. It was not only the astuteness of the rabbi from Seville that had frustrated the hopes of the pair from Paris, but also the intervention of the Radhanite courier, for as soon as the rabbi had concluded his discourse, and before the translation had begun, this heavily built man had risen to his feet and applauded enthusiastically, thus prejudicing the judgment by sympathy for the plaintiff.

By means of this sympathy, which combined with the compassion felt by the simple crowd of wine-workers for the sturdy, dusky North African merchant who had condescended to bring his two wives with him all that distance, the courier from the Land of Israel had been able to free these people somewhat from their feelings of respect and obligation to the proprietor of the winery and the Levitas family, and instead of making do with surreptitiously or unintentionally touching the smooth silken robes of the Moroccan women, they had now been made to confront human nature openly. But what was his motive? Was it possible that this merchant too had, somewhere on his long route between the Orient and Europe, a secret second wife to relieve the tedium and loneliness of his travels? Or perhaps he was motivated by a desire for revenge against Master Levitas on account of the low price the latter had offered for the Indian pearls he had brought with him from afar?

That night, after the Jews of Villa Le Juif had dispersed to their homes and the two sides in the lawsuit were on their way back to Paris, the proprietor of the winery would not leave his sickly-faced wife alone, but in their large bed, surrounded by little bottles of wine for tasting, he asked her again for an explanation of her "betrayal." How had she come to side with a strange Jew against his friends from Paris? Had she really agreed with the rabbi from Andalus? he asked, holding her shoulders roughly, either in anger or desire. If so, if that was how it was, he threatened in jest, he might take a second wife himself. And why not, come to that? thought the woman, who was weary of satisfying her husband's desires, aroused as he was beyond his real powers by the sight of the women stamping grapes in his yard. But she did not dare admit to his face that she longed for the tranquillity of those two southern women, one seated and the other standing, with their colorful robes seemingly frozen in motion. Weary and irritable, she mumbled a confused excuse, which seemed to imply that she had been spellbound by the courier from the Land of Israel with his bushy black beard into supporting the repudiated twice-wed plaintiff.

The three young women who stamped grapes also talked of the spell cast by the man from the Land of Israel, but they knew only too well that behind the "spell" were his warm eyes and the masculine smell of his big strong body, which drew you to put your confidence in him and obey his voice, perhaps out of a strange feeling that anyone who went to such lengths to protect the husband of two wives would also feel strong enough to defend a third. But since they were unable to admit this even to each other, let alone to the curious men of the winery, who demanded an explanation for a verdict that harmed the proprietor and his friend, they tried to justify what had happened by saying that their minds had been addled by the muddle of different languages.

Even the scribe, who was being driven with his two colleagues back to the small estate of Chartres in an old cart, tried, in the silence of the desolate landscape of the Île de France, which was suddenly filled with

139

animated exchanges between hungry jackals and clever foxes, to explain to himself, before explaining to the others, how and why he had changed his mind. He had known perfectly well what verdict the people who had brought him to Villa Le Juif expected from him, and what fee he had been promised for his troubles, though that had vanished into thin air because of his disgraceful betrayal. Yet miraculous though it might seem, even though he knew he had let the others down, and himself too, he felt not dejected but excited, as though another authority, true or imagined, coming from the oriental merchant, had acquired a foothold within him and in an instant toppled old loyalties. But he was afraid to admit this to his two colleagues lest they began to repudiate him, as Mistress Esther-Minna had repudiated Ben Attar. And so, as the decrepit cart that the proprietor had given them made its way amid grim mist-swathed meadows and ruined castles and the gentile driver talked to his horse to see if it remembered the way, the judge who had erred tried to excuse himself to his fellows and embarked on a gentle discourse full of longing for men of yore and their wives and numerous progeny, trying by doing so to change the distance Ben Attar had covered into a distance of time rather than space, so as to place him among the giants of Scripture.

Only the old widowed vintner was not asked to explain what she had done. Yet she, in her heart of hearts, had been convinced that the whole assembly secretly wanted the partnership between north and south to be restored. So excited and pleased was she by what had taken place that she decided to spend the night in the dark winery instead of returning to her tiny hovel. Removing the fox skins from the casks, she improvised a soft bed for herself on the little dais. There, like someone who has acquired proprietary rights, she lay down to sleep, inhaling the remains of the scents of the parties to the case, the judges and the interpreters, and wishing that her late husband had left her a second wife, so that they could lie side by side and warm themselves with shared memories. She closed her eyes and relit in her mind's eye the great torch that had been planted in front of the dais, and passed in review face after face, translation after homily, until her eyes were caught by the large eyes of the interpreter Abulafia.

Who was now sitting very quietly, full of terrors yet also of hopes, in the large wagon on the way back to Paris. Although he was squeezed between his wife and his brother-in-law and facing his uncle and aunts, his eyes, eluding the gaze of anyone close to him, were fixed on the gaunt back of Rabbi Elbaz, who had sat down beside his son, next to the wagoner, so as to crown his joy at his victory with the sight of the unfamiliar stars and be free to mumble to himself the lines of the new poem he was composing, to brand it deep on his memory. All were now silent, but while the successful party was feeling very hungry, their discomfited hosts not only felt no hunger pangs but seemed to have forgotten the existence of the second hamper tied to the side of the wagon. Abulafia did not feel hungry either, not because he felt defeated and dejected but because he could not put out of his mind the moment when he would have to stand alone facing his wife and comfort her for her failure, and at the same time admonish her gently on account of the unnecessary suffering that her strange repudiation had caused. Gently, he repeatedly promised himself, for the formal public annulment of the repudiation invited him to go back next summer to the frontier between the two worlds, to the azure Bay of Barcelona, which here, in the dank darkness of the wagon, seemed to him illumined by a thousand enchantments. Since he wanted to clarify his own thoughts and the thoughts of those about him, he assumed the authority of the head of the household and ordered the wagoner to halt the horses at the same wood and by the same stream where they had eaten by day, so that they might eat by night.

It transpired that all the travelers, on either side of the dispute, whether they were hungry or not, were very happy at the halt that Abulafia had imposed on them, even though they had not yet traveled very far and Paris was not far away. After the hubbub of the verdict, they all wanted to be by themselves for a while, hidden from their companions by the darkness but exposed to the dome of the sky. As soon as the wagon stopped, the rabbi dragged his son into the bushes to stretch their legs and attend to some bodily functions that had been postponed out of the respect due to the religious court. Nor did Ben Attar hesitate to lead his two wives deep among the trees, although in the opposite direction, to enable them to do whatever they had been prevented from doing before. Before they returned, Master Levitas went to the stream to fill a pot with clear water, while Abulafia helped the wagoner untie the hamper from the side of the wagon and went off to gather wood for the small fire he planned to light for his guests. Mistress Esther-Minna was left standing on her own beside one of the horses, holding on to the bridle with one hand while with the other she absently stroked the broad, rough brow of the horse, who waited patiently for the woman's pleasant small hand to leave him so that he could join his partner in cropping the fresh grass.

Abulafia, accustomed to traveling, soon had a good fire going, and the sound of its crackling was soon joined by the rustling of the robe of Ben Attar's first wife, who had returned alone, without her husband. When she saw that Mistress Esther-Minna was still deep in thought beside the well-mannered horse, she offered to help Abulafia spread the cloth and slice bread and cheese and hard-boiled eggs. It was just as well that Jews give thanks after the meal, not before it, so there was no reason to restrain the famished child until Ben Attar and the second wife returned. It was sufficient for him to wash his hands in the water that Master Levitas poured over them and recite two short blessings before he received a large slice of black bread from the first wife. And although it was not fitting that Mistress Esther-Minna should continue to stand to one side like a sulky guest rather than a responsible hostess, she did not stir from the horse until she heard the rustle of the second wife and Ben Attar emerging from the undergrowth. Now the reason for their delay became clear, for the young woman had exchanged her silk robe for a simple but warmer garment of cloth. Mistress Esther-Minna, still without uttering a word, gave them a sad, absent-minded smile and joined the pair as they strolled slowly across the dark field toward the fire, which was growing stronger by the minute.

Only her younger brother, who was better able than her husband to discern the depth of her distress, hastened to rise up as she approached and helped her to find a comfortable place beside the fire. Unable to eat anything, she did at least accept a proffered goblet of wine to fortify her broken spirits. And she did indeed need fortification, in part against the caress of the rabbi's eyes, which lingered on her face and body, arousing additional anxieties now that she had learned to recognize the shrewdness of his thoughts. So great was her anxiety that she trembled at the light, soft touch of the first wife, who with a friendly smile offered her a cube of cheese on which the Hebrew word for "blessing" was stamped as a guarantee of its fitness for

Jewish consumption. What have I done? Mistress Esther-Minna asked herself in despair. Instead of dissolving the partnership privately, with blandishments and excuses, I have reinforced it with the verdict of that stupid, drunken crowd. In vain she sought the eyes of her husband, who did not appear sad or downcast but merely very busy boiling water for a fragrant infusion of dried leaves that the first wife extracted from a pouch.

Suddenly Master Levitas stood up and struck his brow. Only now had he remembered that in the confusion of the departure from Villa Le Juif he had forgotten to pay the scribes their promised honorarium, and they were bound to suspect that he had ignored his promise because the case had not turned out as he had wished, as though the sum were not a fee but a bribe. So distressed was Master Levitas by the thought of this false suspicion that he could find no peace; he could not eat or drink, but walked round and round the fire in a state of dejection. It soon became clear to him that the only way to recover his peace of mind was to return at once to the winery and discharge the forgotten debt. Though Abulafia tried to persuade his brother-in-law to wait for a day or two and not to set out alone at night, Mistress Esther-Minna, who knew her brother better than he did and understood that no power in the world could stop this man from hurrying to clear his good name, instructed the startled wagoner to unharness the horse she had been stroking a little earlier and give it to her brother, so that he could atone as quickly as possible for his sin.

While the sound of the horse's hooves died away to the south, she felt her loneliness intensifying unbearably, so that even her husband's curly hair, which she loved so much that she sometimes combed it herself in bed, seemed suddenly wild and strange in the firelight. Now she had a strong desire to hurry home, although she did not forget that tonight too her double bed would be requisitioned for the southern visitors. But it did not seem as though the people sitting around the fire were in any hurry to leave. They sat side by side, cross-legged and relaxed, sipping the hot infusion and producing little leather pouches containing multicolored seasonings that they sprinkled on everything they ate to excite their tongues. They were conversing in Arabic in a profound southern calm, as though they were sitting on the safe golden beach of their homeland instead of in a wild and desolate landscape.

It was now perfectly apparent that Master Levitas's departure was the sign for the two wives to unbend. As soon as they saw that the gentile wagoner was dozing on the driver's seat of the wagon, they allowed themselves to hitch up their veils a little. Now that the restoration of the partnership had turned the hardships of the long journey into something purposeful and successful, they broke into merry chatter with each other, laughingly teasing not only Ben Attar but Abulafia too, and even venturing to mock the rabbi, who had laid his head in his son's lap so as to be better placed for searching for new stars that were not visible in Andalus. And Abulafia, even though he was aware of his wife's mood, could not be indifferent or cold toward the family conversation that was gushing all around him. To please his wife, he leaned toward her from time to time to translate a sentence or two here or there, particularly from what the second wife was saying, for in the flickering firelight she had begun to take charge of the conversation with a kind of pert vitality, as though when she changed her clothes in the bushes she had also received an assurance or promise from her husband that had reinforced her self-confidence.

But Mistress Esther-Minna's gloom only intensified, as though a crack had appeared in her famous self-assurance. If she had possessed a veil, she would have been happy to hide her face behind it, first and foremost from the glances of her husband, whose evident cheerfulness she found so abhorrent that she felt she wanted to die. Rising swiftly from her place, she headed toward the trees, as though she too were seeking a quiet spot to do what the others had done before her. But as she walked in the dark among the big trees she felt empty rather than full, hungry rather than sated, so she did not stop but pressed on into the thick of the wood, not walking straight ahead but describing a wide circle centered on the flickering fire, until all at once she heard the startled cry of a small wild animal. Stopping short, she rubbed her head despairingly against a tree trunk, as though her God had been completely defeated and from now on she must beg for mercy from the trees of the field.

While Mistress Esther-Minna conjured up the image of her young, desired husband packing his sack and saddlebags next summer and setting off to travel a thousand miles to the Bay of Barcelona, to receive from his uncle and partner not only brassware and condiments but also the scent of double marriage, which clung like the odor of cinnamon to his clothing, the husband in question stood up and began to walk anxiously around the fire, wondering whether his wife's protracted absence demanded his intervention or whether her honor obliged him to hold himself back. Finally, unable to restrain himself, he called her name aloud, hoping for a sign of life. But his wife, hearing his call like a distant echo, held back her reply, not only because she was not certain that her voice would carry that far but also in the belief that only thus, in the dark silence of the damp green thicket, would she find the courage to think a new thought that could dispel the new threat to her honor.

Even though Abulafia knew in his heart that his new wife was silent only to arouse in him a lover's anxiety, he was not certain whether the spirits of the night would allow her to execute her plan without harming her. Once he was convinced that she was persisting in her silence, he decided to bring her back to the fireside and headed straight for the point from which she had set out, believing that she would be a few paces beyond; but when he had sought her for several long minutes without success and his cries met with no response, he returned to the fire, alarmed and upset that the imagined loss had turned out to be real.

Ben Attar improvised two torches from handfuls of dry leaves and twigs, one for himself and the second for the young husband, who had already lost one wife in the sea, so it was only natural that he should exert himself now not to lose a second in the forest. But Mistress Esther-Minna did not want to get lost, and in fact she was not very far either from the fire or from the two men who were looking for her, their torches flickering among the trees. Because she had not gone in a straight line but had described a wide arc, she was now on the opposite side from her seekers, so she could sit huddled up small under the tree she had just rubbed herself against, her hands clasped at her bosom, sunk deep in thought, waiting for them to give up hope. Then she could return with ladylike composure to the fire, excited by a new idea that had taken root in her heart. But by then the two men who were looking for her had split up and were going in different directions. While her husband went in the same straight line, as though he truly believed that his wife had decided to return to Paris alone, perhaps navigating by the stars, the older uncle, more familiar with the minds of women, had turned back, for his fine senses told him that a woman who could make him travel for so many long weeks on the ocean was capable of taking care of herself.

The torch was disintegrating in his hand, its last embers disappearing among the bushes. So when Ben Attar stumbled over Mistress Esther-Minna in the dark, for a moment he did not know whether he had happened on a human being or on some soft unknown European animal. When he leaned over her, touched her, and tried to lift her, muttering some words to her in Hebrew to see if she had passed out, she, realizing that a fainting fit would justify her disappearance and her silence, closed her eyes tight and imagined herself as the third wife of the sturdy man who was lifting her up, feeling all the trembling of pain and humiliation in her new condition. And for the first time in her life, she, who had always kept her composure and clarity of mind, struggled to make herself dizzy so she could try to faint.

When she opened her eyes, she realized that she had not been pretending to faint, for she was lying by the fire covered with someone else's robe while Abulafia's face hovered over her full of astonished admiration, as though in fainting she had acquired a quality she had not possessed before. But although she was very curious to know whether her husband or the twice-wed man who had found her had carried her out of the woods to the fireside, she realized that this was not the time to ask, when all the travelers were surrounding her with affection and fear, as though her fainting had atoned for all the offense of the repudiation. So great was the concern for her welfare that the first wife was unstitching one of the seams in the lining of her undergarment, which also served as a kind of secret pouch, and drawing out a tiny vial of sharp-smelling unguent that Abu Lutfi brought her every year from the desert. To judge by the secretive way he gave it to her, it seemed that this was the fabled elixir extracted from the brains or testicles of impure but intelligent monkeys, whose pungent smell was so special that when the first wife rubbed a single drop of it into the new wife's sallow temple, she had no choice but to sit up immediately.

146

4.

The strange smell of the drop of desert elixir penetrated the new wife's temple, immediately flooded the whole of her being, and even seemed to be regulating her breathing, striking a new chord inside her that only reinforced the novel idea that had just come into her mind. When Esther-Minna rose to her feet and climbed smiling into the wagon, leaning out of mere politeness on her husband's arm and declining with thanks the soft bed of leaves that the two wives had amiably contrived in the depth of the wagon for her, she could clearly envisage the words she would speak to her husband when he was standing before her alone in the small chamber that had been provisionally allocated to them in her brother's wing of the house.

So firmly had the decision concerning the new direction of her life taken root within her mind that she even dispensed with consulting her brother on his return—or perhaps it was also because for the first time in her life a breach had been opened up in her faith in this brother, who had so often served as her oracle. Even now, in the swaying darkness as the road climbed among the ruins of the city of Lutetia, she could not forget the affront of the faint spiritual smile that had flitted across his face as he listened to Rabbi Elbaz's dangerous speech, as the rabbi had sought to transform the sorrow and pain and happiness of the marriage bed into a simple and easy pleasure. How was it possible, Mistress Esther-Minna brooded resentfully, that this brother, who like her had grown up in a house immersed in true religious discourse, should think that any idea, if it was only dressed up with a few biblical verses, deserved sympathetic examination with the mind, even if the soul should abhor it?

But Master Levitas, who was now crossing the night on horseback on his way back to Villa Le Juif, was not thinking about the rabbi's speech, nor was he troubled by what his sister might be thinking. Master Levitas was determined to overtake the scribes and preserve his reputation by giving them the promised honorarium, and also to find the Radhanite merchant and offer him a higher price for his two Indian pearls. It was impossible for this Parisian businessman's sharp mind not to make a connection between the other's forceful and hostile intervention during the judgment and the very low price he had offered him the day before. But when Master Levitas reached the winery, swathed in the shadows of its vines, he found the proprietor and his little crowd of workers fast asleep, as though they had been impatient to explore in their dreams the wonderful verdict that they had just heard delivered. And since the three scribes were on their way to Chartres in a cart and the merchant from the Land of Israel had vanished into thin air, Master Levitas had no alternative, as he paced vainly among the wine casks, but to listen to the prattling of the old woman judge, who at the sound of the surprise visitor's footsteps had hurriedly emerged from the heap of fox furs, which in any case had failed to warm her flesh.

Shivering slightly in the night chill of early autumn as he sheltered between two wine casks on the former judges' dais, wrapped in an old fox skin, Master Levitas waited for the light of morning to hand over the promised fee with his own hands to the proprietor and to inquire where the courier from the Land of Israel had gone. In the meantime, while waiting for the dawn, he listened to the babbling old woman, who, faithful to the rabbinical precept "Do not speak much with womankind," did not permit the Parisian to get a word in but assailed him with her rapturous impressions of the dark-skinned Jews from the south, the beauty of their wives with their fascinating robes, the purity of the rabbi's speech, and the sweetness of his child. In particular she dwelled repeatedly on the powerful appearance of Ben Attar, who might—who knew? the widow permitted herself to dream—enlist her as a supplementary wife on board his ship when it sailed back to his sunny homeland.

Master Levitas sat in silence, his eyes closed, and despite the shiver of tiredness he tried, as a level-headed, practical man, to unravel a first fine thread of thought that would enable him to arrange a compromise between the partnership that had been resurrected by a lunatic verdict and his sister's self-respect. Perhaps the interminable, contemptible prattle of the old woman who had attached herself to him in the depths of the night was beginning to cloud his mind; how else could a decisive, clear-headed man such as himself seriously contemplate proposing himself as a fourth member of the revived partnership between south and north, even if only to interpose his own stable, reliable personality between the uncle and his nephew and thus cushion the threat of double matrimony that so alarmed his sister? The only reason such an original and bizarre idea sprouted in the mind of this anxious, responsible brother in the depth of night was because he was far from his sister, who was now bathed in the warmth of her husband's body in the dark of the wagon, as though since she had been bested in the arbitration and fainted in the wood his love and desire for her were redoubling by the minute. It was precisely because Mistress Esther-Minna felt this so clearly that she was convinced she did not need her younger brother's consent or any novel stratagem on his part to make a new declaration to the man who would soon be standing before her in the candlelight and removing his clothes.

So she merely smiled and inclined her head when Rabbi Elbaz turned and inquired politely as to her well-being, as though seeking merit for himself, on the assumption that his wonderful speech had been partly responsible for her fainting. And when they alighted at midnight in the Rue de la Harpe, by the statue of a man holding a harp, and smelled the smell of the river, she smiled again and bowed submissively to the North African man as he entrusted his two wives to her with the newfound authority of the head of the family, although he himself felt constrained to hasten to the ship to inform his anxious Ishmaelite partner that his prayers to Allah had not been in vain, and that with morning they would be able to begin unloading the cargo. It was only after Mistress Abulafia had taken the two women upstairs and smoothed the rabbi's bedclothes and turned his pillows lest he suffer from sleeplessness beside the two women, who had vanished into their respective chambers, that she instructed the old maidservant to heat some water for her to bathe herself in in the small room that Master Levitas had put at her disposal.

Naked in a large, exquisitely ornamented copper tub that Abulafia had given her as a betrothal gift, her small pink body gleaming, despite her age, with purity and freshness, the blue-eyed woman scrubbed herself with the help of her pagan maid, not so much to remove the lingering scent of the desert elixir as to blend it with the perfume of her usual soap. When she saw that Abulafia wanted to come in and undress, she dismissed her maid and stood before him in all her splendor before putting on the lightest shift she had. And while this curly-headed man who was at once husband and nephew, repudiated and attracted, interpreter and accused, victor and vanquished, began to remove his clothes, she told him in a voice only the depths of night could endow with such firmness that since the repudiation of the twice-wed uncle had failed and the partnership with him was about to be revived, she was declaring herself to be a rebellious wife who no longer desired her husband. According to a powerful and ancient law, whose source was not the rabbis of Ashkenaz but the heads of the Babylonian academies themselves, who were universally considered as unchallenged legal authorities, a rebellious wife who no longer desires her husband is compelled to submit to immediate divorce.

The desire that made Abulafia's soul dizzy did not permit him to digest what had been thrown in his face, and he continued to undress himself, as though the words he had heard had been spoken not by the desired woman, gleaming before him with cleanness, with all her parts revealed to him under her light shift, but by another woman, a hidden, furious, disobedient shade who wished to spatter his ardent seed upon the cold flagstones. With the blunted senses of a man in the grip of lust, Abulafia maintained a blank silence and continued to divest himself of his remaining garments, displaying in the little glass that stood on the chest of drawers his face blackened by the fire and his arms scratched from his terrified quest for one who a few hours earlier, he had been certain, had tried to do to him in the wood what another, previous wife had done to him years before in the sea.

Even though Mistress Esther-Minna took a step or two backward and even raised her hands to repel her young husband, who refused to recognize the seriousness of the rebellion confronting him, she was taken by force, roughly and against her will, into the arms of a naked man who would have been willing to have had her faint again if only he could satisfy his lust at once. But just then, as though coming to the aid of the woman in distress, as she grappled not only with her husband's desire but with her own as well, there arose behind the curtain the insistent strident wail of a girl who still missed her Ishmaelite nurse. Abulafia now found himself contending not only with the rebellion struggling in his new wife's damp, fragrant frame but also with the ghostly cry of his dead wife, calling to him for help from the depths of the sea through the raucous voice of their child.

So his new wife made good her escape, as though Abulafia's flesh and blood made concrete in the child wailing on the other side of the faded curtain took priority for her over his flesh and blood now suffering torments in her presence. When she left the chamber to go to the crying child, Abulafia's strength gave out. For three whole days, ever since his uncle had appeared in the doorway of his house, he had been buffeted and pressed between beloved but powerfully opposing forces. Just as he was, naked, with his erect member still projecting like a dagger looking for a new target, he entered the tub in which his supposedly rebellious wife had just bathed, seeking in the suds the warmth and fragrance of the flesh that had eluded him. And with the wretched child's bawling still piercing the curtain beside him, his eyes closed painfully at the sight of his spent seed floating on the water.

After a while, still in this water, he heard his wife talking to him gently, compassionate and friendly. Although the verdict of seven ignorant judges was no better in her view than that of the seven wine casks on which they had been sitting, she was not so arrogant as to demand that the verdict be annulled, if only out of respect for the rabbi. Since she could not forget either the oriental courier's applause or the smile that had played around Abulafia's lips as he translated the rabbi's words one by one, or particularly the calm curiosity of her brother, her own flesh and blood, on hearing the effrontery of the speech, she had no alternative but to wrap herself in her sorrow and separate herself from all that was most precious to her. And she prayed it would not be accounted sinful by the God of Israel if for the first time in her life she found herself envying the Christian women, who in time of affliction could abandon all and withdraw into a nunnery. But since Jews had no nunneries, all she could do was return to her native town, where her first husband's kinsfolk lived, in particular her brother-in-law, who had released her from the bonds of levirate marriage on the death of her husband so she could join her brother in Paris. And so, in simplicity and good will, she said to her husband, who lay immersed in water that still bore the scent of her flesh, *My repudiation has failed and your partnership is revived, and henceforth you are free once more to travel the trade roads disguised as a monk or a leper, to your beloved uncle and respected partner, with his wives and his condiments. Only divorce me first, my lord, and I shall not trouble you or any man further. Then I shall take my leave not only of you and your child but of my brother and his family, and return to the river of Ashkenaz, the river of my childhood, which is incomparably wider and deeper than the river beyond that window.*

In fear of the refusal that was sure to follow, she quickly plunged the candle flame into the cooling bathwater in which her startled husband was still splashing, and in the great darkness that fell suddenly on the small room she put on a wrap over her light shift, then she quietly toured her guests' bedchambers to make sure that no one was passing a sleepless night because of inattention on her part. But the four North African travelers, weary and lulled by their victory, did not require any attention from their hostess, whose stubborn repudiation had brought them from the far ends of the earth. Finding that the two wives were breathing calmly in their beds, that the blanket had not slipped off the curled body of the boy Elbaz, and that the rabbi's beard had not become entangled in the embroidery of his pillow, she went to the kitchen to see what food she might offer her guests in the morning, which was not far off. Some time later she returned silently to her own chamber, to find Abulafia wrapped in his traveling cloak, sleeping on a chair beside the bathtub with the large extinguished candle still in it, and there was no way of telling whether he had fallen asleep so swiftly so as not to have to face the rebellion that had been raised against him.

How could he surrender a woman whose high cheekbones gave her the look of a fair and noble beast, and for whom his love became richer day by day? A woman who had fainted a little earlier with such delicious sweetness? Yet how could he now reject a dear and loyal uncle, who had risked hardships and dangers on the sea to be reunited with him, and who was now protected by a verdict secured in his favor by the sharp-witted rabbi from Andalus? Therefore, Abulafia mused in his patient and somewhat superficial fashion, it would be best to doze awhile and mingle the contradictory currents of his life in dreams, as was his wont, until Master Levitas, his wise brother-in-law, should return and find a solution. But Master Levitas would not be back soon. He was still slumped between two large barrels in the winery at Villa Le Juif, and he too was dreaming, while beside him the old woman,

152

who had thrown some more fox furs over him, continued to grumble. In his dream Master Levitas, naked as on the day of his birth, was walking on the seashore to a business meeting with Ben Attar, who now possessed the Radhanite's two Indian pearls. Since Master Levitas had never set eyes on the sea, he imagined it like the Red Sea in the prayerbook for Passover—as hillocks of reddish water, while on the dry land that was exposed between them good men walked naked toward one another.

Ben Attar, however, was not free to enter either Master Levitas's dream or Abulafia's, or even that of Esther-Minna, who lay huddled alone on her bed trying to conjure up the moments of her fainting, for Ben Attar was busy speaking with Abu Lutfi, who kept one eye on the black slave as he led the male camel ashore on a rope halter to crop the lush grass of the northern bank. No matter how hard Ben Attar tried to explain to his Arab partner about the victory he had won, Abu Lutfi, who had never understood the need for a battle, failed to grasp the point. But the Ishmaelite was glad of one thing, that at dawn they would be able to unload the cargo, for ever since Ben Attar and his party had gone ashore the sailors had begun to help themselves to the goods. Was it the lack of the owner's quiet authority that had removed all restraint from Abd el-Shafi and his crew, or the absence of the two wives' gentle gaze? Or was it perhaps neither of these but the want of the rabbi's quill pen?

One way or another, the time had come to rescue the cargo from the ravages of the crew, unload the large sacks and sealed chests, separate the pale honeycombs, and refold the rugs and mats. And, most important of all, to extract the gem-encrusted daggers from their hiding places and restore their former brilliance, which would excite the urge to purchase even in those who had no need for them. So the two partners prepared for the week of trading that lay ahead. On the first two days they would transfer the merchandise to the repentant third partner's home, so that he could inspect it carefully, and on the following two days they would make good use of their presence in the marketplace to examine covertly (so as not to offend Abulafia) the state of the market and the prevailing prices, thus gaining a clearer idea of how much of the proceeds Abulafia received he brought to Barcelona to be shared out among the partners and how much was to be attributed to traveling expenses. On the remaining two days they would start to search for goods with which to fill the hungry belly of the ship for the return journey—either timber, which Abu Lutfi usually loaded onto the boats returning from Barcelona, or jars of local wine, which the Jewish partner suddenly thought of taking. While they were discussing these plans, the camel and the black slave disappeared, and they were obliged to break off and expend some effort combing the thicket on the northern bank before arriving at a damp, sandy area where the river had surprisingly carved a new, bare islet and discovering the mournful camel sating himself on fresh lettuces and sugarbeets from the Parisians' allotments close to the convent of Sainte Geneviève, while the young pagan excitedly prostrated himself at the sight of a new star he had discovered in the sky above the Île de France.

In this small hour of the night Ben Attar could not imagine that the victory of the old partnership, which was already secured in the folds of his robe, was about to elude him yet again, and that their departure for the double home on the golden shore of Tangier was still very far away. For how could he imagine the depth of Abulafia's sorrow when, on waking from his snatched, huddled sleep on that hard chair, he remembered his rebellious wife? Since he believed that she was hiding from him, he did not notice her curled up in one corner of their bed, and he set off to look for her in one of the many other rooms of the house. It was only on his grim-faced return that he discovered how hasty he had been in despairing of her. And his hands cautiously explored his wife's beloved body, to see whether the new rebellion pervaded even her dreams. But Mistress Esther-Minna was sleeping peacefully and very deeply, as though ever since she had announced her separation and her impending return to her own land, the storm aroused in her soul by Uncle Ben Attar's sudden appearance had subsided.

Had only three days passed? Abulafia wondered in the darkness, straightening out his wife's clenched hand on the coverlet to help her sleep better. Seeing that she did not react and that her limbs were heavy in his hands, he was assailed by a fear that she was not asleep but had fainted again, as in that moment when Ben Attar had lifted her from the ground and carried her to the fireside. And desire, which had seemed to be released and evaporated in the bath, seized him again, as

154

though its source were not within himself but somewhere in this house that Ben Attar's wives filled with their peaceful breathing. No, he swore to himself, he would never divorce her, although he was well acquainted with his wife's stubbornness. Even though he had no idea how things would turn out, of one thing he was certain. He could not lose again in the Black Forest the love that he had already lost once in the waves of the sea. Unable to restrain himself, he began to caress and kiss his wife, so that she would wake and see that it was his intention to fight her rebellion with all his strength.

Very slowly he cradled his desire, while guiding and directing and compelling his response to it. For a moment it seemed as though Mistress Esther-Minna were deliberately refusing to wake, so as to leave this coupling in the twilight zone between waking and being awake. In this way it could not be claimed afterward that her revolt had been snuffed out in its infancy, and without tormenting her conscience she could ignore the wailing of the wretched daughter, who as usual was trying to wreck her father's lovemaking from behind the curtain. And so she was taken, and for a long while Abulafia's member refused to leave her, as though by remaining erect inside her it could prevent a new repudiation and withdrawal toward the region of Lotharingia in her native Ashkenaz. The carnal thrill that filled her took such hold of her that she could not restrain herself, but joined her own moaning to the raucous wailing in the adjoining chamber.

When she awoke from sleep with a heavy head, with the sun already riding high in the sky, she was startled to discover that while she had slept her house had been seized by a rebellion. Ben Attar's two wives were standing beside the fireplace and the oven in the kitchen as though they were in their own home, slicing vegetables and roasting meat, baking bread and stirring a reddish pottage, and all with such easy authority that not only Levitas's wife and the old maidservant but even Elbaz and his boy were forced to contribute, as the latter were called in to taste every dish and relish and say whether they were true to the flavors of Andalus. Only Abulafia was absent, for he had been summoned to the ship to exercise his revived status of partner and to oversee the seamen as they unloaded the cargo and transported it to the courtyard of his house.

Still there was no sign of Master Levitas, who, after sending a special messenger at dawn to Chartres to pay the three scribes for their trouble, had located the Radhanite merchant, who was on the point of departing for Orléans, and reopened the bargaining with him for the two pearls. Even though Master Levitas was not certain that the unusual pear shape of the large pearls conferred added value on them, as the merchant claimed, or whether it indicated a hidden flaw, he was now willing to offer a higher price. When the price had been agreed and the bargain was struck, Master Levitas could not resist inquiring, in a delicate and roundabout way, whether the merchant himself had two wives or only one. But the bearded man did not seem disposed to reveal his secrets, and he went on his way without giving a clear answer. As Master Levitas wrapped the two large pearls in a soft cloth and secreted them in his jerkin, he wondered whether he should offer them both for sale in the Capetian court in Paris, or whether he should sell one to one of the loveliest duchesses and keep the other hidden until the beauty of the owner of its visible twin increased its value.

That afternoon, alone, hungry, and thirsty, he made his way back to Paris. Every now and then he halted his horse, took out the pearls, and held them up to the sunlight, not only to compare them with each other but also to learn which hour of the day best flattered their pear-like character, which hour should also serve as the hour appointed for their sale. Preoccupied with thoughts of commerce, he entered his home, and was startled to see the quantity of merchandise being piled up in his courtyard by barefoot, half-naked Arab seamen carrying jars on their heads. *Your uncle has put the verdict into effect very quickly,* he said quietly to Abulafia, who was standing in the doorway of the house, pale and silent, casting a gentle, distressed look at his brother-in-law as though his whole fate depended on him alone. Abulafia hesitated to expose to Master Levitas the development that was tearing his soul apart and to seek his advice, as he was waiting to see whether the fast that he had imposed upon himself since that morning would annul his wife's harsh decree. But she was already hastening to inform her brother as he entered the house about the status of "rebellious wife" that she had assumed to escape the affront and menace that were looming over her marriage, and she was now prepared to admit that her brother's reservations about that marriage had not been unreasonable.

Master Levitas's practical nature did not permit him to rake over the sins of the past so long as the urgency of the present threatened him and his home with heaped-up sacks of condiments and woven cloth, large earthen jars and brassware, which were arriving relentlessly from the Arab ship, filling his courtyard and cellar, and even beginning to intrude on the upper story. Nor was his house invaded from the outside alone, for Ben Attar's wives were loading the large dining table with wonderfully colorful and exotically perfumed dishes, as though their love of cooking, held in check during the ocean voyage, had now burst forth in all its exuberance.

However, when Master Levitas turned to Abulafia to beg him to stop the invasion that was cascading from the ship to his house under the pressure of his partners' commercial enthusiasm, Abulafia looked at him with a pale, staring face and extended his arms in the graceful, helpless gesture seen in images of the crucified god of the Christians, as though he too since that morning had been transformed into a tortured saint swaying between life and death. The soul of this man, who had spent so many years in solitary travel, had remained fundamentally emotional and shallow, and it was now torn between love and fear, duty and compassion. And this blend of emotions, in which there hovered also the sweet memory of the twin emissions of the night, made the man who had been deliberately starving himself since morning so dizzy that he was in danger of suddenly collapsing.

Before that could happen, Master Levitas hurriedly sent him to his partners' ship to stop the flow of merchandise, the quantity and variety of which was alarming Ben Attar too. Despite the many days and nights he had spent on board the ship, he had not imagined how full his Ishmaelite partner had managed to fill it. Abu Lutfi, who had not only managed to pack whole worlds of merchandise on board but also remembered them, now scrutinized them minutely as they burst forth out of the darkness and were borne ashore accompanied by the singing of burly seamen, so as to fix them in his memory, ready for the meeting next summer, when he would demand payment for them from the third partner, who had returned repentantly thanks to the trial in Villa Le Juif. Although if he was really repentant, why was he calling to them now from the riverbank to halt the flow of goods that was inundating his house and his yard?

Ben Attar told Abd el-Shafi to halt the unloading and hurriedly joined his nephew, who was standing surrounded by throngs of Parisians crowded among the little old wooden houses on a bridge called the New Bridge. Abulafia tugged desperately at his stubborn uncle's garments to pull him away from the curious crowd, and while the sunlight traced trailing purple marks upon the lovely peaceful river as it circled gently southward, Abulafia led Ben Attar deeper into the island, among the narrow streets packed at this hour with people returning home, some leading a lamb or a piglet on a cord for their dinner. From the dull look in his nephew's large dark eyes, Ben Attar knew that some new torment was afflicting him.

Abulafia told him immediately about the rebellion that had broken out in his home, and how his wife had sworn in her distress to go far away to her native town on the Rhine, there to convene a new court of justice to compel Abulafia to divorce her. Although the Moroccan merchant appeared surprised at the news, he seemed to find in it a blessing that might deepen the partnership that had been so laboriously revived. Perhaps the time had really come, Ben Attar tried to inform his nephew obliquely, with roundabout hints, his arm around the shoulder of his beloved nephew, whose pallor lent an additional beauty to his black locks. Perhaps, the uncle speculated wildly, it was really the hand of the Almighty that had urged him to take an old guardship and sail it to this remote little island, which still seemed to him to be rocking in the midst of the river, to rescue a lost lamb. Surely Abulafia could spare the enthusiastic rebel the hardships of a journey to the land of Ashkenaz by simply asking Rabbi Elbaz to put into effect the wisdom of the Babylonian sages and impose the divorce that Mistress Esther-Minna so longed for. In this way Abulafia would be free to travel back not only to the Bay of Barcelona but to the golden shores of the rock from which he was hewn. Surely now that he had proved to everyone and especially to himself that the curse of loneliness within him was broken, he would be able to find a wife to his taste in Tangier, and even a second wife, if he felt inclined to love her too.

But Abulafia, weakened by his fast, merely stumbled and fell in the surge of horses and pigs and hit his head on the cobbles on hearing the fantastic projects that his uncle Ben Attar was planning for him. Ben Attar did not realize how much his very being was interwoven with his love for his new wife and everything connected with her, including even the cobbles of this narrow Parisian street, which had just made his head spin. It was fortunate that Rabbi Elbaz appeared on the scene, sent with his boy to the ship to get some salt and olive oil. He happened on the North African merchant just as he was helping his young nephew to his feet, after a fainting fit that had mimicked that of his fair-haired wife.

A few local Franks, who invested with a status of sanctity any incident of fainting because of the impact of the story of the crucifixion at Golgotha, also hurried up, and sprinkled Abulafia with fresh water from a nearby well and rubbed his temples with red wine before pouring more into his gaping mouth. Ben Attar, afraid to take the young man straight back to his home in the Rue de la Harpe, conducted him first to the ship. There, among the remaining jars and sacks, they laid the frail partner, who opened his beautiful eyes and smiled a smile that held a deep, sweet sadness. And this is what he said when he saw his stubborn uncle's face bending over him: *Uncle, if you cannot kill me, release me, for I shall never give up that woman.* Then Rabbi Elbaz had to hear the story all over again, both from the point of view of the despair of Ben Attar, who was once more, at a single stroke, about to lose the object of his journey, and from the viewpoint of the pain of love that had pierced the young partner, who hoped that he would speedily think up a new compromise that would please Mistress Abulafia and Master Levitas.

But not a word would he say to either of them before making the two partners and his son stand and face the Cité of Paris to the east, to say the afternoon and evening prayers in the old familiar mode and manner. Abulafia, who always loved to sing these tunes, could not find the strength in his soul even to mumble them. There was something attractive about these southern Jews, in their white robes and blue turbans, standing on board the Arab ship scarred by the hardships of its valiant journey, surrounded by the strong seamen, whose eyes were fixed on the crowds of Frankish folk thronging the riverbank and forgoing their dinner in order to enjoy the sight of the variegated mass of humanity on board. Suddenly it seemed to Rabbi Elbaz that in the evening twilight of this city, there was not just a vague menace from the approaching millennium but also the veiled promise of a great and unique beauty to be born of the future marriage between the two banks.

The convent of Sainte Geneviève on the northern bank was screened by the smoke of dinners being cooked on the island as the Jews concluded the prayer "True and faithful," but still Rabbi Elbaz refused to disclose the new idea he had had, since he feared that Ben Attar would stifle it newborn, and preferred to unveil it only after the great feast that the two North African women had prepared. Since the rabbi had followed the preparations during the day and taken part in the tasting and testing, he pinned great hopes on the power of this meal to assist the idea that had captured his heart.

It may have been precisely because of the panic that had seized Ben Attar as Abulafia had pleaded to be released that he too felt very excited about the meal his two wives had made. Since he had set out on his journey he had missed the dishes that each of his wives had always prepared for him, and these wives would now be joined together at a single table. Even Abulafia forgot his woes for a moment, and a tear of pleasure welled up in his eye as he smelled the North African food, not because of his fast, which he had quite forgotten about in the commotion of his fainting fit, but because his memory conjured up the cooking of his first wife, who had died. Master Levitas too was so tired and hungry that he accepted without remonstrance the new smells and flavors, especially since he was careful not to give offense to his two enthusiastic veiled guests, who, usurping the role of hostess, piled his plate with more and more food. Only Mistress Esther-Minna sat grimly at the banquet that had taken over her dining table, consoling herself with the thought that this would be her last dinner before she returned to the place where she had come into the world.

Then Rabbi Elbaz began to question her, in slow, easy Hebrew, about her native town and the merits and achievements of its Jewish scholars. His purpose was to find out whether she would be finally satisfied if these great and meticulous sages gave their approval to the renewal of the partnership between Ben Attar and her husband. But Esther-Minna found the rabbi's question redundant, since she had no doubt in her heart that the sages of the land of Ashkenaz would not only find in favor of the repudiation but would almost certainly convert it into a formal ban. The rabbi from Seville, however, was not dismayed by the menace contained in her words. Perhaps, he answered with a strange smile, because they had not yet heard the arguments thought up in Seville and simmered upon the ocean waves for many days and nights. He had not said his fill at the winery of Villa Le Juif. He still had a few choice arguments left, which were stirring in his heart, and he laid his hand on his chest as though to still their motion. Therefore, the rabbi added softly, with a casual smile, why should they not all join her rebellion and follow her to the river of her birth, so as to face the judgment of those whom she accepted as wise and just? If the judgment went against them, they would accept their discomfiture and return as they had come, but if not, the repudiation and the rebellion would be utterly annulled, and all of them would be reunited, she with her husband who loved her so, and he in turn with his uncle who had refused to abandon him.

So surprised was Mistress Esther-Minna by the Andalusian rabbi's willingness to face another court in her native town that she feared the Hebrew her father had taught her had misled her understanding. So she excitedly asked her brother, whose command of the holy tongue was better than her own, to find out clearly from the rabbi whether he had truly said what she had understood. Master Levitas questioned Rabbi Elbaz, who, without looking straight at his master the merchant, repeated his suggestion so clearly that Master Levitas had no doubt or difficulty in translating it rapidly and fluently into the local language. The rabbi's words caused the pale, exhausted Abulafia to rise excitedly and bow a deep bow to the startled Ben Attar, in the mistaken belief that it was his uncle who was the true source of this wonderful new suggestion.

5.

While Abulafia was bowing excitedly to his uncle, the same unseen hand that was gently wiping away the painful rift in his soul was transferring it slowly to that of Ben Attar. Although he knew well that the rabbi's astounding suggestion was connected to an irresistible temptation to repeat the wonderful speech he had made to the court of the wine casks before the sages in the blue-eyed woman's native town, Ben Attar also understood well that the rabbi was trying to open up a new avenue, so as to avoid a renewed breach between him and Abulafia that was liable to frustrate the whole purpose of their epic voyage. But he shot an anxious glance at his two wives, who were sitting at the other end of the table, their faces beaming with joy at the sight of all the empty dishes, still not suspecting what the little rabbi was cooking up for them. Again, as when a storm whips up the sea, his heart was anxious for his two wives, who would have to journey even farther. Even if he did not fear, like his nephew, that a rebellion might break out in his household, he did fear that the sorrow of homesickness might age them all.

Thus he turned cautiously to Master Levitas and questioned him about the road to the Rhine, the river where he and his sister had been born and bred. And Master Levitas, who had been sitting contentedly stroking his little beard and sniffing the smell of the Moroccan meal clinging to his fingers while trying to discern what was taking place in his guts, was very careful not to let slip a single ill-considered word of discouragement, for although he saw the suggestion of a contest with the sages of Ashkenaz as a dangerous gamble, he also knew that this was the only way of ridding himself of these swarthy visitors, whose presence in his home was becoming more rooted by the hour, and of giving himself a lull, however temporary, from the feverish complications of his sister's marriage, which he realized now he had been only too right to warn her against.

Thus Master Levitas attempted to depict the route from Francia to Lotharingia, from Paris to Worms, in clear, gentle colors, according to his memories from long ago. Although Ben Attar was disappointed at first to discover that the Creator had not managed in the six days of the creation to link the Seine to the Rhine, so that Abd el-Shafi could be asked to hoist the triangular sail and simply sail the ship to Mistress Esther-Minna's childhood home, Master Levitas's reassuring descriptions of villages and small towns on the way led him to hope and believe that this additional journey by land would not put to shame the voyage that had preceded it. Excitedly he heard about the small town of Meaux, which led to the town of Chalons, and about the River

162

Marne, and the Meuse, where Verdun could be found, a pleasant town of customs men and slave traders that straddled the frontier between the county of Champagne and the duchy of Lotharingia. From there easy roads ran through an expansive country past towns called Metz and Saarbrücken, and the rivers Moselle and Saar, until they reached their destination, Worms, which stood beside the River Rhine, to whose marshy banks a few families of Jews had clung lovingly for the past hundred years. And so Ben Attar turned to his two wives, who were trying, each in her own way, to understand what was being said, so that he could soothe the panic that he could sense only too well from the slight motion of their veils.

But while the first wife, unable to restrain herself despite her normally calm and easygoing nature, let out an anguished cry, the second wife recoiled in terror and quickly placed her hands on the lower part of her belly, to protect something that had been occupying her mind these last days as much as her only son, whose last image, standing on the seashore in a little red robe, holding tightly on to her parents' hands, had floated before her eyes every single day of the journey when she lay down and rose up. Ben Attar, who could immediately discern her panic, even though he did not know yet what was burgeoning in her body, reached out to her with his large hand, and without giving a thought to his neighbors he laid it in her lap, and a light touch seemed to suffice to steady the youthful body.

But during the night he had to go back and forth between bed-chambers, to explain and coax, to soothe and comfort, to promise and threaten, so that by dawn, with his practical, Mediterranean wisdom, he could hurry to his ship, which every day seemed to him to have shrunk, to give new orders. There he found his faithful partner seated near the camel, which was diligently chewing its cud after an evening meal in the kitchen garden of the convent of Sainte Geneviève, and he cautiously insinuated into the consciousness of the Ishmaelite the new matter of the additional overland journey. Although Abu Lutfi strove with all his gentile being not to understand this new turn in the wars of the Jews, since he knew that he would have trouble comprehending their full intent, and because he knew from experience that no Jew could truly get the better of another Jew but would only antagonize him, he accepted the news of the additional overland journey with the desert calm he had inherited from his fathers' fathers, especially since it seemed to his joy that he himself would be exempted.

For Ben Attar had decided to leave the Ishmaelite in Paris, both to protect the ship from its unruly crew and also to begin to sell some of the goods that had been unloaded. However, he had made up his mind to enlist the captain for the overland journey, to ensure that during his prolonged absence the sailors did not try to slink back to North Africa with the ship. Also he was certain that one who had conveyed him so safely and skillfully over the waves of the ocean would succeed in doing the same over solid land. But Abd el-Shafi would not easily agree to exchange the identity of sea captain for that of simple wagoner. It would be necessary not only to offer him a further reward but also to agree to take along an additional stalwart sailor, so the captain would have someone on land to give orders to.

It may have been the additional Ishmaelite element in the journey that made the Jewish merchant decide to travel to the Rhine not in one wagon but in two, one large and one smaller, each drawn by two horses, selected for their speed as well as their strength. The smaller wagon, which was upholstered in soft fabrics and woolen cloth and scattered with fragrant spices and yellow cheeses, was intended for the three women, who for the purposes of the journey were united to form a single contingent, and for the Elbaz boy, who might cushion the wives' yearning for their distant children. As for the larger wagon, it was to carry the three Jewish men, and it was also loaded with the choicest of the wares from the ship, such as bags of condiments, carefully chosen bolts of silk, earthen jars full of olive oil, slabs of honeycomb, and gleaming brassware that would make potential purchasers' eyes light up even in the darkest forests. The first wife, who after a stormy night had decided to reconcile herself to the overland journey, sent for some coarse dark cloth from the ship and of her own accord cut out and stitched a pair of black jerkins for the two Ishmaelite seamen on the pattern of that worn by Master Levitas, so as to conceal their ragged clothes and to make them more appealing, when the time came, to the Jews of Ashkenaz.

After some frantic preparations, made hastier by the approach of the Days of Awe, which they would spend, if all went well, on the banks of the Rhine, the day of their departure dawned. The two wagons had been standing since the previous evening at the entrance to the Rue de la Harpe, not far from the splashing fountain of Saint Michael, and the two seamen transformed into wagoners were already sleeping inside them. Before dawn, in the last watch of the night, Ben Attar went to the ship to take his leave of Abu Lutfi one last time and to shed certain old worries so as to make room for the new ones mounting within him. For the first time since he had set sail from the port of Tangier in late June he found his ship wrapped in deep slumber, and even the little rope ladder that was normally left hanging over the port side was drawn up on deck, so that no stranger might disturb her rest.

For a while he stood silently on the bridge, hoping that someone would notice him without his having to shout. Then he felt the great weight of tiredness within him, and he felt very jealous at the sight of the peacefulness of the ship and those on board her, as though it were only when her Jewish owner was away that they could find real repose. What is it, he mused in a fit of sharp self-hatred, that forces me to be so stubborn about my partnership? Why can I not let Abulafia disappear among these northern Jews and forget him forever? Why must the repudiation of this little blue-eyed woman trouble my rest and grieve my heart? Surely in agreeing to face a law court in her native town I am admitting her superiority to me, even if I win the case? And in any case, what do we lack in the south that forces us to believe we shall find it here in the north? After all, we shall never meet until the Messiah son of David comes, and when he does come, we shall all be redeemed and become something else. Is it really because of the damage to my business that I am undertaking a further arduous journey? Or do I, as Rabbi Elbaz hinted, have an arrogant longing to submit the double love of my household to yet another test precisely because I am so confident and sure of it?

A splashing sound roused the merchant from his musings. From deep in the hold, the black slave had sensed his master standing helplessly beside his ship and was hurrying to his aid by lowering the ladder. Suddenly Ben Attar felt an urge to touch the black head, which Abu Lutfi sometimes laid in his lap to warm his limbs. What could Jews who sat hidden in their distant schoolhouses know, he thought, smiling to himself, of such a noble black creature as this? Would it not be right for him to take the slave along as a further specimen of merchandise, a kind of miniature replica of Africa itself, to teach those stubborn sages, who were so eager to surround themselves with walls of statutes, how large and varied was the world in which their brethren and kinsfolk roamed? All unawares, for the first time he stroked the youth's hot black skull. The caress of such an honored hand at once clouded the slave's eyes and made his head whirl.

And so, as a sudden whim will occur even to a strong, firm man, the decision came into Ben Attar's mind to include the black scout with his keen senses in the forthcoming expedition to the Rhine. To judge from Abu Lutfi's sorrow and protests, it was clear that he was being deprived not only of a faithful servant but of a secret beloved. But this knowledge only strengthened Ben Attar's resolve. If the recruitment of the sea captain was meant to forestall treacherous escape by sea, that of the black boy would forestall his partner's treacherous escape by land. Thus he could assure himself that on his return from the coming adventure he would at least find everything where it should be. And at dawn the first wife found time to cut up one of her old dresses with a sharp knife and remake it as a green robe for the young traveler, to provide a covering for his black nakedness.

After they had broken their fast and taken their leave of those who were staying behind, the ten passengers in the two wagons slowly crossed from the south to the north bank, and for some two hours they rolled southeastward, until suddenly the Seine seemed to divide before them. Then they abandoned the southern arm and traveled northeast along the Marne, and it was perhaps only then that in the little chamber the witless child fell silent from exhaustion, for since the departure of the travelers she had struggled relentlessly with the gentile nurse who had been left to look after her. Now the two wagons began to follow the roads of the Marne Valley, which were swarming with carts and wayfarers on foot waving to each other amiably in the brilliant noonday sunshine. On land the strangeness of the southern travelers was less noticeable, not only because of Abulafia's rich experience of the roads but also because Mistress Esther-Minna won all hearts with the purity of her Frankish speech, so they had no hesitation in entering into conversation with pilgrims, peasants, or traders, who, contrary to the gloomy suppositions of those of differing faith, had become more tolerant of each other and hence also of strangers seeking help because of the approaching sanctity of the millennium.

The assistance they chiefly needed concerned the precise delineation of the road, for after running pleasantly and confidently along well-trodden dirt tracks and over fields of wheat stubble, it might suddenly stop short, owing to an unnoticed earlier error, in a farmyard full of squawking geese and a throng of sheep and pigs. It was important to be very particular in selecting the right road, and not to be led astray by paths that looked attractively wide and smooth. They had to halt from time to time at a wayside inn by a stream and announce publicly the name of their first destination, Meaux, and the next one, Chalons, in order to obtain good advice as to the right way. Everyone was quick to offer helpful suggestions and even reasonably priced provender for the horses, or a large loaf of freshly baked bread, or a huge cockerel with a crest, which the black pagan, after tying its yellow feet together, quickly laid beside him on the driver's seat and addressed reverently all day long. After it was slaughtered, he plucked it and worshipped its naked carcass, which lay before him like a crucified man, oozing blood, before it was handed over to the first wife, who insisted on cooking dinner herself for the ten wayfarers, as though her role of housewife, which had been lulled to sleep by the monotonous charm of the waves, had been wakened now on dry land.

What was amazing was that the second wife, and the new wife too, not only allowed the renascent housewife to take command and do whatever she wished but even refrained from helping her. The pensive inactivity that the two of them manifested at the sight of the first wife's feverish activity over the smoking fire bound them together with a new if silent comradeship, for they did not have, and never would have, a common language. But while the second wife, whose mind was in thrall to the tiny ocean-bred creature that floated inside her, which sometimes seemed to her to have smuggled itself into her womb not from Ben Attar's male member but from a breach pierced by the sea in the floor of her cabin in the bowels of the ship, did her best to elude the inquisitive blue look of a woman who was her superior in years and wisdom, Mistress Esther-Minna, whose heart was filling with happiness at the thought of revisiting the house where she had been born and with confidence at the outcome of the renewed tribunal, seemed to allow herself now to repudiate any repudiation, and not only to be friendly with one and all but also to ponder closely and deeply the second wife's nature, as though the secret of double matrimony were concealed in her alone.

So they advanced steadily, between halts, along the right roads. Meanwhile, the approaching year 4760 lashed them in their imaginations from afar as though it had joined the long whip that Abd el-Shafi had improvised from a rope from the ship, which he waved above the horses' heads as though he were breathing life into an invisible sail.

Abulafia and Ben Attar had thought at first they would stay in wayside inns because of the chilly nights, but they were surprised to discover that the bright skies of Champagne retained something of the warmth of the day even after dark. When they realized at the first inn where they halted, in Meaux, what a large and smelly throng of Christians was crowded into the sleeping quarters, and how thin the partition between the men and the women was, Ben Attar decided, with his nephew's concurrence, to try to spend the night under the vault of heaven. Not far from the inn they drew up the two wagons facing each other and tethered the four horses together; they made a comfortable place for the three women to lie, and they left the rabbi's son to sleep among them, to interpose his lean body, at least symbolically, between south and north. The three Jewish men found themselves a sleeping place among the wares in the larger wagon, and the two mariner-wagoners slept under it between the large wheels, so that anyone who tried to move the wagon would wake them at once. As for the black pagan, he was ordered to roam around and scare off anyone who might try to disturb their sleep.

And so Mistress Esther-Minna slept close to the southern uncle's two wives, their breathing accompanying her own and their sighing punctuating her own dreams. Occasionally she was alarmed by the thought that Ben Attar might be unable to curb his desire and might leave the large wagon in the middle of the night and raise the flap of the smaller wagon, to seek love even from one who did not owe it to him. Then she would retreat on her own, leave the triple bed in confusion, and hasten to stand beside the silent horses as though seeking their protection. Very soon the young slave would emerge from the darkness and offer her a hot drink made from bitter, tasty desert herbs, which would restore her peace of mind.

The following night, camping under the stars near an inn called Dormans, after a long but pleasant day's journeying amid vineyards planted on little hills—they had even been invited by an enthusiastic vintner to view one of the caves in which he stored his wine—she woke again, uncertain whether it was the proximity of two wives belonging to a single man that had disturbed her sleep or the mixture of joy and fear she felt at the impending encounter with her native town and her late husband's kin, the Kalonymos family. Again she stood beside the horses, wondering where the unseen fire was over which the black servant invisibly brewed the bitter herbal drink that she needed more and more each night.

The next day, when they reached the dark stone walls of Chalons and a fine drizzle began to fall, Ben Attar wanted to enter the town and find them a real roof to put over their heads, but eventually he dropped the idea and turned the two wagons into the shelter of a small wood so they could prepare for the night. But the dripping of the rain on the canvas cover of the wagon gave him no rest, and fetched him out of his bed to see whether the Ishmaelite wagoners required more covering. While these turned out to be fast asleep, he found the woman who was his adversary swathed and trembling, with her infusion, and he made her a shallow bow. Before retreating in obedience to the law regulating contact between the sexes and reinstalling himself in the men's wagon beside her husband, he could not resist pronouncing a few words of courtesy in his atrophied Hebrew, careful to filter out any hint of protestation or anger about the sorrow and suffering she had caused him for several years now.

In the morning it transpired that they had been mistaken to fear entering the walls of the town, which turned out to be a labyrinthine place but very welcoming to Abulafia and Ben Attar, who could not overcome their commercial instincts and at first light entered the main gate to offer bags of condiments and earthen jars of olive oil for sale. Despite the early hour people pounced on their wares, and they were generously repaid in food and drink. The two partners, whose former cordial partnership had now been revived, could not help regretting the small quantity of goods they had brought with them and the long journey that still lay ahead, although it did cross Ben Attar's mind that a reduction in his stock would increase its attractiveness and double its value.

After breakfast they made their way haltingly toward the border with Lotharingia, stopping other wayfarers and pronouncing the name Verdun. But those questioned persisted in shaking their heads and talking not about Verdun but about a place called Somme, which would have to be crossed first, before the road to Verdun lay open ahead. It soon became clear that Somme was the name not of a town or a village but of a region of dense forest. The ground under the horses' hooves, which had been soft and crisscrossed by brooks and streams, became hard and gray and dry. The following day they began to descend and ascend terraces of land like gigantic flights of steps leading to the Lotharingian border, and the soil, which had been chalky, turned tawny. The garments of the local people also changed their form and color, with crimson standing out more and more in the men's breeches, which became wider, and in the women's aprons, which became longer. From time to time the travelers alighted from the wagons and walked, not only to relieve the horses but to enjoy the views of the winding River Meuse, until they came to the town of Verdun, which was entered through a gate in its fortifications. Through this gate passed not only traders but lines of fair-haired, blue-eyed Slavic slaves of both sexes, shackled together with light chains. Outside the town, beyond the wooden bridge over the river, stood different guards, gleaming grayly in their coats of mail, fingering the broad, heavy scabbards of their swords, and raising their visors in pleasure and surprise to learn how powerful the yearning of a Jewish woman for the Rhineland was, if she was so successful in infecting both her near and her more remote kin with it.

But despite their sympathy towards the Jews seeking entry to the land of the Moselle and the Rhine, the guards refused to exempt them from paying a tax on the merchandise heaped up on their wagon. When the Jews tried to argue, maintaining that this was not merchandise but merely a few small gifts for the many kinsfolk awaiting them in Worms, the officer of the guard was momentarily confused, but after a moment's reflection he ruled that the wagon with the gifts, together with the Jewess returning to her homeland, should be taken to a nearby customs house so that an authoritative and responsible answer could be found to the question of the difference between merchandise and gifts.

It was too late for them to retract their absurd sophistry, and so Abulafia too had to leap quickly up on the big wagon, so that his wife would not be left alone with the stubborn Lotharingians. While the wagoner, Abd el-Shafi, whose rank and dignity when at sea no man guessed at, battled with two soldiers who were attempting to wrest the reins roughly from his hands, Ben Attar ordered the other sailor to attach himself to the wagon that was rolling away, to thwart any impure purpose that might lurk behind this demand for clarification. Thus Ben Attar was left alone with his wives and the rabbi and his son before the walls of Verdun, under a soft gray autumn sky, in a lush green meadow traversed by rivulets, cut off by a bend in the river. He averted his gaze from the black slave, who was now compelled by the guards to remove his clothing and present himself for inspection as naked as the day he was born, so that they could verify precisely how far his blackness extended. From behind the town wall, where the convent of Saint Vanne rose with its two rounded towers, there now burst a sound of singing accompanied by the lowing of a mournful beast. The guardsmen did not seem to be surprised by the sound, and at first they seemed to dismiss it with ribald talk. But gradually they too came under the spell of the sonorous resonance of the music on the other side of the wall, and they released the naked youth, who donned his green robe made from the first wife's dress and, shivering with embarrassment, rejoined the five Jews, whose fears for Abulafia and his wife gnawed at their souls and prevented them from listening to the singing that filled the grayish brightness of the late afternoon.

All except the second wife, who from the moment the first notes sounded had felt her insides turning over. It was as though the entrancing music that curled around her joined her to her only son, whom she had left behind in her parents' house on that faraway continent. Suddenly her patience snapped and she was unable to resist any longer, and she rose to her feet and begged Ben Attar to take her to the source of the singing, as though there she might find a balm that would soothe her sorrow. Fearing a further dispersal of the company, Ben

Attar tried at first to refuse his wife's strange request and quell her spirit, but the young woman, still transported by the new music, would not relent, but shamelessly kneeled before him, sobbing and trying to kiss his feet, until in confusion he turned to the guards, who were observing them with faint curiosity, and implored them with broad gestures to silence the strains of song that were driving his wife out of her mind.

But the Lotharingian guards neither could nor would silence the singing, which they were clearly enjoying. Consequently, if Ben Attar wanted to quiet this sudden turbulence in his wife's soul, he must do as she asked and take her inside the walls of the town. He told the first wife, who was staring wide-eyed at her companion, to resume her place inside the wagon, and he begged the rabbi to join her with his son, while the young slave was instructed to climb up onto the driver's empty seat and take up the reins in one hand and the whip in the other, so that if anyone tried to harm them during his brief absence he could flick his whip and disappear in an instant down the highway that stood open before them. After explaining to the soldiers with broad gestures and an apologetic smile what he intended to do and what he was leaving behind in their care, he took a firm hold of his wife's thin arm, and she trembled expectantly as he steered her hesitantly through the gate into the town of Verdun, making straight for the place the music was coming from.

It had been more than sixty days, ever since the beginning of the bold, amazing voyage on the ocean and the river and the additional journey overland, since Ben Attar had been able to escort a lone woman in public, as he had done on occasion on the waterfront in Tangier. He looked compassionately at the young woman walking trippingly at his side or at his heels, who had not noticed, or chose not to, that in her inner commotion her veil had fallen away from her brown face, which was delineated by the simple yet precise hand of a hidden artist. He did not know if it was the sound of the music that had given her the desire and the strength to force him to take her out of the little company, or if it was her longing to be alone with him, not just as a woman wriggling submissively on a narrow bed in total darkness but under the vault of heaven and in a wide open space. Indeed, the husband and his second wife were walking now under a gray sky, between the furrows of a piece of land scattered with tombstones so uniform in form and color that it seemed as though those lying beneath them had all died and been buried together. And there, close to the wall of the convent of Saint Vanne, stood a solitary house, and before its open door were standing, to the amazement of the North African travelers, not a band but merely a pair of musicians, a man and a woman, whose combined voices had made their music loud and strong, especially since they were accompanying themselves on lutes. But as Ben Attar hesitated to advance, the second wife broke away from him, stood tall, and threw herself upon the musicians and into the doorway of the house itself. The darkness inside was crowded with dozens of jars, vials, and flasks full of powders, herbs, and potions, and a physician or apothecary stood there, aged about thirty, bareheaded and with a close-cropped beard, listening to the music that was being played for him. Behind him hung a terracotta image of the suffering savior.

The two musicians seemed to be pleased at the arrival of a new and exotic listener, and they played even louder in her honor, but the proprietor, noticing the fine shadow of a woman's robe falling across the square of light at the entrance to his house, hurriedly gestured to them to stop playing and came out to see who was sharing the fee he had just been given for his medical attention to the two musicians, who had first listened to his advice and swallowed his potions and only afterward announced that they were penniless. He stared at the two strangers, who might be seeking healing for themselves. Then he inclined his head and introduced himself, first in Teutonic, then in Frankish, and finally in Latin. Even though he could see that they shared no common language, he persisted, extracting with gentle, flowery gestures not only the names and surnames of his unexpected visitors but also the names of the places they had visited during their astonishing journey from the continent of Africa to their new destination.

Neither Ben Attar nor his second wife, who now opened her narrow amber eyes wide, could tell whether this healer of Verdun, who presented himself, either humorously or seriously, as Karl-Otto the First, could really grasp the vast distances they had traversed or the antiquity of their lineage. But of one thing they were certain, and that was the power of the attraction they had for this crop-bearded, black-clad physician. With an impatient gesture he now dismissed the two musicians and their musical tribute so that he could pay attention to the two strangers, whom he was eager to invite into his home, even if they were not patients in need of his healing potions.

Ben Attar, whose heart was troubled with anxious care for those remaining outside the wall, was firmly resolved to refuse the uncalled-for invitation, but the second wife, sad for the music she had lost, was drawn as though by magic into the stranger's house. With the confidence derived from her new solitary status, she did not consult her husband but was swept into the musty darkness, until she almost touched the large, tormented image of the Son of God, whose blood-shot eyes stared with equanimity at all the drugs and simples in the vials and flasks all around. Ben Attar was obliged to snatch hold of his wayward wife's thin arm, which had become even thinner lately, to prevent her from floating on through the door that the physician was eagerly opening before her and into an even darker inner room, which was apparently the consulting room itself. In it a large taper burned near a bed covered in a yellowish woolen coverlet, at the foot of which some river pebbles were whitening in a basin that was empty of water, while on a low dresser were placed a knife, a saw, and a pair of forceps made of the same polished gray iron as the little crosses hanging in every corner, so that the physician could pray while he worked and beg for forgiveness and mercy for the shortcomings of his skill and the weakness of his mind.

Even after the North African had managed to break the spell that the physician's house held over his surprisingly disobedient wife, and with his own hands replaced the veil that had slipped from her strained face and hurriedly led her back toward their fellow travelers, the physician still seemed to refuse to let his two visitors go, and he followed them to the town gate quietly and pensively, gathering on the way among the tombstones two small children with large iron crosses hanging around their necks. It was as though, since he had failed to make progress with them as a physician addressing prospective patients, he were now trying to win their affection as the parent of two lively children, who crossed themselves charmingly before the guard and cautiously touched the horses' tails.

But what does this obstinate Lotharingian want? Why will he not leave us alone? And what is he so curious about? Ben Attar wondered with faint irritation. He was relieved to discover that during his absence the others had obediently stayed where they were, apart from little Elbaz, who had deserted his place between his father and the first wife and seated himself instead on the driver's seat beside the black pagan, who was still vigilantly holding the reins in one hand and the whip in the other, as motionless as a statue. Seeing that the crop-bearded, black-clad physician was trying to extract information from the officer of the guard, he asked Rabbi Elbaz to explore with the help of his Latin the obstinate Christian's intent.

The physician's good Latin easily supplied what was deficient in that of the rabbi from Seville, so their conversation was able to satisfy the nagging but as yet unfocused curiosity of the Lotharingian physician about the journey of these faraway Jewish strangers who had turned up on his doorstep. Just as Elbaz was wondering whether he could explain to this gentile the nature of the painful conflict between northern and southern Jews, whose character and distance from each other made it impossible for either party to overcome the other, but merely enabled them at times to reach a compromise, a short, pale German woman came through the town gate and hurried over to her two children, who were amusing themselves under the horses' feet. The rabbi's heart missed a beat at the sight of the physician's wife, who, apart from the large iron cross dangling at her bosom, resembled their own Mistress Esther-Minna in her appearance and her carriage, and he raised his eyes in amazement to her crop-bearded husband, his lips moving wordlessly. But in truth there was no need for him to say anything, for the physician immediately understood the little rabbi's surmise, and with a faint smile that held a hint of sorrow, he nodded his head to confirm the surprising truth, and thus the rabbi was able to tell him the rest of the story of their travels without fear, knowing that he was assured of an understanding listener.

6.

Then the gray sky came back to life and lukewarm raindrops began to fall relentlessly on Verdun. The physician's little wife quickly gathered her two children and disappeared through the town gate, but her husband, excited by the contest about dual marriage that the rabbi from Seville was spreading out before him like a colorful fan, found it difficult to tear himself away from the unusual story. Did he experience a brief hope of discovering a different, lustier species of Jew, or was it rather that his curiosity urged him to steal a glance at the other wife, concealed within the wagon, so that he could compare her with the dark-skinned young woman who had floated into his house? But when Esther-Minna alighted from the larger wagon as it returned from the customs house and the apostate noticed the hard blue look he received from this fellow countrywoman, who immediately saw through him, he shivered slightly, as though the fanatical repudiation of which the little rabbi spoke were liable to threaten him too. Without saying a word of farewell, he withdrew from the group of Jews, crossing himself occasionally, and exchanged some mocking banter with the Lotharingian guards before disappearing through the wall. The North African travelers, who a mere ten weeks before had been sailing under the bright azure sky, continue their journey eastward in a rainy, muddy fog toward the valley of the Rhine.

Even the customs officer had not been sure of the difference between merchandise and gifts. But since he, like the captain of the guard, suspected that the Jews were deviously intending to sell the goods disguised as gifts on their way to Worms, he had made an inventory of everything in the wagon, including the travelers' own clothes and cooking pots, and sent it by a fast rider to the governor of Worms, so that when the Jews arrived they could be inspected to ensure that no gifts had been magically turned back into merchandise along the way and that everything declared as a gift really reached its intended recipient. Only in this way could the Lotharingian authorities be reassured.

The Jews were dejected not only because the Christian had cunningly outwitted them, but because they had a nagging fear that thanks to the inventory flying ahead of them to the Rhine, not only their goods but even their pots and clothes and everything else they possessed had been turned into gifts, and who knew whether they would have to buy back the "gifts" they had been compelled to give? That evening, as they camped under a large wooden bridge near the town of Metz, Ben Attar noticed his first wife, on her own initiative, ripping open a bag of condiments, emptying out the contents, and then cutting the material of which the bag was made into two and sewing two bags in its place. In this way she was doubling the quantity of merchandise, so as to save half of it from the threat of being designated as gifts. By the time they encamped the following night, she had not only doubled the number of sacks of condiments but the bolts of cloth and even the pale honeycombs.

Again it seemed as though the more the desert merchandise shrank, the more it increased its attractiveness and worth to the wayfarers and town-dwellers between the Meuse and the Moselle and between the Moselle and the Rhine. The bags of spices were now so small that the purchasers did not need to bring them close to their noses to smell them, but could insert them in their nostrils so as to have an effortless and uninterrupted access to the spicy scent of a faraway dark continent. So fearful were Ben Attar and Abulafia of the inventory, however, and of appearing to be merchants dealing in "gifts," that they sent the black idolater ahead of them with a laden tray, as though this were his personal property which he was offering for sale on his own responsibility and the Jews following behind were merely advising him about the prices.

Because the Lotharingians were meaner than the Franks and Burgundians, they were easily attracted to the small, new, unfamiliar goods, whose transient nature would soothe away in advance any regret they might feel at the impulsiveness of their purchase. The two experienced traders could sense where and how strongly the winds of commerce blew in the land of Ashkenaz, and they were beginning to discuss how to prepare themselves for the still conditional meeting in the Bay of Barcelona the following year, the year of the millennium itself.

Thus, between light warm showers of autumn rain, the litigants traveled slowly toward the town of Worms. Up hill and down dale they advanced along wide, easy roads that sometimes skirted a gray fort or the ruins of an ancient Roman camp. Occasionally the horses' hooves encountered boggy yellow puddles that the wagon wheels would sink into if Abd el-Shafi was not careful. Sometimes the convoy had to halt so that a wheel damaged on a rocky descent could be straightened or the horses' harnesses adjusted. Sometimes they had to wait for hours for a ferry to return from the opposite bank of a river, or haggle with an obstinate farmer before crossing a field of stubble. But still it seemed as though the onward impetus of the road was stronger than the mishaps and delays. Whenever the wagoners felt a fair wind blowing, they could not resist their mariner's instincts, and asked permission from the master of the expedition to untie the covers of the wagons and hoist them like small black sails, to make the horses fly faster.

Small wonder, then, if Rabbi Elbaz, transported back to the voyage by the howling of the wind in these strange sails, relapsed into his old poetic intoxication, which gradually stretched his sense of the passage of time. For while the stubborn litigants were advancing slowly through Lorraine on the spent back of the month of Elul, the last month of the old year, they were being slyly outflanked by a fresh young month of Tishri. The Jewish travelers realized that they were liable to reach the community of Worms in the midst of the blowing of the ram's horn for the new year, so Mistress Esther-Minna, who was apt to keep track of the passage of sacred time, tried gently to speed the journey. But the desire to deal in the doubled gifts, which the first wife produced every night with the help of the second, delayed the members of the conditional partnership, who clung to each moment that deferred the determination of their conditional status.

When the wagons entered the region of the Saar, moving very close to the flow of the cold, shining river, amid the bulk of high hills whose ancient origin molded their tops like black domes, there appeared among the oak and ash trees the burial church of the Alter Turm, which Mistress Esther-Minna recognized excitedly by its eight grim sides. Indeed, there was no need here to shout the name of the Rhine to receive from wayfarers a halfhearted reply that gave only a direction. They could announce the names of towns—Speyer, Worms, Mainz— and receive not only nodding confirmation of their famous existence but an enthusiastic, well-informed wave of the arm pointing to a precise road. Naturally, to the fair-haired woman's constant worry that they might have to stop and hear the sound of the ram's horn while standing beside a black pagan in a dark forest was added the nostalgic memory of the cool air and the smell of the turf of her native land being crushed under the horses' hooves. Abulafia's new wife's fearful longing took hold of him too. Even Ben Attar and the rabbi were eager now to reach the town on the Rhine and welcome the Jewish New Year there, the year 4760, from whose womb in a hundred days or so would burst the Christian millennium, so young and wild.

But it is doubtful whether the progress of the wagons could have been accelerated any more as they advanced over a desolate plain descending to the valley of the Rhine if, like some phantasm, Master Levitas himself had not suddenly appeared, mounted on a proud stallion. It transpired that contrary to his hope, the level-headed younger brother had not found any peace at home in Paris after his sister had left with her adversaries. After hastily depositing the members of his household, including the half-witted orphan, with his friends in the winery at Villa Le Juif, to spend the approaching days of penitence and judgment with them, he had hastened with the first of the Indian pearls to a beautiful duchess who loved jewelry and exchanged it for a splendid and renowned stallion from her husband's stables. The horse would carry him swiftly by shortcuts to his native town, Worms, ahead of the main party, to ensure secretly that the mishap that had occurred in the shadowy winery would not be repeated on the banks of the Rhine, but that on their arrival they would be received by a proper, irreproachable law court, full of outstanding scholars, who would not merely speak but would sing forth the right verdict.

But when, after a couple of days' half-secret stay in his birthplace, it became clear that Ben Attar's company was not arriving, while the sound of penitential hymns at night was growing ever louder, he began to fear that some mishap or second thought had made the twice-wed trader turn around and go back. Thus he had decided to break cover and ride out to meet the litigants and speed them into the ambush that he had laid for them. To his dismay, he had discovered that a mere three days before the holy day the two wagons were still a score of leagues from the town of Speyer, which did not contain a single Jew.

And so, as a former resident, Levitas offered to escort the convoy to its journey's end, and he also suggested that they should cease to halt at night. Ben Attar, who had been infected with Esther-Minna's fear, accepted the clever brother's suggestion and instructed Abd el-Shafi, who was accustomed to sailing in the dark, to attach one wagon to the other with a short stout rope, and to tie the front wagon with a long rope to Master Levitas's saddle, so that the travelers were assured of arriving at their destination together.

Linked together in this way, the two wagons advanced over the reddish soil of the Rhine Valley, led by the stallion. The refined young man displayed his enthusiasm and determination, pulling the North African Jews behind him day and night, attached to his saddle, so that they would not, heaven forbid, miss celebrating the New Year in his home town. But there is a difference between traveling by day alone, with night halts for rest, and traveling day and night, and the travelers soon became faint and dizzy and lay piled on one another like a stirring heap of rags. Even the Ishmaelite wagoners, hardy mariners that they were and accustomed to staying awake for long stormy days, drooped limply on their seats, and if the young slave had not continued to urge the horses on with the whip, it is doubtful whether the two linked wagons would have succeeded in entering the narrow street of the Jews in Worms in the twilight of the last day of the departing year and drawing up among the small bowed houses resting on huge rough-hewn piles.

The litigants alighted semiconscious from the wagons, and they might have collapsed on the spot if the good folk of Worms, particularly the trusty Kalonymos family, forewarned of the arrival of the little convoy, had not hastened to lead them to various homes and families so that they might bathe and revive their weary bodies and their flagging souls in the twenty hours that remained before the onset of the festival. Without consulting the exhausted visitors, they efficiently separated menfolk from womenfolk, Jews from Ishmaelites, horses from wagons, and put at the disposal of each group and class the facilities appropriate to it. What was surprising was that the Kalonymos family treated their kinswoman Mistress Esther-Minna exactly like the southern foreigners, and did not exempt her from any of the obligations that were laid upon the others. Together with Ben Attar's two wives, she was taken gently but firmly for ritual cleansing to a large bathhouse that in ancient times had served the Roman troops and that still had small cubicles paved in green marble, in one of which Mistress Esther-Minna now attempted vainly to conceal her pale, blushing nakedness from the curious, startled eyes of her two female adversaries.

After the three women had come out of the bath and been toweled dry and led respectfully each to her place, the uncle and the nephew, the conditional partners, were also brought in for immersion, as was Rabbi Elbaz, dragging his struggling son along into this abyss of abundant naked masculinity. Meanwhile, in a small back yard, a pure meal was served to the three gentiles, to soothe their minds before they too were asked to bathe themselves, in drawn water rather than river water, in preparation for the festival. And because there was a great deal of work to be done in a short space of time, especially since in this year of 4760 the two days of the New Year's festival were followed immediately by the Sabbath of Penitence, other Jews of Worms, eager to have a share in fulfilling the sacred obligation of hospitality, groomed and fed and made much of the five horses, which had not been spared and had not spared themselves to bring the traveling Jews into an established Jewish community for the festival so that they might all worship together in a single synagogue.

Thus, with affection as well as alacrity, the local people absorbed the newcomers into the fabric of their existence. Since on the eve of the Days of Awe there was no one who did not wish to gain the credit of inviting into his home such wonderfully clever guests, who had come from the other end of the world to plead their cause before the wisdom and justice of the Jews of the Rhine, tables were instantly spread and beds were offered in the homes of ten families at least, so that every family could have at least one guest, and it made no difference whether that guest was a woman, a child, an Ishmaelite, or even a young idolater. As for the travelers, who had become accustomed during the long journey to being part of a single moving human lump, to the degree that they had even begun to share each other's dreams, they found themselves in the middle of the night not only bathed and well fed but also separated, each of them lying alone on a strange bed, protected by a curtain, sinking in a soft mattress from which a few goose feathers protruded, and surrounded by black empty space, no longer daring to share someone else's dream.

But Mistress Esther-Minna not only did not want to dream now, she flatly refused to go to sleep. Despite the shadows crowding in on her, she realized that the Kalonymos family, who had exchanged few words with her, had chosen for her the bedchamber of her youth, where her first husband, a sensitive scholar, had tried in vain to bring a child into the world with her, until he had given up in despair and died. Was this the hand of chance, she asked herself, or had her husband's kinsfolk known how deeply she yearned for this dear chamber? It was said to have served as the sleeping quarters for the first generations of Jews to come at the king's command from Italy, who had brought with them from the Alps some fair-haired, blue-eyed pagan servants who were so devoted to their Jewish masters that they had eventually cast off their strange idols and adopted their faith. Who had vacated his big bed for her? Mistress Esther-Minna wondered with excitement tinged with a hint of fear. Was it possible that this was the bed of her brother-in-law, Master Isaac son of Kalonymos, whose mother, her own mother-in-law, had not been willing after the death of her firstborn for her childless daughter-in-law to wait until her other son came of age but had firmly insisted that she should ceremonially withdraw the handsome youth's little shoe and spit on the ground before him, as the law demanded, before going to seek consolation in the home of her younger brother in Paris.

Although Mistress Esther-Minna was well acquainted with the character of her fellow countrymen, who clothed even the most delicate and affectionate sentiments in sternness, yet she was disappointed and bewildered, for she had expected a warmer reception. She had innocently hoped that her townsfolk would be impressed by her devotion and resourcefulness in bringing such stubborn foreign Jews all this way to submit themselves to local justice, which she had come during her long years of absence to imagine as being the very acme of perfection. But she had overlooked one thing—that the great strength of the Jews of Worms was that they never considered their justice perfect, and that during the ten years since she had left her kinsfolk and her friends, they had exerted themselves constantly to improve and perfect it. Today, on the eve of the double day of jubilation, they were not prepared to be impressed by her bringing into their midst such a disturbing case for adjudication; on the contrary, they were inclined to view her with suspicion and distrust, like excellent judges who, in a conscious effort not to favor one side or the other, view both, before the case is heard, as sinners.

The woman returning to her homeland felt all this in the cool looks her former kinsfolk vouchsafed her. In the night, in this bed where she and her late husband, for all their passion, had failed to make a child, her heart was so anguished that a single drop of sorrow could flood it with fear. Suddenly even the impossible seemed possible. Perhaps here too, in the place that had seemed to her most safe and pure and decent, she was liable to be surprised again, for in the conscious effort not to favor one side or the other, and out of compassion for the simplicity of the southern Jews who had traveled such an awesome distance, the sages of her town might, like the court in Villa Le Juif, allow themselves to be led astray by the seductive words of the Andalusian rabbi and pronounce a verdict against her, which would not only renew the partnership forever but imprint a humiliating fantasy with a double stamp of propriety, northern and southern.

She longed to wake her brother and tell him of her new fears, but she did not know where he was sleeping. She felt a sudden upsurge of anger against the effrontery of her townsfolk, who had scattered and isolated the travelers like witless babes. She also felt a momentary regret that she had submitted herself to a further legal contest, and like Rabbi Elbaz, who had groped his way through the darkness of her house in Paris two weeks before, seeking to escape from it, she abandoned her goose-feather bed and tried to find her way out of the crooked wooden house, which although she knew it so well, suddenly seemed to her like a ship that had run aground on a sandbank. But as she was wrestling with a new, unfamiliar bolt, which had been fitted to the outer door against the menace of the approaching millennium, the master of the house, young Kalonymos, her husband's brother, heard her. Not daring to approach her alone in the darkness, he hurriedly roused his wife to calm his former sister-in-law's distress.

This young and charming Mistress Kalonymos, one of whose early ancestors had endowed his descendants' eyes with a remarkable greenish sparkle, succeeded not only in calming Mistress Esther-Minna's panic but in filling her with renewed enthusiasm for the penitential prayers that awaited them all. Gently she led the woman who, if not for her childlessness, would have been her own husband's first and only wife back to her old matrimonial bed, and compassionately covered her with the quilt that she had thrown off in a fit of rage, so that she could enjoy a few hours' rest before she was awakened to attend divine worship. A synagogue for women only had been built in Worms in these latter years, and there a female cantor intoned the chants and put on the phylacteries for the recital of *Hear O Israel*.

This surprising news soothed away Esther-Minna's fears in a miraculously gentle way. The hope that the women in her native town might have enough good sense to put right what the ignorant, barefoot women in the winery near Paris had done wrong cooled her desperate thoughts and brought on Esther-Minna the slumber that her body so longed for. In fact, four hours later Mistress Rachel daughter of Kalonymos had to exert herself considerably to rouse the dear and honored guest from her profound sleep, so that she should not miss the women's prayer in the *Frauenshul,* seeking pardon and forgiveness on this last day of the dying year not only for their own sins but perhaps also for those of all other women, wherever they might be.

These women included Ben Attar's two wives, who were not spared by the exigent people of Worms. In the darkness of the last watch of the night, with a misty breeze blowing off the river, they were led forth from their separate houses, wrapped in heavy capes but without veils or jewelry, to be taken with their faces exposed to public gaze to that modest chamber abutting the synagogue of the men, who were also converging now like ghosts from all directions for the penitential prayers. Among them were the other travelers, who stood in the narrow lane in a state of utter exhaustion: Abulafia, Ben Attar, and Rabbi Elbaz, who had just remembered to ask where his boy was. They were all dressed in black cloaks on the instructions of their hosts, either to warm their southern bodies and protect them from the cold, dank breeze blowing off the river or to conceal their crumpled, threadbare traveling robes. All three of them were befuddled by deep but insufficient sleep and by an evening meal whose taste they still had not identified, and at first they had difficulty recognizing one another, as though being separated by their hosts had wrought some profound change in them.

Now Master Levitas appeared, lucid and wide awake and in full command of himself. He looked affectionately at his fellow townsmen, who were so carried away by religious fervor on this occasion that they did not even spare the three Ishmaelites, but seated them on a bench in the court of the synagogue, so that sparks of sanctity escaping from the Jews' prayers might lighten their gentile darkness. Ben Attar's heart suddenly went out with painful longing to his two wives, who were being led to the prayer through a tangle of trees and long grass like a couple of bears, their beautiful faces, revealed now for all to see, turned to him with an expression of wonder rather than anger, as though they were asking him, Will your mind know no rest until you have demanded a last and final test of your double love even here in this grim, benighted place?

The little Andalusian rabbi had not ceased to think about this test from the moment he had entered the walls of this small town. On seeing Mistress Esther-Minna, his adversary, wrapped in a light pelisse and surrounded by townswomen who were leading her with respect and devotion to their little synagogue, perhaps to fortify her by binding the straps of the phylacteries on her arm, he intuitively knew that he must beware here not only of the women but of the whole congregation, which was united and tempered by religious zeal. Unlike what had occurred in the winery at Villa Le Juif, here he would have to demand not a broad panel of jurors but a single judge, who would have the wisdom and vision to see from the depths of the marshes of the Rhineland what he, Rabbi Elbaz, had long since seen among the blooming gardens of Andalus.

7.

While the morning prayer was being recited, after the end of the nocturnal penitential prayers, Rabbi Elbaz forced himself to scrutinize the faces of the worshippers around him in order to find a man who might be fit to serve as sole arbiter in the engagement that was about to be joined. His surprise victory at Villa Le Juif had taught the Andalusian rabbi one simple lesson—that in a court of law, whoever selects the judges controls the verdict, without any need of subtle speeches or scriptural proofs. Still, he could not forget how, in the half-darkness of the winery, with the torchlight shining on the little must-stained feet of those women, he had managed to astound even himself with his bilingual oration. During the nights of the journey from the Seine to the Rhine he had repeatedly tried to polish that speech in his mind. But he was also mindful of the saying attributed to the imam of the great mosque of Cordoba: "Never repeat the winning tactics of a previous war." A speech that had captured the hearts of emotional, tipsy Jews in the Île de France would not succeed with these sober-minded Jews of the Rhineland, who were now scrutinizing the new rabbi from Seville over their prayer shawls no less than he was inspecting them.

Before finding new tactics that would finally remove the conditional status hanging over the partnership between north and south and force the stubborn new wife to reconcile herself to her duo of aunts from the golden shores of North Africa, he sought to assess the spirit of the scholars praying all around him, so that he could select from their midst a man whose spirit was free from the tyranny of the congregation. He decided to decline his hosts' offer to take him home after the service, like the other travelers, and put him back to bed, to make up for his lost sleep and garner strength for that evening's prayers. Instead he asked to be taken, just as he was, in his tattered Andalusian robe, for a walk through the muddy lanes of Worms, so that he could become well acquainted with the place and everything in it, Jews and gentiles, dark house of study and grim church alike.

While Ben Attar was wondering whether to join the inquisitive rabbi on his walk through the town, which was now steeped in a milky light, or to go and demand that he be given back his two wives, who at the end of the women's prayers (which were shorter than the men's) had been taken back to their hosts' homes, a pair of armed, mail-clad horsemen entered the synagogue, holding the inventory sent by the customs officer of Verdun. These men had been given the task of overseeing the distribution of goods not only to the descendants of the Christ-killers but, according to a new and generous interpretation of the ducal authorities, also to those who revered the Christ. The two wagons, which were standing outside the synagogue with empty shafts, were soon cleared not only of the bags and bolts, reduced and multiplied by the first wife's resourcefulness, but of the rest of the travelers' personal effects, which had also been changed into gifts by the generous order. So on this festive night the local folk seasoned their pork chops and their wolf stew with new spices from the desert, poured olive oil from Granada on their salad, and decorated the walls of their homes with brightly colored strips of silk embroidered with threads of gold torn from the robes of Ben Attar's wives, while ragged urchins in the church square unpicked the Ishmaelite sailors' big sandals to make a long rope. It was just as well that the Jews of Worms hastened to compensate the distressed litigants with matching gifts, and instead of the bright robes that had been torn to shreds by the excited Christians they dressed them all, Jews and Ishmaelites alike, in dark robes tied with shiny black belts with fringed tassels, and put pointed hats on their heads, so that it was not easy to distinguish them from the local Jews, who would soon scan the skies in search of the new moon, which was believed to draw with a golden thread not only a new month but a new year.

But before the fine crescent appeared at the twilight hour, threading its way rapidly through the dark tatters of cloud, and a satisfied sigh arose at this confirmation that the calendar from the hills of Jerusalem was still operating so accurately, they honored the rabbi's wish to stroll around their town and patiently replied to his questions. The sages, who as they walked had accustomed themselves to his unfamiliar, difficult way of uttering Hebrew from the depths of his throat, invited him to a chamber in the synagogue where there was a chest stuffed with obsolete texts and broken remains of twisted yellowing rams' horns, to hear him deliver a little homily on the subject of the sanctity of the coming day so that they could make an assessment of the intellectual acumen of the southern visitor, of which Master Levitas had given them prior warning.

Elbaz hesitated at first between a wish to lull his adversaries' concern about the danger he represented and a desire to make them aware of the pitfalls of the battlefield. He started with some trite generalities about the binding of Isaac, but he allowed himself to expatiate on the shape of the small gray horns of the original and authentic ram of the Land of Israel, which was offered up in place of the beloved son who was not indeed an only son. As though with the intention of warming the hearts of the local Jews toward the Ishmaelites who had come with them, he addressed to his curious hearers a few kind sentences about Abraham's elder son, who had been cast out thirsty behind a bush in the desert of the Beautiful Land, where all of Abraham's descendants were destined to meet on the day of final redemption, whether they wished it or not. And the rabbi contented himself with this little sermon, after noting that what he had said about a messianic meeting with Ishmaelites in a desert land had surprised his hearers greatly.

But there was no time to explore the subject further, for the festive service was close at hand and they needed to hasten to prepare the body so that it might not disturb the soul during the prayers. One of the scholars who had listened to the short homily, however, could not find any rest, and would not leave the Andalusian alone, for he was eager to hear more about the shape of the small gray horns of the original ram of the Land of Israel, whose slaughtered cries the Jews were said to reproduce each year at this new moon of the month of Tishri. This red-haired scholar had a special reason, for he was the one who would lead the prayers and blow the ram's horn, so it was no wonder that his imagination was captured by the story of a simple small dark ram's horn that trumpeted forth sound without unnecessary twists and spirals.

The thought suddenly flashed through Elbaz's mind that this curious man might be a suitable arbiter in the matter of double matrimony. He resolved to pay special attention to him. He withdrew into a corner with him, and took from the innermost pocket of his baggy trousers a small black ram's horn that he had borrowed at the last moment, before boarding the ship, from the synagogue in the port of Cadiz, for according to the original calculation of the journey, without the overland extension, they should have heard the sound of the horn on their way home, somewhere on the ocean between Brittany and the Bay of Biscay. While the astonished scholar of Worms was feeling the simple Andalusian horn, which to judge by its fineness had evidently been taken from a mountain goat rather than a ram, Rabbi Elbaz attempted unobtrusively to take stock of the man's character with a few test questions well directed to his purpose, which he was keeping hidden until he had had an opportunity to consult Ben Attar.

But where was Ben Attar? And where were the other travelers? Jews and Ishmaelites, white, dark, and black-skinned, had been swallowed up by the wooden houses of the Jews of Worms who now emerged into the drizzle of eventide to assemble in the synagogue, which, even though it was still under construction and the whole western wall was missing, seemed to be as dear to the worshippers as though it were whole. They pressed together in the united brotherhood of a proud congregation, dressed in festive clothing and raising their eyes in satisfaction to three large oblong windows, above which were three circular lights like portholes, glazed with thick yellow panes, which, since they were not adorned with any image, of angel or man or even floral designs, shone into the darkness of the synagogue with the charm of three bright suns.

Master Levitas insisted that the Andalusian rabbi and his son, who had emerged from somewhere or other with a pointed hat on his head, should be seated against the eastern wall, beside the holy ark, so that the rabbi could be impressed by the excellence of the congregation standing facing him—a congregation that would scrub away at its sins on Thursday and Friday, continue to afflict itself on the Sabbath of Repentance, and then mark a slight pause on Saturday evening to ascend the judgment throne and to decide between north and south, between Abulafia and Ben Attar. These two were now standing side by side, swallowed up in the worshipping congregation, shivering slightly in the cold damp wind that in Europe accompanied the evening prayer of the New Year, whereas in Tangier, their birthplace, they both recalled sorrowfully, it was always said under a warm, star-studded sky.

Ben Attar customarily spent the first night of New Year with his first wife and the second night with his second wife. His first wife prepared the meal before the Day of Atonement, and he broke his fast afterward with the second wife. He built the tabernacle first at the first wife's house, and he carried the small scroll to the second wife's house at the Rejoicing of the Law. And so for the other festivals of the year, whose naturally double nature invited and demanded at least two wives, always fresh to help the man, who might otherwise be overwhelmed by the many complex regulations of his faith.

But this evening, in the dark synagogue on the bank of the Rhine, where the service followed the abbreviated rite of Amram Gaon rather than the long Babylonian rite of Saadia Gaon, the worshippers had time to embellish the chants and repeat their favorite passages, and since they all knew the prayers by heart, they were not too troubled by the lack of light. Ben Attar stood holding a parchment text that he would have had difficulty reading even in daylight, let alone in the dark, wondering at himself. So many hours had passed since he had been separated from his wives, and yet he was in no hurry to be reunited with them, and had not even asked after them. Was this only because he was confident that their hosts would be treating them with generosity and respect, as he himself was treated, or because for the first time in his life he felt relieved that they were not with him, as though his soul were sated with them?

In truth, throughout the many days that had elapsed since he had set out, not a day had passed without his two wives' being within reach or at least within eyeshot. Surely the whole strength and purpose of dual love was that it forced each of the parties to be separated occasionally from their partner, so that they could digest thoroughly what they had been given before asking for more. But in the darkness of the swaying wagon driven by Abd el-Shafi's tattooed arms, on the long road from the Seine to the Rhine, when he saw his two wives lying wearily side by side or occasionally, when the going was particularly hard, in each other's arms, he had begun to fear that in the fantasy of his desire he would be liable henceforth to fuse them into a single woman, and so it was fitting now that he did not see them and did not even know where they were. Were they on the other side of the wall, in the little women's synagogue? Or caged among curtains in the wooden houses raised on stilts, listening through the window to the chorus of frogs croaking across the wide marshes of the Rhineland?

It was a rich and insistent croaking that the leader of the prayers tried to drown out with his loud yet steady voice, steering the prayers confidently, without yielding to the whims of worshippers who tried to slow or speed the pace, to skip or repeat some passages. Rabbi Elbaz was confirmed in his belief that one who was accustomed to leading the prayers of such a pious and learned congregation every day with such confidence would also make a single and final arbite in the appeal that was ahead of them, even if he was not considered the greatest and best of scholars. The rabbi from Seville already felt as close to his chosen one, with his yellow beard and his bloodshot eyes, as though he had discovered a twin soul. But at the conclusion of the prayers, when Master Levitas hurried over to the rabbi and Ben Attar with an expectant smile on his face, hoping to hear from the two southern litigants some words of praise and admiration for the spiritual excellence of his native town, the rabbi cautiously refrained from revealing to his adversary even by a hint his intention of demanding a single judge instead of a panel of several judges. For the moment he contented himself with a cautious question about the character of the prayer leader, who was folding his prayer shawl slowly and reluctantly, as though he were sorry the prayers were over.

It transpired that Master Levitas, who knew and remembered everybody, could tell him all about this man, Joseph by name, who although he was also called son of Kalonymos, like the majority of the folk of Worms who had come from Italy at the bidding of Emperor Otto, was only partly a Kalonymid, on his father's side; on his mother's he was descended from an ancient local family that had belonged, according to legend, to the legions of Julius Caesar, who had fought here more than a thousand years ago. He was a widower, but unlike Rabbi Elbaz he had not remained single but had speedily married a widowed kinswoman, so that they could raise their orphaned children together. Perhaps it was because there were so many children in his home that Master Levitas had chosen to house the youngest traveler with him.

Now the rabbi understood why his son had not taken his eyes off the man, and why he had tipped his little black hat at the precise angle favored by his host. He suspected that the invisible hand of a good angel was touching him kindly, and his mind hastened to confirm the choice it had made. It would be good to plead his cause before a judge who, like Ben Attar, had had experience of two wives, even if not simultaneously. For a moment Elbaz wanted to join his boy as a guest in the house of his chosen one, in order to make a close study of the weak points of his mind and his character, but he gave up the idea, fearing that excessive propinquity might arouse suspicion. He decided, though, to offer this Joseph his little black horn during the service next morning, so that he might try to make the softer and darker southern sound on it.

Before the North Africans went their separate ways to eat the festive meal with their respective hosts, the rabbi hurried to share his new thought with Ben Attar and seek his permission to place the case in the hands of a single carefully selected judge. The merchant, who had so far been obliged to bestow retrospective approval on the decisions the rabbi had imposed on him, was surprised at the suggestion, but after some thought he gave his consent, because he too had realized that the unruly simplicity of the makeshift court near Paris would be replaced here by the stern, united knowledge of a community that was sure of itself. Thus it would be better to be judged here by a single, humane person who was accustomed to stand and pray with the congregation behind him rather than in front of him.

Then Rabbi Elbaz approached Master Levitas, whose eyes were searching the women coming out of their synagogue, looking for his sister, and gave him a first indication, not in his own name but in that of Ben Attar, the party to the suit, of their wish for the case to be heard in Worms by a rather restricted panel of judges, in fact by a single arbiter. At this the other, who had learned from his bitter experience in Villa Le Juif the same lesson as the rabbi—namely, that whoever selects the judges controls the verdict—pricked up his ears shrewdly, and apprehensively he asked the Andalusian rabbi, who looked just like a local Jew now with his black cloak and pointed hat, *A single arbiter? Why? Surely we could benefit from the combined wisdom of several judges?*

But Rabbi Elbaz held his ground. On the contrary, it was precisely because this community contained such an abundance of scholars, who learned from each other but also scrutinized and threatened each other, that they should prefer the option of a single judge, who would take full responsibility for the final separation between uncle and nephew, south and north. But who would the single judge be? Master Levitas's fears increased, though he was heartened by the gentle presence of his sister, who now, after the evening service, appeared charming and radiant among the townsfolk. Surely the boy was not to be charged with selecting him, as at Villa Le Juif? It turned out that the rabbi was demanding not any kind of ballot but merely the straightforward right to choose, which by any standards of justice and ethics should belong to the complainants, who, confident of the rightness of their cause, had risked life and limb upon the stormy ocean to come and make their protest. Even when they had won their case, they had generously agreed to submit to a further hearing, in the depths of the forests and swamps of Ashkenaz, in a wretched and benighted town full of sharp-witted, learned kinsfolk of the other side. Honesty and propriety decreed that they should be granted the right to choose the individual who would pronounce the final verdict.

In the face of such powerful arguments Master Levitas had nothing to reply, although he wondered whether his elder sister, whose bright eyes held a fleeting smile, could fathom the purpose of the Andalusian rabbi, who had set forth his case so enthusiastically in the holy tongue. Over the festive dinner in the home of his host, the elderly rabbi of Worms, the rabbi from Seville saw that the right of choice that he had arrogated was already granted, and all that remained was to investigate the chosen candidate. Consequently, between discussions of a scriptural character, he attempted to extract some further information about Joseph son of Kalonymos. When he heard, by the by, that many years previously Joseph's parents had wished to betroth him to Esther-Minna Levitas, but that her parents, being very particular, had preferred a whole Kalonymos to half a Kalonymos, his spirit trembled, as though it were being not merely touched but caressed by the good angel. It was possible that two different qualifications might converge, and that justice might be reinforced by a wish to be avenged for the affront of past rejection.

Neither did Rabbi Elbaz disclose the next day, at the morning prayer, the secret of the single judge—not even to his employer, the merchant, who stood stiffly among the worshippers at the side of his beloved nephew, the curly-haired conditional partner, whose musical talents enabled him to join even in the most complex chants of the Rhenish congregation, so that the leader, Joseph son of Kalonymos, feared for a moment that he had a rival. But when they took out the scroll of the holy law and laid it upon the reading desk, and Joseph son of Kalonymos blew upon a massive twisted yellow ram's horn the threefold blasts prescribed by tradition, a vague terror fell upon Rabbi Elbaz. It was as if the raucous, insistent sound of the German ram's horn contained a new and urgent warning for him. However, he composed himself, particularly after the scroll was replaced in the holy ark and

Joseph son of Kalonymos turned to him and invited him to grace the service by blowing the little black southern horn that the rabbi had managed to conceal from the eyes of the customs officer in Verdun.

And so, slowly, with restrained excitement, the first day of the festival passed, and after it, in leisurely fashion, amid persistent drizzle, the second day too, whose afternoon service was followed immediately by the evening prayers for the Sabbath of Repentance. And still Ben Attar did not know, and may not even have wanted to know, in which of those black-beamed wooden houses raised on stilts his two wives were secreted. The gray autumn skies of the German town seemed to have soaked up the North African merchant's constant dual love and filled his soul with a tangled despair that was apt to cloud his mind, so that for a moment there was a fear that he might leave everything behind him, take the strongest and best of the four horses that had faithfully brought them here from the Seine from the stable behind the synagogue, and gallop back alone to Africa.

If at the outset Ben Attar had wanted to prove, as in Paris, his quiet ability to realize fully and in perfect equality his rights and duties as a husband, he had quickly understood, perhaps because of the way the local Jews had managed to isolate him from his wives right from the start, that it was not from the man that they were expecting proof here, but from the wives. But proof of what? he wondered again as he noticed his wives reappearing in the women's synagogue on the two days of the festival. Was it religious piety, he mused in irritation, or was there also an intention of tarnishing their souls with fear and perhaps even guilt, as though the great love that had delighted and continued to delight them both had been illicit from the outset?

From the moment that Master Levitas had placed before the community Rabbi Elbaz's firm request to appeal to the decision of a single judge, the spirit of the Jews of Worms had flagged, since for several days they had been entertained by the thought that they would dispel the tedium of the ending of the festival and the Sabbath with a pleasant discussion of the fate of three women. But when they were assembled in their synagogue after the closing ceremony of the Sabbath, not to sit in judgment as a community but merely to be passive spectators, waiting to see which scholar the busy little rabbi would choose, they still did not imagine that he would place a further constraint upon them and adamantly insist that the hearing should be held behind closed doors, so that the judge who dared to sever north and south forever would not be supported by the presence of a fanatical assembly.

Thus they were reluctantly made to put up a double curtain in the synagogue, to separate the public from the space reserved for the court. But for all his stubbornness, the rabbi could not prevent them from improving the light by increasing the number of candles and lanterns, so they would not miss seeing the litigants as they were summoned into the small, hidden space next to the holy ark. True, it was not as it had been in the large space of the winery in Villa Le Juif, where the torchlight had cast mysterious, enlarged shadows into the corners of the hall so that the judges, sitting on wine casks, could imagine that they were floating in the depths of hell, where all mortals, men and women alike, are split into their dual human nature; here in Worms the Andalusian rabbi wanted to define a small, well-lit space, where the parties to the dispute and the witnesses would be pressed close together with each other and with the arbiter, whom it was now time to detach from the assembly of Jews filling the synagogue.

Even though the candidate, Joseph son of Kalonymos, was sitting apparently absent-mindedly in a corner, half listening to the chatter all around him, it seemed that he had had a premonition that he would be chosen, not so much from the readiness with which he handed his candle to the man sitting next to him or the alacrity with which he rose to his feet, but rather because he had remained wrapped in his prayer shawl after the evening prayers. He may have wished to excuse himself to his friends for being chosen, as though the judge's seat that he was being summoned to occupy were merely the natural extension of the lectern where he regularly officiated, as an ordinary elderly man, undistinguished from his fellow men and sounding the ram's horn as occasion required.

A stir of disappointment ran through the faithful public as they divined how cleverly the Andalusian visitor had chosen from among them a lenient judge, who, although his strength was in his voice rather than in his intellect or his book-learning, could not be disqualified, for who could claim that one who was deemed fit to represent the congregation by leading the prayers was not fit to represent it by serving as arbiter? But there were a few men, among whom naturally was Master Levitas, who knew and remembered that the man who had been selected was not only a widower who had had experience of two wives, albeit consecutively and not concurrently, but had also been a candidate for betrothal to Mistress Esther-Minna, and who suspected that what had been denied him in the past might well stir his antagonism in the present.

Master Levitas darted behind the curtain, where Rabbi Elbaz was already escorting an embarrassed Joseph son of Kalonymos to his seat and standing Ben Attar and Abulafia facing each other, wishing to exploit the momentum of the amazement he was causing and to open the proceedings at once, apparently counting on a lightning hearing that would be conducted in the holy tongue alone. But Levitas, grasping with alarm the sudden deterioration of the situation and the possibility that because of his own and his sister's excessive self-confidence the sly rabbi from Seville might succeed in securing a verdict against them again, in the heart of their native country, burst into a frantic discourse in the harsh local German dialect, leavened with flattened Hebrew words. Whether he did this to save precious time or to foil the rabbi's understanding, he addressed himself boldly to the judge, who all the time kept anxiously tightening his grayish prayer shawl around his shoulders.

The whole of Master Levitas's impassioned speech concerned only one demand: that his sister, Mistress Abulafia, should be brought into the hearing, for she counted herself as a party to the case no less than her husband. Although the suggestion made Joseph son of Kalonymos's heart quake, he did not grant his consent before turning to the foreign rabbi who had chosen him, questioning whether the wife could be brought in, even though she was apparently not a member of the partnership herself. For a moment the rabbi seemed taken aback, but even though he saw no way of opposing the request, he still refused to make a concession for nothing, and so, without knowing why or wherefore, he suddenly sought to balance her presence with that of the three Ishmaelite sailors or wagoners, for it was thanks to their toil no less than to divine favor that the parties had arrived here safely.

The good people of Worms rose excitedly to their feet at the sight of the three Ishmaelites, summoned to the synagogue from their several lodgings, being taken one by one behind the curtain. While the whole congregation devoutly muttered the time-honored blessing to the Creator of all manner of folk on seeing the young black man passing through their midst, Mistress Esther-Minna slipped in by a side entrance. Master Levitas, after a momentary pang of remorse for allowing Rabbi Elbaz to fill the small space of the courtroom with these gentile servants, still believed that he had behaved correctly, for it was a long time since his older sister had seemed so comely and attractive as on that Saturday evening, standing beside the holy ark with her hair bound up in a fine silken snood. Not only had sleeping in her former marital bed soothed away the effects of the hardships of the journey and her anger at the southern visitors who had burst into her life, but the pleasant prayers that had filled the dank marshy air of her native land had smoothed her wrinkles and put life back into her pink cheeks and her blue eyes, which now smiled amiably into the blushing face of the arbiter, who remembered only too well how a score of years earlier her dear departed parents had forbidden her betrothal to him.

Again, as in the dark hall of the winery, Master Levitas served as master of ceremonies. First he invited the principal complainant, Ben Attar, to set forth the complaint that had traveled so stubbornly from the furthermost Maghreb. Since on this occasion the defendant could not serve as interpreter, since Abulafia's business trips had never brought him this far and so he had never learned the local language, Master Levitas had no choice but to concede that Rabbi Elbaz should translate from the language of the Ishmaelites to that of the Israelites and back again, aware though he was that the quick-witted rabbi would exploit every opportunity to reinforce and adorn the words as they made their roundabout way from language to language.

But when Ben Attar opened his mouth and began to utter his first words, those present were astounded, and even the interpreter-rabbi was surprised. Instead of the jeremiad that they had already heard in the winery near Paris, about the pain of a Muslim partner, and the sadness of lost merchandise, and the treachery of a rejecting partner, who had sought the pretext of the sages in order to augment his own profit, the stubborn merchant suddenly stepped backward, as though the twelve days of additional overland journey from the Seine to the Rhine had never taken place. And as though the second hearing were merely a direct continuation of the first one, he now sought to address the harsh and piercing argument put forward by Mistress Esther-Minna, his adversary's real wife, in the dark hall of the winery at Villa Le Juif—that it was not the shame and disgrace of the bewitchment and curse issuing from her womb that had made Abulafia's wretched first wife bind her hands and feet with colored ribbons to help the waves of the sea do their work, but only the veiled threat of taking a second wife, the selfsame threat that was now seeking the full approbation of a holy congregation.

Despite his lack of experience, Joseph son of Kalonymos managed to understand, by means of the circuitous and excitable yet detailed translation of Rabbi Elbaz, that this swarthy, sturdy complainant, the partner who had come from the end of the world, wished to reopen the whole case from the start. At the price of revealing an old secret, he would defend not only his own dual marriage but dual marriage in general, which had come under assault from the new wife, who, arrogantly and uninvited, had belatedly adopted the cause of a wife who had taken her own life, with the aim of avenging her. To general surprise, it suddenly became clear that Ben Attar's decision to agree to the journey to confront a further tribunal in the Rhineland had been the result not of Abulafia's desperation nor of the rabbi's desire to repeat his wonderful speech, but first and foremost of a desire to refute, in the midst of her native town, the slander that the new wife had uttered before the gathering in the winery at Villa Le Juif.

For who better than Ben Attar could testify to the sinful woman's true motive? On the same bitter day on which Abulafia's poor first wife had come to Ben Attar's shop to entrust her baby to Abulafia so that she might be free to search the stalls of the nomads for an amulet that would bring her blessing or comfort, she had not, as all believed, gone straight from the gate of the city to the seashore with the elephant's-tail fishhook she had bought, but had first returned to Ben Attar's shop to take her baby away. On discovering that even during such a short absence, Abulafia, the father, had been unable to remain close to his daughter and had left her alone among the bolts of cloth on the pretext that he was required at Ben Ghiyyat's for afternoon prayers, she was assailed with such profound despair and melancholy that, unable to restrain herself, she had drawn her veil off her face to mop up her tears before Ben Attar, the beloved uncle. Indeed, not only was that beautiful young woman not afraid that her husband might take a second wife, but on the contrary, in those last hours she had even offered herself as a second wife for Ben Attar, to make it easier for her husband to part from her for fear that she would give birth to another bewitched demon. But Ben Attar knew only too well that Abulafia's love would never leave her, which was why he gently declined her strange suggestion. To set her mind at rest, he offered to keep an eye on her accursed daughter until her husband returned from prayers, while she returned to the market and tried to find a better amulet. How could he have imagined that instead of going to the market she would go straight to the city gate, to seek solace among the waves of the sea?

The North African's last words fell to the floor of the synagogue and turned into little snakes. Not only the woman who had issued the repudiation but Master Levitas, her wise brother, now took a step back. Only Abulafia, who was now, in the depths of the marshy Rhineland, hearing for the first time in his life the terrible story of his previous wife, remained rooted to the spot as though paralyzed, and his lips turned very pale. The confused arbiter, not knowing if he had understood correctly what had been said, was only too aware of the new silence that the complainant had occasioned in the small law court. He rose helplessly from his seat and tried to approach the curtain, as though to ascertain the opinion of the public, but Rabbi Elbaz frustrated his intentions and gently yet respectfully hurried to restore the confidence of the bewildered man, whom he still considered the right man for the job.

At the little rabbi's poetic touch, Joseph son of Kalonymos did indeed reconsider and resumed his seat, and his reddish eyes, which had previously been too timid to look at the woman who had been refused him, now watched her distress in the face of the silence that had overcome her husband. Rabbi Elbaz resolved to exploit this silence at once to move the judge's mind in a different and original direction. Even though he felt a strong urge to repeat the wonderful speech he had made in the winery, in the presence of that thick-bearded courier from the Land of Israel, whose absence now pained him acutely, he knew that the prayer house of a devout congregation might not be the right place to argue in the name of an obdurate man who could sustain the image of a second wife in such a way that no edict of the sages could eradicate it. Therefore he changed tack and set his sails for a distant destination, to reach which he now brought in the two Ishmaelites and the black pagan, who had been standing silently and uncomprehendingly before the shrine of the Jews' god.

If there were Jews, the rabbi mused to himself, as firm in their faith as those who were silently standing behind the curtain, who were so strong-minded that they could banish from their imagination the very tips of a second wife's toes, this was apparently so only because they were eager to give a more honored place to the image of the dear redeemer, the king messiah, who did not need a millennium to come to his Jews, but only greater respect for the commandments. *See you,* the rabbi began excitedly, developing a new thought, apparently addressed to the startled judge who was sitting facing him but plainly, by the loudness of his voice, intended to be heard beyond the curtain, by a gathering that was holding its breath to catch every syllable, *my lords and masters, members of this holy congregation, soon we shall all return to the Beloved Land, to the land flowing with milk and honey, which has neither bubbling marshes nor croaking frogs but pure streams of water and the song of nightingales. There in the last days which are nigh shall be gathered in not only distant Jews like yourselves but also, as is written and promised, all the inhabitants of the world, gentiles thirsty for the word of God. And first of all, naturally, the nearest neighbors, Ishmaelites and Mohammedans, who to find favor with the elect, the redeemed Jews, who cherish one woman above all others as though she were God himself, are likely to hurry and cast forth from their homes their redundant second, third, and fourth wives.*

At this point the rabbi turned to the three sturdy seafarers, whose appearance had not been improved by the black cloaks and pointed hats in which the local Jews had dressed them; their spirit had not been quelled, and they merely seemed wilder. In a voice that contained a hint of protest, he asked, and immediately answered his own question, *Is it fitting that we should tarnish the bliss of redemption with the sorrow, pain, and offense of so many Ishmaelite women, who will suddenly be inconsolably alone? How can we persuade good neighbors who long to share in our redemption not to go berserk or change their nature, if we do not show them that there are pure, good Jews who have*

200

two wives, whose orthodoxy and righteousness do not depend on the thoughts of others?

Then the reddish curtain stirred slightly, and the Elbaz child, who had heard his father's loud voice from afar, cautiously drew back a flap and silently entered the space of the court and stood between his host, Joseph son of Kalonymos, and his sire, as though he had come to reconcile them with a compromise. Rabbi Elbaz stared in astonishment at his son, who had now tipped his little pointed hat at a new and rakish angle. And he looked back at the arbiter, who was smiling slightly at the sight of the boy. Well, Rabbi Elbaz said to himself hopefully, maybe this is just the moment to stop talking, so as to draw from the heart of this German judge's smile a civilized, tolerant verdict that will allow the natural partnership to continue by virtue both of former brotherhood and of future redemption.

In truth, the slight smile that appeared on Joseph son of Kalonymos's face at the sight of the rabbi's son testified clearly that his nervousness and distress were being soothed and that the new role that had been placed upon him not only no longer frightened him but even pleased him. It was obvious that he understood that if Abulafia persisted in his silence and did not rise to defend himself, he himself would be compelled to pronounce, despite his own inclinations, a simple, rational decision that could not be different from the one reached in the winery near Paris. A new course was indicated. He instructed Master Levitas to fetch Ben Attar's two wives, the first and the second, to be examined privily as witnesses.

PART THREE

The Journey Back, or the Only Wife

1.

In the beginning of the winter of that year, in the middle of the month of Shevat, a few days after the year of the millennium embraced Christian Europe in its reality, Joseph son of Kalonymos fell ill, and a short while later he departed this life. His wife, who was now left a widow for the second time, repeated to all those who came to comfort her, with a persistence that was almost disrespectful to the deceased, that evil had entered her home at the moment of weak-mindedness when her husband allowed himself to be persuaded by that strange foreign rabbi to serve as arbiter in the accursed case of dual matrimony that came up from the south. From that day he had definitely lost his peace of mind and his spirit was disturbed, and even long weeks after the parties to the dispute had left Worms and the land of Ashkenaz he still walked around looking as though he had been struck by a wondrous nightmare, until heaven took pity on his soul.

Did he regret his decision? Or did he consider that he had gone too far to please the woman he had been denied, whose appearance before him as a suitor at the mercy of his kindness had aroused such conflicting emotions in his breast that he had been unable to control them? His despairing widow was unable to answer such questions, for he had never told her, or indeed others, what had really happened during his private examination of the two North African women, and in fact he himself may not have been certain until the day of his death that he had understood rightly what he believed they had said.

Indeed, after Rabbi Elbaz, supported on either side by burly Ishmaelites and a black slave, had tried to discourage Joseph son of Kalonymos with a gloomy vision of a messianic age packed with abandoned, dejected Ishmaelite women, the alarmed judge had tried once more to communicate with the assembly on the other side of the curtain, so as to gauge its reaction and know what to do and say. But when the rabbi's son entered in his new cloak and hat, looking, despite his dark complexion, like a long-established child of Worms, Joseph son of Kalonymos suddenly understood that he had no need to seek beyond the curtain but that he could draw strength from deep inside himself. From that moment his self-confidence increased, to the point that his curiosity to see the two wives with his own eyes became a real, urgent duty.

A duty first and foremost toward Mistress Esther-Minna, who stood before him radiating the beauty of her anxiety. Although he did not know whether it was her parents alone or she too who had rejected the match with him, he recognized that he did not have the right to brush aside her distress, which had been considerably aggravated by the continued silence of her young husband, who may have tried to circumvent the legal ruling by an elusive deception. Therefore, as an impartial judge, he felt it was his duty to offer an opportunity to the repudiating wife who had returned to seek justice in her native town. He did not mean to favor the love of his youth, but neither did he wish to be a stranger to the beautiful, delicate face, whose transparent pallor crushed his heart. At last he asked Master Levitas to take her outside with all the others and bring the merchant's two wives into the little courtroom, heated by the warmth of the large candles, to be questioned as witnesses.

It appeared that this was the moment the women of the community of Worms had been waiting for, for in an instant the two wives, who had been held in strange seclusion ever since they had emerged from the wagon in a state of near-collapse, had finally been fetched from two different streets and brought to the synagogue. Ben Attar's heart was embittered at the sight of his wives, wrapped in coarse black cloaks, their faces uncovered and bare of kohl, jewelry, or any adornment, as though the local women had deliberately decided to remove the enchanting decoration that distinguished one wife from the other and to expose them as far as possible in their stark femininity, so as to mock their duality. But as the distraught Ben Attar hastened toward his wives, the women of Worms boldly blocked his way and did not let him approach, as though his purpose were to subvert their testimony rather than simply to comfort them.

Without a single word having been said to them, the pair were led behind the curtain into the cleared courtroom and were stood side by side before the judge, who was shaken by such excitement at this double vision standing exposed before him that it was all he could do to prevent himself from fleeing for his life into the bosom of the wise congregation, which even behind the drawn curtain continued to follow all his movements. Since he did not know whether the prohibition of intimacy between a man and another's wife applied also in the case of a pair of wives, he told the Elbaz child to remain, with the additional purpose of serving as interpreter.

Although it was hard to conduct a private interrogation without a common language, Joseph son of Kalonymos was determined to dispense with the overabundant services of Elbaz, fearing that the clever rabbi would distort and improve the women's replies and the accuracy of the investigation would be undermined. He preferred to make do with the little unskilled interpreter, who would translate simple questions and answers faithfully, even if not precisely or completely, from the Hebrew of the prayerbook to the Arabic of the marketplace and back again. Moreover, it might be supposed that after their long journey in each other's company, the women and the child had got to know each other, and he would be able, by means of gestures and expressions, to exact from the frightened pair who stood all alone before him the incriminating testimony that would compensate for Abulafia's obstinate silence.

Even though the prayer leader of the synagogue of Worms had never before interrogated witnesses, he had learned from Tractate Sanhedrin and from the words of others that everyone must first be warmed and softened, so that the outer husk may be easily peeled off and the pale kernel exposed. Therefore, in warmly conciliatory tones, he extracted from each of the women her name, and then proceeded to ask for the names of their fathers and mothers, their brothers and sisters, their sons and daughters, their uncles and aunts. He made no distinction between the names of the living and of the dead, or between those of near and remote kin. Soon the courtroom in Worms was filled with a small Mediterranean congregation, which mirrored and contrasted with the German congregation audible behind the curtain.

Not content with names alone, Joseph son of Kalonymos wished to know the age of each one named, and this was harder, because the accurate reckoning of years is always shrouded in mist, and the long voyage followed by the considerable overland journey had only served to thicken it. Indeed, so confused had the time of the one wife become with that of the other that it might have seemed at one point as though the first wife were younger than the second, had not the little interpreter succeeded in putting the record straight and enabled the curious northern judge to enter, by means of a fragile bridge of half-forgotten Hebrew and the gesticulations of an excited child, into the interiors of two separate houses on the African coast of the Mediterranean Sea, with their pots and pans, beds and bedclothes, and to seek beyond the scent of flowers, the exuberant spices, and the throngs of children the secret of the shame and reproach of enforced duplication.

To this end the arbiter wished to remove the younger wife a little way and to remain alone with the first wife, who seemed to him in his innocence and inexperience as the weak link from which he could extract a complaint of sorrow, pain, and shame, so that the arbitration that was shortly to be delivered would not only follow as the natural outcome of what had been said, but might even appear as a genuine act of rescue. However, he suddenly hesitated to discharge the second wife and remain alone with the wrath of the first, whose age, he now knew, was that of his own wife, and her height, he now saw, the same as hers. This hesitation resulted not only from his uncertainty about whether the presence of a boy who had not yet reached the age of legal majority was enough to satisfy the prohibition on intimacy, but more particularly from fear that out of the anguish in the older woman's soul a secret or open curse of death might burst forth, directed against her tall, dark, slim adversary, with her delicate, handsome face and her amber-colored eyes that occasionally flashed with an emerald-green spark.

It seemed as though Joseph son of Kalonymos had also caught the infection of the duality that had come up from the south to defend itself, since he was now unable to muster the inner resolve to remove the second wife but sought only to put a little space between her and the first wife. Since he could not hide her away inside the holy ark, he told her, with the help of the gestures of the little interpreter, to squeeze herself into a narrow recess between the holy ark and the east wall, and asked her to cover her head with an old curtain that he had discovered in a drawer, so that she should not hear what her opponent was saying against her.

But to his great surprise, Joseph son of Kalonymos did not manage to extract a single word of calumny against the second wife from the first, even though the latter knew that the other could not hear her. On the contrary, if previously the first wife's love for the second wife had been distant, because she had not known her, after traveling with her for sixty days on board an old guardship and for a further twelve days on a cramped wagon, the first wife's soul had become so closely bound to the other's that this duality, which had journeyed to the heart of Europe to contend for its life, would return home so much stronger and more united that it would no longer need two separate homes but could make do with a single house. *A single house?* The arbiter was alarmed, for he immediately thought of his own home, a wooden house with bales of straw piled on its roof and black piles supporting its rickety frame, with an additional fair-haired wife walking from room to room, receiving what she had been denied a score of years before.

From the noises coming from behind the curtain, the novice inquisitor could sense that his public was beginning to grow restive at his diligence. Any member of the community, even if he had been raised to unwonted and questionable prominence, was obliged by his nature and upbringing to exercise some self-restraint, and therefore the congregation, cut off from its holy ark, now hoped that this prayer leader and blower of rams' horns would not forget that his pleasant voice and knowledge of the order of service did not authorize his moderate intelligence to distract him from his duty.

This duty Joseph son of Kalonymos undoubtedly remembered while he sought to replace one woman with the other so as to conclude the examination of the witnesses. He was surprised to discover that to duty was added enjoyment, as though these two strange Jewish women who had been entrusted to him this evening had been joined by other women who had appeared in his life, such as the comely woman who had brought this case and who now waited outside, beside her husband, or his own wife, who awaited him at home, not forgetting his departed first wife, buried so long ago in the clay of the small cemetery beside the Rhine. For a moment it seemed as though his flesh were invested not merely by a duality of wives but with a veritable multiplication of thereof. This was a dangerous moment. He gestured to the child to remove the ragged old curtain from the second wife's head. And despite his fear of the ban on intimacy, he overcame his shyness, banished the first wife beyond the large curtain, and bid the second wife approach, in the hope that this one might offer him at least a grain of adverse testimony and so enable his conscience to pronounce judgment in the spirit of the sages of Ashkenaz.

Indeed, now there was some hope. Unlike the first wife, who was constrained in her speech, carefully weighing each word, so she did not incriminate or besmirch the duality so beloved by her husband, the second wife let fly a spate of whispered Ishmaelite speech so long and rapid that the youthful translator was completely muddled and took hold of the holy ark as though to hide himself there. Gradually it emerged that in the lowest part of the ship there had been secretly hatched, besides the fetus that had been growing in the young woman's belly, not some mere plea or complaint but a highly charged dream, which the northerner's first short opening question was enough to release in the form of a declaration that resounded in that narrow space as if it were the whole wide world.

Ever since this wife had shed her veil, she had understood, from the looks that were cast not only on her back now but on her face as well, that she was not alone, and that she had many partners to her dream. Although she had not been asked about it, she lost no time in recounting it to Joseph son of Kalonymos, who would soon be thrown into turmoil.

Just as the women of Worms had taken off her fine silken veil on the eve of the New Year, so she now permitted herself, at the end of the Sabbath of Penitence, to let fall from her shoulders the black cloak that the sanctimonious women had wrapped her in and stand slim and blushing before the arbiter in a colorful embroidered robe of fine cloth that had faded a little from being washed in seawater. From the jumble of Jewish Arabic that now poured from her small mouth, the astonishing truth gradually emerged that not only was she willing to be *subjected* to dual wedlock, she herself wished to *contract* a dual marriage. Having no complaint against the first wife, whose patience and kindness she had learned to appreciate during the long shared journey by sea and land, she was experiencing a mounting envy of a husband who had two wives to himself while they only had one husband between them.

Even though at this moment the inquisitive judge knew that his professional curiosity might have made him go too far, he still could not stop himself. And even if Joseph son of Kalonymos was not yet entirely convinced that his young interpreter—who was doing his best by means of frantic gestures and broken Hebrew, eked out by half-remembered roots and fragments of words from the prayerbook—was really translating correctly the words of the woman who was standing so boldly before him, he sensed, from the fierceness and bitterness echoing around the little court room, that it was not *duality* that the second wife perceived as a threat but *singularity*. Consequently he could not restrain his curiosity and was sufficiently carried away to put a strange question: *A second husband? Like whom, for example?* And while he was still regretting his unnecessary question, the young translator was already relaying the answer, whether on his own initiative or out of the heart of the Ishmaelite storm that was raging before him: *Like you, my lord, like you, for instance . . .*

This was a real arrow loosed against him, and it both pierced his soul with a strange desire and poisoned it with a new fear, as though it were only now that he understood, on his own account, the profound source and the true meaning of the prohibition that the whole community was attempting to transmit to him from behind the curtain: *Duplication inevitably leads to multiplication, and multiplication has no limits.* His whole body was trembling and his face paled at the thought that this woman might attempt to put her claim, outrageous yet correct according to its own logic, into effect, and divest herself also of her Mediterranean robe. Without wasting time on further reflection, he picked up the loose black cloak from the floor and gently but firmly placed it around the young woman's shoulders as though covering an invalid, before wrenching aside the curtain that divided him from his congregation.

As though the time had come for the standing prayer, the whole community rose to its feet. Already Rabbi Elbaz was hurrying toward Joseph son of Kalonymos, and after a slight hesitation he was joined by Ben Attar and by Master Levitas. Only Abulafia continued to stand where he was, his face blank, even though he could have no doubt that the moment of decision had come. The ruddy-faced judge asked the rabbi from Seville to lend him the little black ram's horn before he announced his verdict. Elbaz hesitated for an instant, as though sensing the approaching disaster, but he could not refuse one whom he himself had elevated to a position of distinction only a short while ago.

As though waking from sleep, the prayer leader took the dark Andalusian horn as it appeared from its hiding place in the folds of the rabbi's robes, and closing his eyes, he put it to his lips, as though to reinforce his coming pronouncement with a blast from heaven. He blew three southern notes, long and sadly tender, followed by a still small sound, and then, with closed eyes and with fear and trembling, he pronounced not merely repudiation against the southern partner but a ban and an interdict.

To make his meaning plainer, Joseph son of Kalonymos had recourse to two languages—first, to admonish and encourage his friends, the muddy local Teutonic tongue, mingled with a few flattened, lugubrious Hebrew words, and then the holy tongue itself, with a clarity that brooked no appeal. He sealed his pronouncement with a rapid sequence of short sharp notes on the ram's horn, which he then returned to its stunned owner. Only then was the pregnant silence broken by murmurs of approbation tinged with admiration for this modest prayer leader, who had dared to lead his flock to a distant but clear horizon. While a furious Rabbi Elbaz was explaining the verdict in rapidly whispered Arabic to the crestfallen merchant, Abulafia's head spun and he sank as though in a faint. As Mistress Esther-Minna cried for help, Master Levitas, true to the spirit of the new decree, carefully interposed himself between her and the outlawed uncle, not yet certain whether the interdict that had just been pronounced so decisively also embraced the two wives, who were now once more standing side by side.

Until one of the true scholars of the community could explore the full implications of this arbitration, from which traditionally no appeal was possible, the Jews of Worms preferred to segregate their banned guest speedily from the rest of the people. It seemed that someone with singular wisdom and foresight had already rented a small room for the vanquished disputant in the home of a gentile widow in a narrow street not far from the church. In the dark of night, by the light of a flaming torch and to the accompaniment of the chorus of frogs in the river, Ben Attar was conducted there together with the black slave, who was deemed by the community a suitable companion for a man under ban. But Rabbi Elbaz, the furious, desperate complainant, adamantly refused to abandon the owner of the ship that was to carry him home to Andalus and followed after him and climbed the rickety wooden steps at his heels, not only to bring him comfort and to seek advice but also to demonstrate publicly his utter contempt for the ban that had been pronounced here. Indeed, he even vindictively contemplated pronouncing a counterban of his own upon the whole community.

But in the little room belonging to the gray-haired, blue-eyed gentile woman, who offered the banned Jew no more than a bed and a crust, the rabbi felt that he owed his Moroccan employer, who had trusted him and brought him from Andalus to help him repair the broken partnership, a greater consolation than a public outburst of anger or wild visions of revenge. Although he could only guess what had happened during the private interrogation of the second wife in front of the holy ark behind the curtain, he felt he did have a real solution for the banned merchant, who was left with a ship full of merchandise in the heart of wild and desolate Europe—a solution that might be temporary but that would enable him, despite everything, to renew his partnership with his dear nephew, who had collapsed in a heap as if he were a young woman at the news of the interdict.

But would the little Andalusian rabbi, who was now groping in the thick darkness of a crooked Rhenish room with only three walls—one of which might still have a crucifix hanging on it—have the courage to speak out and explain the plan that he had thought up as a possible escape route even before he had persuaded Ben Attar to set out for a second legal confrontation on the Rhine? Tears of sorrow and compassion but also of secret longing stung Elbaz's eyes at the startling but generous thought that he himself might free the banned man from the double marriage that was his downfall, not only by releasing the second wife from her marriage vows but by wedding her himself and taking her into his home in Seville, so that she should not remain alone.

But while Rabbi Elbaz was floundering and longing for an opportunity to explain his new plan, Ben Attar asked him to hasten and demand from the Jews of Worms the return of his vanished wives, for it was his intention to bring them both to him, even in this tiny room in a gentile house. All the concern of the banned merchant was not for himself or his merchandise but only for his two wives, his only ones, lest they were assailed by anxiety that he might be thinking of betraying his dual love. So hard and stern was Ben Attar's voice as he commanded the startled and disappointed rabbi that the man of God felt that since he had failed in his mission, the North African Jew valued him no more highly than the black slave who was now removing his master's shoes.

2.

In the third watch the second wife thought she heard a faint blast on the ram's horn, and her heart sank in fear. While she was trying to compose herself in the unfamiliar, alien silence, there floated before her the bloodshot eyes of the arbiter, to whom she had weak-mindedly allowed herself to reveal the secrets of her heart. Again she tormented herself, not for anything she had said but for what she had not managed to say. Rabbi Elbaz, who earlier that night had had to contend for a long time with the excitable hostesses of the two southern women in order to gain their return to their banned husband, had tried to calm the young woman and console her over what she had said, some of which he had learned vaguely from his son, the little interpreter. But it had seemed to the second wife as though the rabbi's words of comfort had been spoken faintly and halfheartedly. Had he been secretly trying to bind her to him in a compact of guilt, in the knowledge that he too would be called to account not only for the failure of his apocalyptic speech but also for his mistaken choice of judge, a man who had disguised his weakness with an overhasty and cruel verdict? Or had he conceived some strange idea of encouraging the young woman with soothing words to continue to cling to the right of counterduality that she had demanded for herself, to see how far it might go?

One way or another, his words of comfort had only served to confuse her, and now, as she silently rose from the pallet that was all the Christian landlady could offer her unexpected guests, she hastily wrapped herself in the rough black cloak that the local women had given her and slunk past her husband, who had curled up in a fetal position between two large logs that he had rolled out from a corner.

Stepping over the first wife, who was sleeping as peacefully as a corpse, with her hands joined, facing a long, sharp-edged, sloping iron bar that supported the ceiling of the triangular cubicle, the second wife entered the other chamber. Wishing not only to escape the curse of the ban but to try to put right the wrong she had done by her rash words, she held her sandals in her hand and slipped noiselessly past the Christian landlady, who was spending the night in a large chair, covered by the pelt of a black bear, whose stuffed head hung on the wall beneath the figure of the Crucified One, who bore his sufferings even in the dead of night.

Although the old woman sensed the shadow flitting past her and momentarily opened an eye, she did not stir at the flight of the Jewess, who descended the creaking, swaying wooden steps toward the darkened narrow alleys of the sleeping town. The foreign woman was alert to the silence all around her and to the huge silhouette of the church, wrapped in a yellowish mist, and yet she clung resolutely to the aim she had set herself, to seek out among the little houses the home of the hosts who had cared for her so generously since she had come to Worms so that they could take her to the arbiter and she could plead with him to listen to what she had not managed to say, in the hope that he might retract the interdict that he had pronounced because of her. And despite the darkness and the marshy vapors, which made her lose her way in the narrow streets of the little town, she recognized the right door and promptly knocked upon it.

But nobody, either in that house or in those on either side, heard the second wife's light knocking, for the Jews of Worms were fast asleep, having found peace of mind after the days of turmoil, as though the interdict and the ban had swept from their hearts the wonderfully sinful new thoughts brought to their town by the southern disputants. And so the second wife, whose shouting had no effect either, had no choice but to grope her way to the synagogue itself, first to the modest little women's synagogue, where she knelt for a while after the manner of the Ishmaelites, who manifest total submission before making any request, and then hesitantly entering the men's prayer hall by the unfinished western wall, slipping between the empty rows, and finally pressing herself into the narrow recess between the holy ark and the eastern wall.

Was it possible that the North African woman's tormented heart had divined that the judge, Joseph son of Kalonymos, would also be unable to sleep in the coils of this night, and that he too, whether from an access of new strength or from a hint of remorse, would be unable to prevent himself from rising early and coming to his pulpit, either to prepare himself for the morning prayers of the Fast of Gedaliah or to join his body and soul to the place where three women had stood the previous night, waiting for the words to fall from his lips? Therefore, as he picked up the fallen red curtain and drew its corners together, piously pressing his lips to the golden letters embroidered on the faded velvet, then folded it carefully away and put it back in its proper place, no cry of alarm escaped from his mouth when yesterday's witness suddenly appeared before him. It was as though it were self-evident that after such a stern verdict those who lost would come back to plead, like this young foreign woman, who knelt before him like a primitive pagan.

While her narrow, fin-shaped eyes sought to meet those bloodshot eyes that had hovered before her in her nightmares, she began without delay to speak. Since she had no interpreter to assist her, she mixed into her rapid Ishmaelite speech a few words that had been pronounced repetitiously in the New Year's prayers, so that for a moment she imagined that the man who leaned toward her compassionately would also understand in the dawn light that was scratching at the yellowish windows the nature and spirit of the counterduality that she claimed not only for herself but for women in general. For while a man demanded duality of body, a woman demanded duality of soul, even in the form of the tiny soul that was encased in her womb.

But could a fearful, confused man, even if he were assisted by the best of interpreters, understand at dawn the new explanation of the obscure testimony of the previous evening? In his terror that some early-rising worshippers whom three successive days of intensive prayers had left unsated would enter the synagogue and find their prayer leader closeted in uncompromising and utter intimacy with another man's wife, albeit one of a pair, Joseph son of Kalonymos did not even begin to try to understand what the second wife was attempting to say to him in her Ishmaelite tongue, but hastened first of all to raise the form that was kneeling before him cautiously but firmly to its feet and expel it from the sacred place that was forbidden to it.

But the second wife resisted, and with arms still tanned a deep brown from the long sunny days at sea, she clung to his pulpit with all her strength, until the judge, realizing that his arbitration had not been completed, was forced to his embarrassment to unclench her hands by force. Seeing that she still persisted in kneeling and holding on to his knees, he bent over, trembling and blushing, and attempted vainly to free himself. Then, feeling how tightly the southern woman was holding him, he knew that he must take her out of his prayer house, and very firmly he began to walk outside, dragging the young woman into the back yard of an old stable. Only there, under an overcast sky, in the pungent manure, did he manage to free himself at last from the grasp of her hands and from her struggling legs, which were now scratched from the synagogue's rough wooden floor. In stammered Hebrew he asked forgiveness from God and also from her, not for dragging her but for daring to touch her at all. Since terms of pardon and forgiveness were so familiar from the prayers for the New Year that had just passed, the second wife guessed the meaning of this man who was speaking to her so distractedly. He was demanding forgiveness only, with no regret or understanding, as he left her alone in the morning mist laden with cold drops of fresh rain.

Exhausted and abandoned, her hands and knees grazed by the roughness of the black wooden floor, the second wife began to make her way back between the small wooden houses, whose crookedness gave them a dizzy air. Although the black cloak protected her from the lashing rain, it could not allay the indignation of the little fetus that had been dragged along with her, and was not prepared to accept pardon from anyone, so for a moment she felt that it was demanding to be spewed forth instantly. Assailed by weakness, she turned aside between the piles that supported one of the houses, and there, in the shadow of the long grass and bushes that grew from the lush, marshy soil, beside a stream whose cold water gurgled among discarded household utensils, she began to vomit up everything that was within her— determined, however, not to lose the new little soul that had been conceived by the dutiful desire of a man making his way at night between the bow and the hold of an ancient guardship.

That man, who did not yet know what he had or had not brought forth, was still sunk in deep sleep, which dimmed, even if it could not wholly cancel, the interdict that lay upon him. The first wife, who had woken and taken stock of the other's disappearance, hesitated to wake the husband whose face was buried in the fresh dry straw of the pallet. Although more than twenty years had passed since their first night together and she had often watched while he slept, she had never felt so tender toward him, seeing him for the first time bury his face in the bedding to hide it as he slept. She stared through the open doorway, cocking an ear to catch the returning footsteps of the second wife, so that on her return she could waken their husband to a single trouble rather than two.

But the footsteps of the second wife did not come, and the first wife began to understand that she must be stopped before she reached a point from which there was no return. Yet still she pitied Ben Attar, and granted him a few more moments of blessed ignorance before reaching out and carefully removing the blades of straw that clung to his beard and hair. For a moment the waking North African's eyes were as bloodshot as those of the arbiter who had pronounced judgment against him. But it seemed that he remembered well where he was, and why he was here. As he rose from his bed, his sharp eyes noticed the second wife's absence. *She has gone,* the first wife said very quietly. *I have waited for her, but she has not come back.*

The merchant of Tangier, who remembered only too well the rapid loss of one young woman, knew that they must hasten to stop her before she reached the riverbank. Since today was the Fast of Gedaliah, he did not need to consider whether the black bread brought by the gentile landlady was fit for eating, but inclined his head politely and thrust it away, and donning a local black cloak over his bright robes he hurried in search of the missing woman. He did not have to go far before he met Jews hurrying to prayer, who had not expected to come across the banned visitor so early in the morning. Despite the distress and embarrassment that urged them to avoid him, they could not disregard the real panic that marked his countenance as he appealed in broken Hebrew and with frantic gestures for help.

Since they feared to enter into a conversation that would shatter the newly pronounced ban, the Jews retreated in confusion, but instead of fleeing they hastened to summon Rabbi Elbaz, so that with his Andalusian virtue and learning he might cushion the Rhenish ban and explain what was troubling the peace of the southern Jew, for whom they had come to feel a strong affection. When the Jews of Worms learned of the disappearance of the second wife, panic spread through the community, and a demand arose that the morning prayers might be shortened so they could gather a large company to search for her and restore her to her husband, even if she was the cause of the ban and the interdict. News of her disappearance soon reached the synagogue and crept up to the reading desk, causing Joseph son of Kalonymos to cut short his chanting and boldly confess to his comrades what had happened beside the holy ark a short time before.

The Jews drew some comfort from his words, which seemed to rule out abduction, a thought that pierced every Jewish heart with double dread, leaving only the fear that she might have become lost or fled. So little time had elapsed since the woman's dawn meeting with the judge that there was some hope that she had not managed to go too far. But before the search began, some punctilious Jews still demurred, wishing to assure themselves that the ban pronounced the previous night had referred to the husband alone and not to his wives; otherwise they might run the risk of seeking a forbidden object, and it would be better to invite the participation of gentiles, even the Ishmaelite guests, who had not yet risen for their own morning prayers. For added security, they too were summoned. First the two burly wagoners, Abd el-Shafi and his mate, were brought from their respective billets, and then they fetched the young pagan, who at once and without hesitation set off in pursuit of the missing woman, whose scent he had absorbed deep within himself during the long journey. Before much time had passed he found the secluded spot where she had collapsed, in a dark space choked with long grass and discarded household objects, framed by the piles that supported one of the houses.

She was brought forth at once, very weak but safe and sound, apart from some bleeding scratches on her hands and legs. Even though the Fast of Gedaliah had commenced, the Jews tried to make her drink something as they dressed her wounds, and the women of Worms desired to take her into the house beneath whose piles she had hidden herself, to help and strengthen her before sending her on her way. But

Ben Attar allowed nobody to touch his second wife, and since the interdict forbade anyone to speak to him, it was impossible to persuade him otherwise. Sternly and proudly, he stood and ordered his Ishmaelites to ready the wagons and harness up the horses. For an instant it seemed as though it were he who had placed the local Jews under a ban and not the other way around, for he seemed to avoid meeting the gaze of those around him, even the blue eyes of Master Levitas, whose habitual thin smile was wiped off his face the moment he was summoned.

But where were Abulafia and his new wife? Had they been forbidden to come, or were they trying to spare themselves the pain of the final parting from the grim-faced, discomfited uncle, who was resolved to set out at once on the return journey?

The speed and skill with which the little procession was prepared for the road were amazing to behold. Two or three commands from the southern Jew were enough to bring the three Ishmaelites to a fever pitch of activity and to send Rabbi Elbaz off in search of his son. As for the Jews of Worms, who were already tired from the beginning of the fast and confused by the strange morning's events, they stood around the two large wagons, sorry to be deprived of such wonderfully colorful and exciting guests, and even though in their heart of hearts they longed to keep them in their midst for the ten days of penitence and for the joyful festivals to follow, they knew only too well that the arbiter's judgment, however hastily arrived at, was final and brooked no appeal, and so it was best, perhaps, for the banned man and his company to go on their way, to soften the pain of parting.

Before Ben Attar set forth on his journey and their sorrow was forgotten, the Jews of Worms hastened to load the wagons with food and drink, blankets and warm apparel, candles and dishes, little silver candlesticks and wine for ritual purposes. Although the ban forbade them to speak to the women or touch them, they brought dozens of small gifts for them, and they also brought sacks of feed for the horses, who were already sniffing the air of the journey ahead. But where was Abulafia? Ben Attar's heart quivered with pain. Where was his dear partner hiding himself? And where was the blue-eyed woman, who had turned her repudiation into final rupture? Did they know that at this moment, in the mist rising from the river and drifting into the Black Forest, their kinsfolk were leaving them forever, vanishing into the west on the first stage of their long journey to the south?

Master Levitas saw it as his duty to hasten and inform his sister of the sudden departure of Ben Attar and his company, and he also stirred himself to obtain special dispensation from a revered scholar, Rabbi Kalonymos son of Kalonymos, for Abulafia to meet his uncle briefly so as to take his leave of him. But Abulafia declined the generous offer. Not only did he refuse to leave his chamber, he lay in his wife's former matrimonial bed and would not even join Mistress Esther-Minna, whose throat suddenly choked with tears as she watched from the little window while Ben Attar pleaded with the good folk of Worms not to load any more gifts on his two wagons, which were slowly sinking into the yielding Rhenish clay.

Even if Abulafia was yearning to fall into his beloved uncle's arms and beg the pardon of the partner who was returning empty-handed to the azure shore of their native land, the soul of this curly-haired man, who had not yet donned his phylacteries nor said the morning prayers, bridled at the thought of a further meeting with his second aunt, the secret basis of whose being he had finally discovered yesterday in his uncle's passionate and unexpected confession. Even if she replaced the veil on her face and covered herself in layer upon layer of cloaks, she could not conceal from him any longer the form that was hidden within her, the form of that miserable, admired, beloved sinner, naked and drowned, who in vengefully destroying herself had punished him and banished him to a faraway land. Therefore, with all his might he must shut himself up in this former bridal bed which creaked beneath him, for he knew only too well that if he went to take his last leave of his uncle, he would not be able to restrain himself, tender and sorrowful as he was, from tearing the second wife away from Ben Attar, ripping out the form that was hidden inside her, and throwing it, if not into the salt sea of their birthplace, at least into his new wife's freshwater river.

Thus Abulafia knew that he had better wait until the rumble of his uncle's wagons faded away in the distance. The same rumble disturbed the chief wagoner, Abd el-Shafi, who felt the wheels straining. When they pulled up in the square in front of the belfry in Speyer, a town

221

where no Jews dwelt, they decided to lighten the load and offered a goodly part of the gifts that the community had generously heaped upon them for sale to the local inhabitants, who pressed around them curiously. Although the distance separating Worms from Speyer was not more than fifty miles, the gifts, converted into merchandise, aroused such great interest that Ben Attar was amazed at his ability, with no common language and with no knowledge of the local customs, to sell the Worms Jews' old clothes, jars of honey, dull copper candlesticks, and bottles of ritual wine, accepting in exchange, on Abd el-Shafi's advice, an elderly but sturdy mule. On this the black youth was at once seated, so that he could ride out ahead of them and sniff out the right road, which they had taken two weeks earlier in the opposite direction.

For they were alone now, in a strange and alien expanse, without Mistress Esther-Minna's command of the Teutonic and Frankish tongues and Abulafia's experience of the roads. All they had at their disposal were Rabbi Elbaz's limping Latin, the young slave's finely tuned desert nose, and the two expert mariners' knowledge of the winds and the motion of the stars. The Day of Atonement, which flickered ahead of them like a menacing black beacon, spurred them on to greater speed and effort, so that they would cross the border between Lotharingia and Francia in time to seek refuge in the Jewish congregation of Rheims, who they hoped would not yet have heard news of the ban.

Indeed, there seemed no reason why the master of the little convoy should not realize his modest ambition, for the wagons were more lightly loaded now that they lacked the two passengers who had caused the ban, and now that the gifts had been bartered for the whiskered mule, which walked proudly ahead of the wagons, bearing the lithe form of the master tracker, who was happily sniffing out the right route. Nevertheless, Ben Attar had the feeling that a mysterious heaviness had laid hold of the wheels as they advanced between fields and hills toward the silvery furrow of the Saar Valley. In fact, it was hard to explain what was slowing them. At first they suspected the autumn breezes, which occasionally soaked them in gentle drizzle; yet the spirits of the wagoners seemed to be revived by each soaking, as they cracked their whips at the drenched horses.

It was only when they made their third night halt, near the small village named Saarbrücken, not far from the octagonal burial church that Mistress Abulafia had excitedly recognized as marking the approach to her native land, that Ben Attar understood that the hidden source of their loss of impetus was to be sought not in the mud that impeded their wheels or in any slackness in their manner of driving but in a spiritual cause. At first he wondered if it were not due to gloom brought on by the ban and interdict, which, plausible though they were, were nevertheless particularly irksome because they had been pronounced so abruptly and by such a simple man. But gradually he realized that the thing that was holding them back was not hovering around the wagons but was hidden deep inside them, in the continued silence of the second wife, who sat slumped at the side of the wagon, wrapped in two black cloaks, stubbornly refusing evening after evening to taste the food that the first wife prepared. Indeed, at first sight the cause of her ill humor seemed plain enough—two deep gashes that crisscrossed her slender legs, marked by pearls of dried blood. But was it really only physical pain that prevented her from joining the others for the evening meal, or was it also resentment and anger at all that had taken place?

Even though she was still careful not to reveal her secret testimony on the eventful night of the arbitration, she worried that the truth had become known to her husband, either from Elbaz or from his son, the little interpreter, who very tenderly brought her a steaming bowl of meat stew from the campfire. Therefore the look the second wife bestowed upon the little go-between was blank and withdrawn, and she added to the two cloaks that she had brought from Worms the first wife's black cloak, which lay beside her. She kept her mouth firmly closed, not only against eating any of the food that the first wife cooked for her but also against letting out any cry of despair at what she had said behind the curtain on that terrible night, and at the words she had tried to add next morning in the same place before the same man, who should have listened to her instead of hurting her.

To whom could she now say what would never be understood? Perhaps only to the oceanic fetus, which was cloaked in the envelope of her womb and demanded additional warmth from its mother, who was shivering inside and trying with all her might to hoard what warmth she could, for its sake and for her own. Again, as at every hour of this journey, there came before her inner eye the wondering face of one who would cease to be her only son in a few more months, the dear child she had left behind with her parents in Tangier, who although he might not yet have forgotten his mother had certainly forgotten his father, who was now raising the flap of the wagon to inquire after his second wife and see whether she had tasted her food. When Ben Attar saw the bowl lying shamefully where it had been put, his spirit was greatly disturbed, and all the resentment and blame he nursed toward her on account of the counterduality that she had dared to ask for herself—which he mistakenly understood as physical rather than spiritual—burst forth at her refusal to strengthen herself with the stew that had been set before her.

Now she was alarmed, for she had the feeling that he was about to feed her himself, against her will, something he had never done before. She began to sob, but very quietly, so as not to be heard by the company gathered around the campfire, particularly the first wife, who was asking Abd el-Shafi to tell her about the movement of the stars in the sky. But the Elbaz child heard the muffled crying inside the covered wagon and his heart curdled within him, and before his father the rabbi could stop him, he had lifted the flap and seen the owner of the ship, the leader of the expedition, raising his second wife and feeding her with the stew made for her by the first wife, who had suddenly fallen silent.

Deep in the night, when the rest of the company was fast asleep, the second wife arose from her bed and went a short distance away, to a tree where a little jackal or dog was tied by a rusty chain. It had come up in the evening to scavenge the remains of the company's supper and been caught by the black slave, who with Ben Attar's tacit permission had taken it in as a pet in place of the young camel that had been left behind on board the ship. The little beast, which had already become used to the travelers, whimpered and wagged its tail as the second wife approached, and without a moment's hesitation lapped up the vomited remains of the stew she had been forced to swallow. Only then did she feel better. Desperately pale and buffeted by successive waves of heat and cold, she gulped the cold air of the autumn night and looked toward the remote campfire of another company of traders, who were transporting slaves from the east to the west.

Eventually she returned to her bed, wrapped herself in her sweat-soaked cloaks, and closed her eyes to seek a little rest, not suspecting that her footsteps had woken the Andalusian rabbi, who had followed her movements through a crack in the canvas cover of the other wagon. For a moment Elbaz wondered if it would be right to wake her husband and inform him that the meal had not reached its destination. But he restrained himself, as though he was in no hurry to reveal to anyone else, even the husband himself, the faint signs of illness that had appeared in the dead of night and that filled his heart, in the depths of darkest Europe, with an old longing for the last days before he was widowed. But in the morning, when he went to wash the sleep from his eyes in the little stream and found the second wife busy laundering her robe, he did not hold back from asking shyly yet affectionately how she was, and even though she smiled in thanks, as though there were no care in her heart, he could sense from the redness that suffused her bare cheeks that the fever in her body was mounting.

Ever since the women of Worms had made them remove their veils, the Moroccan women had been in no hurry to replace them, not only because they had seen how women could stand boldly with bare faces before the Lord himself, but especially because on the return journey the company of travelers had drawn even closer together and become a single family with three attendant servants and a rabbi, who could be considered a kind of kinsman. He had become so concerned for the second wife's health that he now demanded that Ben Attar halt the wagons at intervals to let her rest, lest a graveyard rather than a synagogue await them on the approaching Day of Atonement.

Thus the little procession wound its way more slowly, and by evening prayers on the fourth day Ben Attar found himself staring alone at the distant horizon where the fading light glowed pink above the walls of Metz, the town where he had planned to spend the coming night. But could he allow himself to take no notice of the fever? It was sufficient to put a hand to the brows of both his wives by way of comparison, to perceive the growing threat to the second wife, whose handsome face, despite her efforts to make light of her distress and smile pleasantly, not only at her husband but at anyone who greeted her, undeniably bore an unfamiliar flush because of a disease that had originated in the manure in an old stable and had infected the blood that oozed from the scratches on her legs.

On the morning of the fifth day, the day preceding the eve of the ever-approaching Day of Judgment, after hours of sleeplessness beside the campfire had blackened his love with anxiety, a bold decision seized Ben Attar. Instead of feeling his way in discomfiture and confusion among the Jews of nearby Metz to discover whether the news of his ban had preceded him, he would press on before the coming of the holy day to the next halt, the little border town of Verdun, so that in the event of any mishap they would be close to the home of that strange apostate physician who had shown such interest in them on their way to the Rhineland. It was even possible, Ben Attar continued to himself, by way of strengthening his resolve, that before the physician's solitary house beside the church they would hear once again that wonderful song, with two distinct yet intermingling voices, which had so entranced the second wife and might now revive her spirits. But as Ben Attar did not know whether there were Jews in Verdun who would welcome them into their congregation, he divided his little company in two. He himself would take the smaller wagon, with the feverish wife and the cool-headed one, to the little border town, while he would dispatch Rabbi Elbaz and his son to Metz, the favorite town of Emperor Charlemagne, to gather, in exchange for gold coin but also under constraint of pious duty, eight qualified Jews to make up a company of ten males, like the eight Jews whom Benveniste had used to bring up from Barcelona to the ruined Roman inn to celebrate the ninth of Ab. Thus he might mark the holy day in a private, if temporary, congregation, hired by his own gold and untroubled by any ban.

At noon on the sixth day, the eve of the Day of Atonement in the year 4760 of the creation of the world according to the reckoning of the Jews, in the ninth month of the year 999 since the birth of the wonderful suffering child who by his death was to win so many hearts, the North African trader spied the stone bridge over the Meuse, which abutted at its eastern end the stone and clay walls of little Verdun. Even if by some chance the news of his ban had preceded him here, he did not need to fear an inquisition from the physician, who without waiting for overzealous Jews to ban him had separated himself from them first. Therefore, as the horses drew up on the spot where they had halted before, a few paces away from the Lotharingian sentries with their sparkling mail and glinting swords, he instructed the mariner-wagoner and the black youth to protect the two wives, who had seated themselves against the wheels of the wagon to rest after the tiring journey and to breathe the cool autumnal air, while he himself entered through the town gate without delay, crossed the graves of slaves who had met their death here, and hastened to the solitary house near the church, to the physician Karl-Otto the First, whose being at once a gentile and not a gentile conferred a great advantage upon him now in the mind of the southern Jew, who believed that a few words of the ancient holy tongue would suffice to secure his assistance.

And assistance was needed. He had discovered from the trembling that racked the second wife's frame as he helped her down from the wagon that the illness he was pitted against, like himself, had not rested during the previous night. If there was any man here who called himself a physician, his aid was needed, however meager his skill. Again, as on the last visit, Ben Attar found the door of the house standing open. In the half-darkness of the double chamber, under the earthenware crucifix, he stared again at the long row of jars filled with multicolored potions and powders and at the gray metal forceps and tongs, as though everything were ready to deliver him except for the renegade physician himself, who was absent.

The physician's wife, however, was at home, and she had no difficulty in recognizing the stranger in the white robe, for it was only two weeks since he had stood here last. Once again Ben Attar shivered on observing her likeness to Mistress Esther-Minna, who had utterly upset him. But this did not prevent him from bowing to her and pronouncing the physician's name, as he remembered it. The woman nodded her head, as if to confirm that her husband the physician was indeed alive and well, but her countenance expressed sadness, as though she had not yet reconciled herself to the apostasy. Ben Attar, who had no time to meditate on others' regrets but only to proclaim his own distress, stretched out his hand to indicate the road along which he had come, closed his eyes, inclined his head to indicate an imaginary bed, and sighed the gentle sigh of a sick woman. But though the physician's wife opened her eyes wide with sympathy as she followed his gestures, still she did not respond. Then the North African merchant took a step toward her, pointed to the sun which stood high in the sky and to the direction in which it would set, and whispered in Hebrew, clearly but in a pleading tone, *Yom Kippur,* and repeated again and again, *Yom Kippur, Yom Kippur,* and he clapped his hand over his mouth to indicate to the woman what would be forbidden soon to those who had not changed their faith, in case she had forgotten. But it was evident that she had not forgotten, for at once she nodded, wrapped a shawl around her shoulders, called her children inside and locked them in with a large key, and led the southern traveler into the heart of Verdun, to her husband the physician.

Ben Attar followed the woman through the narrow streets of the little town, and on their way they passed a large slave market, where warriors and farmers bargained over yellow-haired, blue-eyed pagan Slavs who were attached to a large stone. The local people smiled at the physician's wife and led her to a large house, which she promptly entered, accompanied by her visitor. It was a noble mansion, whose occupants welcomed the newcomers warmly and conducted them respectfully into a hall spread with carpets, with weapons hanging on the walls. There, on a large couch, sat a venerable Christian with his hands crossed on his chest and his eyes closed, listening attentively and smilingly to the renegade physician, who was letting blood from his neck.

Ben Attar said to himself that this might be the way to save his second wife, by letting some of her blood to calm her spirit, and he took a step toward the physician, to examine what he was doing more closely. The latter, noticing his wife and her companion, gave them a sign to indicate that he had grasped the urgency of their mission, and he speedily concluded his work and came outside to meet them. At once Ben Attar bowed to him deeply, but he renounced the attempt to explain his distress in the holy tongue. Instead, he closed his eyes, inclined his head upon an imaginary bed, and shivered a little and sighed in imitation of his sick wife. Then he gestured to the horizon, to the place where the sun would soon set, and repeated again, *Yom Kippur, Yom Kippur.*

3.

There was no way of knowing whether it was the announcement of the approach of the Day of Judgment that caused the physician to postpone a bloodletting that had been arranged in the home of another nobleman and hurry to attend a patient outside the town walls, or whether it was simply the curiosity of an apostate who had already been excited on their previous visit by the sight of Jews who were so different from those from whom he had detached himself. Indeed, the sight of his young wife lying beside the wheel of the wagon made Ben Attar feel that his anxiety was well founded, for her condition had worsened during his short absence. Not only had her shoulders not stopped shaking, but the gentle autumnal breeze had begun to trouble her, and she had had to ask the first wife to find the cast-off silken veil and cover her face and even her eyes with it. And when Ben Attar lifted her for the physician of Verdun, he felt her gaunt frame stiffen a little in his hands.

The physician's eyes had not yet turned to the patient but first sought the little Andalusian rabbi, not only so that he could translate the nature of the North African woman's pains (which were causing her to twist her head) into a civilized tongue, but also so that he could enlighten him about the end of the great contest with the Rhenish Jews, whose outcome might help him to understand what had befallen the young woman. But the rabbi was missing, and the larger wagon had vanished too, and so had that repudiating woman, so fine yet sharp of eye and stern of countenance, who had abhorred him for the faith he had adopted and railed at him for what he had turned his back on. And so the physician had no other way open to him but to try to understand from the halting language of the prayers of his forefathers what was tormenting the young woman, whose bright red eyes indicated that she would be better off in bed in a darkened room than in the open air by the Meuse, exposed to the stares of the guardsmen. It was plain that something or someone had tainted her blood.

Even though it would have been right and proper for this new-made Christian to decline to admit Jews, even sick ones, into his home, the apostate could not suppress his pity for this suffering woman, especially since he was still excited by the desire to extend his knowledge of these exotic Jews. He suggested to Ben Attar that they take the patient to his house, so that he could more readily combat the illness with the help of all those potions and drugs and medical implements that were ready and waiting to save life, which is sometimes likened to a passing shadow or a fleeting dream. It would be better too, the physician opined, for the first wife to accompany them, so that she could prepare ritually fit food for them, for there was not a single Jew available for the purpose in the whole of Verdun.

Ben Attar, his anxieties vindicated, was glad to hear the counsel spoken by the physician, whose apostasy did not detract in Ben Attar's opinion from his medical skill or his humanity. Since he had been doubtful all along about Rabbi Elbaz's chances of persuading eight qualified Jews from the community of Metz to leave their families and their house of prayer on the eve of the Day of Atonement, even in exchange for gold coin, and travel some thirty miles to a little border town so as to make up a temporary wayside congregation for a foreign Jew whose wife had fallen sick, he knew that no purpose would be served by waiting outside the walls. He had explicitly said to Elbaz that if he could not accomplish his mission, he was not bound to hasten to rejoin them, but on the contrary, it would be preferable for him to spend the Day of Judgment together with his son in the midst of a large Jewish community, cleansing his soul and sanctifying himself by prayer and enlisting the whole congregation in supplications to the Almighty to grant recovery to the sick woman and peace of mind to the well one—for surely the prayers of a banned man's advocate are more efficacious than his own.

As the midday sun moved from the Lotharingian side of the border into Champagne, the captain of the guard also took pity on the young woman, and gave permission for the foreign company to enter the town with their wagon. Slowly the two horses advanced between the graves of idolatrous Slavs who had expired in slavery, and very cautiously the mariner-wagoner led the wagon into the square in front of the little church. At the entrance to the house stood the physician's wife, watching them, with her two sons, who already looked just like Lotharingi-

230

ans, only sadder, holding on to her apron. Ben Attar firmly refused the help of the burly Ishmaelite and the young idolater in lowering the second wife from the wagon, accepting no other assistance than that of the first wife's strong, warm hands in guiding the invalid, whose face was lit by a faint, plaintive smile at the sight of the house to which she had been so attracted only two weeks before. For an instant her footsteps faltered, as though she hoped to hear again the sound of two intertwined but different voices singing on the threshold of this house in exchange for skillful healing.

Very slowly the second wife was helped into the physician's home and with double care was laid on a narrow bed, and the large iron basin in which large river pebbles gleamed was brought close to her. Ben Attar covered his wife with the two black cloaks that the Jews of Worms had given her as a gift. The physician did not delay but sprinkled fragrant medicinal herbs all around, and made her drink a potion that was the color of egg yolk. The young woman did not attempt to resist her physician, but obediently drained the bitter potion to the dregs, and for the first time since the company had left Worms a cheerful smile broke out on her face, as though she were trying to say to those who surrounded her, *Now all will be well*. At the sight of this smile Ben Attar, unable to restrain himself, retreated into a corner of the dark room and wiped away copious tears of gratitude. The darkness and the quiet seemed to do the patient good, and the yellow potion also hastened to do its work, for the tremor in her shoulders was gradually becoming less severe. Moved, the merchant tried to give the physician an advance payment in the form of a small precious stone, but the physician, aware that he was dealing with a wealthy, principled Jew who would not pay him with a song, declined the jewel, which sparkled in the dark, with a calm smile, as if to say, *The time will come*.

Meanwhile, on a small plot of land behind the church, the Ishmaelite and the idolater without delay prepared a meal for the Jews so that they could take their fast. A verdant smoke rose from a fire of twigs and thorns, on which the first wife could cook a stew in a large cooking pot. Ben Attar hastened to the town market to fetch white doves to atone for the sins and transgressions committed by others with the cooing of their pure little souls. Again his throat choked with tears at the thought of his sick wife's smile as she lay in the physician's house. Even if the physician was finally unmasked as a charlatan, he wished to trust him as a kinsman. *Yea, as a kinsman,* Ben Attar muttered to himself in surprise. *As a kinsman,* he repeated with bitter defiance, as though the ban that had followed him from Worms, clinging to him as stubbornly as an evil demon, had suddenly made of him too something of an apostate.

But not such an apostate, heaven forfend, as to shirk the observance in all rigor, even in these difficult circumstances, of the commandments of the holy and awful day that was descending slowly upon the world. He carefully felt the flesh of the Lotharingian pigeons in the market of Verdun, which fluttered in fear in his hands. After filling his sack with a dozen milk-white birds well tied together, he headed back to his small company. His heart suddenly missed a beat at the sight of the pole of the wagon lowered to the ground, the horses nowhere to be seen. Was it possible that the gentiles had taken advantage of his absence and his troubles to take the horses and flee? But at once, cocooned as he was in hope and security like a baby inside its caul, he calmed himself with the thought that his Ishmaelite had not fled but merely taken the horses to graze in a nearby meadow. Without delay he pressed on to the back of the church, where in the leaden light of an overcast sky he came upon the solitary first wife crouching barefoot over the fire that the Ishmaelites had made, in a crumpled, smoke-blackened robe, patiently stirring the stew with a large wooden spoon, her stern face flushed in the light of the fire, which was almost scorching a trailing lock of her hair.

Seventy days and upward had passed since the ancient guardship had set sail from Tangier to ride the wild ocean waves so bravely toward a distant town named Paris, yet amid all the hardships that had visited the expedition, by sea and by land, Ben Attar had not known a single moment that could compare for bitterness and gloom with this terrible moment when he stood so alone, without rabbi or fellow worshippers, without business partner or nephew, without servant or sea captain, without horses or congregation, without even a house of prayer. Placed under a ban in the heart of an alien land, with his cargo-laden ship far away, pent up in the harbor of Paris. And all this a few hours before the start of the Day of Atonement, behind a little church built of grayish timbers, staring brokenheartedly at the wife of his

232

youth wrestling with a fire like a servant while his second wife lay in pain in the house of an apostate physician. Although he wished with all his being that he could blame himself for what was befalling them all, because of his obstinate urge to demonstrate to the world the depth of his love not only for his two wives but for his nephew, he felt that he did not have the right, whether in defeat or in victory, to detract from the force of the destiny that had guided him, for good or for ill, since the day of his birth.

Yes, despite his desire, the North African merchant was not so proud as to take all the blame and responsibility upon himself alone, as though he had become the only true master of his deeds. Moreover, he knew only too well that if he fell to his knees before his first wife and beat his breast and confessed his guilt, she would be very confused and sad, not knowing what to do with the guilt or its owner. But if he spoke repeatedly of blind fate, which sometimes smites a man and sometimes caresses him, she would nod agreement and know how to comfort him. Without complaint or anger or regret, she would remind him of how beautiful the light of this holy eve was in their own azure city, and how radiantly white the raiment of their two sons was as they went, at the conclusion of the meal, to the synagogue of the old uncle, Ben Ghiyyat. And if that selfsame fate willed it, it was very possible that in a few more days they would board the ship in the port of that small dark town and sail back home to their own dear city, and wash away in the waters of the ocean whatever ban or interdict had been pronounced against them by the Jews of the Black Forest, whose self-assurance was as great as their numbers were small.

With these words, which his first wife might have spoken if he had mastered his pride so far as to ask her for words of comfort, he soothed the dread that had caused his legs to tremble since he had left the Rhineland, and with a heart filled with love he approached the large, barefoot woman as she crouched over her cooking pot, took hold of her ample shoulders, and drew her gently away from the fire, which for a moment seemed to be trying to follow her. He produced from the sack a single pure white dove, bit through the thread that bound it to the others, and holding it by its two red legs, he waved it in a circular motion above the disheveled hair of his first wife, who closed her eyes gratefully. *This is thy substitute, this is thy exchange, this is thy expiation, this dove shall go to its death and thou shalt enter into a good long life and into peace.* And just as his great uncle used to take a sharp butcher's knife and slaughter the lamb of atonement in the presence of the atoned members of his household, so Ben Attar severed the head of the dove and handed its bleeding body to his first wife, who waited for the fluttering of the little wings to cease before plucking it and preparing it for the meal preceding the fast, to be joined in due course by the doves that would atone for the remaining members of the little family.

Ben Attar now concealed a dove in the folds of his robes, and added a second dove to it, for the sick woman, who would require a double atonement. There in the physician's dark room, Ben Attar found his second wife where he had left her, sunk in a deep, peaceful sleep, as though the yellow potion that the apostate physician had administered to her not long before was doing its work. But he hesitated to draw forth the doves from the folds of his robe, for at her bedside he found not only the physician but also a black-clad priest, who had come in response to the news of the arrival of the Jews at the house of his disciple the apostate, to warn the new Christian against backsliding or relapsing. The physician, Karl-Otto the First, as he called himself, had to prove to his former catechist that he had no secret attraction to his previous faith but was merely displaying the simple charity of a physician toward a young woman who was suffering, and that even if she belonged to a company of Jews, these were different Jews, who were under the protection of distant Ishmaelites and therefore had no intention of settling in Verdun or anywhere else, but were planning to leave Europe and journey far, far away.

But no man of the Church, and certainly not this one, who stood so dignified and stern, was able or authorized to believe in the existence of another category of Jews, even if they did come from a distant, dark continent. Since on principle the priest considered all Jews alike, he had to be on his guard in case his protégé, who had voluntarily abandoned a sect of blind, error-ridden God-killers in favor of a faith of salvation and love, was deceived into supposing that any Jew might be saved, even if he possessed the sad, dark nobility of this North African who had now entered the room. Ben Attar was examining the light fading in the window, and realized that he had only a little time to awaken his second wife gently yet firmly, sit her up in bed, and revolve two white doves first around her head and then around his own, like some savage idol-worshipper, and to declaim the ancient formula: *This is our substitute, this is our exchange, this is our expiation, this dove shall go to its death and we shall enter into a good long life and into peace.* On no account could he flinch at the physician's embarrassed countenance, or at the faint smile of contempt on the face of the priest; he had to complete the ritual by slicing off the heads of the two curiously blinking little birds and drop them, oozing blood, onto the black earth floor at the foot of the bed, confident that they possessed as much healing power as the sparkling array of multicolored flasks lined up under the crucifix.

The young woman sat flushed and confused, her golden nose-ring twinkling like a tiny star in the half-darkness. She was still wondering whether sharing an expiatory dove with her husband was a sign of desperation or of great hope. Meanwhile she obediently took the skin full of water that her husband placed in her hands, closed her eyes, and swallowed slowly, nodding agreement with a faint smile when he whispered to her in Arabic about the meal that the first wife was cooking outside over a fire, which was intended not only to satisfy their hunger and delight their souls but particularly to restore to all of them, and especially to her, such a beloved woman, the strength that had left them since ban and interdict and insult had been cast in Worms, ostensibly upon the twice-wed husband alone but in fact upon them all.

Ben Attar did not linger at his second wife's bedside, even though his heart yearned to remain by her side and watch over her recovery, but went out to give the two slaughtered doves to his first wife so that she could add them to the stew. Outside the clouds broke and soft sunlight played around him, and suddenly tears welled in his eyes, as though out of the sorrow and despair a new ray of hope had burst, not only at the memory of the faint smile that had flitted across his second wife's flushed countenance, or at the sight of the meal that his first wife was preparing in readiness for the fast, but also at seeing the two horses and the mule returning from pasture, emerging slowly from behind the gray wooden church. His heart went out to his two servants for returning his property, as though he had really feared that they might vanish with it. A strange idea flashed through his mind of atoning for them too, so as to fortify them on the Day of Judgment that was fast approaching, in case the powers above mistook them for Jews. He told them to approach and bow their heads before him, and out of the large sack he took two more doves, and holding them by the legs he circled them three times above the egg-shaped black skull of the young idolater and three times above the grubby blue turban of the mariner-wagoner. So they would not suspect him of black magic, he also circled the doves above his own head, and he provided a shortened translation of the formula into rich Arabic before deftly removing the birds' heads and throwing them to the jackal, who devoured with gusto whatever was put before him.

Surprisingly, although he was alone and abandoned, his mind was calm, and the love that welled up within him for all who stood around him and belonged to him comforted and strengthened him for a new and unique experience, which he had never had before in his forty-four years—to be his own prayer leader on this awesome day. Although it was still early and three whole hours remained before the sun would sink behind the treetops, he began to feast, so that he would be filled with food and his soul would be free from hunger pangs and composed for prayer, the better to plead for his second wife's recovery. Seated beside the fire, he dipped his bread in the steaming stew that his first wife served him and patiently chewed one helping after another. A light slumber descended upon him, and through his fluttering eyelids he saw the priest leaving the physician's house, followed by the physician himself, clutching a leather bag. A sated tiredness took possession of him and the smoke of the fire befuddled his wits, so he lay down on the ground and stretched out his legs, drowsily but gratefully watching as his first wife spooned some of the steaming stew onto a platter and broke off some delicate morsels of pigeon flesh to add to it, to take to the second wife, who might perhaps need to be helped to eat.

But he did not doze for long. Soon the whinnying of horses interrupted his dreams, and the delightful prattle of the rabbi's son awoke him from his sleep. Opening his eyes, he found himself surrounded by strangers who looked like Jews. Farther away stood the large wagon, with its pole hanging limply, as Abd el-Shafi and the black slave led the horses to the meadow behind the church. Before he could rise to his feet, Rabbi Elbaz fell into his arms, smiling proudly. Ben Attar's heart rejoiced, not only because his company was reunited and Jews had been found who were prepared to join it as it stood trapped before the Creator on the Day of Judgment, but more particularly because now he could finally dispel the terrible suspicion that the rabbi too was seeking to reject him.

It seemed as though his luck had turned again and was smiling on the tenacious traveler. The Jews of Metz, whom the news of the ban had not yet reached, had been ready to come, with the satisfaction of fulfilling a command as their only reward, to make up a quorum of ten for a Jewish wayfarer whose sister-in-law, his wife's sister, had fallen sick. So Rabbi Elbaz had chosen again, as in Rouen, to attach the two women to each other by a more usual and acceptable relationship, in order not to arouse unnecessary thoughts. Only one slight cloud darkened the joy. On the way, one of the Jews had had second thoughts and had turned back to Metz, leaving seven men instead of eight. If no other Jews could be found in Verdun, how would they make up the quorum?

Since the sun in the sky could not wait for another Jew to be born in Verdun and reach the age of legal majority—for from India to Abyssinia and from Babylon to Spain, the Jews of the entire world were standing and waiting to inaugurate the solemn fast—and while the seven Jews from Metz were hastening to atone for themselves with the doves left in the sack and decapitating and plucking them to add them to the stewpot steaming in the smoke of the fire, it was clear to the shrewd Andalusian rabbi by what device he might produce another Jew, although only a temporary one, for the purposes of the prayer. As usual without disclosing anything of his plan to Ben Attar, who had gone into the physician's house to hurry his first wife, who for some reason was lingering with the second wife, he separated himself from the group and went behind the gray church to the pasture where the horses were grazing, to tell the wise Abd el-Shafi that if the prayers of supplication for the recovery of the sick woman were to be accepted in heaven on the holy day, there was no alternative but to transform the black African into a Jew for the space of a single day.

While Ben Attar joined his first wife and the apostate physician's wife, who were both trying, one with words and the other with pleading looks, to persuade the ill woman to taste at least a thimbleful of the reddish stew, in the green meadow Abd el-Shafi and the rabbi from Seville were stripping the young slave of his robe and immersing the smoothness of his black nakedness in a little pool of water that the River Meuse had managed to send this far. Since Abu Lutfi had far-sightedly circumcised the black youth before taking him on board, so the sailors would not attempt to do it themselves, all that remained for Rabbi Elbaz to do was to turn him into a Jew by immersing him twice, once to wash away his idolatrous delusions and once to purge him for his reception by the chosen people. At once the other Jews were called to immerse themselves and to confess to one another sins both genuine and feigned, and if possible to flagellate themselves a little, before saying the afternoon prayers and gathering around the fire to eat their last supper—eight born Jews and one proselyte, waiting for the leader of the expedition to make up the number ten.

But the leader of the expedition was not yet able to leave his second wife. After sending the two other women out of the dimly lit room, he tried, using the soft language of love, not only to feed her some tender morsels of pigeon with his own hands but to repeat to her that the only effect of despair and guilt was to poison the world. A new hope was brewing in the North African's mind that everything that had befallen them would fly away like dust, and the ban and interdict, having failed to overtake them on their rapid flight westward, would turn tail despondently and sink forever into the soggy mire that surrounded the prayer house in Worms. The second wife listened attentively to his words and yielded to his entreaties to swallow some of the bean stew, including some pieces of the flesh of her tender expiation, encouraged by her husband, who set her an example by eating some with her. Despite an occasional tremor in the muscles of her back, Ben Attar did not relent until between them they had licked the platter clean.

When Ben Attar emerged into the evening twilight, completing by his presence the congregation of ten males required for public prayer, there was no reason for further delay. Indeed, the first wife had resourcefully located in the luggage a prayer shawl for the new black Jew, who was seized with excitement and dread on realizing that he had been attached to the faith of the Jews at their most sacred and awesome hour. Although Abd el-Shafi assured him that his affiliation was temporary and short-lived, the slave's heart still quaked within him as the strange Jews closed in all around him and turned to face the east. It was evident from the first moment that two different prayer rites would have to be combined somehow in the course of the holy day— that of the Jews of the Christian kingdoms, who were faithful to the abbreviated but intense rite of Rav Amram Gaon, in which the service for the Day of Atonement began with the words "O God and God of our fathers, let our prayer come before thee and do not reject our supplication, for we are arrogant and stiff-necked," and that of the Jews of the Muslim caliphate, who were accustomed to the more expansive and detailed wording of the older rite compiled by Rav Saadia Gaon, which brooded over the opening of the Atonement liturgy in these words: "Thou knowest the mysteries of the universe and the innermost secrets of all living beings. Thou searchest the chambers of the belly and seest the innards and the heart. Nothing is hidden from thee, nor is aught concealed from thine eyes . . ."

Therefore the two rites were attentively and respectfully blended together, and even the melodies adapted themselves to each other, and all was done cautiously, quietly, and properly, so as not to attract undue attention from the Verdun folk, who were gathering to pray in the gray church of Notre Dame, and also not to disturb the devotions of the two Ishmaelite sailors, who had been moved by the religious fervor of those around them to prostrate themselves on the ground in testimony to others and to themselves too that they also had a prophet, who was all the younger and fresher for having come more recently. In the face of such pluri-religious piety, the apostate physician, who had returned from his visits and his bloodletting, did not hasten to church but sat down in the dark on the doorstep of his house, hugging his two small sons and staring unseeingly at the outlines of the Jews which filled the little wood nearby.

Does our worship make him feel regret or hatred? wondered Rabbi Elbaz, who had been sent by Ben Attar at the end of the evening service to the second wife, to bolster her spirits with a special prayer, and who now stumbled over the physician as he sat in the doorway of his house, flanked by his two sons, as though to block the entrance against the Jews, who had turned his home into their own domain. But when the physician saw that the rabbi bowed his head humbly and withdrew, he felt a pang of remorse in case he had offended the small man of God, and he hastened to straighten himself and dismiss the sons, and he invited the rabbi into the inner chamber, possibly so they could resume the conversation they had embarked on during the previous visit, which had been peremptorily cut short by a look from the blue-eyed woman. The inner chamber was very somber, being lit by only a single small candle fixed to a crucifix. The physician's wife was sitting at the bedside of the second wife, who was lying peacefully with her head inclined backward, as though an invisible hand were drawing it like a bowstring.

At the sight of the rabbi a spark of life flared in the sad amber-colored eyes. She sat up a little in bed, and in hoarse Arabic she implored Elbaz to ask the physician to extinguish the candle, for even its faint light pained her eyes. Although he was surprised at her request, he translated it into his quaint Latin for the benefit of the physician, who, unperturbed, nodded his agreement, as though confirming to himself his diagnosis of the illness. Picking up the candlestick in the form of a crucifix, he handed it to his wife to put in a seemly place in the other chamber. Now that the room was in darkness, the moonlight shone more brightly through the single small window, and the second wife at once turned toward it in wonder, as though not understanding how she had failed to notice it before and wondering how she could diminish it, if not extinguish it altogether. She turned her flushed face toward the rabbi from Seville with a kind of smile in her bloodshot eyes, as though surprised that she could ask him to put out the moon for her sake. He responded with a wide, open smile, perhaps the first smile since they had met on the old guardship, and the sweet smell of his late wife's sickbed assailed his nostrils, so that a hard knot of tears constricted his throat. Suddenly he could stand it no more, and in a whisper he turned to the physician and asked in the ancient Hebrew tongue, *Will she live?*

But the physician did not reply, as though the tongue in which his forebears had prayed and supplicated had been erased totally from his memory. It was only when Rabbi Elbaz translated into his broken Latin that he answered, *Yes. She is young. She will live. If we make haste to let her tainted blood.* The rabbi's heart leaped with emotion, as though he had been taken straight back to his little house in Seville and his dead wife had come back to life. Tears of happiness clouded his eyes, and while he was wondering whether to begin the prayers for the young woman's recovery at once or wait so that his words of supplication might wrap themselves compassionately around her spurting blood, there came a tumult from the doorway. Her eager, tormented husband was pushing the congregation of seven Jews into the room with their confused new co-religionist, and in tones that brooked no refusal he demanded that his hired rabbi immediately begin the full and complete prayer for the recovery of his second wife, so that heaven above would not have any excuse or pretext to shirk the obligation to bestow mercy on a being in whom there was no sin.

The apostate physician, who had opened the door of his house to a sick Jewess, albeit a foreigner and a second wife, through Christian charity reinforced by the ancient medical oath, found himself, to his great alarm, pressed into a small space with Jews of assorted varieties who had come to reinforce the prayers of the gaunt rabbi, who now, from the depths of his memory, embarked on a small anthology of supplications that had been well formed in his mind during his wife's prolonged illness in Seville. The woman who was lying facing him turned her beautiful amber-colored eyes back and forth between Ben Attar and Rabbi Elbaz, as though the latter had become a second husband to her. But the apostate did not allow the Jew from Seville to be too carried away by his prayers, for not only did it suddenly occur to him that they tended to cast doubt on his own medical skills, but they also in a sense undermined his newly chosen faith and dragged him back toward the fate he had escaped. So he raised his hands to silence the Jews who had invaded his house, and fetching a large thick needle and a small knife, he bade all of them leave the chamber, for the time had come to pass from words to action. Moreover, once the patient's tainted blood had been let, the only prayer that would be due was one of thanksgiving.

So he banished all the Jews except for Ben Attar and the rabbi, whom Ben Attar insisted on keeping at his side so that he could continue to pour out his supplications, although silently, while the physician bared the second wife's shoulder and proceeded to draw forth a fine jet of blood that was imbued by the moonlight with a strange gray

241

color. The woman's eyelids gradually closed, as though the spurting blood gave her not only some comfort but even pleasure and relief. Her handsome, sharply etched features, which had become emaciated during the past days, now took on in the shadowy chamber a masculine toughness that strengthened her resolve to hold on to life with all her might. And a single heartbeat seemed to unite the two men who stood at her bedside and watched the physician as he gathered the blood in the metal basin containing the river pebbles. Was it not time to stop the flow of blood? Ben Attar wondered anxiously, and he took a step toward the physician, who seemed as spellbound by the bloodletting as the two spectators. But the physician appeared to be waiting for the white pebbles to turn dark with blood, for then he gently and painlessly withdrew the large needle from the woman's bare shoulder while she sank into a deep sleep, as though the tainted blood that had now been drained had been standing in the way of her peace.

Only now did her husband approach her and cover her slack body with a checked blanket, and ask the Andalusian rabbi to raise his voice, so that even the drowsiest angels in heaven might hear the last supplication for the recovery of this young and so beloved woman. When the prayer was concluded and he drew the rabbi with him out of the chamber (though the rabbi was reluctant to leave), he saw the apostate's wife, who bore more visible signs of the sorrow of apostasy, approach to take the vacant place at the patient's bedside. *Will she live?* Rabbi Elbaz asked in Latin as the physician joined them outside to breathe the cool Lotharingian night air, and after considering he finally nodded silently. *Yes, she will live,* he replied solemnly, with the assurance of an experienced physician, lightly touching the tip of his boot to the rabbi's son, who had fallen asleep beside the silent embers of the Jews' fire. And he continued unexpectedly, *And this child too will live . . . ,* and sensing the rabbi's alarm he added, *And you too will live, and the merchant and his family will live.* He hesitated for a long moment before continuing softly, *But they will not live,* and he indicated the forms of the seven Jews who were arranging their bedding beside the large wagon that had brought them from Metz.

How will they not live? asked the startled rabbi from Seville. Seeing that the physician was looking away and saying nothing, as though he were regretting the words he had let slip, he gave vent to his alarm once more: *Why will they not live?* At last the physician had no alternative but to take the stubborn rabbi by the arm and lead him a short distance toward the darkened church, and there, in a field that smelled of newly cut wheat, by a little fire that his sons were busy lighting, he was able to whisper a strange, somber confession: it would be the duty of the Christians, when they discovered at the end of the millennium year that the Son of God was not coming down from heaven to save them, to kill those Jews who refused to convert to their faith. *So he is not coming down from heaven after all?* the Andalusian rabbi said in surprise, to this renegade Jew who was foretelling the future with such assurance, as though unknown secrets were revealed to him with the blood that he let in the homes of his noble patients. And the physician shook his head. No indeed; since the faithful were so numerous and so dispersed, any visit from the Savior would only cause schism and strife, so it was more natural and fitting that instead of the Lord's coming to his followers they should go to him, to the place where he might most readily be found, to the sepulcher in a far-off land. *The Land of Israel?* the rabbi guessed at once. It was plain that the news that the Christians would go there, perhaps even before him, made him sad and disappointed. *Yes, there,* the physician confirmed. *And so that Europe is not abandoned to the mercy of the Jews, who will remain here alone, the faithful will have to kill them all.*

Even the children? the rabbi asked in alarm, trying not to miss a word of the dark vision that blazed in the physician's mouth as he drew him ever nearer to his sons' fire. *Yes, even the children,* said the physician, *but not these,* and he stroked his little sons' shaved heads affectionately as they snuggled up to him. *And not their children, or their children who will come after them.* The rabbi stopped still, trying to avert his gaze from the flame that was swaying so cheerfully in the dark heart of the holy Day of Judgment. And even though he knew perfectly well that neither he nor any other Jew was making this fire burn, still a faint dread shuddered inside him, as though conversing with the apostate were a sin in itself. He carefully and politely separated from the physician and laid out his bedding beside his young son's, and put his arms around him to get a little warmth. Between his drooping eyelids there flickered the image of a new Jew, a dark-skinned young barbarian, standing awake among the sleepers, wrapped in his new prayer shawl and sunk in thought, trying to understand how the old gods might join the new ones.

In the depths of the night the second wife felt a spasm in her spine, and quickly she arched her head back to relieve the pain a little. There was pitch darkness all around, for even the moon had vanished from the window. After a day of such hardships and commotions, her mind was soothed by the dark quiet that embraced her, if only she could still the spasm that drew her back like some little goblin determined to turn her aside from the straight and narrow. There still hovered in her mind the seven strange Jews with horn-shaped hats on their heads, who had come to reinforce the Andalusian prayer leader drawn to her bedside. Was it only pity for her weakness that had saddened the little rabbi, or was he also trying to admit to her that her private little speech about two husbands was no less dear to him than the vehement speech he had delivered among the wine casks in the winery outside Paris?

At that, a fancy began to float in the second wife's desperate mind that if she tried to fulfill the desires of the Jews who had prayed for her recovery and arise from her sickbed, Rabbi Elbaz might accept in return, if only symbolically, the role of her second husband, and so not only strengthen the message of the southerners to the northerners but also continue to serve her first husband as a learned rabbi and able interpreter of any new question that might arise. This surprising thought so rejoiced her soul that her lips parted in a smile, as she imagined that on their way home they might all disembark in Cadiz in Andalus and go together to the rabbi's home in Seville, to fetch his belongings and his clothes and his holy books, then load them onto the old guardship and sail away to that little well-tended house that looked out on the meeting of the ocean and the Inner Sea. And although the goblin's vicious hand still twitched the muscles of her back, the smile and this fantasy strengthened her will to recover.

As she rose from her bed and crouched to relieve herself in the basin stained with her tainted blood, she caught sight of her husband's sturdy form creeping into the chamber to watch over her. Lifting her from the basin, he laid her down very carefully in her bed, and although he knew that the physician and his wife might have heard his stealthy footsteps, he did not yield his right, the right of a loving husband, to caress her cheeks and kiss her feet, so as to strengthen her spirits and relieve her suffering. If this were not a holy day, when marital acts were forbidden, he would have offered her proof positive that in his eyes she was neither tainted nor enfeebled but a healthy, whole woman deserving of love according to the season of her desire and her status.

But despite the North African husband's conviction that abundant love would hasten his second wife's recovery, she continued to be racked by spasms, and her head with its disheveled mane of black hair continued to arch backward as though she were trying to make a living bridge with her frail form on this simple bed offered to her by an apostate physician in Verdun. If her husband had promised to give her a second husband, her tortured body might have been soothed by hope, for this woman who had been plucked in the tenderness of youth from her father's house believed she possessed enough love to attract and keep two husbands. But with all the power of his attentive love, Ben Attar could not imagine in his heart that his suffering wife was indeed capable of being, like him, twice wedded. Thus it did not occur to him to fetch her a second husband, but only a physician, who, hearing the sound of Ben Attar's kisses in the next chamber, rose and came to watch over his patient.

When the physician saw how she suffered, he at once fed her some of his yellow potion and strewed healing herbs upon her and around her. When she was a little relieved, he hastened to draw aside part of her robe and lay his beard upon her heart to hear the throbbing of the tainted blood in her veins. Then he palpated her small belly and inhaled the smell that rose from her navel, and a mysterious smile flitted across his face. Silently he went to the window to ensure that no stranger was spying on them, and for want of an alternative he strained to retrieve a few words of the holy tongue from the recesses of his memory to induce Ben Attar, who stood clenching his fists, to redouble his love and care for his young wife, for she was no longer alone but carried another, tiny life inside her.

The news pierced Ben Attar's heart like a knife, and not only doubled but tripled his anguish, so that it seemed for an instant that with a merchant's bold and stubborn despair he might try to bring the fetus forth from the womb of the invalid, who had fallen into a deep slumber, and entrust it to that of the first wife until the second wife's fate was decided. So thoughts of this kind would not drive him mad, he asked in the morning twilight, when Rabbi Elbaz entered the chamber to raise his spirits, for the first wife to be roused and for her to be joined by all the other members of the congregation, so that they could form a dense wall around the second wife and block her way to the hereafter.

4.

Alone she is left now, her covering cold.
Beholding his loved one her lord laments.
Calmly she journeys, barklike her bed,
Darkness directs her, we know not where.
Ebbs now her spirit, thy dear one departs,
Fails now the vision, dashed is the dream.
Gone without gaining pardon or peace,
Hoarding up vengeance, dead is the dove.
In secret caressing melts now the love,
Kissing a dear foot—crowning content.
Loved in her lord's arms, never alone,
Moves now the curtain another's desire.
Now in the northlands somber and sad,
Ocean-wide grimness holds thee from home.
Pause to remember one mournful man
Quite worn with weeping, a suitor despised.
Ruthless and fearful lawyers proclaimed it:
Stern interdiction and baleful ban,
Tearing asunder first wife from second,
Undone forever comradeship close.
Voyaging unfriended, seeking release,
Wrapped in yon widower's whispering words,
Yet stay a moment, fatal reflection,
Zealous I follow, faithful to death.

5.

In the course of the morning prayers, the seven Jews from Metz realized from the deep anxiety the North African displayed for the health of the young woman inside the little house that she was someone special to him, someone he held in particular affection. But as they were unable to interpret what they saw, it was hard for them to avoid thinking that it was a question of carnal sin—in other words, that the sister-in-law was also a secret, beloved concubine. At once they began to investigate, and once they had manage to persuade the young Elbaz to speak, the patient's true position was revealed—namely, that she was neither sister-in-law nor concubine but an additional wife, a legal wife but a second wife nonetheless. What troubled the contingent from Metz, it emerged, was not the truth now revealed, but the untruth the rabbi had told them when he had solicited them to come. Before they consented to proceed with him to the solemn service of the high priest of old, according to his own rite, the great Babylonian master, they withdrew for a consultation in a corner of the woods, not far from the wall of a convent, and eventually the little Andalusian rabbi was invited to join them to explain why he had lied to them. At first the rabbi was evasive, fearing to disclose the matter of the ban in case, tempted to associate themselves with their brethren of Worms, the Jews of Metz dissolved the congregation in the middle of the prayers and departed with the scroll of the Torah that they had brought with them. Being uncertain, however, whether the forgiveness granted on the Day of Atonement would extend to a lie pronounced in the course of the worship, he yielded and disclosed the whole truth, though in a terse and laconic fashion.

The seven Jews of Metz, hearing with astonishment and a whit of pleasure how much firmness their brethren of the Rhineland had displayed, were fearful of rendering null and void the prayers they had prayed so far in the company of a banned Jew and a lying rabbi, for they knew that they would have no opportunity to repeat the holy Day of Judgment and put right whatever might have been disqualified in the prayers. So they decided to see themselves as people who had heard but not understood, postponing the full explanations until after the conclusion of the service, which they wished to press on to swiftly. But now one of the ten was missing—the banned man himself, who took advantage of the short pause in the prayers to hurry to the bedside of his second wife, eager to see how she fared. Since dawn he had entrusted the bedside vigil to his first wife, but he was not certain that it was fitting for the latter's face to be the last image his second wife saw if the angel of death came to her.

Since midnight Ben Attar, abandoning false hope, had no longer held back from pronouncing the name of the foe who had insinuated himself into the bosom of his family. Indeed, since the early hours he had had the feeling that here in Verdun it was not a single fiend that threatened them but a whole band of fiends, gliding easily through the cold gray mist that wafted through the narrow streets and over the meadows, stealthily attaching themselves to the little congregation of Jews, and gathering around the new, temporary Jew, who stood wrapped in his prayer shawl, attending earnestly to the strange words evoking the service in the holy of holies in the ruined temple in Jerusalem: *O Lord, I have sinned, I have done iniquitously, I have transgressed against thee, I and my household. I beseech thee by thy name to pardon the sins, the iniquities, and the transgressions that I and my household have committed against thee. As it is written in the Torah of Moses thy servant, from thine honored mouth, "For on this day he shall make an atonement for you to cleanse you from all your sins before the Lord."*

Unable to contain his impatience and wait for Rabbi Elbaz with his soft, wavering voice to conclude the high priest's confession, Ben Attar had slipped away once more to the physician's house. The doctor had left his Jewish patient alone and gone to do his rounds of peasant huts and noble houses, perhaps to avoid the suspicion caused by excessive and prolonged contact with the company of Jews. Thus, in the half-darkness of the inner chamber, whose window was veiled by a prayer shawl, the twice-wed merchant's eyes encountered only those of his first wife, who was afraid to utter any word of protest or despair in the presence of this good, devoted man, who realized as soon as he entered the room that his young wife's condition had deteriorated further.

Indeed, in addition to having her head thrust back in pain, her eyes veiled against the light, and her ears plugged with wax, her breathing was now labored. A terrible dread filled Ben Attar's heart, for he did not know what he would say or how he would excuse himself to her father, his childhood friend, who had trusted him and given her to him as a girl in the tender first flower of youth. Now he could not even offer her father a grave upon which to prostrate himself. And how would he comfort his son? Not the fetus in her womb but his elder brother, who had been left with his grandfather and grandmother in Tangier and who would require satisfaction from his father for the many days he had dreamed of his mother's return, when she had already departed this life.

The North African merchant scrutinized the countenance of the mistress of the house, the physician's wife, who had crept into the room, to learn from her experience whether the terrible despair that had seized hold of him was justified. But the pale little woman's eyes gave him no clear hint, but only reminded him of the blue eyes of another, of the new wife whose repudiation had begotten death, which was groping its way toward his second wife's bed. For the first time since Ben Attar had heard of the existence of that woman, beside the campfire by the Bay of Barcelona, he felt how heavy was the hatred he had borne her in his heart for so long, and how deep his vengeance would be. But on account of the sanctity of the day of forgiveness and atonement, he forced himself to stop the feelings that were rising up within him, and gently and compassionately he approached the patient's bedside.

There, beside the physician's colorful flasks, he removed the fine veil from her pure, emaciated face, so that she could see the tenderness and sadness in his eyes. He removed the soft wax from her ears, so that she could hear the sound of the prayers coming from the little wood next to the house. All so that she might be certain that neither he nor any other member of the company intended to abandon her in this terrible moment, but on the contrary, they were all joining together in body and soul in the fight against the angel of death, who, even if he was close to the house, was still motionless in the doorway, listening in as much astonishment as the Lotharingian worshippers to the wonderful, richly colored description, full of poetic eloquence, flowing from the mouth of Rabbi Elbaz as he sang the service of the high priest on the terrible and awesome day.

So as not to fail the congregation that had gathered for him alone, Ben Attar cut short the words of affection and comfort that he was heaping upon his second wife, and with profound yet unspoken gratitude he nodded to his first wife, who was covering the patient's eyes again with the fine gauze veil and stopping her ears again with pieces of soft wax, and hurriedly he left the small chamber to rejoin the other worshippers. It was as well that he hastened back, for Rabbi Elbaz needed southern reinforcement. He was motioning to the seven northern Jews not to hold themselves back and content themselves with a polite genuflection, like Christians, but to prostrate themselves devoutly upon the ground, as though the holy of holies had merged with the physician's house that stood before them, and the little wood had been transformed into the Temple court and Verdun into the beloved City of David. Thus they could join not in spirit alone but in body too in the memory of *the priests and the people who stood in the court, who when they heard the honored and awesome Name spoken distinctly by the high priest in sanctity and purity, bent the knee, prostrated themselves, and fell on their faces, and said, "Blessed be his honored, majestic Name for ever and ever."*

At first the northern Jews had difficulty joining in the full-length prostrations of Rabbi Elbaz and his son, and of Ben Attar and the young barbarian, who extended themselves lithely on the ground like Muslims at prayer. But slowly their souls were won over by the splendor of the rhymed and ornamented verses, and obeying the passionate rabbi's gesture, they rubbed their foreheads repeatedly, if cautiously, on the reddish soil of Verdun, in the hope that such deep and humble prostration in the company of one banned Jew, one lying Jew, and one black Jew of doubtful Judaism might be added to the afflictions of the fast and fortify the virtuous act they had committed in making up ten for prayer. So might their purity be strengthened on this strange Day of Judgment, and their powers of resistance be doubled in the new year that was beginning, a gentle Jewish year that held in its womb the dragon of the frightening millennium.

As though to reinforce the newfound self-righteousness of the northern Jews, who dispersed at the end of the service to rest for a while under the trees, the overcast sky suddenly parted and the autumn sun exposed a bare patch of sweet blue sky which stabbed Ben

Attar's entrails with a sharp pang of longing for his children, his kins-folk, and his friends in Tangier, who must be enjoying an afternoon rest at this very moment, reclining on gleaming white couches in large, calm rooms. The next instant his nostrils were assailed by a foreign smell of forbidden meat emanating from the smoke curling up from the chimney of the small house. Was the apostate physician about to return home, and was his wife preparing his dinner? he wondered as he hastened to the corner of the convent wall to see whether he could see the eagerly awaited figure of the renegade. And indeed, Karl-Otto the First, as he styled himself could be seen approaching, holding his medical bag. Ben Attar hurried to meet him, ostensibly to hasten the physician's footsteps, but perhaps unwittingly he was also attempting to postpone as long as possible the moment of his own return to the inner chamber, to his accursed holy of holies, where the rites of death might already be commencing.

Will the woman live? Rabbi Elbaz asked again fearfully, in his quaint Latin. *Yes, she will live,* the physician assured him, with the same confidence he had displayed the previous day. *But they,* he insisted on adding, gesturing toward the Jews of Metz, who were dozing beneath the trees, *will not live, neither they nor their children.* He pursed his lips with a look of grim resolve, and entering his house, he embraced his two children firmly, perhaps to comfort himself for having exchanged such a holy day for an ordinary working day. Then he washed his hands to remove the dust of the roads and the blood of peasants and nobles which he had let all morning, dried them on a soft towel, and prepared to eat the roast meat that his wife had cooked for him. But disturbed by Ben Attar's looks, he set down his knife and went into the inner chamber, making a sign to the first wife to give up her place beside the second wife, whose head was still tilted back and whose mouth gaped wide open as though she were short of air.

For a moment it looked as though the physician were at a loss for what to do, but then he rummaged in his little wooden chest and extracted a soft reed tube, which he proceeded to insert carefully in the second wife's throat. He poured down it some of the yellow potion that was so efficacious at soothing pain, and indeed, in a moment the strung bow relaxed and the amber-colored eyes opened wide. Gradually the eyelids drooped wearily and the lips parted in a faint smile, as though now,

251

at the height of her torments, she had been vouchsafed a moment of acute pleasure. The alert physician seized this moment of grace, and before she sank into slumber he took out his knife and needle, bared a lovely shoulder, and let out a further quantity of tainted blood into the basin, which now contained fresh white river pebbles.

The second wife's body now seemed to find relief, and the painful spasm relaxed and disappeared within her sleep. Ben Attar judged that this was an opportune moment for him to elude the savours of the dinner that the physician's wife was serving to her apostate husband and join the others for a rest in the little wood, until the daylight had mellowed enough for the afternoon prayers to commence. When Abd el-Shafi and his friend brought the four horses and the mule back from pasture, proudly waving their tails, washed and gleaming from the rest and grooming they had received on this holy day, and the physician emerged from his house for another round of bloodletting inside the walls of Verdun, Ben Attar went to rouse the young slave, the temporary Jew, who had remained kneeling all this time before the scroll of the Law, which had been placed in the branches of a tree. He made him join the rabbi, who had assembled the other worshippers together so he could pronounce the prayer that opened the afternoon service, which stabbed Ben Attar's innards with renewed dread: *The men of faith who were strong in good works have passed away. Valiantly wielding shield and buckler, they averted calamity by their supplication. They were to us like a fortified wall, and like a protection in the day of wrath and affliction. They appeased anger and fury, they restrained ire by their petitions. Before they invoked thee thou didst answer them, for they knew how to implore and propitiate by their supplications . . .*

The fervent murmur of the Jews' devotions entered the window of the physician's little house and penetrated the clouded consciousness of the second wife, and with it the spasm returned to her spine, drawing her head back again like a bent bow. With a great effort she opened her eyes, in which there flickered now the grim mane of the angel of death, who had crept in stealthily and now lurked behind the first wife's back, pretending to share in her light sleep.

Surprisingly, a renewed slumber came over her, as though the remote wailing chant of the men in the nearby wood were soothing the fear that was sapping her spirits. In the midst of the painful spasm that had laid hold of her back like a vampire, she suddenly felt a tender longing for the women's prayer house in Worms and that female cantor who had stood wrapped in a prayer shawl, wearing leather phylacteries. *Behold, thus I shall not prevent you taking me out of this world.* She was flooded with sadness and self-pity, which were blended, miraculously, with a gentle flush of pride. And in the twilight of this new thought, which stubbornly darkened within her, she tried to understand to whom that *you* was addressed—whether to her husband, or to that red-haired arbiter at whose feet she had sunk, to the rabbi from Seville, who was chanting the pentitential prayers in a tired, hoarse voice, or perhaps to the angel of death, who had disguised himself in the plump form of the first wife, who was bending over her affectionately and nodding to show not only that she understood the good new thought that had been born but that she agreed with it.

While the second wife struggled with all her might to expel the breath that threatened to stifle her, and a ray of light that had managed to infiltrate through the curtain revealed in her motionless eyes a glint of satisfaction at the sobbing of her angel of death, two young nuns came forth from the Benedictine convent, sent by the abbess to ensure that the Jews were not so carried away by their devotions that their vain thoughts defiled a world that was preparing itself for vespers. Surprisingly, the mere appearance of the proud, self-confident sisters was enough to halt the Jews in their prayers, so they could hear a clear demand in the local language that they should move their worship from the little wood toward the bare, tomb-strewn field, and should also lend the convent the young slave, whose slim build and dark skin rendered him suitable for shinning down into the well and fetching up a lost bucket. The Jews from Metz, who understood only too well with whom they were dealing, declined even to translate the sisters' strange request for the benefit of the rabbi and Ben Attar, but took it upon themselves politely but firmly to refuse to lend a temporary Jew, who by his patient but fervent presence was contributing to making up the ten required for worship. They offered the women instead the two burly Ishmaelites, who were checking the wheels of the wagons for the next stage of the journey.

The two nuns smiled at each other on hearing the generous offer, knowing perfectly well that it was utterly unacceptable to introduce two such strong men into a convent of women who led a constant struggle against delusions and fantasies. They abandoned their impertinent request and disappeared through the gateway of the convent, not before making sure that the worshippers had indeed taken the scroll of the law and were heading toward the graveyard, where they would conclude their prayers.

When the tops of the trees of the abandoned wood were stabbed by shafts of light, the seven Jews from Metz were seized by fear and trembling at the approach of the concluding service, when the gates of repentance in heaven would be closed, and they sought to remove the rabbi from the office of cantor and chant the all-important concluding prayers themselves according to the rite and melodies of their own dear, distant congregation. Ben Attar made a covert sign to the rabbi from Seville not to resist but to yield his place to a local Jew, whose prayers might help to avert the harsh decree that menaced him. He also told the young African to approach him, so that he could seek consolation in the desert scent that rose from his body, a fragrance of dried thorns and smoke of ancient campfires, which the long ocean voyage and the additional journey overland had not been able to erase.

Then as the local cantor began to wail the prayer in a tune familiar to the city guard of Metz: *What shall we say before thee, O thou that dwellest on high, or what shall we recount before thee, O thou that inhabitest the heavens, for surely thou knowest all the hidden things.* Ben Attar, as he swayed in distress, knew that from now on he would have to increase his dependence on his God, for his first wife, the wife of his youth, emerged wearily from the physician's house and collapsed on the threshold in a posture of mourning, indicating wordlessly to her husband, who was wrapping himself in the concluding prayer, that the days of his double marriage were ended.

Although it was clear to the North African merchant that the confession of the closing prayer had no power to eradicate the guilt of the death he had brought upon his wife, not because of a stubborn journey made to demonstrate dual love but because of a desperate attempt to justify it, he did not forsake his place among the other worshippers to run to his dead wife. Instead he importuned the Lord of forgiveness to pity and to inscribe in the book of life his only remaining wife, who would soon need not only comfort for the death of her companion but also renewed assurance.

It was only when the end of the evening service marked the conclusion of the holy day—which was also the Sabbath day, when lamps must be lit and spices sniffed, and the appropriate blessings pronounced over sweet wine so that they might safely cross the frontier between sacred and profane—that he hastened to the little house, at whose doorway the physician's wife stood, barring the entrance to her two children so they would not find themselves standing in the dark in the presence of a corpse. A little way away stood Abd el-Shafi, sea captain and chief wagoner, waiting respectfully for his lord, his eyes running with tears. He knew only too well how hard and sad their journey would be from now on, without the second wife. He embraced the Jewish merchant and uttered words of condolence to him, saying how fine and wonderful was the destiny of the one who at this moment was ascending with her little bare feet the golden staircase of paradise, and how harsh was the lot of those who must continue to plod their weary way through this world. Since all day long he had watched the Jews fasting, he forced Ben Attar to taste a morsel of the warm bread that he and his companion had baked for them, before the merchant went in to take his leave of the one who had departed without permission.

Then Ben Attar stood silently in the total darkness beside the young woman's body, his eyes roving over the gray outlines of a stilled arc and a startled gaping mouth, and pondered the final leavetaking on this narrow cot in this strange house in this grim and gloomy Christian town, whose terrible memory he would carry with him all his life, even if he never returned here. Surprisingly, he thought also of Abulafia, his nephew and protégé, who could not imagine at this moment, wherever he might be, that the failure of the partnership of heart and body that his uncle had taken upon himself, to atone for the sin of Abulafia's previous wife's drowning, had now renewed, amid rage and wrath but with redoubled force, their severed partnership, and annulled not only the ban and interdict of Worms but even the repudiation of Paris. When Ben Attar sensed Rabbi Elbaz's presence beside him in the darkness, removing the prayer shawl that had been hung up as a curtain at the window, not so as to grace the departed by letting in the gentle moonlight but to use it to hide the slowly whitening face under the cloth and thus begin to separate the second wife from her husband, he turned sternly to face the little rabbi to tell him that he had no intention of either holding a funeral service or burying his dear second wife in this accursed town. Instead, he meant to take her body back to Paris, to prove incontestably to the stubborn repudiatrix and her brother, Master Levitas, that he stood before them now as a fit and proper business partner, the husband of a single wife, and that consequently the severed partnership could now be renewed, although in the midst of wrath and pain, and indeed it could be confirmed forever by the testimony of a grave and a monument set up in the very courtyard of their home.

Ben Attar, feeling that the rabbi was moved to anger and might even break the bonds of loyalty and assail him with harsh words about a journey that would be so disrespectful of the departed one, and refusing to entertain a reply that might contradict his resolve, even if it were embellished with a scriptural citation or a legal precedent, took down from the shelf the flask containing the yellow potion and swallowed the entire contents at a single gulp. Then he left the little house somewhat unsteadily, bumping into the apostate physician, who was arriving with his catechist, the priest. Without saying a word, with an air of utter desperation, Ben Attar thrust the two of them aside and strode as though sleepwalking toward the Jews from Metz, who were standing in terror, unobtrusively eating their meager meal. Pressing right into the middle of the little wood, he stumbled and fell in a heap among the trees, desiring not to die but to sleep and then to sleep.

She is dead, the rabbi bitterly taunted the physician, who appeared neither disconcerted nor repentant over the false hopes he had persisted in raising during the previous day. He turned calmly to the ecclesiastic and translated the news of the death into the local dialect, to demonstrate to him that he had attended to this Jewish wayfarer from a sense of medical duty alone, not as a mark of any special favor, and that Jews too, and not Christians only, might expire upon his bed.

By way of reinforcing his words he invited the learned man into his home, into the moonlit inner chamber, to show him the patient whom the angel of death had mercifully put out of her suffering. The little

Andalusian rabbi followed on their heels, to ensure that they did not take advantage of the dead woman's helplessness by any unseemly or disrespectful action, such as making the sign of the cross or pronouncing alien prayers for her repose. It seemed, however, as if the ecclesiastic, lacking the power to evangelize and thus admit to heaven one who was already dead, had lost interest in the infidel soul that had already departed to its fate, and demanded to hear instead the tale of the body that had failed, and the mystery of that powerful spasm, which the physician named in the learned tongue of the ancient Greeks *tetanus*, thus ascribing to the illness grandeur and beauty in addition to its seriousness.

Rabbi Elbaz, brokenhearted at the sight of the departed woman's motionless little foot, once more reproached the physician for his false promise, in a voice stifled with tears, but this time not in the broken Latin he had learned from the Christians of Seville but in the ancient tongue of the Jews, which had the power of giving particular force to whatever was spoken in anger or frustration. The apostate seemed to be deeply disturbed by the antique garb of the reproach being repeatedly hurled at him, and as though to defend the angel of death, who appeared to have made a mistake, he went over to the window and opened it wide and looked at the seven Jews of Metz, who were standing weary and perplexed around the first and now only wife, who was handing them slices of the bread the Ishmaelites had baked. Indicating them all with his finger, the physician repeated, this time not in Latin but in strange, crushed Hebrew, the second limb of his accursed prophecy: *But these will not live.* And the rabbi, although he had heard these words more than once already, trembled all over, as though the utter failure of the comforting part of the physician's prophecy reinforced the effect of the baneful part.

Noticing that his son, the neglected orphan, was standing at the doorway with his dark eyes fixed on the body of the dead woman, near whose cabin on board ship he had sought the sweetness of sleep, the rabbi pulled himself together. He hurriedly pushed the child out of the chamber so that he would not merge the death of this strange woman with that of his mother in his imagination. He handed him over to the first wife, so that she could give him some of the warm black bread that the goodhearted Ishmaelites had baked, and although he himself felt not the slightest pang of hunger, he forced himself to eat some of the warm, sourish bread too, and to recover some strength, for now, faced with a lord who had permitted himself to fall so soundly asleep, the Andalusian rabbi would have to change from counselor to associate, and who knew, perhaps also into a leader.

Because the North African merchant had neither spasm nor pain to disrupt his sleep, the yellow potion acted on him with double force, and for hour upon hour he lay so motionless in the little wood beside the convent that it seemed as though the sleep of God itself were enclosing him on every side. In the morning, when Abd el-Shafi was harnessing two of the horses to the larger wagon as arranged, to drive the seven Jews of Metz home, Rabbi Elbaz suddenly decided to remove two fine gold anklets carefully from the dead woman's smooth, cold feet and give them to the borrowed congregants, not, heaven forbid, by way of recompense for a virtuous action that was its own reward, but merely as a token to sweeten their return. Knowing how firm was Ben Attar's resolve not to bury his beloved wife in a bare field, he instructed the black temporary Jew, who was the last remnant of the dissolved congregation, to gather some gray planks of wood for the construction of a strong sealed coffin in which the second wife might be transported respectfully and safely to the burial ground in Paris.

It was only the sound of hammers that Sunday afternoon that finally woke Ben Attar from his yellow slumber. In the delicious misty languor of awakening, it seemed to him that he had never set sail on his ocean voyage, neither with the first wife nor with the second, but that he was lying comfortably on his big bed in his azure house, and the sounds issuing from the inner courtyard informed him that his older children were hastening to fulfill the command to build a tabernacle for the approaching festival. But as the coils of his deep slumber detached themselves, he became aware of the hardness of his bed, and through the screen of russet leaves that stirred before his eyes he was joined to the gray sky of Europe, which had turned repudiation to interdict and interdict to death.

In an instant memory assaulted him and a sharp pang of hunger and loss pounded in his head, and he rose to his feet and went to a nearby stream to wash his face. As he did so, a smell of burning reached his nostrils, and he saw that his living wife, who had probably remained beside him all the time to watch over him lest anyone disturb his sleep, had also succumbed to slumber, and was lying in her rumpled robe beside some smoking logs on which his dinner was keeping warm. In the silence of the wood, without seeking out the rabbi or anyone else, he fell like a wild beast upon the slightly burned food, which was seasoned by the supreme condiment of two days' hunger. And without waking the wife of his youth, he turned to the physician's house, from which bluish smoke was rising, to see if by some miracle someone had sprung back to life there.

Entering that house, which in the past two days he had entered and left as freely as if it were his own, Ben Attar saw the physician's wife standing beside the stove, stirring the supper with a large wooden spoon. Her little blue eyes looked at him with a hint of reproach, as if to say, *And a fine time to be waking up.* Guiltily he hung his head, and with an aching heart he entered the other chamber, where he was startled to see his second wife wrapped in her shrouds like a parcel ready for dispatch. He did not know who had dared to dress his dear one so without asking his consent. Was it the physician, or the Andalusian rabbi, impatient to resume the journey?

Without further thought, he hurriedly closed the door of the chamber behind him and feverishly unbound his second wife and looked again on that splendid face, which had become sharper during the night that had elapsed, so that it seemed now like that of some large quaint bird. His trembling hand hesitated to raise her eyelids gently and look for the last time at that old, dear emerald sparkle, which had never failed to set his heart aflame. And while he was taking his leave, slowly, with a kiss and a caress of the body that had given him so much pleasure and joy, he heard behind him the rabbi, who had entered without knocking and was gazing with total freedom at the woman laid out before him, as though her death had made him at last into a second husband.

At once the rabbi gave Ben Attar an account of his actions during the day, without excuse or apology, as though it were natural that he should assume authority while his lord slept. Again, as when he had decided to travel to Worms for a further judgment, Ben Attar stood stupefied at the little rabbi's audacity, not only because he had taken it upon himself to remove the anklets from the North African's wife's feet with his own hands and give them to the Jews from Metz, whose destruction might well be nigh, as a recompense for their trouble and pain, but also because he had authorized himself to give the mule that they had bought in Speyer to the physician, in payment for his simples, his hospitality, his yellow potion, his bloodlettings, and his accommodation of the corpse. But Ben Attar did not utter a word of reproach, for he was pleased and grateful to discern that Rabbi Elbaz had consented to his request to postpone the burial. Indeed, the Ishmaelite seaman and the slave had already been told to hasten and make a strong sealed coffin.

So the North African expedition lingered no longer within the walls of Verdun. At midnight, when Abd el-Shafi returned from Metz with the large wagon, the coffin was loaded onto it and Ben Attar and the rabbi arranged comfortable seats for themselves on either side of it, so that they could accompany the deceased during the journey with verses of psalms, which might console and strengthen her soul, which merited a final rest. Meanwhile the two Ishmaelite wagoners were checking the horseshoes and adjusting the harnesses, while young Elbaz greased the wheels. The young African, whom Abd el-Shafi had not yet released from the bonds of Judaism, was packing the cooking pots under the supervision of the only wife and loading them onto the smaller wagon. Meanwhile, the physician, who had tethered the mule to a tree near his house, seemed to be having some trouble composing himself sufficiently to take his leave of the Jewish travelers. Ceaselessly he roamed among them, sketching on the ground the best and safest way to Paris, and a tear welled for an instant in his eye. With the first light of dawn, just as the first crack of the whip sounded out, he suddenly exclaimed with emotion, *You shall live.* In flowing Latin he assured the travelers, *You shall return to your Ishmaelites, and there you shall live.* And to reinforce his words he repeated the last phrase in the holy tongue: *There you shall live.*

With the slow motion of the wheels of the wagons as they moved westward, Ben Attar's soul was pierced with sadness as he took his final leave of the place where his second wife had smiled her last smile. On hearing the rabbi's voice beginning what was necessary and urgent for a journey, the first tears rolled down his cheeks: *I lift up mine eyes to the hills, whence shall my help come. My help is from the*

Lord, who made heaven and earth. He shall not let thy foot stumble, thy guardian shall not slumber. Behold, he that guardeth Israel shall neither slumber nor sleep. The Lord is thy guardian, the Lord is thy shade upon thy right hand. By day the sun shall not smite thee, nor the moon by night. The Lord shall guard thee from all evil, he shall guard thy soul. The Lord shall guard thy going forth and thy coming in, from now and forevermore.

And so they journeyed from Verdun to Chalons and from Chalons to Rheims and from Rheims to Meaux and from Meaux to Paris. The route was well etched in the memory of the wagoners and in the idolater's nostrils. Since the nights were chilly and on occasion they were lashed by the rains of autumn, they preferred this time to lodge in wayside inns or peasant cottages. But they never left the second wife's coffin alone under the sole care of Ishmaelites; there was always at least one Jew beside her, Ben Attar or the rabbi, the first wife or the Elbaz child. By the third day, which was the eve of Tabernacles, a heavy, cloying smell had begun to come from the sealed casket, and looking up they could see a black vulture circling patiently in the sky overhead. Out of respect for the dear departed one, who longed to return to the dust, the rabbi from Seville decided to exercise rabbinic license and to deem the dry land sea and the wagon to be the equivalent of a ship, and in this way they did not have to rest from their journey on the festival but could recite the festive prayers and fulfill the obligation to construct a tabernacle while moving. They pressed on with all speed to the Île de France, abbreviating their meal stops and making do with little sleep. Even when Abd el-Shafi discovered a peasant on the way using a new kind of plow that had an additional, curved blade, which turned the earth by its side, thus cutting a wider and deeper furrow, Ben Attar did not allow him to linger long enough to study it or sketch it for the benefit of the peasants of Tangier and its hinterland, but insisted that they crack the whip and urge the horses on.

By the morning of the second day of Tabernacles, as in the course of their morning prayers they crossed the bridge over the Marne and turned westward to join the busy north bank of the Seine, they were compelled to fold back the dark cover of the larger wagon and expose it to the world, so that the fresh smell of the riverbank vegetation might relieve the fetid air coming from within. Even though this exposure obliged them to fend off an occasional vulture or crow that alighted on the coffin, their spirits rose at the sight of the familiar island of the little Frankish city, resting gracefully in the middle of the river in a riot of roofs and towers beside its little white uninhabited twin. A pleasant warmth surrounded the North Africans as they entered Paris, as though their brief stay a full month before had attached them to the city with proprietorial bonds. As they approached in the light of the setting sun, they were more and more eager to see among the craft clustered in the port the green flag of the old guardship.

It was not until the horses drew up right alongside that they managed to recognize her. Even the captain's face fell on beholding the change that had overtaken his ship. In the thirty days that they had been away, the partner Abu Lutfi, left with nothing to do, had decided to change from a buyer to a vendor, in order to test the worth of the desert merchandise among the local inhabitants. To this end he had dressed the old guardship in multicolored rags and clothed the five crewmen in finery to attract the Parisians. Indeed, the burly seamen were running around among the olives and the heaps of dried fruit, the pale honeycombs and heaps of copper pans like so many salesmen, adorned with silken scarves and rainbow-colored turbans, and they even seemed to have mastered some words of enticement in the local language.

For his part, Abu Lutfi also seemed to have some difficulty in recognizing his Jewish partner as he stood on the riverbank with his company, pale and gaunt and dressed in threadbare clothes, for he ignored him and continued haggling with a local merchant, gesticulating expressively. But when he felt the warm hand of the black slave, who had lithely climbed aboard, his breath was taken away, and dropping the copper jug he was holding, he fell to his knees and prostrated himself in thanksgiving to the god of the Jews, who had not prevented great Allah from bringing his dear ones back safely, Jews and Ishmaelites alike, from the Black Forest of the Rhineland. To judge by the bows and embraces and kisses and rapturous praises of destiny, which had spared the adventurers its blows, it seemed that Abu Lutfi was not interested in knowing about the fate of the expedition, or whether his Jewish partner had succeeded in trouncing his adversaries with the rabbi's help in the further contest on the Rhine. The Ishmaelite evidently clung to his view that the whole of this great journey, on sea and by land, was totally unnecessary, for Jews by their nature are incapable of achieving a final and decisive judgment.

Therefore, to tell Abu Lutfi about the judgment that really had befallen, although not by virtue of speeches, Ben Attar took him to the stern, where, amid sacks of condiments and crates of dried fruit, before the opening that led down to the hidden cabin of a wife who had not returned, he recounted in a roundabout way the tale of the angel of death who had struck them, and even gestured toward the sealed coffin that lay all alone on the quayside, with the Elbaz child standing guard beside it. Although Ben Attar had supposed that the news of the young wife's death would be hard and painful for his partner, who had gone to great lengths each year to find her some special gift in the desert, he had not imagined that Abu Lutfi would be so distraught that he would suddenly wave his hands in the air and hold his head in despair, as though the death that had made so bold as to snatch off such a beloved passenger could cut off such a great and hairy head. On witnessing the grief of the Arab, who drew a small dagger and made a cut in his robe as a token of sympathy, Ben Attar too let loose, perhaps for the first time, a cry of terrible loss, which had been reined back until that moment.

But the pleasant autumn sun of Paris did not stand still in the sky to wait for all the grief, pain, joy, and hope that mingled in that great meeting on board the old ship to be expressed and stilled. Rabbi Elbaz, already impatient at the sight of the two partners comforting each other as though they were two husbands of a single wife, canceled all the license to delay the burial that he had granted since they had set forth from Verdun and stood resolutely before Ben Attar demanding immediate interment. To this end they must proceed instantly to the house on the opposite bank of the river, to announce to the kinsfolk who had issued the repudiation and the ban that all they had held to be settled and sealed was undone, and that they were to prepare a plot of ground that very evening for the departed wife.

At once, however, a doubt arose as to whether the kinsfolk in question had returned to Paris, or whether they had decided to remain on the banks of the Rhine to keep the Day of Atonement and the feast of Tabernacles in Worms, so as to rejoice with their holy congregation over the ban that had been declared. While the rabbi thought about whether to send his clever son secretly to the other bank with one of the crewmen to find out who was in the house, Abu Lutfi testified that there was no need, as he had seen Abulafia a couple of days before among the throng of Parisians on his deck, looking pale and miserable and disguised as an elderly peasant woman.

That being so, said Abu Lutfi, who knew their younger partner's disguises from the meetings in the Spanish March, there was no sense in further delay; they should set out at once. It was decided that the rabbi should lead the cortege, while the banned husband should remain concealed some way off, to avoid a further, irreparable repudiation. At once the five seafaring salesmen were ordered to take off their colorful garb and replace it with clean, somber robes, so that they could carry the gray wooden coffin in a dignified manner through the narrow streets of the Cité to the Jews' house on the south bank, or left bank, according to the river's flow. And in the Rue de la Harpe, near the statue of David staring at Saint Michael's fountain, in the last of the evening twilight, the Andalusian rabbi on his own entered the thick iron-studded door that he remembered well having had difficulty opening. In the courtyard, near the well, he found a small hut constructed of twigs and branches, in which the opposing party was eating its festive meal by the light of a small lamp. He did not enter the tabernacle, but announced his presence by clearing his throat. Mistress Esther-Minna was the first to hear him, and she peered out of the hut. Not recognizing him, she called Abulafia, who emerged wearing a hat with a horn of black velvet in the Worms style and black robes, as though he had anticipated the imminent mourning. Despite the darkness he recognized the uninvited guest as the Andalusian rabbi, and he started to shake, as though realizing that something had occurred. Without a moment's pause he hurried over to the little rabbi and embraced him warmly. But on this occasion Elbaz was seeking neither greeting nor embrace but merely information about the location of the nearest Jewish cemetery where they might inter a coffin they had brought with them. *A coffin?* Abulafia asked apprehensively. *What coffin?* And the rabbi drew him into the street, where the five seamen were standing around the coffin, which was lying on the pavement.

What is inside? whispered Abulafia fearfully, in a broken voice, having already perhaps sniffed the terrible cloying smell. The rabbi was filled with pity at the sight of the apprehensive third partner, who was trembling in front of the large coffin, fearing that it might house his banned uncle. But then the new wife, Mistress Abulafia, emerged from the house to see what had so attracted and detained her young husband. It seemed that she had not yet noticed the coffin or the seamen standing in the narrow street but only Rabbi Elbaz, and her delicate little face flushed with pleasure at the sight of the shrewd Andalusian rabbi, who had bested her once and had now been bested in his turn, and she dropped a little curtsy of respect and asked him with a cheery smile, *So you have returned?*

At that, the North African merchant emerged from the recess where he had concealed himself. His hair and beard were unkempt, his robe was torn, and his eyes were sunk deep in their sockets. Before Mistress Esther-Minna could draw back, he answered her question clearly: *We have returned, but not all of us.* With an air of grim despair that contained a hint of lunatic glee, he hurled himself upon the coffin and pulled out one of the planks, to furnish clear proof that henceforth the old partnership could be revived without contravening any new edict. While Abulafia clutched the wall to stop himself from collapsing, Ben Attar fixed his black eyes straight on the wide blue eyes and asked with utter hostility, *Is the new wife satisfied?*

6.

The Andalusian rabbi's firmness having paid off, the second wife was laid to rest that very night in a little burial ground squeezed between a fair vineyard, the property of Count Galand, and a small chapel dedicated to the unfortunate Saint Mark. At first Ben Attar had demanded that his second wife be buried in the courtyard of his in-laws' house, so that the grave might be watched over and tended by his kinsfolk. Abulafia was at once eager to do his uncle's bidding, but Master Levitas gently refused the request, which seemed to him to be merely vindictive, and persuaded the merchant and more especially the rabbi from Seville not to leave the deceased alone in the courtyard of a Jewish family, which might be here today and gone tomorrow, but to lay her to rest in a real cemetery, close to other deceased folk, so that she would not be overlooked at the time of the resurrection of the dead. While the sailors, transformed now into gravediggers, cleared away the undergrowth and dug an ample grave pit, Ben Attar, grim-faced and weary, distracted by grief and exhaustion, listened as Master Levitas sang the praises of the place where he was laying his wife to rest. It was odd that Master Levitas, a clear-thinking Jew who could hardly bear Jewish old wives' tales, let alone those of the Christians, so far forgot himself as to tell Ben Attar the story of Mark the hunter, who cruelly killed a doe and her young fawn in full sight of the terrified stag, which thereupon opened its mouth and prophesied in human language that he who had not spared a mother and her child would one day inadvertently kill his own wife and child. To prevent this terrible prophecy from coming true, Mark shut himself away forever in a little house surrounded by ancient Merovingian tombs, secured with an iron door and stout bolts and a grille on the window, and lived on the generosity of pilgrims setting out on the Road of Saint James for the holy shrines of the southern lands. Since he had managed to flout such a clear and terrible prophecy by willpower alone, his calamity brought him strength and his sin was a source of sanctity, and his little house became a chapel that served as a landmark for pilgrims setting forth on their long journey.

The grieving husband did not fathom the intent of Master Levitas's strange tale, but one realization had been growing steadily stronger within him since the beginning of the nocturnal funeral cortege—namely, that his second wife's death had decisively ended the ban and interdict declared against him in Worms by the red-haired arbiter, the poetic and heartless prayer leader. Not only did Abulafia, whose heart had been smitten with sorrow and guilt by the young woman's death, cling to his grim-faced uncle as a slave clings to his master, but even the reserved Master Levitas was unable to disregard the misfortune of these people who had been defeated from an ethical and a legal viewpoint alike, and so he summoned up all his resources of attention so as to listen with sympathy and compassion to the story of her last hours and her death as recounted with deep feeling by Rabbi Elbaz.

Mistress Esther-Minna's fair foxlike countenance, however, be-

trayed not only sorrow and sympathy but also the first tokens of a new
alarm. While her feet sank into the freshly dug earth piled around the
edge of the grave, and while she listened to the rabbi reciting the
prayer for the dead, she realized that the North African uncle's daring,
epic journey had indeed achieved its purpose. As the frail body
wrapped in pale green silk slid as though of its own accord into its last
resting place, between the chapel and the vines, it took with it the last
restraint that might have prevented her footloose husband from recom-
mencing his travels.

Supposing that she insisted on joining him, she thought quickly,
would he agree to take her with him? Or would he make her stay at
home to keep her promise to look after his poor child, whom she
herself, in a moment of weakness, had wrested from the Ishmaelite
nurse and taken under her own wing? In which case, Mistress Abulafia
thought, tormenting herself, who would warm her cold feet at night,
now that she had become accustomed to the soft hands of the southern man? And who would give her a glimmer of hope of turning her
barrenness to fruitfulness, if only to demonstrate to her stern mother-
in-law in Worms that the fault had not been hers? Meanwhile, until
the new direction that the contest might take became clearer, she
must try to soothe Ben Attar's feelings, for even the darkness of night
could not conceal the hatred he felt toward her. At the conclusion of
the burial she gathered the inner strength to approach him and offer
her condolences, and even to beg him to fetch from the ship his first
and only wife, who was as precious as an aunt to her, so that both of
them, together with the reverend rabbi and his son, might accept the
hospitality of her home and fulfill the command to dwell in a tabernacle. Since she had not hesitated to welcome his double menage into
her home previously, there was even less reason to do so now.

But Ben Attar, whose robe was now disfigured by a long, ugly rent
of mourning made by the little rabbi, waved her offer away and declined to enter her house. He was firmly resolved to return at once to
his ship and shut himself up with his grief in the very cabin in the
stern that had been the last home of his wonderful deceased wife.
There was no hope that the entreaties of the fair-haired woman, or her
brother's pleas, might deflect him from his purpose. He frostily signaled to his men to take up the empty coffin and return to the old

guardship, for only there would it be seemly to receive any visitor who might wish to honor the command to comfort the bereaved.

Early the next morning, after a long night bereft of sleep, Mistress Esther-Minna assembled some choice food and gave it to her Teutonic maidservant to carry, and joined Abulafia for a morning visit to the ship, which had donned mourning though there was only one mourner aboard (for the first wife, though willing, was unable to be a mourner, not being blood kin to the deceased). On the bridge in the bow, in the midst of sailors waking from sleep, Abulafia and his wife encountered the first wife, with a serious look on her bright face, very carefully laundering her dead co-wife's fine silken gowns, which Ben Attar wished to give to his orphaned son, so when the time came he would be able to dress his bride in them and by so doing be comforted somewhat for the loss of his mother, without even a grave or a tomb-stone upon which to weep.

Abu Lutfi greeted the early callers with a bow, accepted the large leather bag of food from the gentile maid with thanks, and led his restored partner and his agitated lady to the stern. This was Mistress Esther-Minna's first visit to the Moroccan ship, and consequently she took short, clumsy steps, particularly when she was slowly helped down the rope ladder into the dark hold, where fine slivers of morning light hovered in the air together with the odors of various desert wares that had lingered between south and north because of her stern repu-diation. While the visitor marveled at the depth of the small ship's belly, she was suddenly startled by the grunting of the camel, which rose slowly and with great dignity on its long legs to greet her with its small head. For a woman who had been born and bred to the sound of croaking frogs and howling wolves, there was an attractive peaceful-ness about this patient, calm desert beast, whose small head might indicate a lack of wisdom but not any viciousness of character.

The northern woman finally stooped and entered the cabin where the second wife's spirit still hovered, and where her husband had cho-sen to sit and receive condolences, in this gloomy corner, accompanied by the gurgle of the river underfoot, surrounded by timbers that had been weakened in some ancient sea battle but strengthened in readi-ness for the present expedition by the captain and his crew. Since Mistress Esther-Minna had absorbed some words of Arabic during the month of confrontation in Villa Le Juif and Worms, she realized that the conversation between uncle and nephew did not concern the pain of death or the memory of the deceased woman's good qualities but went straight to the future hope of the revived partnership. Even Abu Lutfi, the quiet Ishmaelite partner, was excited now, and with precise gestures he described the quality and quantity of all the goods that had been longing for three months to leave the darkness of the hold and burst forth into the brightly lit world outside. At the sound of the commercial Arabic babble in full spate, Mistress Abulafia's pale blue eyes darkened with sorrow, and she left the little cabin to wander down the avenues of large jars and swollen sacks, laying a soft hand on a pile of skins and cloth and making a shiny copper cooking pot ring with a tap from the toe of her shoe before halting silently before the Elbaz child and the black idolater, who were feeding the young camel with one of the loaves of bread she had brought on board.

This may have been the moment when a strange notion was born that would create a new reality after the end of the Tabernacles week and the days of mourning. Since the previous night Mistress Esther-Minna had not ceased to consider how she could defend her marriage against her husband's renewed traveling, not only because she wanted to deprive her jubilant brother of the pleasure of validating the warning he had issued back in the year 4756 against the frivolity of a match between an older widow and a questionable wandering southerner, but more particularly because she regretted every night that passed without furthering the hope that beat within her breast. And so, after returning to the cabin of mourning to take her leave of Ben Attar, whose coldness toward her seemed weaker, she obtained her husband's permission to return home alone, leaving him with his restored partners so that he could discuss business with them to his heart's content.

But Mistress Esther-Minna had no intention of sitting quietly in her corner and waiting for her husband to depart on his travels; she wanted to discover whether a spark could ignite a conflagration. That afternoon, seeing that her husband had not yet returned, she decided to go back to the ship with food and drink, as was fitting for a visit of condolence. But this time she took the poor child with her, washed and scrubbed and clothed in a fine robe. Although the startled girl walked clumsily and somewhat lopsidedly, she led her calmly along the winding streets of the island, among Parisians hurrying to their evening meals, and helped her without mishap across the new bridge that led to the ship moored on the north bank. It transpired that Abulafia had gone off with Abu Lutfi to sell their merchandise in the market of Saint Denis, and so, for lack of choice, she waved her arm to summon the pagan, who was standing all alone on the bridge, staring westward like an admiral, to help her get the heavy child on board and lower her slowly into the hold, in the conviction that an encounter with the noble, sad desert beast would soothe her desperate soul, however slightly.

Even though the girl gripped her stepmother's gown in terror, Mistress Esther-Minna felt, with her sensitivity and experience, that behind her fear the child was absorbing the smell of her southern childhood, and that in looking at the camel she was recognizing something she had lost. For lo, the trembling ceased, and her large black eyes fixed on the peacefully waving little tail. Perhaps this is the solution to the problem that has been tormenting me, the new wife's soul suddenly claimed, though she could still not determine precisely what the solution was, or even what the problem that required a solution was. Then Abulafia could be heard on deck, speaking in Arabic to Abu Lutfi, and the merry liveliness of his noisy conversation showed that far from deepening his old melancholy, the second wife's death had released him from it, so that it seemed as though a new happiness animated him. From now on, she felt sure, her young husband would be able to guard himself against any further designs that might threaten his beloved partnership.

When the two of them descended into the hold and Abulafia discovered his daughter standing calmly beside the camel, trying to feed him a slice of black bread from her pudgy hand, a cry of encouragement burst from his mouth at the strength of his dear wife, who, according to his understanding and his own notions, was tempting the accursed enchantment that had taken hold of his daughter to change its dwelling place from his child's soul to that of the camel. Although it was impossible to tell whether the stubborn sprite really would exchange the soft body of the child for the little rounded hump of the patient creature, Abulafia seemed to betray a new weakness of purpose, for now, for the first time since the end of the reign of the stern

Ishmaelite nurse, who had been sent to Barcelona in his stead to put an end to the partnership, he saw a charming smile again on the face that should have been as fair as her mother's, if it had turned out differently.

Indeed, in the half-darkness of the hold of the old guardship, among sacks of condiments and jars of oil, a new affection seemed to flow not only between the camel and the odd child but also between Abulafia and his wife, who even in moments of carnal intimacy seemed to have had difficulty in looking straight at each other ever since the North African expedition had burst upon them. So the following day Abulafia himself took his daughter down into the hold, which was gradually being emptied of its cargo, and asked the Elbaz child and the slave to keep an eye open to make sure that the growing friendship between the girl and the beast did not cause her any harm.

Meanwhile, the grieving husband sat in his torn robe, hidden away in a cabin in the bowels of the ship, pursuing his silent mourning despite the festive season. From time to time the first wife descended to him, bearing food or drink, to rub his hands and feet with almond oil and to sing the praises of the departed. Even the rabbi, who was not happy about this secretive mourning, which impugned the joy of the feast of gathering in and the commandment to dwell in a tabernacle, visited him occasionally to speak words of admonition. Ben Attar listened and nodded, his eyes dull, his head drooping on his chest, his expression that of one who wishes to die by degrees. But when his partners, Abulafia and Abu Lutfi, came in, he shook off his gloom to utter a short, sharp sentence about the price of a copper pot or the urgent need to find someone in the Capetian capital to rid them of the burden of the camel.

Before the camel could be offered for sale it must be taken ashore and fed, and it would be best to send it to graze in the fine fields and vegetable gardens of the Duke de la Teulerie, which adjoined a dense forest called by the locals Lupara on account of the packs of wolves that roamed it, attracted by its burrows. Therefore, toward the close of the festive week, on the eve of the Solemn Assembly, one of the sailors was sitting in a garden holding a long cord, at the other end of which a long-necked item of merchandise delicately cropped the tenderest greenery in Paris, pricking up its ears curiously from time to time at the

Jewish boy and the young idolater chatting in the language of the desert and at the disturbed girl, who was reminded by the sounds of Arabic of the nurse who had been taken away from her.

Now that the autumn blew an occasional cold breeze over the Île de France, the young people, knowing that in a few more days they would be summoned to board the ship and sail away and that for days and nights on end they would sway to the monotonous rhythm of the wind flapping the sail, sought to enjoy to the full the rustle of the russet leaves on the firm ground. Since the rabbi's son had absolute faith in the son of the desert to take them safely home again, especially if it was somewhere as simple and straightforward as the right bank of the river, he offered to take his companions on a short excursion to the top of a low knoll that could be seen some way off, which he had no doubt was the same hill, topped with a ruined arch, from which he and Ben Attar, the first of all the passengers on board, had seen the enchanted city.

But he had unwittingly mistaken for the western hill another, northern one, which seemed low only because of a white smudge that spread in its center. Since the girl walked with a slight bias that constantly had to be corrected, the Andalusian child, who had become the leader of the small expedition, wondered whether they should keep climbing the slope, whose steepness was only too evident to their young legs, or whether they should turn around and go back to the ship before the drizzle that was accompanying them turned into a full-scale rainstorm. While he was still debating, the rainclouds burst, turning clothing and flesh to a single pulp, until they had no choice but to take shelter beside a large cottage that they had previously taken pains to avoid, since black smoke was spiraling up from its chimney. While they huddled unobtrusively under the overhanging thatch, the demon in the girl's soul suddenly broke into its old howl, which outdid the tumult of the rain and brought two smiling women out of the silent house, dressed in colorful gowns stitched together, to the boy's surprise, from the green silk that they had brought on their ship and bartered for eggs and cheese on their way to Worms.

When the women caught sight of the young visitors pressed against the outer wall of their cottage, they were as joyful as hunters who have caught a splendid prey. The boy and the black slave calculated the chances of running for their lives, but the women caught the girl and invited her into their cottage, so that her two companions had no choice but to follow in the hope of rescuing her. They found themselves in a large room with a rush-covered floor, and in a corner a small fire burned, over which hung on a spit a delicious-smelling piglet, its eyes closed with a self-important air. The boy's soul shuddered at the proximity of the forbidden, unclean beast, but the African turned excitedly toward a row of brightly painted wooden images, all representing the same young man, with impassive countenance and a short beard, spreading his arms out wide to save his soul or to embrace the world, it was impossible to tell which. While the two women laughed heartily, in fact somewhat indecently, at the young visitors' confusion, the door of an inner chamber opened and a third woman appeared, carrying a skinny baby in her arms and followed by a lean yet agile older man carelessly dressed in paint-stained garments, whose name, Pigealle, the youngsters had difficulty catching.

Just as the pagan was astonished at the sight of the row of figurines, so the man seemed excited at the sight of the dark-skinned denizen of the desert who had happened into his house, and dragged him firmly over to the window the better to inspect his face. The women had already sensed the man's urgent desire, and as though by tacit agreement they smiled at the visitors and set about busily making them welcome. First they removed their sodden robes and made signs that it would be better if the visitors took off their baggy trousers too, so as to dry them by the fire, and meanwhile they hurried to cut thin slices from the hindquarters of the piglet dozing over the fire.

The only son of the rabbi from Seville, unable to bear the disgrace that had come upon him, leaped to his feet to thrust away the slice of abominable meat being offered to him on the tip of a knife. But he was unable to prevent the girl, whose nakedness was covered by a sheepskin coat, from snatching the morsel and putting it to her mouth. Even the African, who might or might not have reverted from his temporary Judaism to his original paganism, was seized by a frenzy of eating and also drinking, since the lean old man, who had not taken his eyes off the young man since he had removed his trousers and revealed his black nakedness, plied him with ruby wine, possibly with the intention of befuddling his mind and diminishing his resistance. Indeed, the Frankish wine achieved its purpose well, for the youth, after giving thanks in the form of a deep obeisance toward one of the figurines, submitted himself to the ministrations of the women, who led him into the inner chamber and laid him on a bed, then gracefully folded one of his legs and gently stroked his young manhood so that it roused itself until its narrow slit stared at the enthusiastic artisan, who was already screwing up his eyes and drawing a first bright scarlet line on a wooden panel.

And so the youngsters were held captive by these strange but insistent hosts, who barred the door of the cottage until the old artist had finished studying, with line and color, what could be learned from the naked body of a member of an unknown race lying before him. But in the midst of the silence of the slowly passing hours there rose the old wail of the accursed girl, which threatened to become a scream. The women hurriedly silenced her with fine fragrant slices from the haunches of the piglet, whose face still bore a pensive and melancholy air. The boy from Seville, who knew himself and was aware that the hunger raging inside him was liable to drive him out of his wits, closed his eyes and covered them with his hands, and tried his hardest to imagine how his father the rabbi would reason in his place. After a short while he came to a simple conclusion, in the spirit of the logic of his sire's bold discourses. If heaven, which watched over all and exacted payment for every deed, had not hastened to take the soul of a Jewish girl who was gorging herself ceaselessly and with evident pleasure on the forbidden and abominable meat, it might be meant as a clear sign to him that instead of being a martyr to his hunger, which was bringing him close to fainting, it would be better to strengthen himself so he could be ready to escape and raise the alarm.

A plan took shape in his head, and slowly he removed his hands and opened his eyes. He found a great silence all around, for the sated girl had fallen asleep at the feet of one of the women, while from the adjoining chamber there came only the sound of chisel on wood. Rising to his feet, he started to walk across the large chamber in feigned aimlessness, blushing at the sight of the Frankish babe sucking at the pale round breast of the young woman, who eyed the boy calmly. Then, casually, he turned toward the remains of the piglet, still hovering above the dying fire. With an effort he stared into the eyes of the roasted creature as though trying to learn the secret of its stubborn persistence in its unclean nature. Suddenly his face lit up, and he decided to punish it for its obstinacy, and reaching out, he grabbed a pinkish chunk, brought it warily to his mouth, and licked it with the tip of his tongue, wondering at the flavor, which resembled salted butter rather than meat. Before nausea could well up, he thrust the piece of meat into his mouth and chewed it rapidly, then, before its uncleanness had a chance to affect him, he tore off another chunk and thrust it into his mouth, and then another, and one last one to strengthen his spirit in the face of the terrible deed he had done. Only then did he approach the door, unbar it, and run for dear life, paying no heed to the voices of the women, who tried to stop him.

From the pink color of the sky, which had cleared, he realized that they had been detained for a long time and that evening was approaching. He made for the river, which to the best of his knowledge lay straight ahead. For the first time since he had joined the expedition he was utterly alone, among the empty fields that surrounded the small Parisian isle. Since he was careful to avoid isolated cottages along the way, particularly a large one with many windows from which loud sounds of singing were coming, the boy seemed to have caught the girl's slantwise movement, and his little legs took him along paths that led westward rather than south, so that as twilight descended he found himself not, as he had hoped, on the bank of the river but on top of the little star-shaped hill crowned with a ruined Roman arch where he had stood with the leader of the expedition on that first evening. Then the boy's body shook with a sob of gratitude that he had been shown the way. Because he could not spew forth what he had eaten, he fell to his knees, as he had learned to do from the black pagan, and swore to expiate the sin he had sinned by means of fasting and prayer. As the twilight extinguished the sun's dazzling death throes, and on the island in the midst of the river the Parisians began to kindle the lights that would show the little wayfarer the right direction to take, he chose once more the avenue that led him to the open square beside the riverbank, in the hub of which he was surprised to discover the little pile of stones that he had made with his own hands on that distant evening, which still stood, indicating the way back.

When the boy reached the boat, he was not surprised to hear that the black slave and the girl had returned before him and had been taken by Abulafia to his house on the opposite bank, but he was surprised that his father had not waited anxiously for his return but had accepted Abulafia's invitation to say his evening prayers in the tabernacle. Had the dumb girl managed to recount the sin of the abominable meat, and had his father decided to disown him? Deep sorrow seized the boy, and he tried to drive out the impurity that clung to his guts with a cake of dried figs sprinkled with cinnamon. But the fragrant sweetness spreading in his mouth did not calm his soul, and he decided to seek consolation from Abu Lutfi and Abd el-Shafi, who, being gentiles and therefore living their uncleanness without blame or guilt, might be able to soothe away the sin that burned inside him. He was surprised to find them on the old bridge, sitting and conversing conspiratorially with a third man, a stranger clad in the local garb. Seeing the boy approaching, they fell suddenly silent, and he too halted, as it occurred to him that their impurity, even if it were as wide as the sea, did not extend to the eating of pork, and that if the smell of his abomination assailed their nostrils, their wrath might be doubled at his assault on two faiths at once. So he turned back to the stern and descended into the hold, which during the day had given up all its cargo, now scattered in the world, and stood dark and empty, with only the tawny camel stepping through the emptiness as through the desert.

In this dark space the boy was suddenly flooded with longing for the second wife, beside whose cabin only had he been able to surrender himself to long hours of sweet slumber. He groped his way to the bowels of the ship, to rediscover the scent of the abandoned cabin. There, by the light of a lamp, surrounded by the fragrance of herbs and nard burning on a little incense burner, he discovered the ship's grieving owner in the company of the first wife. They were sitting together on a blanket spread on the ground, dining in silence. Deep in the bowels of the ship, attentive to the faint flow of the river beneath them, Ben Attar and his wife seemed cut off not only from the existence of the city of Paris but also from whatever was being hatched above their heads on the bridge.

When they caught sight of the young visitor coming to offer his condolences, they smiled at him affectionately and invited him to join their meal and help himself to some of the remaining stew. At first he wished to refuse, not only because he was not in the least hungry, but also because he was afraid to dip his defiled fingers into a clean cooking pot. But he also feared that they might suspect him of refusing to touch the pot because tears of mourning might have fallen into it or because of the touch of the dead woman's spirit that still inhabited the cabin. Therefore, so as not to offend the owner, in whose hand lay his own safe return to Seville, he dipped cautious fingertips into the pot and picked out a chunk of meat that still smelled of sheep droppings. When he put it into his mouth and closed his eyes, he could see a simultaneously nauseating and attractive image of the furtive faces of the green-clad women in the cottage, standing around the head of the piglet, about to cut off its ears. Finally the nausea that had been restrained thanks to the friendly looks of the gentile women burst forth, and the boy turned deathly pale and swayed fearfully. He tried to escape, but his strength deserted him, and leaning over among the soot-stained timbers, he vomited up clean and unclean meats together. When he saw what was happening in the beloved wife's cabin he let out a wild shriek, as though the raucous little demon that inhabited the girl had entered him too.

Surprisingly, the owner and his only wife showed no signs of revulsion, nor of anger at the way he had sullied the cabin of their memories, but rather of terror, as though the death that had struck their household once might succumb to the temptation to strike again. With hands experienced in childrearing they discerned a fever lurking behind the pallor, and so they hurriedly wrapped the little body in a blanket and laid a damp cloth on the eyes that stared at them guiltily. Ben Attar hastened up onto the bridge to tell Abd el-Shafi to send a sailor to clean up the cabin. And he dispatched the young pagan, who had just returned from the house on the other bank, to summon Rabbi Elbaz back from Master Levitas's tabernacle, the splendor of which had driven all thoughts of his only son's absence out of his mind.

But before Elbaz could arrive and take charge of the boy, who had fallen asleep, Ben Attar took advantage of the respite afforded by this chance occurrence to interrupt his self-imposed mourning in the bowels of the ship, if only for a short while, and to inspect the goods that were ready to leave the ship. He gratefully inhaled the cool night air of the Parisian isle, from which rose the smoke of many fires and sounds of merriment. Screwing up his eyes, he tried to discern on the other bank the place between the vines and the chapel where his young wife rested, waiting to take her last leave of her husband when the memorial was erected on her grave.

He shivered slightly. His wife's hand was touching his nape. Though it seemed to him that her touch was firmer than usual, he was not certain, for ever since they had arrived at Worms they had avoided touching each other. He looked closely at the dear face that had accompanied him since his youth and that now invited him to descend to the cabin, which was ready for his return, cleaned and tidied and fumigated with lavender to dispel any unpleasant odor. Only the feverish child was still there. Should he be moved somewhere else, or stay there until his father arrived? Ben Attar decided not to touch the boy but to wait for Rabbi Elbaz, who indeed arrived after a short while, alarmed and breathless, stumbling on the rope ladder, and hastened to bend over the child curled up on the floor and call his name anxiously. Then the boy's bloodshot eyes opened, and despite their tiredness they stared severely at his father's face. *Did he know about the sin he had committed? And if he did, could he save him from the harsh verdict?*

At least it is not the cold arching spasm that draws the head toward its death. A strange hope burst forth in the Andalusian rabbi's soul at the sight of his son curled up on the floor of the cabin like a soft bundle. Was it possible that the absent woman had sent an evil spirit to harm the rabbi, because of the permission he had given to transport her unburied from Verdun to Paris? *Me, not him,* he shouted bitterly at the spirit, and hurriedly picked the child up in his arms to take him away from the ship to the Jews' tabernacle.

Yes, the rabbi from Seville had suddenly lost his faith in the ship's owner, and even rejected rudely the compassion of the first wife, who offered to help him to cover the child. In this way Elbaz fell prey to an evil thought, for he suspected Ben Attar of trying to punish him for his unsuccessful speech in the synagogue in Worms. Since Ben Attar knew that it was forbidden to accuse a man in the midst of his grief or to impede him in his despair, he immediately told Abd el-Shafi to order his sailors to make a stretcher out of ropes so they could move the sick child safely to the opposite bank. The gates to the island were already closed, so they put out a boat and carefully lowered the boy, strapped to the stretcher, onto it, and also his anxious father, and in case of any mishap they also sent the black slave, for whom this was the third crossing to the south bank this day. There was something wonderfully graceful about the little boat pulling away from the colorful, wide-bellied Muslim ship onto the calm surface of the moonlit river, gliding over it almost without a ripple from north to south, toward the convent of Saint Germain des Prés, which was in the process of being rebuilt.

It was nearly midnight when a heavy knock sounded on the iron-clad door of the Jews' house, and the nephew and partner and his wife, who was now a partner despite herself, were asked urgently to take in a sick child with a secret abomination burning within him, lending his eyes a sunken look as though they were outlined with kohl and painting his cheeks with a porcine pinkness. Mistress Esther-Minna welcomed the sick child with great animation, which betrayed, despite her evident distress, signs of mysterious joy. It was as though by means of this sick child coming to be nursed back to health in her house she might be reattached to the members of the expedition, and above all to its leader, whose failure had brought her down as well. Despite the advanced hour, she spared neither her maidservant nor the sleep of her husband, although he immediately sank back onto his bed. She did not even spare the howling of the girl, who had returned from her outing excited and disturbed but not dejected. It was Mistress Esther-Minna's aim now to be simple and generous, and not only clever and right. She welcomed her little guest by turning the sleeping arrangements upside down. First she moved Master Levitas to one side of the little tabernacle and put Rabbi Elbaz to sleep there too, so that he could share in honoring the commandment, and then she entreated Abulafia to take a coverlet and disappear into his daughter's chamber to find his sleep by her side, all to enable her to set the boy down next to her in her husband's bed, so that she could watch over him with her full attention until morning.

Mistress Abulafia lay awake and alert beside the motherless child from Seville, determined not to miss a breath or a murmur, a sigh or a groan, whether due to pain or to a dream. Outside, the kindly moon had sunk in the sky, and black velvet sailed slowly upon the Seine, which embraced between its two graceful banks the heart of little Paris. Then a new and terrible dread mingled with a gentle, uncomprehended happiness in the soul of this childless woman who was no longer young, as she swore to herself that she would not allow the angel of death to strike a second blow at these dark-skinned southerners, who had been dragged to Europe by the force of her repudiation. Instead, she would enlist the full force of her virtue and resourcefulness in the service of this sick child, to whom it was not only her duty but her desire to be a second mother.

So awake was Mistress Esther-Minna that she dispensed not only with sleep but with the lightest catnap. She rose from her bed and stood like a sentry over the sick child, who tossed and turned in his sleep as his sin donned and doffed various nightmarish forms. So deep was the silence all around that Mistress Esther-Minna felt that she could not only catch every rustle and creak of her house but even interpret it correctly. From the other side of the wall came Abulafia's rapid breathing, as he tried to ignore his daughter's disturbed spirit while she lay beside him. Below, in the little tabernacle, the rabbi was pouring out his prayers in a whisper, so as not to disturb Master Levitas's sleep, perfumed as it was with the joyful command to dwell in booths. So wonderful was the silence all around her that she imagined that if she opened her window and strained her ears she would catch not only the thudding of the water against the side of the ship but even the idolater's footsteps as he made his way longingly to the sculptor's cottage. And if she tried very hard, closing her eyes and inclining her head and extinguishing every stray thought or wish inside herself, she might even hear the faintest sigh of the first wife as she sought love in the bowels of the ship.

7.

She crumbled the ashy lavender and straightened the rug once more on the floorboards to make the place more inviting for sleep, already waiting to fold the mourner into its embrace. The first wife was also intending to extinguish the lamp before leaving, so the shadows flitting among the timbers would not disturb her husband, whose eyes were following her every movement. But before she could reach out to the lamp she was stopped by two commands that were evidently interconnected: *Do not put it out and do not leave.* It was as though the North African Jew felt that to the presence of his first and now only wife was added something new, which could not be deciphered in darkness but needed a full flame to bring to light everything that was latent within it. Small wonder, then, that these few words, spoken gently and longingly yet firmly, made the large, calm woman tremble, and her eyelids slowly sank.

Although she knew only too well that it was forbidden to mourn on festive days, that what Ben Attar was doing here in the belly of the ship was a private and rebellious mourning and the Andalusian rabbi had warned him that heaven would not recognize it, she was nevertheless a little frightened of the sudden upsurge of desire that, despite its strict legality, not only burst forth from sorrow and mourning but might also contain a strange desire to join the dead wife to the living one in a single congress on the rug. She raised her eyes imploringly to her husband and tried to indicate to him with a slight gesture of hesitation that if what was stirring here was a need of the body and not of the heart it would be better to wait a few days more until the ship had set sail again, its swaying motion helping to soothe the body that had become so stiff and hard on the arduous land journey, which had not yet ended.

But Ben Attar's mind was directed not at all to his own body but to his wife's, whose warm being surrounded and caressed every pore in his flesh. Though he had not touched her as a man since that dream-like nocturnal entry into the narrow alleys of Worms when his two wives had been snatched away from him, he knew by looking that on the funereal journey from the Lotharingian to the Frankish river, the living wife had neither stiffened nor hardened, but on the contrary had softened and widened, and that a new opening might have opened up in her. This he set about exposing, not only with the seriousness of his lovemaking but also with a hint of resentment, which surprised him both with its novelty and with its strength.

Though the resentment was directed not against the wife who was with him, whom his lips and hands were exploring with powerful de-sire, but against the one who was absent, who had so quickly despaired of her secondary status that she had wanted not to remain on the earth but to be embraced by it, the only wife nevertheless sensed that it was

281

aimed at her, and for the first time since she had known herself as a woman, she felt herself repudiating her husband, as though the arduous journey she had made between those two great European rivers had made her into a new woman. Even though in the narrow confines of a tiny cabin, hemmed in by timbers blackened by the fires of ancient combat, any repudiation could be only mental and not real, Ben Attar was obliged to hold her fast as he stripped her of layer after layer of clothing, something he had never had to do before, for her nakedness, with all its mysteries, had always been offered to him generously and totally, from the outset, without any effort on his part.

Their strange, frenetic struggle confirmed her fear that the husband who was disrobing her was not only trying to unite with what she had now acquired as sole wife but was also seeking within her the remnants of his second wife. This certainty, which made her soul shake with sorrow and pain, also surprisingly aroused within her a sharp, unfamiliar thrill, so that for a moment it seemed as though her two breasts, breaking free from the fiercely ripped fabric of her restraining clothing, were not only her own breasts but those of another woman, whose nipples and navel were arousing and fueling her own desire.

Indeed, by the lamplight flickering on her plump form and on limbs that had been filled out and rounded by those leisurely dinners beside the campfire on their wayside halts between the Île de France and Lotharingia, it became clear to the increasingly agitated husband that the prophecy of his heart had not been mistaken, and that on those accursed, miserable days, as his second wife was ebbing away, his first wife was secretly flowering. The excited Ben Attar hastened to untie one of the yellowing cords with which Abd el-Shafi had bound the beams together, this time not to tie himself up, as he had done during the sea voyage to assuage and console a young wife for the sorrow of being the second and not the first, but to bind the hands of this large, heavy woman, his only wife, who was now required to satisfy his lascivious desire, which despite all that had occurred still refused to relinquish the power of its duality.

Was it the same desire that was welling up in the belly of the ship that drew the young idol-worshipper back along the dark lanes of the north bank to the cottage with the idols, where he had been imprisoned that afternoon with the two Jewish children? He was attracted there not only by a strange urge to worship at last before a representation of his own image rather than images of strangers, but also because he could not forget the laughter of the women who had so boldly reached out to touch his private parts, which had since remained full and stiff in homage to them. Although the black youth's desire was as yet virginal and vague both in its objects and in its limits, the autumn night of Paris, concealing its stars with a fine mist, was charming and seductive enough to lead this son of the desert, the sensitive heir of the navigational skills of his ancestors, safely among the dark cottages and fields, the croaking of frogs and the howling of jackals and the barking of foxes, straight to the woodcarver's cottage, where to his joy a small light was still shining.

The face suspended in the open window was so dark that the man did not notice the youth staring at him from so near, even though it was his image that the sculptor was trying to conjure up in his mind. Even in the depths of the night, while the three women lay sleeping among the figurines scattered around the room, the desire of his craft did not leave the old artisan alone, for before the Son of God revealed himself in his last and final form in the approaching millennium, the sculptor wished to season the vision of his savior with the features of a man of alien race. With his copper chisel he continued to gouge the white flesh of the block of wood before him, struggling to dredge the black face up from the dimness of his memory, not suspecting that it was right beside him, framed in his own window. But the eldest of the three women, turning in her sleep, noticed the dark visitor, who was drawn in wonder to his own image emerging from the flesh of the white wood. Without saying a word to the craftsman, who was totally absorbed in his work, she rose and tiptoed barefoot outside and stretched out a warm hand to touch the bare neck of the African, who was so startled and excited by the renewed touch on his flesh that he was too afraid even to turn his head.

The old woman, who despite her white hair was full of the sap of life, did not release the fair prey that had been attracted to the light out of the depths of the night. With a grip that might have been a caress she drew him inside the cottage. She was in no hurry to hand him over to the surprised artisan, but took him close to the darkening embers of the dying fire so he could warm his body before being stripped of his tattered clothes. Although the young man did not know whether she was trying to strip him in the middle of the second watch of the night as a model for the artisan's image or for her own benefit, he did not hold back but undid his belt himself, so as to display to the man and the woman, who were both smiling amiably, his trimmed manhood, which was aching and lengthening, having been unable for so many hours to find relief.

A similar circumcised male organ, albeit a limp and childish one that still knew neither pain nor enmity, was exposed between the legs of young Elbaz as he tossed and turned in the coils of his fever upon Abulafia's bed, trying to tear off his tunic and trousers with his little hands. Although Mistress Esther-Minna attempted delicately to cover up his private parts and conceal them from her eyes, the child kept trying to push the coverlet away again, as though it were not a simple covering but an abominable shaggy beast clinging to him. But Mistress Abulafia neither wakened her husband to share in her anxiety for the child nor called Rabbi Elbaz up from the tabernacle to join her in praying for the little Andalusian. This woman had such confidence in herself that she preferred to pray to heaven on her own, without partners whose prayers might be rejected.

Since she was not so naive as to rely on prayer alone, she hastened to rouse her old Lotharingian servant and told her to boil some water so that she could wipe away with a soft, damp towel the perspiration and the remains of vomit that clung to the child's thin limbs, as well as the tears trickling down his face. She adamantly rejected any attempt to explain events as the result of witchcraft or demons—faithful to her late father, Rabbi Levitas, who liked to find in every detail and in every place, however obscure or mean, the holy spirit, which should be listened to—so she now tried, while washing the rabbi's son, whose tangled curls reminded her suddenly of her husband's, to extract from his mutterings the secret of the young people's excursion on the right bank. A strange excursion, which had made the clever boy feverish and confused and had relieved the wretched girl of her depression.

But when the boy fluttered his scorching eyes and saw the bright eyes of the new wife, whose repudiation had brought real calamity upon the owner of the ship and failure to his father the rabbi, he sealed his lips. Although the wise and fair woman was leaning over him with tender maternal affection, he knew only too well that if he let out the secret of the swine's flesh in his guts, it would become a two-edged sword that would be plunged straight back into his belly. But Mistress Esther-Minna, who had suffered for several years because of the silence of the holy spirit dwelling in the mute girl, would on no account allow the holy spirit contained within this strange boy the right of silence. Moreover, in the half-light of the second watch, this dark-skinned, tousled child looked like a little Abulafia who had miraculously arrived in her house in order to be shaped and educated from scratch. Thus she decided to draw out the Andalusian holy spirit by roundabout means. Picking up her chair, she placed it at the head of the bed, behind the child, who was lying on his back, washed and perfumed, so that he would not see her face and fear her reactions but might think that he was talking to himself in a dream. In fact the whispered questions of the hidden woman brought instant replies from the innocent young heart, although not in the language in which they were asked but in wild, fragmented Andalusian Arabic. Even though Mistress Esther-Minna understood not a word of the passionate Arabic confession that sought to yield up to her the sin of eating abominable things, she did not interrupt the flow of the words but listened very intently, in the confident hope that having begun in the tongue of the Ishmaelites, it would eventually end in the tongue of the Jews.

Meanwhile, the Arabic confession pierced the curtain to enchant with its old familiar tones the spirit of a young girl whose depression had been turned to wonder as by the wave of a magic wand, and whose dullness had been turned to terror by the sight of the carved images, the women's laughter, and the taste of swine's flesh. Instead of rising and howling as she usually did, to summon up from the sea depths the mother who had abandoned her forever, she crept cautiously out of her bed to stare attentively at her father, Abulafia, who had fallen peacefully asleep at her side. And instead of tugging insistently at his hands as usual, to remind him to give her back the mother who had forsaken her, she merely reached out a small but firm hand to touch his curly locks and stroke his face, so that he would open his eyes and produce for her out of the misty night not her lost mother but the young idol-worshipper, who might lead her back to the cottage of wonders on the opposite bank of the river.

The words of the boy Elbaz's Ishmaelite confession had the power not only to pierce a curtain and excite the dream of the wondering girl in her cubicle but to continue down the winding wooden staircase and to float, faintly yet clearly, through the greenery bedecking Master Levitas's little tabernacle, which symbolized the transitory nature of human existence, particularly of that of the Jews. There, beside the palm fronds, myrtle sprigs, and boughs of willow, bound together and placed like a slim, fresh second wife on Master Levitas's couch, was one who could not only hear the feverish child's muddled Arabic confession but understand it too. But the rabbi, his own mouth tainted by the abominable food eaten by his only begotten son, took care not to stir from his place or utter a sound, so as not to offer a sign to the young confessor that his father was suffering with him.

Meanwhile, in the little cabin in the bowels of the old guardship anchored in the harbor, a strange new thought on the subject of sin and punishment was deliriously coursing. The North African husband, whose eyes roamed excitedly over the ample, pity-inspiring nakedness of the large quiet woman shimmering on the floor of the cabin, suddenly believed that he could merge the young mistress of the cabin who had gone to her rest with the first wife who was lying in front of him. Therefore, before he submitted to the lust fermenting in his blood, urging him to fall to his knees to embrace caress kiss lick bite the pure rounded parts of his wife's body, he closed his eyes for an instant, and with the imagination of his desire he conjured up the face and body of his second wife. Now he could see the narrow amber-colored eyes with their green glint, could scan the long brown legs, the legs of a girl who had been married before she had run her course, could feel with the palms of his outstretched hands the smoothness of the flat stomach, the firm, desire-laden breasts, the jab of the reddish nipples erect with passion. To the sound of the gurgling of the Seine underneath him, he clung resolutely to his desire to blend two lusts in a single act of coupling. But while he melted and dissolved in longing for the duality taking shape within him, and while his hand was groping to remove his robe so as to add passionate nakedness to an unbridled congress replete with possibilities, he felt his rigid member anticipating him in its quest for satisfaction and relief, and, still beating against the mourner's rent in his robe, helplessly enveloping itself, and itself alone, in a warm slippery coating of its own seed.

Is this the congress I was longing for? Ben Attar thought in a fit of despair and disappointment at the seed he had discharged in vain into the little cabin. For if so, this is not a congress but a punishment that I am seeking to inflict not only upon myself but upon the one who is left with me. Indeed, the first wife, who had learned since her nuptials to interpret every detail of her husband's actions, could already detect the smell of the vainly spilled seed in the dark cabin. Her heavy hips, which had been arched in anticipation of coupling, subsided disappointedly on the rug on which had slept another woman, who had not disappeared even in death. The hands that had longed to comfort with gentle caresses the beloved man's weary, aching form quietly unfolded. Although she was ostensibly freed now, she did not even cover her cheated nakedness but merely blew out the now pointless lamp, curled up like a huge white fetus, and tried to join her humiliation not only to that of the absent woman, who had been expected to put off her shroud and couple against her will, but also that of the manhood that had lost its head and missed its aim.

Indeed, this manhood was now shamefully soft, limp and weeping. Although it feared to approach the sole wife in this state, for she might already have despaired of it, it knew that its only hope of redeeming itself was through real contact, which would bring consolation if not consummation. So the owner of the ship went down on his knees in the dark and cautiously felt with his lips along the woman's naked body to locate the right and proper place in which to bury this shamefaced object. And there, in the wide space between her breasts, Ben Attar felt a moistness in his beard, so that for a moment he was startled by the idea that the woman, having despaired of his manhood, was attempting to suckle him. Cautiously he reached out his hands and brought her two nipples close to his ears, perhaps to hear the sound of this new flux. But the hillocks of sweetness that gently tickled his earlobes were dry, and to judge by their soft limpness, desire was still far from them. Only then was the man who had led the arduous expedition from the south to the north obliged to recognize that the tears he had held back so stubbornly for so many days were now pouring unstoppably from his eyes.

Ben Attar could not have imagined how wonderful and sweet the woman found the man's tears flowing between her breasts. She kept quiet, careful to give no sign that might cause them to stop. Sometimes it is precisely when manhood fails and gives way that maleness takes on a sweet and attractive taste. Even though she knew the tears were for the second wife, who was lost forever, for whom henceforth he was precluded from finding a substitute, she was neither offended nor angry. On the contrary, she felt proud that the tears for a woman who was lost were not lost themselves, but flowed between her own breasts and dripped into her navel. She had a hope that the second wife's tears might moisten her own desire and enter in all purity into her womb, this womb that now parted its lips to whisper with its little tongue the sole wife's announcement that she did not want the man's fantasy but only his real presence and his love.

The spirit of the imagination can not only be extended, it can also run riot, as it did now among the women waking each other up in the woodcarver's cottage at the sight of the young visitor, who had been drawn in the depths of the night to worship naked before the representation of his own image. First they laughed a little and jabbered in their own language at the sight of the ebony figure standing in silence and seeking the lines of its face wrestling with the white flesh of the wood, but slowly their eyes seemed to widen in sweet dread at the sight of the neat groove dividing two dark gleaming buttocks carved by a perfect hand, until the white-haired woman sighed deeply and put her little hand to her mouth to bite it.

The woman's open display of desire, instead of making her friends snigger in embarrassment, swept away any anxiety over pleasure at the sight of this nocturnal tempter standing in all the splendor of his youthful manhood. The innocent devotion with which the African stranger stripped himself before the old craftsman inflamed the lascivious imagination not of one woman alone but of all three, opening a dark breach to a new, disturbing, but infinitely degenerate horizon.

Already a flash of lecherous complicity passed from one woman's eyes to the others', and was silently aimed at the elderly master of the house, to check whether he still needed the visible image standing motionless before him, or whether the young man might now be requisitioned for another need, neither artistic nor religious but full of the wonderful sap of life. The old woodcarver, whose spirit was so amused by the women's excitement filling his cottage that it seemed to be infecting him too, laid down his chisel, dusted the wood chips off the block of wood struggling to find its wounded identity, then covered it with a piece of cloth as though to hide from its view the orgy that was about to break out. Then he withdrew to his cot in a dark little corner, but he did not cover his face before he knew which of the three women was favored by fate in the draw.

It emerged that the three women were unwilling, or unable, to wait to draw lots, preferring to cast in their lot together in unbridled licentiousness. Before they could strip off their garments they approached the youth, whose black flesh gave them the freedom to pass him from hand to hand, from mouth to mouth, from lust to lust, as though he were an animal rather than a human. The more the triangular desire raging in the third watch of the night intensified in its brazen savagery, the more the wonderful thrill that transported the crumbling virginity of the son of the desert became blended with sorrow and pain. From the groans of pleasure bursting from his mouth, resembling the sound of a wild camel, he knew that to the end of his days he would have no rest from the fury of his longings, which would always draw him and his descendants to make their way from the south to the north.

Surprisingly, with the first glimmer of daylight on the horizon, the same tones of sorrow and pain were intermingled also in the thoughts of Esther-Minna, whose heart was pierced by a fine new longing. Unlike the slave who was being tossed about in the old woodcarver's cottage on the right bank with the kisses and bites of three unbridled women, the painful longing in the Jews' house in the Rue de la Harpe next to Saint Michael's fountain aimed gently and compassionately in the opposite direction, from north to south. Ever since that night when Ben Attar first appeared in her house with the boy, she had ostensibly been waiting only for the moment when she would finally be freed from the nightmare of the southern expedition that had come to turn her world upside down, but now, as the moment of their departure came closer and closer, Mistress Abulafia felt a certain sadness at losing her discomfited visitors, perhaps especially because of her new anxiety about the Andalusian child who had finally sunk into a deep sleep in her husband's bed. For after he had finished mumbling and groaning his confession in the outlandish, impenetrable language of the Ishmaelites, he began, this time in the familiar and holy tongue of the Jews, to recount his fears concerning the imminent sea voyage.

Esther-Minna had never before had a real child whom she could train in the paths of righteousness by day and watch over by night, and so when Rabbi Elbaz's outline appeared in the doorway of her bedchamber with the first breeze of morning, she hurried out to meet him, to prevent him from depriving her of this graceful, curly-headed little boy who had finally found rest in sleep. She intensified her description of the past night's fever, and made the father promise to let her atone for what she had occasioned with devoted nursing and suitable vigils. Yes, now she felt regret for the obstinacy of her repudiation, if not for any sin. And the rabbi from Seville rubbed the sleep from his eyes in amazement, for ever since he had first disembarked from the old guardship in the port of Paris, he had never heard a word of regret from his elegant opponent, whose blue eyes now reminded him of the blue sky of distant Andalus, which he did not know if he would ever see again.

Mistress Abulafia hastened to the tabernacle to waken her brother from a night's sleep sweetened by the command to dwell in booths and by the rustle of the breeze in the greenery and the scent of the citron that lay beside his couch. With unusual firmness she asked the befuddled Master Levitas to allow the rabbi to lead the prayers for the day of the Great Hosanna, so that he could be the first to strip the willow by beating it with all his might in memory of the ruined Sanctuary and its worship. And so it was. To the accompaniment of the raindrops that had been skipping on the surface of the Seine since dawn and the voices of the Frankish travelers on the river, Rabbi Elbaz was the first to begin the recitation of the hosanna: *May you be delivered and saved from war and from famine, from captivity and from pestilence, and from all manner of destroyers and from all manner of punishments that are experienced in the world. May you all go up to Jerusalem the pure, and may your feet trample upon those who hate you, and may your feet dance in the court of the sanctuary, and may you raise in your hands the fruit of the citron tree, palm fronds, myrtles, and willows of the brook, and say, "Hosanna, Lord save us!"*

But the rabbi's hosanna did not penetrate into the bowels of the old guardship tied up on the northern shore and swaying now under the feet of the Ishmaelite crew, woken from their slumbers by the rain. Even less could the recitation that shook the tabernacle on the left bank reach as far as the old artisan's cottage at the bottom of the hill of the white smudge. But while the idol-worshipper's body was still lying wearily among the idols at the feet of his own shrouded image, bitten by the greedy desire of the Gallic women and stained by the endless outpourings of his seed, Ben Attar too was woken by the rain, and accompanied by the sound of the camel shuffling around in the belly of the ship and the smell of the remains of the condiments, which had spilled from the sacks and mingled with each other, he began to stroke, kiss, and squeeze with all his strength the only wife he had left. And the first wife hastened to respond to the wakening man with all the power of her love in a perfect and unique congress that was free from all extraneous thoughts and from any remnant.

8.

Had the time not come at last to unfurl the triangular lateen sail on the tall mast of the old guardship and raise the anchor from the bottom of the Seine? Had the time not come to depart from this Europe with its darkening sky and sail back to the safety of home? Even the patience of such a hardy and experienced captain as Abd el-Shafi was strained at the sight of the wind and rain lashing the Île de France on the Day of Rejoicing in the Law, for who knew as well as he how urgent it was to set sail and leave before the northern winds grew stronger on the ocean? So anxious was the captain that he was prepared to protest against the calm Ishmaelite fatalism that left it to Allah to govern the infinite world according to his mysterious will, and he demanded urgently that Abu Lutfi stir his Jewish partner from the hesitations of his grief and force him to put off the torn robe of mourning and bring himself up from the bowels of the ship to the old bridge, to pronounce there the order that all the Ishmaelites had been so eagerly awaiting— to leave desolate Europe behind and return to luxuriant Africa, to hear once more the sweet sound of the muezzin's call.

Perhaps it was the blood of Abd el-Shafi's grandsire's sire, who had been taken captive by the Vikings more than a century before and had spent many years as their prisoner, that sharpened the captain's senses to perceive the dangerous, unhealthy hesitancy that was spreading like ivy over all Ben Attar's thoughts and deeds. This fear concerned not only the voyage, which had lost the charm of novelty and adventure and was left mainly with the memory of hardships and distress, but also a deeper doubt about the leavetaking, both from the nephew, whose partnership had been renewed through blood and suffering, and from his blue-eyed wife, whose stern elegance had suddenly changed her old repudiation into a powerful new attraction.

In truth, a strange new attraction emanated from this woman toward the sorrowing uncle, the extinction of whose duality had left around him, or even within him, a new, unclear space, like that left by the loss of a severed limb. There was no way of telling whether Esther-Minna herself was in command, or was even aware, of the new quality emanating from her toward the uncle, who consented in honor of the closing days of the autumn festivals to emerge from his close mourning in the bowels of the ship, bathe and dress his beard and hair, and exchange his rent robe for a fresh one, so that he could clasp to his breast in holiness and purity the soft little scroll of the Law that was handed to him by Master Levitas and execute the modest dance ordained by custom.

What precisely was the secret of this strange new attraction passing between the northern woman and the southern man, which was able to delay the moment of parting despite the impatience of the Ishmaelite seamen? The North African's enmity toward Abulafia's new wife still blazed within him, and if his young wife had not departed to what was supposed to be a better world, it would not have occurred to Ben Attar to withdraw from the campaign he had launched, and despite the ban and interdict pronounced against him by the prayer leader in Worms he would have sought out another river on the European continent and challenged the woman to a third round. There, on the north or south or west or east bank, he would not have allowed the rabbi from Seville to appoint a court or a judge, but he would have taken the stand himself, alone and face-to-face with the stubborn woman, and overwhelmed her repudiation with a speech woven not of texts of the sages but of the wisdom of life.

His second wife's unexpected death had indeed brought him a victory, but it was a hollow and bitter victory that had not extinguished his anger. Thus the nature of the new attraction that joined the two adversaries was unclear. Surely it was not possible that now, on the brink of the departure from Europe and the parting of north from south, the mind should be expected to endure the mounting suspicion that the extended intimacy enforced upon these two who had traveled together from Paris to Worms had kindled in one, or even perhaps both, a demented, forbidden fantasy, and that the hope of realizing it was delaying the departure? The date had already been set for the summer meeting of the renewed partnership in the Bay of Barcelona, and there remained nothing for Ben Attar to do at the close of the festival but to give the order for the Ishmaelite crew to spread the sail, weigh anchor, and glide downstream to the mouth of the river and out onto the great ocean, which, who could tell, might be longing to rock the old guardship on its waves.

Ostensibly what delayed them was the sickness of the rabbi's son. This sickness Mistress Abulafia fomented with dark potions, so that she could plead with the rabbi and more particularly with the leader of the expedition to take pity on the little invalid, and instead of exposing him to wind and rain linger a little and let him recover in the comfort of her bed. But a sixth sense told the merchant of Tangier that behind his new niece's pleas there lurked a brazen wish from which he himself might draw some advantage. Therefore, before determining what reply he should give, he sent his only wife to the sick child to discover, by questioning and feeling him, what was real and what was feigned in his body and his soul. The experienced, sensitive woman returned with news for her husband. Although it was almost certain that the eating of abominable flesh, which had so upset the child and infected him with guilt, was no mere fantasy, it had touched his soul alone and not his body. In other words, the sickness itself was entirely feigned.

Still Ben Attar held back from speaking ill of the feigned invalid, who had been taken under such a gentle yet enthusiastic wing. Since he even felt a certain compassion for the desire for a child that had suddenly arisen in the bosom of a barren adversary who was no longer young, he tried to think afresh how he might turn the pretended malady into a further pledge to fortify his partnership. Precisely because of its dramatic rupture, there might still lurk in the renewed partnership some hidden cracks through which that accursed repudiation might grow back, by attempted prevarication, by dispatching a strange agent, some private local associate instead of Abulafia to the summer meeting in Barcelona to bring the North Africans their money and take the new merchandise. Although it would not occur to Ben Attar to postpone the sailing on account of a woman's desire for a curly-haired child, it seemed that he would be willing to abandon the young passenger and leave him behind in Paris until the following summer, so that he could recover body and soul. This he would do on condition that Abulafia would give an explicit promise, backed by an oath on the soul of his wife—not the living one but the first, drowned one—not only to watch over the child as the apple of his eye but to join him to the purse of money that he himself would bring to the ancient inn overlooking the azure bay of the Spanish March. Only when they had finished chanting the lament for the ruined shrine together would they hand the child over to Abu Lutfi, who would choose a young horse for him from Benveniste for the night ride by way of Tortosa, Toledo, and Cordoba back to his waiting father in Seville.

It was surprising that Ben Attar, who was already enthusiastic about Esther-Minna's excitement at taking under her wing, without the pain or trouble of childbearing, a full-grown, black-curled, clever child, whom she might take by the hand and promenade through the lanes of the little island without shame or reproach, did not take the trouble to obtain Rabbi Elbaz's assent to having his young son expropriated in order to buttress the partnership between north and south, which had been renewed by dint of a death alone. Indeed, on the basis of the familiarity acquired in the course of the journey, the merchant suspected that the rabbi he had hired in Andalus would not only be pleased to spare his only child the hardships and dangers of the return sea voyage, but would even seek to join him. But Ben Attar, unwilling to dispense with the rabbi's company and learned conversation on the ocean waves and unwilling to be left alone with his only consort in the midst of alien Ishmaelites, chose to keep his own counsel for the time being. He spoke not a word to the anxiously waiting Jews, but went first to the ship to consult his faithful old Ishmaelite partner about his new plan.

But Abu Lutfi turned out to be not so faithful, for during the proprietor's absence he had taken it upon himself to give permission to the ship's captain not only to prepare the ship for sailing but to embark a new cargo in place of that which had been discharged, so as to stabilize the ship on the ocean. *A new cargo?* exclaimed the amazed Jew, who since his second wife's death had let his commercial vigilance slacken. *Is there anything fit to buy here in this godforsaken land that might interest people in the South?* Abu Lutfi made no answer, but merely winked and led his partner into the hold, from which there rose a strange and unfamiliar smell mingled with a new sound. There, in the darkness of the space that had been cleared of its cargo, Ben Attar saw human beings attached to the timbers of the old guard ship.

Slaves? the Jew whispered in horror, and at once he asked himself whether there were not a disturbing sign here of things to come, for Abu Lutfi, who had begun as a humble assistant in Ben Attar's shop in Tangier, had never before dared to act on his own initiative without obtaining the blessing of his Jewish master. Was this the price the Ishmaelite was levying for his participation in the vicissitudes of the conflict of the Jews, a conflict that despite its hardships had incidentally broadened and strengthened the Arab's mind and perhaps his soul as well? Or was it merely evidence of a new contempt or even anger that the Ishmaelite felt for the weakness of a husband who had allowed his young second wife to depart this life in her prime, only to please a new woman, whose hair was fair, her eyes blue, her countenance pale and sad?

Come and see close up, whispered Abu Lutfi to his partner, who was still hesitating to advance into the bowels of his ship, from which a new menace seemed to emanate. But the Ishmaelite relentlessly compelled the Jew to inspect the new, disturbing human cargo, which froze at the sight of the new master, who was wondering about its nature and also its value. As his eyes became accustomed to the darkness, Ben Attar could discern the slaves and distinguish them one from another. His heart pounded as he saw that there were five tall, thin males dressed in long leather tunics. And his breath stopped for an instant as he noticed that the slivers of daylight filtering between the timbers glinted on yellow hair and blue eyes, whose sadness and submissiveness the darkness was unable to disguise. With a rush of excitement whose strength caused him real distress, he sighed, closed his eyes, and turned a grim face toward Abu Lutfi, who was smiling proudly, to inquire not only as to the price of the disturbing cargo shackled in the hold of his ship but also as to its faith.

It was remarkable how his natural commercial instincts had led this Jew with no previous experience of slave trading to make precisely the right connection between the two questions. Abu Lutfi proudly recounted how, while the Jews were praying for remission of their sins in Verdun, Abd el-Shafi had made the first contact with a slave dealer, and how after the death of the second wife they had covertly agreed that in return for five sacks of fragrant condiments and ten copper caldrons he would receive five northern slaves, whose modest price was due not to any mental or bodily defect or weakness but purely to a defect in their faith, or, it would be truer to say, in their *lack* of faith. For their origin was in the wild remote regions in the extreme north of this gloomy continent, where even a thousand years had not sufficed to bring the good news of the birth, death, and resurrection of the crucified god. In simple speech, these were also idol-worshippers, albeit fair northerners rather than dark southerners, whose inscrutable and unsteady thoughts and deeds made them unpredictable and therefore dangerous, so it was no wonder that their price on the local slave market was so low.

Idol-worshippers? Ben Attar whispered despairingly to Abu Lutfi, who nodded his head, his eyes gleaming. *And what shall we feed them on? And who will look after them?* But the Ishmaelite was so pleased with the deal he had done on his own initiative that he promised his Jewish friend to take full responsibility for the new cargo. Not only would he stay close to them to ensure that they caused no mishap, but during the long voyage he would also try to teach them to speak some Arabic and to understand orders, which would increase their value and their selling price. He had no doubt that their fair and reddish hair and hue, their blue and green eyes, would attract and excite the folk in Andalus and the Maghreb, who would clamor for a further consignment.

Ben Attar said nothing, but a strange sadness overtook him and made him want to escape. He hurried up on deck, where Abd el-Shafi and some of the burly seamen, who had treated him respectfully before, roughly seized hold of his garment and rudely asked him to set sail at once, before the northern winds blew up and turned the ship into a deathtrap. Ben Attar felt that this new violence and impudent speech were occasioned not only by his hesitancy but by the absence of the second wife, for whose death the Ishmaelites held him indirectly to blame. Hurriedly he mumbled a new promise. But it seemed that the Jew's promises were worthless now, for the men threatened him openly that if he did not assemble the Jewish passengers forthwith, they would weigh anchor at dawn and sail without them, and even without him.

Ben Attar knew that their threat was genuine and that if he did not agree to leave, he would lose his ship. Suddenly he felt lighter, as though the Ishmaelites had managed to trample under their rough sandals once and for all the hesitancy that had been consuming him ever since he had arrived in Paris. He hastened to Abulafia's house on the left bank to summon his wife and the rabbi urgently back to the ship, and to discuss with Abulafia and his wife not only the conditions under which the supposed invalid might be left in their home but particularly those under which he would be returned the following summer. Ben Attar still could not shake off his doubts and uncertainties touching the patched-up partnership. It was as though the dagger of the ban that had been thrust into him had not vanished or been returned to its sheath on the death of the second wife but had merely been wrapped in a soft old cloth, and on his departure from Europe some pretext would be found to plunge it into his image, which would haunt this gloomy house like a ghost. He suspected that Esther-Minna had not forsaken her hostility to this partnership, which would take Abulafia out of her control once more and set him to wander the distant roads of the south, where he would be reunited with his uncle. Who could guarantee that Ben Attar would not craftily revert, there on the faraway dark continent, even in secret, to the ways of his forebears?

It would be better, Ben Attar said to himself as he hurriedly crossed the river by way of the charming lanes of the little isle, to accede to the sudden desire of a childless woman for a temporary adopted son, in order to strengthen the renewed partnership indirectly. Surprisingly, he was still not troubled by the possibility that Elbaz would resist any attempt to deprive him of his only son as a pledge. Did the Jewish merchant really think that in hiring a rabbi, one hired not only his knowledge and his wisdom but also his feelings and his soul? Or was there a secret desire to punish the Andalusian for the self-confidence and love of debate that had lured them into agreeing to a further tribunal in that boggy midden on the Rhine?

But when Ben Attar was standing with the other Jews around the bed of the young traveler, whose black eyes opened in terror to hear his fate decided, and announced his willingness to leave him behind, he realized that his authority was waning among his fellow Jews as well as among the Ishmaelites. Not only did Rabbi Elbaz not require his consent to entrust his son to Mistress Abulafia for convalescence, but he had already decided to invite himself to stay as well and to accompany his son on the journey overland.

In an instant and for the first time, the merchant experienced a powerful new fear that would—so he felt in his desperation—accompany him through his life as though it had become his second wife. His face flushed and he began to tremble with rage at the treachery of the rabbi, who was willing to abandon him and his only wife, who was sitting quietly in a corner of the room, unveiled, staring at her husband with her gentle eyes, and to let the rabbi would let them sail all alone, without the protection of his sanctity or prayers, in the old guardship, her deck swarming with impudent Ishmaelites while in her hold were shackled idol-worshippers who might be concealing Lord knew what schemes behind their blue eyes. If this rabbi dared to usurp Ben Attar's authority and honor in this way, who could tell whether this desertion betokened not only a grim turn in the destiny of the journey home, but also a secret plot to sabotage the renewed partnership by another cunning betrayal, which would make the rabbi, returning with his son to Andalus next summer, into a courier for Abulafia, who might still be held back by his wife?

Vengeful thoughts continued to race through the North African's mind. If a plot was afoot, perhaps he ought to warn the rabbi that if he abandoned his employer, he would forfeit the promised fee for his wisdom and learning, especially since in the end these had availed nothing. But on further reflection, the experienced merchant held back from uttering the threat that was choking him, certain that Abulafia and his wife would find a way of recompensing the rabbi for his lost fee, and also because it was clear to him that what was needed in this desperate twilight of the festival's end was not a threat, which would exacerbate the rift and heighten the loneliness and dread of the journey home, but only sense and sensitivity, which would ensure that the imminent parting between the southern and northern partners should retain within it an additional pledge which would make certain that at the beginning of the month of Ab the ancient Roman inn would indeed witness a cordial meeting between a loving uncle and a beloved nephew.

Ben Attar stared deep into the eyes of his nephew's wife, trying to determine the proper pledge to exact from this stern contestant so that the blood of his young wife should not have been shed in vain on the altar of the renewed partnership. Esther-Minna, unperturbed by the man's piercing gaze, neither lowered her eyes nor dimmed their radiance, but merely narrowed them slightly in a gentle and reproachful warning, soundlessly inviting the apprehensive southerner to listen instead of staring. Indeed, the many hours that these two strong and determined adversaries had spent in each other's company had taught them to interpret each other correctly. Moreover, the North African was unable to forget how this woman had collapsed in a swoon on the night of her defeat in the judgment at Villa Le Juif, and how he had bent down to raise her from the undergrowth and carried her some distance in his arms to the campfire. No wonder, then, that he understood her hint and obeyed her invitation to avert his eyes and prick up his ears and hearken to *her* pledge, beginning now to howl behind the curtain.

After all, if they could all agree to leave an Andalusian boy-child in the heart of Europe, where the stormclouds were already gathering at the approach of the millennium, as a pledge to guarantee the partners' summer meeting in the Bay of Barcelona, it was only right to reinforce it with a parallel pledge and take another child in his place from north to south. And if no boy-child was available for the purpose, a girl-child would serve as well to make the curly-haired young husband overcome any scheme that a stern, childless, proud, and suspicious wife might hatch to sabotage his renewed relations with the rock from which he was hewn. In this way Ben Attar might ensure that Abulafia would indeed come himself to the Spanish March, to take his daughter back from the enchanted continent to the accursed one.

That was the strange idea that now flickered, to their shared astonishment, at one and the same moment in the minds of two hardened adversaries, who had skirmished at first from a distance of two continents, then face to face, and who now, on the brink of parting, in the midst of the hesitations and suspicions they nursed in their hearts, were united in fear and weariness in a new idea. By seeking to exchange one child for another, they would ensure not only the existence of the summer meeting in the Bay of Barcelona, as Ben Attar wished, but also its propriety, as Esther-Minna desired.

Anyone who listened attentively to the girl's renewed crying could recognize that since meeting the southern children, her howls of despair had turned into howls of longing. And anyone who, like Esther-Minna, did not believe that witchcraft and demons had played a part in her birth could only be pleased to return her, if only for a short time, to the azure shores of her native land, so that she could revel in the smells and colors that had faded in her memory and exchange the torments of longing for sweet reality. Moreover, in this way, liberated from the obligation to attend to her, Mistress Abulafia would be able to accompany her husband on his springtime journey, not only to enjoy the partners' meeting in the inn but to observe close up how the Christian millennium passed in Ishmaelite territory, without Jewish duality of wives, and also to see with her own eyes how the clever uncle divided up the spoils of trade.

And so, on a Parisian autumn evening, to the sound of the bells of the abbey of Saint Germain des Prés, which abutted the riverbank, the old repudiation melted away and the partnership reborn from the dust of the nearby grave of the second wife was strengthened and reforged in the flickering candlelight, so powerfully that it seemed it would henceforth be even stronger and firmer than it had been before Abulafia made the acquaintance of his wife in the inn in Orléans. While Abulafia was still trying to comprehend the converging intentions of his wife and his uncle, the whispered instruction was already being given behind the curtain to the Teutonic maidservant to make the girl ready for a sea voyage and to prepare her cubicle for the supposed invalid, who was rubbing his little feet against the covers as he might have

300

rubbed them against the great mast. Even Master Levitas, who knew how to beget a further thought out of any new idea, wasted no time in wondering at the doings of his older sister, but was already musing on the possible advantage he could take of the Andalusian rabbi's wit and wisdom, so that by the next spring they would not be eating the bread of charity.

Finally, wearied and worn out, Ben Attar made a sign to his wife to rise up and follow him, and without glancing either at the rabbi or at Abulafia he hurried out of the house, as though fearing some further attempt by the new wife to tighten his partnership to the strangling point. Emerging into the cool evening air, he crossed the river by the swaying ferry and made his way confidently through the lanes of the Parisian isle, which had become a kind of second home for him in the course of the past month, to bring to Abu Lutfi and Abd el-Shafi the good news that the long-awaited order was now lying upon his tongue. As he approached the little anchorage on the right bank and looked at the mass of masts and sails huddled together in the darkness of the little port, his breath was taken away by the fear that the Ishmaelites might have put their threat into effect and set sail without him. But no, the old guardship was still bobbing there, and despite the long time that had elapsed since she had first cast anchor in the harbor of the Île de France, she had not been sullied by her surroundings but still stood out from the Christian craft all around.

The deck was empty, apart from the light of a single lantern, and it seemed that no one had sensed their coming, to unroll the ladder. Since Ben Attar did not yet know that the black slave, who could not discern his masters' presence by their scent alone, had not returned to the ship from his amatory expedition on the right bank, he began to think that some plot had been hatched against him. Then, as his feet sank into the mud of the riverbank and his wife's face disappeared again behind a heavy veil, he felt his whole being shaken by despair and disappointment at the rabbi's abandonment of him, and he raised an Arabic cry that startled the Frankish sailors all around him, but not those who should have been listening on the ship. Just as he was about to call again, his wife removed her veil and, anticipating him, gave a loud, wild shout that he would never have imagined her capable of producing. The woman's piercing cry summoned the seamen up from belowdecks, and here was Abd el-Shafi hurrying to fetch his master and his only wife up onto the deck of their ship in his strong arms.

Tomorrow we sail for Africa, Ben Attar announced to his captain, as though Africa were not thousands of miles away but just beyond the horizon. Abd el-Shafi said not a word but smiled and nodded, as though he did not need the Jew's consent to set sail but was only waiting for Abu Lutfi to finish attending to his slaves. Indeed, to judge by the way the seamen were excitedly coming and going to the hold, it seemed as though the stabilization of the ship had been reinforced in the past few hours and some new human cargo, requiring more room, had been taken down belowdecks. Consequently, it was not to be wondered at if the news that the rabbi and his son had left the expedition was received with satisfaction, or if the additional news concerning the new passenger, a bewitched young girl, was met with some misgivings. But when Abu Lutfi was reminded how ten years before she had crawled among the piles of merchandise on the first boat that had sailed to Barcelona, he agreed to take her on board once again.

It seemed as though this Ishmaelite, who had been so easygoing and restrained before, was gradually taking control of the whole ship, to the point that Ben Attar was fearful of descending belowdecks to see what had been added to the shackled cargo. In the gloom gaining control of his soul, he did not join his first and only wife, who had installed herself in her cabin in the bow, but went first to look for the young idolater, to get him to brew him some of his beloved herbal drink. To his amazement, it seemed that the town had swallowed up the black youth. Not only did Abu Lutfi not know where he had gone, but he was not even taking the trouble to look for him, as though now that he had taken on so many new slaves he did not need the old one. Meanwhile the night was growing darker, and the Jew, whose fear was growing stronger all the time, stood leaning on the rail, while all around the crew was busy preparing the ship to sail. With painful longing in his eyes he stared at the lights of the little town as though he were looking for the burial place of his second wife, in whose dust he suddenly wanted to warm himself, instead of being presently cast upon the cold depths of a savage ocean.

At the end of the third watch the triangular lateen sail was hoisted and unfurled in all its splendor, and it seemed that nobody and nothing could stop the old guardship from sailing down the Seine to the ocean and making her way back to her warm homeland. In the murky morning light Abu Lutfi woke his Jewish partner, who had dozed off despondently huddled among empty sacks on the old bridge, and announced the arrival of the new passenger, who was standing like a woolen bundle on the riverbank, between her sire and his new wife, with a glowing flush on her cheeks, dressed in warm new clothes to protect her from storms at sea.

She was not the only passenger joining the ship, whose sail was beginning to fill, for in the first broken rays of daylight Ben Attar could make out to his surprise the small, familiar form of Rabbi Elbaz. It turned out that although the rabbi had remained true to his resolve not to endanger his son with the sea voyage, even if he was only a feigned invalid, and to trust the promise given by Abulafia and his wife to return him to Andalus overland and to receive in return their unfortunate little girl, so far as he himself was concerned he had changed his mind and was determined to rejoin the old guardship, not only in order to return to Seville as fast as possible and receive the promised fee, but to prove to the North African Jew who had hired him that he would neither abandon nor betray the mission he had accepted, to defend the status and propriety of a second wife. Even if God had decided to take her to himself and to bury her on the left bank of faraway Paris, her erect, noble form was deeply engraved in the rabbi's soul, and her robe and veil still floated before his eyes. No, Elbaz would never forget her, and the speeches he had made for her and about her, both in the winery at Villa Le Juif and in the synagogue of Worms, shone like diamonds in his memory, side by side with the legal texts and moral sayings that he had not managed to weave into his speeches but that he kept ready, if needed, for a further contest of wits in the case of a second second wife.

Thus, confused, excited, and even a little frightened, Elbaz boarded the ship with his bundle and fell into Ben Attar's arms, burying in his lord's chest both his loyalty and his apprehensions about the coming journey. It looked for a moment as if they were silently exchanging tears. Since he would be alone in his cabin near the bow and it was out of the question for the girl to be put in the hold, the bewitched young passenger was put next to him, after a light wooden partition had been erected. Already Mistress Esther-Minna was hastening to make both his bed and that of the quaking child comfortable with thick covers, and she hugged the girl tight to quell her fears while Abulafia acceded to Abu Lutfi's request to go belowdecks to peer at the cargo of slaves, who were shifting restlessly, waiting for the ship to sail. But when Abulafia came up on deck again, flushed and confused by what his eyes had seen, he said nothing, either to his new wife or to his uncle, in order not to delay the long-awaited moment of departure.

When the moment did come, it was not quiet but tuneful, for before they weighed anchor and disembarked those who were staying behind, Abd el-Shafi placed his hands on his ears to hear only the silence of his God and began to wail like the muezzin of the great mosque in Tangier, issuing the call of the Prophet to the faithful to fall on their faces and beseech Allah to turn all adverse winds to fair ones. Although there were too few Jews to compete with the eight prostrate Muslims, they could still muster a company, numbering not three but four, for Master Levitas, not neglecting the sacred duty of leavetaking, had risen early and stood now on the bridge of the ship to reinforce the parting prayers of the southern Jews. When both the Muslims and the Jews had concluded their prayers and the neighboring Christian seamen had added their blessings, there was nothing whatever to prevent the ship from retracing its route to its point of departure.

Back again came the slight rocking motion, which seemed to have been forgotten during the forty days on land. Although it was the gentle motion of the river rather than the violence of the ocean, the current was still surprisingly rapid, either because they were now going downstream or because of the autumn winds. No sooner had the travelers remembered to turn around to take their leave of the little Parisian isle than it was gone, hidden by the first bend of the river and swallowed up in the brilliance of the eastern sun soaring relentlessly behind them, soon to dance before the prow of the ship as she gathered speed. But the calm presence of the beauty of nature on either bank no longer soothed the Jewish travelers' hearts as they leaned silently on the ropes that fringed the deck, but a faint dread forced them to scan the undergrowth for a human figure with whom they could at least exchange a parting wave. The chill and gloom of the European autumn seemed to intensify the silence of the world, and since there was no child at the masthead to survey the world beyond the vegetation on the riverbank, anyone wishing to make some contact had no choice but to seek a sign of life in the beautiful purple leaves that fell slowly and soundlessly from the boughs of the great, sad trees that cast their shadows deep on the fast-flowing water.

Although the captain, who had once more bound himself to the mast and attached crewmen to his traces to navigate better, clung resolutely to his decision to press on night and day toward the great ocean, he could not fail to accede to a firm request from Abu Lutfi, whose authority on board was growing hour by hour, to put in briefly at the port of Rouen. Perhaps the duke who had bought the little she-camel from them had realized that for the sake of the health of the young desert creature in his care it would be best for him to furnish her with a male partner, at a modest price. Thus, in the twilight of the second day after the tawny ship pulled out of the port of Paris, the anchor was lowered again not far from the little houses of Rouen. Abd el-Shafi, who was unwilling on any account to detain the ship until daybreak, had a dinghy lowered into the dark water and sent the Ishmaelite merchant, with the Andalusian rabbi as interpreter, in search of the duke or his Jewish counselor, to make them the astute offer. But before much time had passed Abu Lutfi returned despondently to Ben Attar, clutching some yellowish tatters in his hand. The she-camel had not endured for long in her new owner's care, and because of neglect or pining for her mate, she had breathed her last and collapsed in an open space behind the cathedral. Instead of wrapping the noble desert beast in a shroud and giving her decent burial until the millennium arrived, with its promise of universal resurrection, the Christian duke had exposed her to the curiosity and greed of the local inhabitants, who had soon cut her up into little pieces and realized whatever they could for them, so as to recover something of the purchase price. They had not spared even her hide, but had stripped it off and tanned it, and discovered its wonderful property of restoring the shine and sparkle to tarnished gold or copper.

But Ben Attar paid no attention to the plaints of his old partner, who since the disappearance of the black pagan had become bitter and domineering. Without saying a word, he took a strip of soft, yellowish hide from the remnants of the she-camel and brought it close to his face, to see whether the little tatter of skin still retained the smell that used to assail his nostrils each time he made his way through the hold on his way to the second wife's cabin. While the captain gave orders in the dead of the night to weigh anchor, light a great lantern at the prow, and sail on, the North African Jew was so overcome with the sadness of sweet longing for the wife he had lost that he could not resist descending into the bowels of his ship to take a brief look at the abandoned cabin.

In the semidarkness, beside the outline of the he-camel, whose fate was apparently sealed since the death of his mate in Rouen, the Jewish proprietor discovered that his captain had cleverly given the new slaves oars that protruded outward through ancient openings in the side of the ship, which had been closed up and now had been reopened. As he groped his way amid the creak of oars and the splash of water, he observed, from the number of the shapes moving around him, that his partner had increased and reinforced the stabilization of the ship. Feeling a new excitement rising up and shaking his guts and his loins, he approached to inspect the nature of the new arrivals, who were huddled in the cabin where he had sat as a mourner. But before he could lower his eyes he was pierced by the frightened, curious looks of three flaxen-haired, blue-eyed women shackled to each other by their long legs. Abu Lutfi explained with a conspiratorial smile what a good bargain he had made just before they set sail, but he was pushed away impatiently by the Jew, who hurried up on deck to discover that despite the late hour, everyone was awake—not only the captain and his crew, but even his wife, who was sitting swaddled in several layers of clothing on the old bridge, listening to the chatter of Rabbi Elbaz, who was still wondering if he had been right to leave his only son, an orphan, in the care of a strange woman, an obstinate adversary and childless contestant.

Even though Ben Attar knew that it would be impossible to conceal from his wife and certainly from the rabbi what his eyes had just beheld belowdecks, he tried to delay giving the news, and wordlessly, with a weary gesture, he gently indicated to his wife that she should leave the rabbi from Seville and return to her cabin. Right then, as an improper and unworthy suggestion rose up to him from the bowels of the ship, he needed to discover again, with a fearful body, how far one could push the limits of a sole wife in carnal knowledge, which always contained some spiritual knowledge as well.

But when he left the cabin at the close of the third watch of the night, while the indefatigable Abd el-Shafi, full of the excitement of being under sail again, looked down on him from the mast, he knew what he had always known—that one woman could never fulfill the promise of another. His eyes sought in vain for the black slave, who would always emerge from a corner and between watches, between wives, would prostrate himself and touch the hem of Ben Attar's garment submissively before handing him the steaming herbal brew. Where was the idolater? the Jew asked himself longingly. Who had detained him? Was he alive? Had the new slaves so turned Abu Lutfi's head that he had so easily abandoned his faithful servant? For if Ben Attar were to exert his imagination to the utmost, he could not imagine that he could never track the slave down, even if he exercised the full weight of his old authority and managed to stop the ship and turn her around to search for the lost African all over the Île de France. This was not only because the black youth was too well hidden in that faraway cottage, secure in the clutches of three women who were determined, as the millennium drew nigh, to satisfy the desire of the old woodcarver to add the lines of an alien race to his vision, but also because the captive himself, the gleaming black youth, had fallen in love with his captivity, within which the spring of his passion flowed so strongly.

So Ben Attar strode off dejectedly to seek out another co-religionist, who would stand with him against a loneliness that he had never acknowledged before and that now flooded his whole being. Since the rabbi was fast asleep, he drew aside the thin partition to inspect the girl, his own kin, who was sailing back to her birthplace as a counterpledge. Only now, in the silent moonlight that contended with the first rays of dawn, did he observe how the baby who had crawled on board the first boat to Barcelona had grown and filled out. A strange idea gripped him—to surprise Abulafia and his wife and to give them back at their meeting in the Spanish March a little girl who was betrothed, if not actually wed. If he persisted, there was no doubt that despite the enchantment or, who knew, even because of it, he would be able to find someone who would want to make love with the heavy but lush and youthful form that was now sleeping, cramped and curled up, in the tiny cabin. Despite her accursed enchantment, she recalled the beauty of a young woman who had abandoned her and disappeared into the depths of the sea.

Now he rose, so surprised at the new thought that had been born in him that he could not find rest or return to his bed before descending into the belly of the ship, of which he still considered himself the sole master, to check not only whether Abu Lutfi was really keeping watch but also whether the three blue-eyed women were still attached together at their long legs. There in the bowels of the ship, it turned out that one of the women had fallen suddenly sick and had been loosed from her bonds, and was sitting in a corner, pale and trembling, with her head thrown back, covered in a soiled and torn silk robe that had been found among the sooty timbers. Ben Attar, recognizing with pain the source of the torn robe, stood silently staring at the blue eyes, which opened and turned in defeat to his feet, and at the thin hands of the idol-worshipper, who was clutching the image of an animal. Because he knew that he would never, ever touch her, or her companions, he went back up on deck.

The North African Jew thought to himself, This is what the new wife and all her wise friends who dwell on the Rhine desire—that from now on I shall take on every day anew, but only in my mind will there be crumbs and tatters of a second wife who has vanished. He was enfolded in such deep sorrow that he could not resist waking Rabbi Elbaz to look him straight in the face and tell him how great was the defeat he had suffered, for the renewed partnership between north and south could never atone or comfort him for what he had lost forever on this journey.

But the rabbi from Seville, caught up in his own sleepy thoughts, heard the words of the ship's owner as he lamented for what he had lost as if all the troubles of the world were subsumed in this sorrow. It was as if they would not soon have to face the waves of the raging ocean, where the river flowed into the sea and an ancient sunken Viking ship stood like a great bird, and fierce northern winds would turn the fate of the second wife into a gentle, easy story compared to the story of what awaited her husband and his party. Suddenly the little rabbi was filled with joy at having agreed to leave his son with

Mistress Abulafia, so that despite the millennium he could return safely overland to his home. He already imagined Master Levitas and his sister clothing the child in the black garb of the people of Worms and placing a hat with a horn on his head, and waking him in the morning, a little feverish, to sit and study an ancient text and a new law. Then tears welled in his eyes for the child who was saved, and once more the poetic urge woke within him, to write one more poem, the fourth. He felt around him to see whether that old quill pen and inkwell were still there among the timbers of the cabin. But he found nothing. And so he was compelled, to the accompaniment of Ben Attar's long drawn-out keening, to save in his head the first line that had composed itself inside him: *Is there a sea between us, that I should not turn aside to visit thee* . . .

Haifa, 1994–1996

About the Author

A. B. Yehoshua is the author of *The Lover, A Late Divorce,* and *Open Heart,* in addition to *Five Seasons* and *Mr. Mani,* both of which received the National Jewish Book Award. For his body of work to date, Yehoshua has received the prestigious Israel Prize. He was born in Jerusalem and lives in Haifa, where he teaches literature at Haifa University.

About the Translator

Nicholas de Lange's translations from Hebrew include *My Michael, Black Box,* and *Fima,* all by Amos Oz. He teaches at Cambridge University, where he specializes in medieval Hebrew and Judaism. He is the author of the *Atlas of the Jewish World* and editor of *The Illustrated History of the Jewish People.*